The Three Daughters

MANFRED BIELER

The Three Daughters

translated by Kathrine Talbot

ST. MARTIN'S PRESS   NEW YORK

Library of Congress Cataloging in Publication Data

Bieler, Manfred, 1934-
  The three daughters.

  Translation of Der Mädchenkrieg.
  I. Title.
PZ4.B585Th   [PT2662.I38]   833'.9'14   77-76627
ISBN 0-312-80245-5

Contents

Book One

I

At the Wildfowler

An hour's walk from Zerbst, near a pond surrounded by willows, lay the Wildfowler. The bushes and hedges behind the dance floor and the stables were overgrown with wild roses, black thorn, lilac and wild hops, and the meadows frothed with clover and marguerites to the very edge of the track through the marsh grasses.

Here, two hundred years ago, the River Nuthe had seeped through the peat cuttings and had flowed with some difficult/ into the broad Elbe which pushed its way through the plain, swollen by other rivers higher up and reluctant to swallow its smaller tributaries. Later the Nuthe had been dammed and diverted into a new bed by convict's of the Zerbst dukes, and the ducal fowlers had delivered snipe, larks and buntings to the castle kitchens.

The estate was eventually acquired by a gold-merchant who, by adding summer-houses, arbours, pergolas, an artificial lake and a gondola, tea-rooms and a roulette room, had made it into a veritable paradise for the Prussian and Russian officers who bought epaulettes, stripes, tassels and sword-knots from him.

When the Sintenis family came to own the Wildfowler, it became an inn but kept its magic garden. The creaking and grating of the swing in the playground was transformed into the song of a bird, and even Dr. Sellmann, the director of the Dessau branch of the Saxonia bank, was a changed man when he met Betty Sintenis, the landlord's sister, there.

Through the years, the Wildfowler's customers had become used to a strict timetable. On Mondays, their day off, the Zerbst innkeepers came to the Wildfowler, on Tuesdays the mayor and the directors of local factories, on Wednesdays the 'hungry government penpushers' as Wilhelm Sintenis, the landlord, called civil servants. On Thursdays the Lutheran clergy appeared for their weekly beer-synod: Pastor Kuck from Natho in a pony-carriage,

9

Deacon Liebetruth from Little Lubs by donkey-cart. One midnight in this late spring of 1932 the spiritual gentlemen had been deposited in the wrong vehicles, and taken home to the wrong vicarages and the wrong wives.

On Fridays the ladies' circles came strolling across the meadows to eat apple tart and drink coffee and cherry brandy, and to speak French – or if their schooling did not run to this, just high-falutin'. On Saturdays the clubs marched in, pushed the tables together, stood on the chairs and sang to make the chestnut leaves tremble. On Sundays the band played for dancing, the mosquitoes swarmed around the necks of the students from the Politechnic and around the bosoms of the lady typists.

This was where the children of Betty and Anton Sellmann spent their holidays. The four of them usually travelled from Dessau to Zerbst in July, and were collected in the trap at the station by their Uncle Wilhelm, and returned there by him towards the end of August.

But this year they stayed only three weeks. They were told, one Wednesday evening, that their parents wanted them at home to meet an important visitor. For the last time they ate ham with noodles, and a soup made of ham, rice, carrots and peas; they walked round the pond once more, smelled the musty breeze of dead leaves and last year's stubble, slept smothered in the bulging featherbeds, then next morning they got into the trap, and an hour later they were sitting in the train.

Christine, Sophie and Katharina Sellmann did not look like sisters; indeed, they did not even look as if they were related to each other, yet each of them bore some small resemblance to their blind brother. The eldest, eighteen-year-old, fair-haired Christine, had Heinrich's narrow lips and his small ears which fitted closely against his head. Sophie, two years younger, had dark hair, and showed, when she laughed, the same gap between her upper teeth. Fourteen-year-old Katharina had his determined chin, and her brother had had the same grey-green eyes before his pupils had become inflamed when he had had measles. But Katharina's red hair and her broad nose came directly from her Sintenis grandmother.

The meadows beside the railway line held up their tall seed-heads in vain to the sky. Uncle Wilhelm had predicted rain, but it didn't come, though the air was moist.

'It sounds like cannon fire,' Heinrich said when the train thundered over the bridge across the Elbe.

'It's the sleepers,' Sophie explained.

'How long before we get to Dessau?'

'A quarter of an hour.'

'Why do we always have to travel third class when Papa isn't with us?'

'To teach us about the drawbacks of life,' Sophie said and smiled.

'Are there ashtrays everywhere?'

'Yes.'

'Even in the non-smokers?'

'Yes, for heaven's sake!'

'But one doesn't smoke in the non-smokers?' Heinrich continued his questions.

When the eight-year-old had to wait too long for a reply, he blew noisily through his lips, until Christine snapped her fingers against his knee.

'What are you wearing?'

'Christine is wearing the dress with the twelve buttons, Sophie the embroidered frock with the bow, and I'm wearing my kilt,' the redhead said.

'And what's the name of the gentleman who wants to see us?' Heinrich asked as the train drew into Dessau station.

But none of them knew.

2

Herr Lustig and Herr Croissant

THE GENTLEMAN'S NAME was Herr Eugen Lustig, and he came from Prague. He owned large lignite mines in Western Bohemia, was a partner in cement works and foundries, lead and sulphite mines. He owned open-work mines in Germany and shares in potassium and chemical works there. He also held the controlling minority of the Böhmische Landesbank in Prague. Kleinworth & Sons of London, the Banque de Bruxelles, and loan banks all over the world did business for him. So did the Saxonia, the bank for which Dr. Sellmann worked. He read legal documents and financial reports in five languages, but all his negotiations were carried on in German.

He was an insignificant looking man, wore pince-nez à la Masaryk, and would have liked to have worn the same peaked cap as the president he so much admired, but when he had tried one on at Hess the Hatter's, he had had the uncomfortable feeling that he might have been taken for his own chauffeur. When his architect suggested building a swimming pool in the garden of his Prague mansion, Lustig had said, 'Do you think I'm an American and need to bathe twice a day?' When he had been presented with a car for his sixtieth birthday, he had driven it along one of Prague's main streets but had got out at every corner to make sure nothing was coming the other way. After a while he had let the chauffeur drive him home and had given the car to his son-in-law who was an ophthalmologist. 'If I used everything I sell to other people,' he had said, 'I'd be dead in a week.'

At the suggestion of the heads of the Saxonia bank, Dr. Sellmann asked the Czech magnate to join him on an excursion to the Wörlitz Gardens. Herr Lustig's visit to Dessau had been preceded by a transfer of his shares in German browncoal mines to the Saxonia. From Berlin he had sent Betty Sellmann a bouquet of tea-roses and had asked her and her children to join them for the excursion to Wörlitz.

There were therefore eight of them, in two cars, including Herr Lustig's valet Rohlik, who would have preferred travelling on the running board rather than give the impression that he laid claim to a seat like the gentry. Lustig and Dr. and Frau Sellmann drove in the first car, the valet and the four children in the second, and soon Katharina was asking what his name Rohlik meant.

'Croissant, Miss,' he answered and waited with a steely expression for the expected laughter. But it did not come. Instead Sophie said:

'Names really are a cross we have to bear. Our surname, if you translate it from the English, means "men who sell things". An aunt of ours is married to a man called Cheeseman and our hairdresser is called Chicken.' From that moment Rohlik loved the Sellman children, and most of all Sophie.

When he had first met Heinrich, Lustig had been surprised to see that the boy was wearing sunglasses, but it was only when they were visiting the Wörlitz Palace and Christine began describing the paintings to her brother that he understood the reason. He stood still for a moment, brought his white silk handkerchief out of his breast pocket and blew his nose so resoundingly that he

12

made Dr. Sellmann jump. Only the valet could have told the company that this was his way of coming to terms with his feelings. Outside, on the steps, the small gentleman from Prague took Heinrich by the hand and went down the stairs with him: one step, and another, and another. Then, to everyone's surprise, Eugen Lustig, the Prague Jew, showed his blind companion the unknown park, took him ahead of the family to the landing place, drew the outline of a swan's neck on his palm, the ragged contour of a gingko leaf, the towers of a Gothic summer-house and the tympanum of the Temple of Flora. Heinrich sat on the rustic bench, his head against the old man's lavender-scented jacket, threw breadcrumbs to the invisible swans, listened to the sound the water made as they swam past, and finally got up and put his hand in the lake and laughed. At first Frau Sellmann had tried to take the boy away from the visitor, but she soon realised that she need not worry. Lustig held him safely by the arm, and Herr Rohlik too looked ready to jump in amongst the water-lilies if necessary.

Only at lunchtime did Lustig return the boy to his mother. Then he and Sellmann went alone to the Orangery, and while they strolled back and forth, Lustig spoke of his own son.

'He is thirty-four but doesn't live with me. Perhaps I'll have him with me later, when I retire. Was Heinrich born blind?'

'No. He was three. Measles.'

'Victor was five. No, he isn't blind. He can see well enough, but he can't remember his surname. He had brain fever. The doctors just call him "Victor", then he joins them and laughs. He is the gayest person I know. He shakes everyone by the hand and says, "Delighted, delighted." He is much taller than I, has dark hair and black eyes like my wife. He lives in Vienna, in a private clinic. When I told him that his mother had died, he looked at me for a long time. "Mama is in heaven!" I don't know where he gets such ideas. But I'd have him baptised if it would restore his health. I sent him to Vienna because I couldn't bear the idea that he was living just around the corner. I love him, you understand.

'When I was young, I wanted to make a lot of money so that when I was an old man I wouldn't be sent to sit in a corner with the evening paper and told to shut up. I'm beginning to think that there's nothing nicer than to sit down somewhere, read the paper and be quiet. But ... since we've had the good things God has sent us, we can't refuse the bad things, can we?'

'But I have three daughters as well,' Sellmann said. 'I'm hardly in the same position.'

'And which of your children do you love best?'

'Yes,' said Sellmann, 'you're right.'

Now the ladies in their light dresses with Heinrich in his navy blue sailor suit were approaching along the gravel path, and a little behind them the valet in black.

'Come and see me in Prague with your wife and Heinrich,' Lustig said, 'and bring the girls. My son-in-law is an ophthalmologist. Pupil of Elschnig. I can see that's a name you've heard before. Come as my guest. Come in October when we usually have good weather. But you know Prague, don't you. Would you like to?'

'Perhaps.'

Next morning a messenger appeared at the Sellmanns' house with silk scarves for the girls and a violin for Heinrich. Frau Sellmann received a bouquet as large as the previous one, with a note in which Lustig thanked her for the excursion and repeated his invitation to Prague.

3

The Sellmanns

DR. ANTON SELLMANN was a gentleman of the old school who held his life together by diligence, manners, and the creases in his trousers. He had studied economics at Strassburg and Oxford. During the battles in Flanders he had often fought in the same section as Freiherr von Richthofen, only not in the air but in the mud.

For a long time, some thought too long, he had been the protégé of an influential person in the Berlin banking and government world, and some thought that he had been put into cold-storage in Dessau, a backwater despite its chemical factories and the Junker aeroplane works nearby. But he seemed to remain well known in business and banking circles, for when he first appeared on the race-course near Prague many hats were raised in greeting, hats which had rested on the heads of the most influential bankers and businessmen of the Czech capital. Six months later he was one of the promoters of the German football club there, and explained to the English trainer, Mr. Otaway, in his native language, of course, the decisive points of the game in which the 1st F.C., Nürnberg had won the German championship.

But he was the opposite of a self-made man. He insisted that everything he knew about finance he had 'learned from Justi, Conrad, Garnier, Lotz and Rathenau'.

He taught his children how the finances of a good government or a good family should be run by saying, 'What I breathe in, I have to breathe out. What I breathe out, I can breathe in again. If my lungs are healthy.' For him, money was the air he breathed.

For his sake, Betty Sintenis had left the Wildfowler and had become a Catholic. For his sake she would have become a Moslem or a Sunworshipper. She put a holy-water stoop in the hall, ate no meat on Fridays, kept the fasts, included the Pope in her prayers, went regularly to confession and communion, and for the last twenty years had repeated the Lord's Prayer without the Protestant ending.

Christine, two years older than Sophie, was allowed to have her blonde hair bobbed when she was eighteen. She played Chopin polonaises and told the cook exactly how to make the most complicated desserts. She knew that one served sherry with turtle soup, Gewürztraminer with cold meat, Châteauneuf du Pape with game, Pinot Noir with cheese, and champagne with dessert. She took business friends of her father's on excursions, was able to deal with office messengers and bible scholars without embarrassment, and she was the first of the sisters to wear cream-coloured stockings held up with violet suspenders. Christine had become a lady before she had had time to be a girl.

Sophie also played the piano, but loudly and out of tune, and when she danced with Katharina, vases fell over or buttons tore off. If a pedlar came to the door and called her 'little Miss', she blushed and bought shoelaces and mothballs out of her pocket money. When Christine talked about her partners at her dancing classes, Sophie thought that her first boyfriend would have to come as a swan or golden rain. No 'dates'. One didn't make an appointment for an adventure. Nothing was as boring as to know what would happen tomorrow. If her prince came and murdered the whole family except Katharina and Heinrich, that was all right. They'd drink all the wine and eat all the cakes, and use the last of the money to travel to Berlin. She might even become a criminal. Sophie wanted a destiny, not a rendezvous. Sometimes, when she woke up in the morning, she forgot where she was, and only remembered her name when Christine's blond mane rose from her pillow.

Katharina, the redhead, liked to wear kilts and green blouses. Her hair was braided in loops over her ears. She had not succeeded in altering her broad nose with either clothespegs or vinegar compresses. When she prayed at night, she would ask her name-saint, the patron saint of surgeons, 'Clip my wings, dear saint. Don't let me become like my grandmother, that wicked old woman whose portrait in the hall has a potato-dumpling for a nose. Please give me, Virgin of the Wheel, Sophie's dark, wavy hair instead of my red jungle, and instead of my meagre little points, a bosom that you can call a bosom. And above all, dear beheaded Katharina, give me Sophie's love of life, else I'll hang myself. Amen.'

She was often sad. Perhaps she read too much at night: *The Life of Butterflies*, by Friedrich Schnack, *The French Revolution*, by Jules Michelet, *The Love Story of a Wild Goose*, by Bengt Berg, and *The Riddle of the Gobi Desert* by Sven Hedin, in fact anything she could lay her hands on.

Heinrich shared her room, and there were green muslin curtains at the windows so that he could have the kind of light that did his eyes good. The sun hurt them, and he was afraid of the dark. He loved over-cast skies, and when he learned at the school for the blind that the creatures of the ocean lived in perpetual gloom, he asked why he couldn't have been a fish.

4

Prague

IT WAS NOT until the following spring that Dr. Sellmann, accompanied only by his wife and Heinrich, went to Prague, and the red flag with the white circle and the swastika already flew over the customs post at Bad Schandau. They stayed at the Palace Hotel, and Lustig was even more friendly than at Wörlitz.

'They're beginning to get some order into things, *chez vous*,' he said to Sellmann. 'That Schacht has once more been made president of the Reichsbank shows that Hitler has learnt his lesson.'

Sellmann had expected a different welcome. He thought he'd be asked about the '*Ermächtigungsgesetz*' and the burning of the Reichstag.

Professor Kulik, Lustig's son-in-law, cooled Heinrich's cup of tea and put it into his hand. From the terrace of the Lustig mansion the view was of the orchard in bloom. When they left, the valet helped them into their coats, and they made an appointment at the clinic for the following day.

The examination showed that a cornea transplant was indicated. The surgeon decided that only one eye should be operated on at first, to test the reaction of the tissue. They would have to find a cornea from a young and healthy accident victim and might have to wait for some time and be prepared to decide on an operation from one day to the next. Under the circumstances it would be best if Frau Sellmann and Heinrich stayed in Prague for six months, since the success of the transplant could only be finally gauged after three or four months.

After many earlier examinations in Leipzig and Berlin, Betty Sellmann had lost all confidence in doctors, even when they sounded as plausible as Professor Kulik. Nor did she want to live in this foreign city for six months without her husband and daughters. Sellmann shrugged his shoulders.

Next day Lustig showed them a castle near Prague. Lustig's daughter was one of the party, also a Herr von Lilienthal whom Sellmann knew to be the director of the Böhmische Landesbank. The ladies strolled in the French Park with Heinrich, and the gentlemen walked on either side of their guest. Herr von Lilienthal offered Sellmann a post on the management of the Böhmische Landesbank. He would be in charge of all its German business affairs and might eventually become a director. As far as remuneration was concerned, Herr von Lilienthal mentioned a figure which weighed on Sellmann since it was the measure of the amount of work that would be expected of him.

'You could come and live in Prague.'

'You'll have to think about it in peace and quiet,' Lustig took over. 'But I may as well tell you that Berlin will put no obstacles in the way of such an arrangement.'

That meant, Sellmann translated, the old gentleman had already had the agreement of the Saxonia Bank. He could, of course, decline, but Hans Luther, on whose support he had counted and built his career, had ceased to be president of the Reichsbank and was now Ambassador in Washington. With his departure the future had become uncertain. The idea of leaving Germany without emigrating was certainly tempting.

'Thank you,' Sellmann said. 'But I'm afraid . . .' and he paused deliberately, and only the crunching of the gravel could be heard as they paced on. He was about to add: 'It can't be done', when Heinrich called, 'Papa, come and see. A giant cactus.'

Herr Lustig laughed and so did Herr von Lilienthal, and Sellmann said, 'I'll really have to think about it.'

When he suggested staying an extra week, Betty agreed.

Dr Sellmann chose one Sunday after they had returned from church to tell his family that they would be moving to Prague. They were in the music-room.

'For how long?' Christine asked.

'One or two years,' said Sellmann and explained how their education was to be tackled. Christine had finished her schooling in any case. Katharina was to go to the German Lycée in Prague, and Sophie should take the time off, and resume her studies once they were back in Germany.

'Why are you trembling?' Heinrich asked her.

'I'm not trembling.'

When she said goodbye to her friends, they asked, 'When will you be back?'

'Soon.'

'How soon?'

'When the chickens fly south in the autumn,' she said like Wilhelm Sintenis, her uncle of the Wildfowler, when someone asked him when he'd at last find himself a wife.

5

Frinz

SOPHIE WAS SEVENTEEN and determined to take her destiny into
her own hands. In the morning, when she put on a dress, she did
it in the same frame of mind as a wayfarer might look at the
endless prairie and say to himself: 'There's plenty of opportunity
here'. Her Dessau singing teacher had given her the address of
Fräulein Kalman who had been a student of the 'divine' Emmy
Destinn. Frau Sellmann, who accompanied her daughter on her
first visit, expressed a certain suspicion as they descended the
stairs from the fourth floor.

'There's a smell. Had you noticed?'

'What sort of a smell?' asked Sophie innocently.

'Of champagne, to be honest.'

'But Mama!'

'And isn't it also too far from home?'

They tried it out immediately, did not go by car but clambered
on a tram and jolted across the Stephanik Bridge.

'Endless,' Betty sighed. At first she had found it difficult to
orientate herself, for Sellmann had not rented an apartment in the
centre of the city as she had expected, but in the modern district
of Bubenech. She would have liked to have lived near public
gardens, as in Dessau, but the paths in the Rieger Gardens were
too steep for her. Only when she was near the river did she feel
content, remembering the Elbe at home.

Katharina, who was best at topography, unfolded a big map of
the city and traced with her forefinger how best to get to the
centre. The girls chose three routes and set out, walking together
as far as the tennis courts. Here Christine turned off, and Katharina
took the stairs down to the Vltava. Sophie remained for a little on
the plateau and looked over the city. The spires stood green
and pointed in the grey pin-cushion, everything else was in-
comparable. The bridges looked like bridges, the river like a

19

river. If God had built himself a city it would have been this one.

'This is where I would have started the Thirty Years War,' Katharina said in the Old Town. 'Because it would have been so easy to hide.'

Adventures beckoned behind the window curtains, but the language was incomprehensible. How did one say, 'Good morning' and 'Goodbye'? Dr. Sellmann did not need to speak Czech. In the bank everything was done in German. Frau Sellmann had a German maid-servant who had grown up in Prague. She sent her with a list to the shops and to market. Katharina bought a phrase book and learnt sentences like, 'The Duke's sons were all heroes, but the inkstand is on the table'. Sophie invented a new language called 'Frinz' which had neither grammar nor vocabulary. It had only one word, 'Frinz', but this single word was pronounced in different ways, as in Chinese, and took on different meanings with the voice. Thus it could mean headscarf or lipstick, a railway station or a singing lesson.

The only other person who knew 'Frinz' was Jarmila, a nineteen-year-old girl who lived nearby. From November to April she lived in Prague with her parents. The spring and summer the family spent on their estate near Melnik watching the 'Frinz' (the hops) in bloom, and how their 'Frinz' made hay and dug potatoes and milked the cows, and Jarmila's father, Herr Mangl went with friends on a pheasant-'Frinz'. In winter, Jarmila took English lessons and attended courses in eurythmics, went to premières at the National Theatre, concerts, or sat behind the window of the Café Edison and waited for her 'Frinz' to come and set her free. She was clever, quick-witted, gay, generous, courageous and faith-, ful, but she wasn't 'Frinz', which in this case meant she was no beauty. Her big blue eyes were set too close together, and her nose was a fraction too long. Her thin, colourless hair hung about her head. She was also knock-kneed. 'I waddle like a gorilla,' she said to Sophie, later when they both spoke Czech, not 'Frinz'.

They had met in the park. Heinrich had escaped from Sophie's hand and collided with Jarmila. Sophie apologised in German, Jarmila in Czech, and both continued to speak in their own language as if the other understood what was said. Jarmila snapped open her handbag and pressed a roll of acid drops into the blind boy's hand.

'Drops, Heinrich,' Sophie said. 'How do you say that in Czech?' she asked.

'Drops,' the other girl said, and they all three laughed.

Sophie began to discover things. In Dessau the Sellmanns had belonged to the people who set the tone. Her father had an English tailor in Berlin. Her mother employed a local dressmaker for herself and the girls. The materials used were good, the cut and decorations provincial. Where would one go in a creation by Maggy Rouff? To the Café Altmann, where the wives of civil servants swayed rhythmically when a tenor from Leipzig sang Rhine ballads? To the ladies' circle at Fräulein von Hüllweck's, where the Meissen figurines behind the glass doors trembled when the silver sugar tongs fell on the tablecloth? Men in spats were ridiculed as dandies, and veils on hats – except for funerals and weddings – were 'plain silly'.

At home Dr. Sellmann sat at a Van-de-Velde desk, but for years his business friends had been amused by the 'crooked thing', and when he had suggested furnishing at least one room in the Bauhaus style, with stainless steel easy chairs with linen covers, Frau Sellmann had thrown up her hands in horror. They had gone on with carved oak and red plush. They lived in a provincial way, neither above nor below their circumstances, but suddenly circumstances had changed, and Frau Sellmann felt the difference. It wasn't a matter of money. But when she returned from their first evening at Herr von Lilienthal's she was uneasy if not downright disturbed.

For three hours she had sat in a bare room with nothing in it but a long dining table and twelve chairs, two sideboards and three or four paintings. Afterwards the guests had stood about in the adjoining room, and a waiter, whose hand she had almost shaken, had served champagne. Her partner had entertained her during dinner with stories from the Prague film-studios and anecdotes about the Minister of the Agrarian party, but then left her with a younger man who, immediately he heard she came from Dessau, drew her towards a canvas covered in green and yellow patterns.

'Observe, my dear lady, this is, I'm afraid, all that we can produce! A few months after the Paris Salon we discovered Cubism, Surrealism, Collages. In spring Braque paints a mandolin – in the autumn the Prague galleries are full of string instruments.

'Filla? "Un Picasso pour les pauvres", is what Picasso said himself. Every painter needs a faith. When I was in Cracow and saw "The Lady with the Ermines" I suddenly had faith. Thus everyone waits for a "Lady with the Ermines". What is Kandinsky working on? Has he really gone to France? I believe a painter should paint the "being", "l'être", not the effect.'

Frau Sellmann admitted to herself that nothing impossible had

21

been expected of her. She had been asked about things that had happened on her doorstep, and she knew nothing about them. She felt as if she were in a trap into which she herself had put the cheese. After a few such evenings she felt unwell, and Christine went in her stead.

Sophie went to tea with Jarmila's parents. Herr Mangl spoke German, translating for Jarmila, and asked Sophie to come again. He told them how he had been hunting chamois in October and had fallen into a snowdrift. His companions had had to dig him out.

'And you didn't shoot anything?' asked Sophie.

'Oh, a bit,' Herr Mangl said and smiled while Jarmila held up two fingers.

When Sophie returned to her parents' apartment she would have loved to have thrown some of the china ornaments out of the window, also the sewing box, the dim table-lamps, the pedestal clock and the embroidered pink doilies. She carried a chair across and looked closely at the painting of Zerbst her mother was so fond of: a military tower with a conical red roof above the battlements, with houses behind, a street with a flat cart, and in the foreground, the city wall and five chickens, three old women and two old men.

Sophie managed to get permission to go to Fräulein Kalman's Tuesdays and Fridays, Jarmila fetched her after her lesson, and they walked arm in arm through the dim afternoons like two birds who didn't know where they wanted to fly to. Every Wednesday Sophie met Jarmila outside her eurythmic class, and slowly proper words began to creep into their Frinz-intimacy. Jarmila pointed to a hat and said 'klobouk', Sophie listened to her friend's greetings and thanks. One day she spoke her first Czech sentence. They had already said goodbye to each other, and Sophie had to hurry home not to be late for the evening meal, but she suddenly turned back, ran after Jarmila, and, holding her by the arm, said, 'Já tě mám velice ráda'. 'I like you.' And because she'd meant it, Jarmila's eyes filled with tears of joy. 'You are my Frinz,' she said in German, and kissed Sophie. They held hands for a moment, then parted quickly.

At Christmas the Sellmann family went to the Little Jesus Church, at Epiphany to the Church of St. Salvador, on Good Friday to St. Jacob, and at Easter to the Church of St. Nicholas. Jarmila had left on Maundy Thursday, and that same day Herr Sellmann had had a visitor from Berlin. Herr Frenzel, a director of the Saxonia Bank, had come to see the forsythia in bloom. He loved flowers. Behind his villa in Charlottenburg he grew Gloire-de Dijon roses, and when the Victoria Regina bloomed in the botanical gardens, white during the first night, pink on the second night, he stood amongst the spectators and felt deeply moved.

'I'm delighted to see you again,' Sellmann had said in the smoking-room of the hotel where Frenzel was staying, and he really had been pleased. But in the course of their talk there had been a moment which kept coming back to him all through the Easter Mass at St. Nicholas.

Frenzel had said something like: 'You're very much missed, my dear Doctor Sellmann,' which was very flattering. But then Herr Frenzel had said: 'There are people who think we ought to have our Doctor Sellmann home again. All that is needed, after all, is for the authorities not to renew his passport.' Then he had laughed and blown cigar-ash from his cuff, and Frau Frenzel had come towards them in a floating blue dress and extravagant hat, and they had arranged to meet on Easter Monday and go for a walk in the park, followed by coffee at the Sellmanns'.

Sophie, two seats further on, was still attentive during the Kyrie, but the lesson from the Epistle to the Corinthians led her mind to other things. The better she understood Czech, the more real Jarmila became for her, and those things that had been obscured by Frinz and double-Frinz now slowly came to light.

Jarmila did not go to Church, not even on a Sunday.

'Do you really believe there's a "Frinz" up there?' she had asked, pointing to the ceiling of the Café Slavia. 'Why should I love mankind? I'll hate mankind if I feel like it. And I shall lie if it gives me pleasure. I just want to be myself. What I detest is indifference. I am I. I am what I am.'

The priest crossed himself as if drawing a violin bow across his chest. And who am I? asked Sophie. Am I so merged with everything else that I can't realise my own self any more? Shall I be sitting on a sofa one of these days and wonder where I stop and it starts? Perhaps I've already been changed into somebody else? We wear the same clothes, the same shoes, we have our hair shingled or bobbed, we put our knife and fork on a knife-rest, we are in love with Clark Gable, we play the St. Petersburgh Sleigh-ride, we don't speak with our mouth full, we don't go to the bathroom in other people's apartments, we sit straight-backed, we smile. That's how we are. We aren't allowed to live like the servant-girls at the Wildfowler who sway on top of the hay wagons at sundown, breasts like bath buns and backsides like cottage

23

loaves, white kerchiefs over their heads and straws between their teeth, and the long rakes crossed like tent poles.

Nor could one live like Jarmila who believed what she said and was accountable to no one. Sophie's singing teacher was much the same. Fräulein Kalman had modelled herself on Emmy Destinn who had written a play about abortion when she was eighteen, had acquired a private prisoner during the World War, a Frenchman of Arab extraction whom she had kept captive in a castle in Southern Bohemia. Until her teacher's death, Fräulein Kalman had sung at the Prague National Opera. Soon after she had fallen from a mare, and since then she had limped about her little apartment in brown baggy knickerbockers and turquoise sweaters, the corridor, house and piano keys on a string around her neck. When Sophie visited her for the second time, the singer unbuttoned the girl's blouse, pulled her vest out of her skirt and put her hand on her bare stomach to test the vibration of the diaphragm. Sophie froze to the tips of her toes while her teacher looked into her gaping mouth. 'You have a chest like a barrel and a good roof to your mouth. In five years you'll be singing in Bayreuth or helping your mother wash the dishes. A top note,' Fräulein Kalman explained, 'can be achieved with the help of air or tension. The one is called bellowing, the other singing.'

'Yes,' Sophie said, buttoning up her blouse.

She had a horror of her own indefiniteness and was afraid that she wouldn't have the willpower to become as colourful and original as the Sophie of her dreams.

When she left the church with her family, the bells of the city were ringing. The stones trembled. The pigeons flew in white and grey circles above the roofs. Frau Sellmann cried a little and kissed the girls, and Heinrich shaded his eyes against the light with his hand. Sellmann walked two steps ahead in the direction of the bridge, for they had parked the car on the other side of the river.

6

Binz

AT THE BEGINNING of August the Sellmanns took the train to Berlin, spent a few days shopping and seeing relations, and then continued their journey to Binz on the Baltic island of Rügen where they stayed until September. The weather couldn't have been finer and the water was warm, but there were no concerts at first in the pavilion, for the Reichs President, Field Marshal von Hindenburg, had recently joined the great army of the dead.

Other politicians too had died that summer, mostly in less peaceful circumstances than the victor of Tannenberg, but Sophie knew nothing of that. She read neither newspapers nor books. Only Katharina left suntan lotion stains on the pages of John Knittel's *Via Mala*. The Sellmann girls played ball, lay in beach baskets, took photographs, ate ice-cream, and strolled along the promenade in white, ankle-length dresses. In the mornings Frau Sellmann took her son by the hand and collected pebbles, which, to please him, she called amber. He had still not had his operation. In the winter Professor Kulik had been unable to find a cornea donor, in spring Heinrich had had pneumonia and the operation had to be postponed indefinitely.

Dr. Sellmann, in a black bathing suit, swam as far as the buoys, took part in a cross-country run, then changed for tennis. In the evenings he was occasionally called to the telephone, and at the end of August Herr Frenzel came to Binz. His wife gave the girls silver thistle brooches. She greeted the waiter with 'Heil Hitler', which produced prompt service but became tedious in the long run. Even her husband knitted his considerable brows when, walking along the Corso, she lifted her right arm and showed her acquaintances that she shaved her armpits. He himself saluted like the Führer, his right hand over his right shoulder, like a waiter balancing a tray. The Frenzels stayed in another hotel, but joint excursions could not be avoided.

The gentlemen spent one evening on their own and Frenzel made Sellmann an extraordinary proposal. At first they had spoken about the deficit in foreign trade, about the clearing-houses of the Reichsbank where the accounts of exporters and importers of the partner countries were balanced.

'Like the practices of the bronze age,' Sellmann had said when they spoke of the exchange of Italian wines for German locomotives, Brazilian coffee for Daimler-Benz cars, Czech shoes for coke from the Ruhr. The suspension of payments of interest to foreign countries, and the repayment of credits into blocked accounts made business more difficult, and they discussed remedies, if only partial ones, that might help the Saxonia and the Bömische Landesbank.

Quite naturally they began to speak of the past, when Frenzel and Sellmann had first started to work together. This gave their talk a noble vagueness, and the more they talked – not now on the terrace but in a little deserted bay – the more they seemed to have in common. They had both fought for their country and that wasn't so long ago. Now Frenzel made his proposal, but Sellmann shook his head and the very seriousness of the proposition made him smile.

'One cannot serve two masters,' he said unequivocally.

'But there is only the one,' Frenzel answered.

'That's who I mean,' Sellmann said drily, but Frenzel did not give up.

Betty was already in bed when Sellmann got back to the hotel. He took off his sand-filled shoes and walked up and down in his socks. The same pictures paraded before him again and again: he would ask Herr von Lilienthal for the termination of his contract. Lustig would give him an etching or a meerschaum pipe as a farewell present. The same removal people would move them back to Dessau. The statue of St. Wenceslas, a reduced copy of the original, would be packed in wood shavings.

But had Frenzel asked Sellmann to leave Prague? On the contrary. 'Remain at your post!' he had begged, and he had emphasised the military turn of phrase. Wasn't it advantageous to Lustig, Frenzel suggested, if one of his principals could provide contacts and information which would be useful in the future to save greater losses? Or did Sellmann believe that the take-over of the Jewish Simson factories in Suhl would remain an isolated case? Sellmann had already helped Eugen Lustig to get rid of some of his German shares, but what would happen to the rest of them?

What he, Frenzel, expected, was no more than mutual discussion and the exchange of information whenever desirable, and as frequently as possible, 'so that we don't grope in the dark'.

Sellmann sat down in front of the dressing table, poured brandy into a tumbler and felt, while he drank, as if a Japanese paper-flower were opening in his head, covering his brain with a layer of violet leaves, blossoms and floating stems. He put down the glass. In Flanders he had once seen an execution. A white post in a gravel pit, a member of a court-martial, a priest. The whole thing had been very quiet, almost tasteful, yet nonetheless the spy had been quite dead at the end of it.

Betty, who had been watching Sellmann in the mirror, said quietly, 'It's all beginning to be too much for you, Anton.'

'Would you like to return to Germany?'

'What about Heinrich?'

When the Frenzels left, Sophie saw her father raise his right hand for the first time in a Hitler salute.

7

The Miracle of St. Gunter

FROM BINZ, BETTY and the children went to the Wildfowler to visit Uncle Wilhelm and the Zerbst relations. Sellmann went on to Prague by himself and stayed at the Hotel Paris. When he went to the apartment in Bubenech to collect clean underwear, it smelled musty. The servant-girl had got married in July. The furniture was covered in dust, all the clocks needed winding, a tap had dripped rust into the bath, and the remains of mashed potatoes in the larder had grown blue-grey fungi. It was no place for a man who'd rather cancel an appointment than go with dirty shirt-cuffs.

The Hotel Paris was considered neither Czech nor German. It was as international as the hotel's hairdresser, Pippo, who had a Hungarian grandfather, a Viennese mother, a broker from Fiume for a father, a step-sister in Chicago, and a brother who was a trumpeter with the Sarrasani Circus. He shaved Sellmann every morning. According to their interests, he offered his customers theatre tickets, tips for the races, smuggled Austrian cigarettes, or female companions of all colours, races or languages. To Sellmann he offered, without success, a Madonna 'absolutely Gothic and complete to the left index finger.' His gossip was relaxing and amusing. Some of the aphorisms he produced like 'a man without a belly is like a woman without a bosom', Sellmann called 'Pippo's gifts'.

At noon he ate near the bank, at night he went to a restaurant further afield and walked back through the Old Town. What he enjoyed most was letting himself be pushed slowly along St. Wenceslas Square. He knew Piccadilly Circus and the Champs Elysées, the Kärtner Strasse and the Váczi útcza, the Via Veneto and the Puerta del Sol, but he liked this broad boulevard best.

When he received Betty's telegram telling him that she was postponing her return owing to the death of an aunt, he wrote out a telegram of condolences and counted, as he wrote, how many evenings were left for St. Wenceslas Square.

The illuminated signs flashed about him, Osram, Bata, and the stork above a lingerie shop which dropped white cotton balls as far as the fourth floor where they were extinguished. The cinema advertisements shone on the tram-lines, and the ladies in fur-pieces and newly fashionable turned-in hairstyles, the girls with bare necks and open coats, walked in the yellow light. Men in raglan coats or great coats, pearl tie-pins and cashmere mufflers, turned at the end of the street to follow some stranger in a black velvet or striped cotton skirt, or read the evening paper walking along, flicked their cigarette butts under the parked cars, and closed their umbrellas in front of bars. A stranger soon felt at ease, for everybody seemed to have just run away from home to have a night out with all the other deserters. They were more afraid of boredom than of being caught out. Sellmann knew this feeling from other cities. What he liked so much here was the blind confidence of the crowd which he had at first taken for hypocrisy, their tendency not to take themselves seriously, or to take their nonsense seriously only for a while. What a contrast with the sad, taciturn inhabitants of Dessau, for whom life seemed to be nothing but hard work and melancholia, and who seemed to think the sun only rose because they put their full weight on the astronomical pulley to bring it up. As if love were merely a deductible allowance, and spring a recoverable debt.

Before Betty and the children returned to Prague, Sellmann had an evening invitation to the Lustig mansion. This was not at all usual. Apart from a few receptions, the old gentleman held his conferences in his office, in the tea-room of the Böhmische Landesbank, or in a private restaurant, mistrusting his own kitchen. What he liked best was to take anyone he wanted to talk to for a walk. Lustig liked to punctuate these excursions with various quotations, and Sellmann soon found that the same quotations were always produced in the same spot. At a short distance behind them walked the valet Rohlik with a coat, and a secretary with a black leather case which could be made into a writing-desk. Sellmann, who had taken part in such excursions several times, liked to remember how very much at his ease he had felt. All that's lacking are the horses, he had thought, and I'd feel, following the little gentleman, as if I were following Napoleon.

The secretary had told Sellmann that there would be three people at dinner, and he wondered who the third might be. Since his return from his holiday he had wanted an opportunity to make a clean breast of affairs, even if it meant losing his post with the Böhmische Landesbank. He wanted to tell Lustig of Frenzel's offer without at first indicating whether he had accepted it. Lustig's reply would then have its own consequences. But he hoped to bring it up casually: to make a special appointment would look too much like a confession, and he did not feel he needed to go as far as that, especially since he did not quite trust his own change of mind. How could he explain to Frenzel that he would return to Germany? Would Lustig and Herr von Lilienthal be willing if necessary to dismiss him so discreetly that there would be no scandal either in Prague or Berlin?

With these thoughts in mind he entered the hall, gave his hat and coat to the maid and let the valet lead him up the marble stairs. He admired the twilit luminosity of the house, the dark tapestries, the firm carpets on the stairs, the silent opening and closing of doors and the subdued gleam of the parquet. Eugen Lustig greeted him in the library. He had heard, he said, that Sellmann was living in a hotel and he and his daughter had wished to make up for the absent family by inviting him for the evening. Frau Kulik was therefore the third at dinner.

The old gentleman was not wearing his usual dark double-breasted suit buttoned to the very top, but a light jacket from which his tie escaped occasionally. While his guest talked, Lustig bent his head as if he were anxious not to miss a word, but Sellmann had the impression that he was, in fact, listening in quite another direction. When Frau Kulik joined them this one-sided conversation came to an end. After Sellmann had kissed her hand, he listened to a quick but calm exchange in Czech between Lustig and his daughter. Then the maid announced dinner.

The small drawing-room where they dined had windows on to the orchard and was really part of the conservatory. Behind a tall glass door one could see orange trees in tubs, dwarf palms and cacti in which Lustig took a special pleasure. He now seated himself at table in such a way that he could see the illuminated plants. The dinner remained in Sellmann's memory as one suitable for people with a severe stomach complaint: tomato soup, then a luke-warm, unseasoned chicken fricassée with rice, accompanied by a Moselle so light that it might have been an elevated kind of apple juice, and to finish there was yoghourt with grated nuts. When Lustig took his pince-nez off to eat the main course, Sellmann thought he did it so as not to see the miserable stuff on his plate.

Conversation remained formal. The old gentleman was conscious of this and tried to lighten the tone.

'Have you been to the Brevnov monastery?' he asked.

'Not yet, I'm afraid.'

'There's a ceiling there with a painting of St. Gunter's miracle.' He smiled, stuck his fork into a piece of chicken-breast, and lifted it from his plate. 'St. Gunter was invited to dinner by a pagan prince during Lent. There was meat, a roasted peacock. So as not to break his fast, Gunter begged the good Lord to give the peacock its life back, and as is the way with saints, the bird, though done to a turn, sprouted wings and feathers, rose from the platter, spread its tail, and flew away, while the angels handed down Lenten food. Beautifully painted.' Lustig glanced at his daughter's perplexed face. 'I ask myself whether we might not arrange a similar fate for this fowl, by virtue of our prayers . . .'

Sellmann laughed as best he could. Frau Kulik just cleared her throat.

'But I don't suppose it would work,' Lustig continued, 'since we aren't saints.' And he put the morsel into his mouth.

No, something was definitely wrong, something had happened. He hardly glanced at Frau Kulik, feeling that what he had suspected at their first meeting a year before was true: that she was nothing but a 'sourpuss'. But why was she using her peevishness tonight to increase the distance between Lustig and Sellmann? It certainly wasn't an evening to make him forget the lack of his own family, and Sellmann was glad when, after the dessert, Lustig reminded his daughter that there was another guest who might need her. Frau Kulik said goodbye, and Sellmann and Lustig took a turn in the conservatory while the table was cleared.

Why hadn't this other guest dined with them, Sellmann wondered? Had the conversation in Czech between Lustig and his daughter been about him? Why did Lustig not explain the situation, or had he, Sellmann, been specifically invited because of this person's presence? He could find no answer. Even the fact that they went back to the same little drawing-room where the sour smell of the fricassée still hung, instead of one of the other thirty or forty rooms, seemed to him suspicious. Yet there might never be a more favourable opportunity for him to talk with Lustig than this psychologically as well as physically untidy situation. But before he could speak, Lustig had already begun, interrupting himself only to point to the cigars and claret.

'There are two things on my mind, dear Doktor,' he said. 'The first is a matter of business, and perhaps we'll start with that. We know too little of what is really going on in Germany. We have friends in Berlin, but that is not enough, especially since I am forced, after the latest events, to doubt their loyalty. Let me repeat : their loyalty, not their honesty. I understand this, but the fact makes it necessary for me to read between the lines. Do I make myself clear?'

'Yes,' said Sellmann, 'completely.'

'But I don't want to know just half or three quarters of what is going on. Nothing must escape me. You've heard of the Arianisation of the Simson factory in Suhl? I ask myself : who'll be next? What will happen to my other investments? Will they all go? Or was Simson just a chance occurrence? I don't believe that, of course. And again : what will happen to the Reich's investments in foreign countries? How large are the liquid reserves of the German banks since the foreign currency transfers have been blocked? What is the Reich's credit policy vis-à-vis industry? These are questions, my dear Doktor, which concern me not only because I want to keep or increase what I own, but also because I consider myself at least one third German. The other two parts are Czech and Jewish. I speak quite openly.'

'Oh, quite.'

'My idea is this,' Lustig continued, 'you have – Herr von Lilienthal has kept me *au fait* – helped us a great deal since you have been with us. The German side of the business is in order. Its limitations are not your fault. But now we need more. We propose providing you with an extra budget the size of which I have already agreed with the board of directors. Besides, our balance sheet has for years carried an amount for "public expenses" – though you will realise that it means the very opposite. I needn't explain. I'll only ask you one thing, and that is whether such an offer appeals to you. Stop! Something else before you answer. If you accept you must know that this is no affair of state but a matter of business, or to put it quite simply, it is purely in the interest of the bank, which means in my interest and yours. Now it's your turn.'

'You said there were two matters you wished to discuss,' Sellmann said.

'I like the way you're taking this,' Lustig said, 'but I want to take one thing at a time.'

'I'll have to think about it.'

'Please do it now. Does my suggestion go against your feelings?'

'That may not be the question,' Sellmann answered. For the last few minutes he had had the impression that something was moving between the plants in the conservatory. At first he had thought that someone was watering an oleander bush in the dark. In fact he saw no more than a silhouette which moved, sometimes slowly, sometimes fast, between the lights which were let into the floor, and the way the shadows fell diagonally could have enlarged a dog or a cat to gigantic proportions. But Sellmann knew of the old gentleman's dislike of anything that might rub itself against him unexpectedly, or suddenly lick his hand. No domestic animal therefore. What then?

'I'm thinking,' Sellmann said without letting the shadow out of his sight, 'whether someone might not one day make me the same offer from the other side.'

Lustig looked at Sellmann for a while without speaking. 'Nothing could suit me better, Herr Doktor,' he said at last. 'I'm surprised it hasn't already happened.'

'And if so?'

But before Lustig could answer, someone knocked on the door, and Frau Kulik came in. 'Excuse me,' she said to Dr. Sellmann, 'but I must ask my father something.' She spoke a few words to the old gentleman who straightened up. He spoke softly but sharply and with finality. Sellmann understood nothing but the name of the valet. With another word of apology, Frau Kulik went out.

'I'm sorry,' said Lustig, and Sellmann thought that this was a dismissal.

'No, don't go,' Lustig went on, then thought for a moment.

'Why shouldn't I tell you?' We talked about it when we were in Wörlitz together. Do you remember?'

Sellmann remembered.

'He is here,' said Lustig. 'But he's left his room, and now we are looking for him.'

'Perhaps he's in there,' Sellmann said and pointed to the conservatory.

'Victor?' Lustig asked, but there was no need for Sellmann to reply, for the face of a young man with large eyes and a smiling mouth appeared in one of the glass panes. His hair stood on end and he moved his chin and lips and said a word which neither Lustig nor Sellmann understood.

'I'll have him taken away,' Lustig said, and put out his hand towards the bell.

'Please, not on my account.'

Lustig's lids fluttered as he tried to look into Sellmann's eyes. Sellmann took it for a challenge. He opened the door. Victor was still saying the silent word. Sellmann read it on his lips : 'Birthday.'

'Come in,' Lustig said. 'Sit down with us.'

Victor took a few steps into the room and stood by the table. He wore white pyjamas and leather slippers. In his hands he held a few flowering branches which he had torn off in the conservatory.

'This is my son,' said Lustig, 'and this is Doktor Sellmann.'

'I'm delighted,' Victor said softly.

Sellman bowed.

'I'm delighted,' Victor repeated. 'I'm afraid I can't shake hands. I've been picking flowers.' He laughed as if he had suddenly remembered something strange. 'The thing is, it's my birthday today,' he said.

'Tomorrow,' Lustig corrected.

'Not until tomorrow?' Victor asked and sat down. He lowered his head, frowned and twisted his mouth like a child who tries hard to be sad. He did not succeed. He looked at Sellmann and said, 'But I can be happy about it even today, can't I?'

'Of course you can,' Sellmann said.

'Would you like to know how old I'm going to be?'

'Yes.'

Victor laid the branches on the table, put his chin in his hand and considered. 'You say,' he asked Lustig after a while.

'Thirty-five,' his father said.

'Is that very old?' Victor asked, looking at Sellmann.

Sellmann couldn't speak. There was a lump in his throat. He

was afraid to swallow it because then the tears would come. He shook his head.

'You're very kind,' Victor said. 'Would you please take your glasses off for a moment?'

Without taking any notice of Lustig's protest, Sellmann took off his glasses, closed them and put them in his breast pocket. Victor came up to him and looked into his eyes. Sellmann blinked until he was used to the lack of focus, then looked, outwardly calm, but inwardly startled and upset, into Victor's pale face.

'Herr Doktor,' he thought he heard, but did not know whether Victor had spoken aloud or whether he had only moved his lips. 'I'm glad that my father has such friends. Are you glad too?'

'Yes, Victor,' he wanted to reply, but behind Victor's shoulder the head of the valet appeared, and Victor turned.

'Herr Rohlik,' he heard Victor exclaim, 'how nice to see you again!'

'I want to take you to your room,' Rohlik warned.

'I'm coming,' said Victor, 'but take the flowers.' He turned again to Sellmann who still stood without his glasses on the edge of the carpet. 'Would you like to congratulate me?' Victor asked.

Sellmann gave him his hand. 'I wish you all the best,' he said. 'I am glad I have met you. You are,' he searched for the right word, 'an angel,' he said. He knew immediately that he had never said anything like that to anybody, not even Betty, and was surprised that he was not ashamed.

When Victor and Rohlik had left the room, he took out his glasses, cleaned them and put them on. He couldn't very well just go, but waited for Lustig's invitation before sitting down again.

'Thank you,' Lustig said after a moment and pointed to an armchair. He opened his mouth as if he wanted to add something, but it only turned into an almost embarrassed smile. 'Or would you rather leave.'

'No.'

'I can't begin all over again now . . .' Lustig said. 'Let's leave it for another time.'

'That's not necessary,' Sellmann said, and nodded when Lustig looked at him.

'You don't want to think it over in peace and quiet?'

'I'm quiet now,' said Sellmann. 'And I'm quite ready to listen to your second matter now.'

'No,' Lustig said, 'there isn't time for that tonight. But there was something else I wanted to mention to you. I've heard—you've got to excuse me, I know everything—that you're looking for a

34

maid-servant. Well, I've told Rohlik to make it his business to find you one. Would it be all right if one or two applicants came to see you on Saturday? I think your wife would be pleased if you could surprise her with a new girl. Rohlik will guarantee their reliability, Goodbye, Herr Doktor.'

8

The Frog Prince

WHEN SOPHIE LATER tried to remember the winter after their return from Binz, she only recalled the twelve declension examples which Professor Vavra had tried to get into her head. The days simply went by, leaving her where she was. The sun rose, the moon came up, the street where she lived had a name, but they were only like a façade of life. She remembered sheet lightning in the mountains, a picnic, a broken suspender in the tram, an arm in plaster and influenza.

Years before, Professor Vavra had advised the National Theatre on a production of *Tristan*, and had fallen in love with Fräulein Kalman. He had declaimed the first as yet unpublished part of his' translation of the *Edda* to her. When the reading had been over, he had stayed on another quarter of an hour, scratched his head, suddenly dashed around the table as if he were about to throw himself at Fräulein Kalman's feet, but had only gone to the window and looked into the street.

'Mozart lived over there,' he had said softly and left.

But unlike her other admirers, Vavra remained faithful to Fräulein Kalman after her accident, though his attachment took on a melancholic air more suitable to a widower.

When Sophie explained to Fräulein Kalman that she wanted to put an end to her gibberish and learn proper Czech, it was taken for granted that he would become her teacher. Though Sophie protested, he spoke only Czech to her right from the start, using Latin names for the parts of speech. She sometimes thought he spoke a different language from Jarmila, for not only did he use other words, but what really surprised her was the formality of his figures of speech and the intonation. She had taken pains to copy the way her friend's voice went up at the end of each sentence, the almost reproachful tone of the long vowels, as if Jarmila meant, though she was saying something quite different: what can I do about it? It isn't my fault!

In the cafés too she sometimes thought that it sounded as if people were mostly occupied in defending themselves against old accusations and thinking up new ones. They seemed to have ordered coffee chiefly to give their neighbour a piece of their mind, not all of it, and not to their face, but with the help of a twisted turn of phrase which emphasised their own innocence. This had seemed to her the essence of Czech conversation, though what made her pause was the observation that while at home people would have been at each other's throat after such vehemence, or tearing out each other's hair, here they suddenly leaned back, laughed, called the waiter to order a third, fourth or fifth cup of coffee with a glass of water, and sat together at the same table next day, gloves inside their hats, morning papers across their knees.

At Professor Vavra's she had to re-learn everything. He was no second generation inhabitant of Prague. The Vavras had held University Chairs, administrative posts, clerical encumbencies in Prague for almost a hundred years, and so as not to get them mixed up, the family had given them various names. Professor Vavra's grandfather, a former head of the surgical clinic, had been called 'bloody' Vavra, his father, professor of church history, 'pious' Vavra, his brother, professor of classical philology, 'roman' Vavra. There had even been a 'stupid' Vavra, stupid not because he had been 'lacking', but because he had voluntarily become an officer in the Austrian army. Sophie's teacher, the translator of the *Edda*, was the 'nordic' Vavra.

On the only free wall of his study, surrounding an etching by Munch, huge portraits of Czech patriots and photographs of Strindberg, Björnson, Ibsen, and the historian Pekǎr. Apart from this and a few simple pieces of furniture, there were only books and a piano in Vavra's apartment. When Sophie brought him some flowers one day he had to put them in his tea-pot, for he found to his amazement that he didn't own a vase.

Sophie had managed to persuade her father to let her have three lessons a week, and the 'nordic' Vavra, who had first seemed ridiculous to her, with his knickerbockers doubly secured by a belt and braces, soon appeared much less old fashioned and absent minded.

Vavra taught Sophie beautiful 'greek' Czech, with its constant stress on the first syllable resembling the metres of the ancient epics. He recited extempore, slowly and with some pauses, the speech of Odysseus to Nausicaa, and though Sophie only understood little, his soft, scanning voice put her under a spell, and she sat on her wooden chair without moving. But this did not stop her from giving her family, that same evening, a performance in which, at Heinrich's insistence, she wore a belt round her waist and braces over her shoulders.

'Beeeauteeeous queeen,' she cried, putting imaginary spectacles on her nose, 'Královná Nausikaa, ever beeeauteeeous! A deemon has peeetched me upon your shore. I've only a twig to hold before my loins ...'

'Sophie,' warned Frau Sellmann.

'Geeeve me a leenen-cloth, goddess, noble washerwoman, that I might cover my neeekedness.'

Katharina laughed until she cried, even Christine's mouth twitched, and Dr. Sellmann said drily: 'Entertainment certainly seems provided.'

But when she was in bed and heard Katharina's giggles next door, she did not feel happy at the thought of having to look Professor Vavra in the eye next day. I'm really horrible, she thought, and when she heard Christine's regular breathing she got up, went behind the curtains, and looked down on the snowy gardens and said aloud: 'I'm horrible.' She could not understand how she could at one and the same time worship a person and make fun of him.

The urge to laugh at Vavra began when she went down in the elevator from his fifth-floor apartment. She looked at her face in the mirror, frowned and pouted as if she just wanted to try it out, but halfway down she was well into her imitation. But when the elevator stopped, this parody of the 'nordic' Vavra changed into a slim, tall young lady who bit her lower lip to save herself from bursting into laughter. And when she took the elevator in the opposite direction, she could see in the mirror, behind the façade of her own face, Vavra's friendly sea-lion look. And when she despaired of the irregular verbs and the declension of the nouns, almost crying with rage, a word from her teacher was enough to cheer her up.

'I'd like him to catch me at it sometimes,' Sophie said to her singing teacher.

'Why?'

'So that he sees what a beast I am.'

Fräulein Kalman laughed so much, the keys on their string tinkled.

'Isn't he a one,' she said. 'He doesn't know that we love him, that he's only to snap his fingers and we'd eat out of his hand.'

'That isn't true,' Sophie said and blushed.

'Yes, it's true,' Fräulein Kalman insisted. 'But it can't be helped,' she continued. 'When I first met him he was still quite juicy. But that *Edda*, which he'll probably never finish, has sucked the marrow from his bones. In a few years' time, just you wait, my girl, he'll be no more than a beanpole with a head on top. What can one do with such a man? He won't be good for anything except to hang the washing on to dry. I know the type. When he's past sixty you'll think he'll die every time he sneezes. No. For old age give me a small fat, rich man who can listen and doesn't laugh only at his own jokes. But you, you need something different. What do you want with a man who wears long underwear and lace-up boots summer and winter?'

'But I don't want him at all!' Sophie exclaimed, and had to laugh.

'Everybody wants him,' Fräulein Kalman said. 'I had Schubertova from the ballet here last week. Vavra looked in by chance. When he left she said, "What a man!" and I thought she'd go right after him. "Not for you," I said. And she is twenty-six and has to clear away the fellows from her dressing-room with her umbrella.' Fräulein Kalman sighed. 'Everybody wants to take him away from me.'

'But I don't,' Sophie protested.

Fräulein Kalman brushed the curls from her forehead. 'You are the most dangerous of them all.'

Sophie laughed and sat down on the piano stool.

'How cunning you are!' Fräulein Kalman said. 'You don't ask how or why. You simply turn away. You know your own potential, one doesn't have to tell you. You'll keep your powder dry. Quite right! But just remember one thing: Vavra belongs to me.' Then she too burst out laughing and vanished, keys clanking, into the alcove to change into her black dress for the opera.

Fräulein Kalman had free tickets for all the theatres and even for the variety shows, but to go to the theatre with her was not an unadulterated pleasure. True, she tucked her keys under her collar, but she did not hesitate to bring them out after the performance, whistling on them to show her appreciation. The effect produced was especially outrageous since she did not sit in the gallery but near the former royal box where the audience was sensitive to such insolence. Since her accident she had to take a taxi to the theatre, but the drivers hated her, partly because it was such a short distance, partly because she usually had no money, or if she did have some, it was always a thousand note. 'Give me a piece of paper,' she'd say on these occasions. 'I'll give you my autograph.' After a while the taxi drivers simply stepped on the gas when they saw Fräulein Kalman at her street door rather than brave half a kilometer of the evening traffic jam. After Sophie started lessons with Fräulein Kalman she, instead of the porter's son, called the taxis, and sat, a hostage, beside the driver.

If the evening was sultry, as was often the case in the autumn, Fräulein Kalman took off her shoes the moment she had taken her seat in the theatre, and stood, during the interval, in her stockinged feet on the marble floor of the foyer. She unwrapped the sandwich she had brought and talked – in German in a Czech theatre, in Czech in a German one – with her mouth full about the 'miserable scenery'.

No, it was not a pure pleasure, but if Sophie had had the choice of spending the evening with her sisters or with her teacher she'd always have gone to the opera with Fräulein Kalman. For Katharina, who was still at the German high school, was always offering solutions to problems nobody worried about, and Christine was rather like the English soprano of whom Fräulein Kalman had said: 'Her head has gone to sleep the way my feet go to sleep.'

Christine was bored, and, as behoves a young lady, she made it into an enigma. She liked to speak in unfinished sentences, suddenly stopped in the middle of a word, and smiled an embarrassed smile.

Katharina, always ready to crack uncrackable nuts with a sledgehammer, suggested to Sophie: 'Let's lock her into the lavatory until she confesses.'

'But what do you want to know?'

'Why she is suddenly so different.'

'Leave her alone.'

'With females her age, it's bound to be a man.'

'Why not simply ask her.'

'No, I wouldn't stoop so low.'

'Or talk about it with Karol.'

Katharina tried to frown prodigiously to show her disgust, but her face was too small for her efforts.

'You're no better,' she spat. 'You're a monster too,' and she ran out of the room.

Katharina was the only one of the three sisters who really had a boyfriend. In actual fact she only knew his first name, and didn't even know whether he was fair-haired or dark. At the beginning of the year, her history teacher had asked her whether she wanted to work in a history club which also included students from the boys' high school. Frau Sellmann had refused her permission since she did not want to leave Heinrich with the maid, and thought Katharina too young to meet strange boys, especially in someone's private house. But she could not stop one of the young historians getting in touch with her daughter on the telephone. His name was Karol, and he arranged with Katharina to keep her informed about the work of the club. No, Frau Sellmann did not object to this.

The club stopped functioning in November, but Karol's calls did not stop. His phone calls were a bit mysterious, for Karol thought it unnecessary to give his full name. 'We'll disregard everything personal,' he said the second time he phoned. 'I don't want to know where you live, or who your parents are. I only want to speak to you occasionally to make sure I'm on the right track.' That was music to Katharina's ears. 'What do you think, for example, about the battle of the White Mountain? Do you think it was really a battle between the Czechs and Germans as they tell us these days?'

'I don't think so,' Katharina replied. 'After all, Christian von Anhalt, who commanded the Czech troops, was a German.' She heard Karol laugh heartily at the other end of the line.

'Excellent,' he said. 'But it's not quite so easy. Your Herr Christian also fought in France. Is an army German because it has a German general?'

Sometimes the telephone rang as late as ten o'clock at night.

'What was the name of the harbour in Egypt where Louis IX was captured?' asked Karol.

'Damietta,' Katharina answered, already in her nightdress.

'Thank you,' said Karol. 'I just wanted to make sure. Good night,' and hung up.

'If this continues,' said Sellmann, 'I'll have to have a phone connected in your room so that he can ask you in your sleep when Napoleon was born.'

'We don't bother with *that* sort of nonsense,' said Katharina crossly, lifted her nightdress to her knees and ran with bare feet, her red hair flying, along the corridor and into her room.

Once, to trip him up, she asked him what had been the Hungarian capital in the sixteenth century.

'Bratislava,' he answered at once.

'How do you know that?' she asked, astonished.

There was a pause.

'That's where I come from,' Karol said, and Katharina was careful not to ask any more.

Since she never saw him, she made up from his voice the kind of model pupil she knew amongst her brother's friends. But after a few days she took off his spectacles, combed out his parting, took off his tie, unbuttoned his collar, wiped the pimples from his forehead, and let him wander through her dreams with long legs, wide shoulders and an angular chin. Now he had blue eyes, dark, curly hair, white teeth and a soft mouth, and her picture of him, though she did not tell even Sophie, was so real that she imagined her sisters were jealous of her on Karol's account.

It was much worse. The sisters believed that the names and numbers which Karol and Katharina exchanged on the telephone were nothing but a code leading to secret assignations. Mistrusting themselves, they believed each other capable of anything.

Christine suspected a love-affair between Sophie and Vavra, for the very parodies of the professor seemed a most cunning device of hiding Sophie's feelings. Hadn't she taken him a bouquet of roses last week?

Sophie on the other hand had made up her mind that Christine's air of boredom was pure sham, and to find out her secret she followed her sister when she should have been at Vavra's. Christine went into a café and did not come out again, and Sophie did not find out for some time that it had a second entrance. She eluded her time and again, and although Sophie never completely lost track of her, she began to realise that it was not easy to follow someone unobserved. When she did finally lose her altogether she began to wonder whether Christine had really vanished, would never be found again, and she turned cold with fear. What if she had really gone, had eloped, had been kidnapped, murdered? Terror invaded her and she prayed to all the saints for Christine's safety, promising to confess her pursuit as a penance. Then she saw Christine standing in St. Wenceslas Square, looking as if she were waiting for someone.

'I've been following you all the time,' Sophie said.

'I know,' Christine replied drily.

'I've been shadowing you properly.'

'I'm not blind. You're too stupid for that sort of thing. I've been waiting for you for a quarter of an hour.' Christine wrinkled her lips, then straightened them. It looked as if she were blowing someone a kiss, but she only did it to make sure her lips did not chap. 'Why were you following me?'

'Good Lord, because I'm curious.'

'If I ever catch you at it again . . .' threatened Christine, but did not finish the sentence. 'Well, let's forget it,' she finally said. 'We'll meet at supper.'

They parted without saying goodbye and never mentioned this encounter again, though they slept in the same room and often lay awake until midnight.

At the end of February, Professor Kulik operated on Heinrich, and all quarrels were firmly put on ice.

The operation was arranged at short notice. Professor Kulik telephoned one evening and announced that a donor was available. The transplant of the cornea could take place the following morning. Frau Sellmann asked for an hour's time for thought and spoke with her husband in Berlin. Dr. Sellmann agreed.

Heinrich had his bath. Then Frau Sellmann went with him to his room and told him what was going to happen. Half an hour later she called for Hanka the maid to bring a hot drink. When Katharina listened at the door a little later, she heard her mother telling the eleven-year-old boy the fairy tale about the Frog Prince. This had been his favourite story for years. When Katharina returned to her sisters in the drawing-room, she whispered, 'The Frog Prince,' and they all understood.

Next morning, Frau Sellmann and Katharina took Heinrich to the clinic. Heinrich was immediately made ready for the operation.

'He didn't cry at all,' Frau Sellmann told them at home. 'He just asked the Professor whether he'd be able to read afterwards.'

At lunchtime they just had soup, and when the telephone rang, Frau Sellmann waved Hanka back into the kitchen and answered herself. It was Karol.

'I'm sorry,' Frau Sellmann said, 'But we're waiting for an important call. My daughter will phone you in the afternoon.'

'She hasn't got my number.'

'Please give it to me,' asked Frau Sellmann and wrote his number in the phone book. The sisters had listened to Frau Sellmann through the open door. Christine who knew, as did Sophie, about the arrangement that Karol would always be the one to telephone, hissed, 'Well, now you've got it at last,' but before

Katharina could think of an answer, the telephone rang again. All three girls left their soup and went into the corridor. Frau Sellmann, pale and speechless, clung to the receiver with both hands. She was silent for a long time, and the sisters only heard the gabble at the other end of the line. Then she breathed deeply and asked: 'When may we visit him?'

'Tomorrow afternoon,' said Professor Kulik. 'But the bandage will stay on for at least a week.'

'Thank you,' said Frau Sellmann. 'Thank you, Professor.'

She put the receiver down and sat down where she was, on the floor.

When the maid, worried by the long silence, came out of the kitchen, she saw a strange sight: the three daughters sat around Frau Sellmann in the middle of the hall carpet. Madam was crying, the young ladies were beaming, and though Hanka was not yet of age, and had only been in the house five months, she already knew what to do at such a moment: put on some coffee.

Next day Professor Kulik took the Sellmann ladies to see Heinrich, warning them to speak confidently and, if possible, not all at once! He said this with a glance at the girls, but Frau Sellmann took it personally and later pronounced his remark 'highly unnecessary'. She went ahead of him into the dark sickroom while the girls remained in the corridor. At first she saw nothing but a white figure which she approached, then the nurse by Heinrich's bed whispered, 'He's asleep,' and Professor Kulik took Frau Sellmann's arm to lead her outside again.

'The nurse will call you when he wakes,' he explained in the corridor. 'In the meantime I shall have to make my excuses.'

They waited for an hour, then were called to Heinrich, but they had to leave him again after ten minutes since the boy broke into a sweat.

The day before Heinrich's bandage was to be removed, Sellmann came back from Berlin. He sent his luggage home and visited Heinrich in the clinic, then spoke to his wife from the bank, announcing his return in time for dinner. He then went to see Herr von Lilienthal, and after a quarter of an hour the two men went to see Herr Lustig. He had brought back news which they had to tell the old gentleman immediately. At the Lustig mansion Sellmann reported on the recent activities of the combined German banks, the consequences of the annexation of the Saar in January, and the secret preparation of a defence law which, as far as could be predicted, would lead to general rearmament.

43

When Sellmann returned home that evening he was tired but gay, and his face was flushed. He kissed Betty and the girls, and they all smelled that he had been drinking. Instead of asking after Heinrich, he began to speak of Lustig. 'He's a genius. He isn't a Czech but a European. He sees what others don't even suspect.'

'A clairvoyant?' Betty asked.

'No,' Sellmann exclaimed. 'He has vision because he is greater than we are.' He laughed. 'He's also got the best burgundy! Forgive me. The walk home wasn't long enough to air my head thoroughly. Soon I'll be good and serious and strong again.'

'I'd rather you stayed like this,' Sophie said, but her mother began to speak of Heinrich, and Sellmann's forehead got its normal wrinkles back, his mouth took on its brooding look, and, as always when he was thinking, his fingers stroked the loose skin between his chin and his collar.

When Heinrich's bandages were removed, he was able to recognise Kulik's outline in his white coat. Two weeks later he sat by the window at the clinic with Sophie and looked down into the garden where the first crocuses were in bloom.

'Open the window,' he said, 'and we'll pick some.'

'We'd have to go downstairs for that,' Sophie said. 'And you aren't allowed to.'

'But can't we do it from here?' he asked and pressed his nose against the window pane.

'It's at least ten metres down.'

Heinrich felt for the latch but couldn't move it. He went slowly to his bed and lay down on it. Then he took the small mirror which Sophie had brought him and looked at himself.

'Do you like yourself?' Sophie asked.

'I'm so small,' Heinrich said. 'I thought I was as tall as you. Did you always crouch down when you talked to me? Last night it was suddenly light in the room, and I called the nurse and asked her to turn out the light. "That's the moon," she said and wanted to draw the blind. But I just had to go and have a look at it. It looked rather like a big cheesecake, and I imagined that I could touch it. But the moon must be much farther than the flowers down there. How many kilometres is it to the moon, Sophie?'

'A few hundred thousand.'

'I think when I've had the operation on my other eye, I'll see everything much better. Don't you think so?'

At the beginning of April, Heinrich was able to say goodbye to Kulik. The Professor was pleased with his progress, but did not want to undertake the second transplant until September. Sellmann had made him give him the address of the mother of the donor, and had sent her, anonymously, a sum of money far in excess of the funeral expenses. When he asked Kulik for his account and the clinic charges, he was told that Eugen Lustig had asked to be allowed to pay for everything connected with both eye operations.

9

Herr von Sternberg

IT WAS THE first really hot day of the year. Sophie sat in the Café Slavia. The sky was blue. The door-keeper winched down the striped blinds, for the ladies near the windows were dabbing their foreheads with eau-de-cologne, the gentlemen delayed their ascent from the big, cool, white-tiled toilets in the basement, or fanned a little coolness with the edge of their newspapers.

Jan Amery, a slim, fair-haired man in his early thirties, junior head of the glass and china firm of Amery & Herschel, left Hess the Hatter's with a straw hat in his hand which he was firmly resolved he would never wear. To kill the time until his appointment, he had, ten minutes ago, walked across the street into the shade and stopped at the window of the hat shop. Amery owned a top hat for funerals, a yachting cap for sailing, a tweed hat for the hunt, two checked peak caps for driving, and a soft slouch hat from his years in Vienna. On his wiry hair each of these head coverings looked as if it had originally belonged to someone with a much smaller head, and was being given its last chance before being finally discarded. The hat he had just bought looked at first sight like a lightly cooked, ruffled omelette from which the actual crown stood out flat but definite.

Now, spinning the hat like a circular saw, his thoughts became quite cheerful, and he let his steps become more lively, without relaxing his straight, military bearing which seemed arrogant to most people and not what it was, the almost awkward habit of self-discipline of a young man who, from his earliest years, had had more trouble keeping the world at a distance than conquering it. He had few friends, strictly speaking only two, a jockey in Kuchelbad, and a gamekeeper in Dubislav in the Böhmerwald, and could not remember speaking with them about anything but horses, guns, or winter-fodder. Neither of them knew about the other, and it would never have occurred to them to ask him about any of his other interests.

Amery's relationships with women, apart from a schoolboy crush which lasted two years, were distinguished by their brevity. He called a relationship that lasted more than two weeks 'romantic' and broke it off. His success was mostly due to the fact that he didn't want success. He was indulgent rather than disappointed with any woman who made it clear that a second evening would be as uneventful as the first. 'You're simply saving yourself an unhappy experience,' he would say, and it didn't even sound blasé, but rather like a general pardon. If the lady changed her mind, and did it quickly and without inhibitions, he felt that good manners more or less obliged him to accept such a capitulation.

To think in military terms seemed natural to Amery. If he had had a brother he would have become an officer. The knowledge that he would, one day, be the sole owner of the largest glass and china firm in Prague, sometimes made him melancholic. But he had never entertained the idea of shirking his fate. Amery & Herschel wasn't a store one could dismiss like a corner sweet-shop. With four show-windows on to the main shopping street, three hundred employees, a dozen warehouses, and a share in the largest factories in northern Bohemia which employed thousands of crystal polishers, potters, glass blowers, and tens of thousands of women and children working at home, Amery & Herschel was an empire whose ruler's task was, as that of the kings of old, to preserve and increase.

His father, Bohuslav Amery, did not like it to be known to the general public that he actually 'owned' the business, though there could be no doubt in the minds of his employees. He disliked the word 'owner' because it implied the servility of others. He kept the name of his Jewish partner, dead half a century ago, on the official business register, and knew no greater pleasure than to be taken for one of the managers by strangers to Prague. Since the death of his wife in 1924 he had lived simply. He had sent his son to the commercial colleges in Prague and Vienna, let him travel to trade fairs in foreign countries, and entrusted him with commissions which demanded decisiveness and judgment. On

Jan's thirtieth birthday he had told him that he wanted to relinquish the business to him within two years. The condition was that he should marry. He, Bohuslav, would welcome any daughter-in-law as long as she was capable of bearing children, and wasn't a German.

Jan smiled and waved his new straw hat. There was still a quarter of an hour to go.

Sophie, in a white linen dress with navy blue dotted cuffs and edgings, had chosen a table for two in the Café Slavia from where she could see the tram stop where Jarmila would arrive. She ordered café-au-lait. She'd rather have had iced coffee in this weather, but Fräulein Kalman had forbidden anything cold. 'The nightingale doesn't eat hailstones!' That was that. Jarmila, if she had been waiting, would have taken out a cigarette and blown smoke rings. Sophie knew she'd be kept waiting for some time yet. Jarmila was never on time and called Sophie a 'Prussian' for being so punctual. Yet there was a lot to talk about today, for tomorrow Jarmila was going to the Mangl estate. They wanted to think up a reason that would convince Sophie's parents that it would be better for her to go to the country to stay with her friend, rather than to travel to Vienna with her family.

They would also have to mention a certain Sixta, in a straightforward manner, of course, so as not to arouse silly suspicions. Pavel Sixta was a protégé of Fräulein Kalman's who studied conducting at the Conservatoire, had written songs for soprano to texts by Holan, and had asked Sophie to sing them. If Herr Mangl was agreeable, he was hoping to spend two or three afternoons at the estate, play his compositions, and if Sophie liked them, start to rehearse them there and then. As a man he wasn't what anyone would call 'suitable' – a dreamer, an oddity, with spots on his forehead and badly worn heels to his shoes. He called Schönberg's twelve-tone compositions 'the key to the kingdom of heaven'.

Sophie had prepared herself for her chat with her friend as for a small exam, but Jarmila did not arrive. Out of boredom she started to play a game which she and Katharina had invented to endure the endless tea-time sessions when the Sellmann girls had to sit ramrod-straight and silent. It was called 'Inquisition', and the rules were simple. One chose somebody nearby and asked them questions in one's mind to which the person could give three kinds of answer. All movements downwards meant 'yes', towards the ceiling, 'no', and horizontal movements 'perhaps'. The questions had, of course, to be formulated in such a way that one of the three answers fitted. When, why and how were not allowed.

Sophie chose first one then another of the people in the café, but became bored with them after a gentleman whom she called Herr Sigismund had admitted murdering his wife and doing the deed with an axe, but then became immobile, his eyes fixed on his neighbour's lips. I'll look for somebody in the street, Sophie thought, and glanced once again at the tram stop. A man stood there, about thirty years old, taller than almost anyone else in sight, in brown tweeds, a straw hat in his left hand, his right hand on the railings, rather like a passenger on an excursion steamer posing for his photograph. He had a narrow face and a strong chin; she couldn't make out the colour of his eyes at this distance. It took her some time to find a name for him. Tamino, Max, Rudolph? Was he a Dalibor, a Rameses? Sophie finally called him 'Herr von Sternberg', which seemed to suit him.

What she wanted to know first was whether he was married, but she didn't want a 'yes'. If she asked too soon, he might take his foot from the lowest bar of the rails and put it on the ground. That would be a pity. She waited until he lifted his head to look up the road and was pleased with the straight 'no' to her question: 'Are you married, Herr von Sternberg?'

But she had spoken aloud. The waiter who was at the next table turned and asked: 'Your bill?' but she shook her head, smiling.

Herr von Sternberg was waiting for the interrogation to continue.

'Do you want to fall in love with a blonde?'

He lifted his hand to his tie: No!

'Brunette?'

He let his hand fall: Yes!

'Slim?'

He laid the hand on the railing.

'Not slim? Fat?'

He looked across at a beer dray. That meant: Perhaps. Herr von Sternberg wasn't quite sure. He wanted a wife between slim and fat. No 'Venus de Kilo' but not something made of skin and bones either. A proper woman. Sophie crossed her arms and felt her muscles. Yes, they were just what he wanted.

But Herr von Sternberg was tired of her questions. He took a little walk towards the bridge, turned and, walking back, looked straight at her. She leaned back and drank her coffee but could feel his eyes right through her sleeve. When she looked back, Herr von Sternberg was in the process of putting on his straw hat and returning to the tram stop. The hat was a joke. She would have laughed if she hadn't just then heard the brakes of a tram. Suddenly her throat felt very hot, which had nothing to do with the coffee. Her fate, she felt, got into the tram and left her sitting there to lead a dog's life. She recognised the jacket inside the tram, but his head was obscured. The conductor pulled the cord, the tram began to move. No car stopped its progress, no tree fell, the conductor rod pressed against the electric cable, and both carriages moved away.

But Herr von Sternberg was still standing at the railing. Only now he was looking down at the river and his right arm was round the hips of a fair-haired girl. She was tall, slim, and wore a white linen suit, and constantly moved her high padded shoulders, either in laughter or to rub herself against the brown tweed jacket. When Herr von Sternberg whispered something into her ear and tried to kiss her, she bent coquettishly so far back, that he had to hold her. Then he stood back a bit to look at her. The blonde in the white suit leaned her arms on the railing and turned her head. It was Christine. She twisted her mouth, and Herr von Sternberg went up close to her. He said something and bowed, and Christine took the straw hat from his head and threw it into the river. They followed it with their eyes and laughed. Then Christine took his arm, and they went along the quai in the direction of the Charles Bridge.

When Jarmila arrived, Sophie was sitting in front of a glass of iced coffee. On the marble table lay an open packet of cigarettes.

'You're smoking?'

'Yes,' she said and gave Jarmila a light.

'Has something happened?' Jarmila asked and blew a smoke ring.

'What could have happened? I suddenly wanted one.'

'You're speaking an octave lower than yesterday.'

'Perhaps my voice has broken.'

Jarmila ordered a lemonade. 'I want you to come to dinner,' she said. 'I'm on my own tonight.'

'I can't today.'

'Well, you'll be with us for Whitsun. I've got an awful lot to tell you.'

'It isn't definite yet,' Sophie said.

'Are you going to Vienna with your parents?'

'I'll probably have to.'

Sophie was choking on things that couldn't be said. She kept the straw in her mouth for a long time, gave Jarmila cigarettes and matches, said 'please' and 'thank you', crossed and recrossed her legs, and looked into the street.

'Is he married?' Jarmila asked softly.

Sophie shook her head.

'Why are you so sad?'

'I'm not sad.'

'So who is it. A tenor or a conductor?'

'How did you know?' asked Sophie and thought of Sixta's friendly face.

'Because it's what suits you,' Jarmila said and blushed with enthusiasm.

'Yes, that suits me,' Sophie said. She wanted to smile, but only twisted her lips. 'He isn't a conductor yet.'

'But he wants to become one?'

'He's studying at the Conservatoire.'

'Does he play the piano well?'

'Very well,' said Sophie.

'Does he play Jazz?'

'I don't know. He's mad about Schönberg.'

'I don't know Schönberg.'

'His skin isn't very good.'

'Pimples? How old is he?'

'Twenty-two.'

'He's got stuck in his puberty. That can't be cured by ointment. Do you want my key?'

'No, thank you.'

'I'm going to the country tomorrow morning. The house will be empty until the end of the week. After that my mother will be back.'

'But I don't want to.'

'You like to take your time!' Jarmila laughed. 'But don't wait until he's conducting the Philharmonic. One mustn't overdo things.'

There was only one excuse for getting away. 'I've got a date with him,' Sophie said.

On the way home she bought a roll of peppermints so that her mother shouldn't notice that she had been smoking. Christine was already at home, mending the lining of her skirt.

'Did you tear it?'

'Yes, in the tram,' Christine said, biting off the cotton and putting the needle between her lips. 'Were you at Vavra's?' she asked without removing the needle.

'No, I met Jarmila,' Sophie said, and after a pause, 'in the Café Slavia.'

Christine found nothing more to mend, and turned the skirt the right side out.

'Why don't you go to the Deutsche Haus, you're half a Czech already.' She held the skirt in front of her and looked at herself in the mirror. She sighed. 'But what else is there for us to do?' and then suddenly in Czech, 'What can we do?' She put the skirt against her breasts, went up to Sophie and kissed her on the lips. 'You've been smoking,' she said before Sophie had had time to recover. 'And after that you've sucked peppermints. But the smoke stays in one's hair. I'll give you my spray.'

She threw the skirt on her bed, took a bottle of spray cologne with a long-fringed tassel around the rubber ball and began to spray Sophie's hair.

'Thank you, Tina, that's enough.'

While they were putting on warmer clothes, for the evening had turned chilly, they heard the gong for supper. The door of the next room crashed shut, and Katharina exclaimed, 'Boy, I could eat a horse.'

'I smell fried sausages,' Heinrich said.

Some days they ate the kind of food they used to eat at home in Dessau. Then, for good reason, there were no guests at the Sellmann's. Sweet and sour white bean soup, pork cooked with pears and plums, rice which was first covered with fried sausage, then with rendered butter, and finally sprinkled with white sugar – that wasn't what Prague people liked. On such evenings they were amongst themselves, 'amongst us barbarians', Sellmann said, and when one of the girls wanted an occasion to ask her father for something, she often asked Hanka what there was for supper. Boiled chicken took their courage away, he might just listen when there was fish, roast beef often overcame obstacles, but lard-cakes and rice assured success.

Christine might have chosen this evening especially, but this was not the case. She would have spoken even if there'd been chicken.

'Say it again, please,' Sellmann asked, and Betty put her fork on the rim of her plate to hear better.

'I'm asking whether Herr Amery could come to tea on Sunday afternoon,' Christine repeated.

'The barber?' Heinrich asked. And when nobody answered, he asked again, 'The barber who cuts my hair and who always...'

'Shut up,' Christine said, and not even Frau Sellmann came to

Heinrich's defence. Only Katharina gave her sister a threatening look.

'Not the barber then,' said Sellmann.

'No,' said Christine.

'But . . . ?'

'Of Amery & Herschel,' Christine said and took a little rice on to her fork. As if the rest of the family had been waiting, they all started to eat again.

'That's where we bought the crystal bowl for Wilhelm,' said Betty Sellmann.

Christine nodded, smiling with her mouth full.

'Should we ask somebody else as well,' said Sellmann, 'so that it isn't so solemn?'

That was a bit too fast for Betty. 'Wherever did you meet him?'

'In the street,' Christine said as if that was the most natural place in the world.

'Did he speak to you?'

'No, I spoke to him.'

'German?' asked Katharina.

'Yes, in German.'

'He's a German?' asked Frau Sellmann, and one could see how much pleasure a 'yes' would give her.

'No,' said Christine. 'But he speaks German like we do.'

'How old is he?' asked Katharina.

'Thirty.'

'Perhaps you should invite his sister,' Sellmann said.

'Yes,' said Frau Sellmann. 'Otherwise it'll look so serious.'

'Jan has no brothers or sisters,' said Christine, 'and it is serious.'

'We'll eat now,' Sellmann said calmly, 'and then we'll speak of it again.'

When Christine came into her bedroom near eleven o'clock, Sophie was in bed and Katharina sat at the foot of it.

'Done it?' asked the redhead.

Christine nodded and, looking tired, sat down on the blue and white striped stool at the dressing table.

'We'll have to get hold of two other men,' she said, 'so that it doesn't look like an engagement party. You can do that. How about Karol and Professor Vavra?'

Sophie and Katharina objected, but on the Sunday of the following week (a week's delay had been diplomatically conceded by Christine), they both sat at their mirrors in fearful and confident anticipation of welcoming their dissimilar friends.

In the meantime Dr. Sellmann had been busy. A discreet

enquiry from Herr von Lilienthal concerning Amery & Herschel had had the expected result: solid family business, solvent despite the crisis, owing to a quick change from exports to Germany to general overseas exports, exclusive manufacture of goods for special clients, and, most important of all, mass-production of cheap glass ornaments at very low prices. Quite unlike his usual, rather ceremonious and fussy manner, Lilienthal had made a thumbs up sign, and Sellmann had feared for a moment that the director of the Böhmische Landesbank had guessed what he was giving the starting signal for.

His researches in the case of Karol's father, Dr. Djudko, were not so simple, but they were after all only asking a schoolfriend of Katharina's to come to tea to take any exaggerated significance out of Herr Amery junior's first visit. Dr. Sellmann did find out that Dr. Djudko was a registered attorney of the city of Prague, and that he was chiefly known for his proceedings against Slovaks, a reputation not free of nationalist zeal.

Of Professor Vavra, on the other hand, Sophie had told them all that was necessary, and much that was unnecessary, and they were quite prepared to see him wearing both belt and braces. But even a well-known scholar would scarcely come to tea without a jacket.

Dr. Sellmann gave as the reason for the surprising invitations and the strange assortment of guests that he did not wish to let the second anniversary of their arrival in Prague go by without his daughters thanking those who had made these two years so 'well, let us say, so full of adventure'. That was, of course, quite untrue in each case, for Christine had only met Amery in March, Sophie had had lessons from Vavra only since November, and Katharina, though she'd been having telephone conversations with Karol for six months, had never even seen him. But each of the gentlemen no doubt thought that the others had a longer acquaintance with their hosts, and they all three agreed to come.

10

Purgatory

THAT SUNDAY MORNING, while the Sellmann family were still at church, an enormous bunch of yellow roses was delivered at the house. It was so large that Hanka had to divide it between two vases.

'There's something ostentatious about it,' said Frau Sellmann when she saw the flowers. She was in fact pleased, but wanted to put a damper on Christine's spirits. The card, in which Amery once again thanked her for the invitation, she declared 'nice'.

After the midday meal Hanka and the cook laid the round table in the drawing-room, but when Frau Sellmann got up from her siesta she wasn't really pleased with the effect. The whole thing should be more relaxed, she said, but the servants didn't know enough German to understand what she meant. She therefore took a hand herself, opened the glass door to the living-room and distributed sugar basins, cream jugs, bowls of biscuits, plates of lemon slices and ashtrays in that room as well. She stood the cognac and chartreuse decanters on a silver tray on the grand piano, she loosened the flower arrangements, shut the windows, and had less than half an hour left to tidy her hair when the bell rang.

'Go and open the door,' Betty said to Hanka. 'I expect it'll be more flowers.'

But it was no delivery boy with flowers, but Professor Vavra carrying a bouquet.

'Many thanks,' Hanka said and took it from him, but since he made no move to leave, she realised that he was the first guest. She gave him his flowers back and asked him into the hall. Frau Sellmann ran into the elder girls' room. Christine and Sophie sat silently facing each other on their beds.

'Your professor is here,' she exclaimed and hurried to her husband who was putting on his tie.

In the meantime Sophie had gone into the hall.

'Forgive me, I'm a little early,' Vavra said in German and kissed her hand. 'I'd quite forgotten how quickly one gets here in the tram.'

'So much the better,' Sophie said. 'Now I'll have you to myself for a few minutes.' She preceded him into the drawing-room, and he put his flowers on a music stand. Vavra had had his hair cut, and he wore a correct, grey double-breasted suit.

'As you can see, I've come in a bit of a disguise,' he said. 'I hope you'll be able to recognise me when you come for your next lesson.'

They went to the window and looked down on the orchard. Their conversation was so lively that they hardly heard Sellmann's entrance. Sophie introduced them to each other.

'Someone like me tends to be forgiven for being late,' Vavra said. 'Please be kind enough to excuse its opposite, and consider it a sign of my regard rather than a wish to be first.'

'I'll put it another way,' said Sellmann. 'We have come to feel so close to you through Sophie, that there could be no time when we wouldn't be delighted by your visit.'

'Except when we aren't at home,' Sophie added, and both men thought it a good beginning. Then Christine, very beautiful and pale in a rust-coloured dress came in, followed by Katharina who tripped over the carpet in her excitement. Dr. Sellmann explained the subjects of some of the paintings, Christine added some Zerbst stories which she thought appropriate, Sophie smiled, and Katharina was almost fainting. When Sellmann mentioned that while he was a student he had taken a trip on a trawler from Scotland to Reykjavik, Vavra began to speak Icelandic.

'Oh, I never got as far as that,' Sellmann exclaimed, but Vavra would not allow this objection. 'My pronunciation is bad,' he said, 'I have difficulties with the silently aspirated "t".' He showed Sellmann and the girls how difficult he found it, opening his mouth and pressing his tongue against his upper teeth, so that its blue-veined underside was visible. 'In English too I pronounce it "f",' he said. 'For example, "Firf of Forf". Look. I simply can't do it.' He repeated the demonstration, 'F-f-f-f-f.'

At this moment Betty Sellmann came into the drawing-room.

'My dear lady,' Vavra said, 'you must think you've got a wild beast here. First I break into your apartment too early and when you appear I am snarling like a tiger.'

'As long as you don't bite, Professor,' said Betty.

She went towards the door to fetch a vase for Vavra's lilies, and at that moment the bell rang.

'That'll be Karol,' Katharina said in a loud voice, though she had meant to whisper.

'I'll look after him,' said Betty over her shoulder, and closed the door behind her.

Sellmann, noticing Katharina's embarrassment, led the professor into the living-room to allow his daughters to meet the boy on their own.

Behind Frau Sellmann appeared Herr von Sternberg. Christine introduced him to her sisters, and while he bowed his head with the whorls of hair over her hand, Sophie felt his cold fingers. He wore a grey suit cut as severely as Sellmann's and a striped tie. She noticed that he had brown eyes, though he seldom looked at her, but concentrated completely on Frau Sellmann. He spoke quietly with lowered voice as if someone were lying ill in the next room. When Frau Sellmann spoke, he leaned forwards a little as if not to miss a word. He greeted Sellmann and Professor Vavra with a strong handshake and looked pleased when he heard the professor's name.

'The "roman" or the "nordic" one?' he asked.

'The "roman" is my brother,' said Vavra.

'Have some tea, please,' Betty said and steered Amery and his cup to sit with Katharina and took over the professor herself. Though Sellmann had already done so, she again explained the Zerbst paintings. Vavra listened for a while in silence, then pulled himself together and said, 'I've been thinking for some time about this name "Zerbst". It is a Slav word.'

'So I believe,' said Betty and noticed that, while he was explaining the derivation of the name to her, he put his tea cup on the grand piano and tried as unobtrusively as possible to adjust the waistband of his trousers. He pressed his hands on his hips, stood on tip-toe, and jerked his jacket about as if he had fleas. It seemed pretty clear that he had left either the belt or the braces at home. But it was also possible that he might be doing without both and was in imminent danger of losing his trousers. This gave Betty the idea of putting him on the sofa. He managed to get there without mishap, though the bottoms of his trousers dragged on the ground.

The bell rang, and Betty saw Katharina go to the door. Her only concern now was to keep Professor Vavra from getting up to greet Karol. She had an idea. She asked Amery to take the big painting of the Wildfowler from the wall to show to the professor.

'Perhaps you'd better put it on your knees,' she said, smiling.

'With pleasure,' said Vavra, who could not understand why he should have to look so closely at a painting that had hung right opposite him. Dr. Sellmann had already explained that the ochre-coloured building under the virulently green chestnut trees was his wife's birthplace. Why did he have to hold it on his knees, the carved frame uncomfortably hard on his legs?

Then Katharina and Karol came into the room. The young man in the black suit might have been a liar, a burglar, or a murderer, but at that moment, as he stood, a little uncertain about whom to give his flowers to, everyone present, even Vavra and Amery, would have sworn to his innocence and been ready to defend him. He was so good looking that Sophie thought: I hope he lisps a little, or stutters, otherwise it's too much to bear! He was slim without being thin, and the neck above the white collar of his shirt was as brown as his face. He had dark, curly hair which lay close to his head. He went quietly to Frau Sellmann and gave her the carnations, then greeted his host and the rest of the party.

'Excuse me,' Vavra said, 'but I can't get up at the moment,' and gave him his hand above the Wildfowler.

Karol's manner had something gallant about it, something 'Hungarian', Sellmann thought, and if he hadn't known that this tea-party was being given for Christine and Amery, he would have been quite content just with Karol. It gave him pleasure to watch this handsome boy, and it took him much longer than usual in such cases to come to the conclusion that, though dazzlingly handsome, he was sure to be stupid. His wife and daughters were obviously of different opinion.

Vavra sighed and leaned back. He felt like one of the giants of the Clam-Gallas Palace with the burdensome difference that he had to carry the weight alone, and not on his shoulders but on his knees.

Sellmann poured brandy for himself and Amery, and when they had drunk, Amery asked rather unexpectedly whether Sellmann had ever been on a mountain-cock shoot. 'The season continues until the end of the month,' he said.

But Sellmann was concerned about Vavra and said, 'Come on, let us liberate the professor from this monster.'

Amery gave Christine a quick glance, then went to help Sellmann with the picture, and Karol too jumped up to help. Betty, begging Vavra to stay on the sofa, and signalling Sophie to join him there, went to the kitchen to order more tea. On her way back, Katharina ran into her arms, crying.

'Whatever is all that about?'

'He is so beautiful, Mama,' Katharina said, 'and I'm so ugly.'

'Go and take an Aspirin and wash your face. In two minutes I want you back without tears.'

When she returned to the drawing-room and had made sure that Vavra was still in his place, Betty went to Amery and Christine, and signalled her daughter to go and look after Karol. Then, with a fresh cup of tea, the Sellmanns talked to Amery for a quarter of an hour. Conversations like this weren't, of course, occasions for confessions or serious discussion. All three of them agreed on that. The rules for such a first meeting didn't include baring one's breast or revealing much of one's nature. The goal was not to make any great points, but to echo each other's opinions, to make opportunities for finishing each other's sentences. Producing some indisputable fact and expressing it in a new way gave them the feeling that there was general agreement. Though purely superficial, this gentle purgatory was a necessary preliminary. And if purgatory was said to have two exits, Jan Amery left it without doubt through the door to heaven.

There was a general move to leave, but Betty, seeing that Vavra was about to get up, called out to him, 'Do stay a little longer, professor.' When Karol said goodbye to Sellmann he asked, turning very pale, whether he might take Katharina to the anthropological museum over the Whitsun holidays. Sellmann was delighted.

'You'd better go tomorrow or the day after,' he said. 'We're going to Vienna over Whitsun.'

When Amery said goodbye to Sophie, she realised that they had hardly exchanged a word. Now she could think of nothing but a conventional word of farewell.

After they had seen their visitors out, Frau Sellmann and her daughters went to join Heinrich, leaving Sellmann to take the brandy bottle and join Vavra on the sofa.

'I'm very grateful to you for having kept me,' the professor said. 'You'll probably not understand why.' His voice changed. He spoke hesitantly and in short sentences. 'You said something very kind earlier.' Vavra looked at Sellmann meaningly. Sellmann nodded, since he was sure that he had spent the whole afternoon saying kind things to all his guests. But he found it difficult to return Vavra's look since the professor's glasses had misted up. 'You said . . .'

'Oh, let's leave it at that.'

'No, allow me,' Vavra continued. 'You said that you had come to feel so close to me through Sophie . . .'

'Yes, of course. And so we have.'

'I feel exactly the same.'

'That's good,' Sellmann said and lifted his glass to the other. 'Let it remain so!'

They drank, and when they set down their glasses, Sellmann noticed that the professor's spectacles were scarcely transparent.

'How old do you think I am?' asked Vavra.

'You're younger than I, much younger.'

'But not in my first youth. Do you mind if I walk up and down a little?'

'Not in the least.'

'I'll tell you the truth,' Vavra whispered, looking about him to make sure they were alone, 'I'm wearing a new suit.' Sellmann nodded. 'The trousers of this suit don't have buttons for the...' he was ashamed to pronounce the word.

'Braces,' Sellmann said, to the point.

'Yes. For an hour or more I've tried to get up and tighten my belt, but something always intervened. You see, I usually wear a belt and braces. But these trousers have no buttons. Might I go into the other room for a moment, before the ladies return... you understand?'

'But of course.'

When Vavra returned he smiled, relieved. 'Now it'll all be easier,' he said. 'I heard that you are going to Vienna, and by chance I'm also going there. For a conference. But now this opportunity has arisen...' He allowed the sentence to remain unfinished, waiting for a question, but Sellmann wouldn't help him. 'I own the leasehold of a house,' Vavra continued, 'a little land, a few shares left to me by my father, and from September I shall have a proper salary with, eventually, a pension, so that Sophie would be provided for after my death.'

'Who?' asked Sellmann. 'Who, do you say?'

'I was going to ask you at Whitsun.'

'Whatever has it got to do with Whitsun?' Sellmann exclaimed. 'Just say it again, please.'

'I want Sophie to...'

'No, don't say it,' Sellmann interrupted. He got up, pushed a chair back, walked around a table, and looked about the dim drawing-room for suitable illumination for his reply. He decided on the standard lamp.

'Of course the difference in age is considerable,' Vavra said.

'Please don't say anything,' Sellmann took a few steps across the carpet. The tea-party had taken a completely unexpected turn. All at once, three men had appeared who wanted to marry

59

his daughters – or take them to the anthropological museum, which was, after all, much the same thing.

'Have you spoken to Sophie about this?'

'Not a word. She suspects nothing. I had hoped, in Vienna . . .'

'For God's sake stop talking about Vienna.' Sellmann quite lost control. 'I warn you, my dear sir!'

Vavra looked at Sellmann with amazement.

'If you should even hint of this to Sophie . . .'

No. He couldn't say it. It was nonsense. Sellmann sat down. At that moment there was a knock at the door.

'Yes?'

Hanka put her head round the door. 'May I . . ?'

'Go away,' said Sellmann.

Hanka vanished and Vavra got up. 'I too must go,' he said.

Sellmann allowed his shoulders to sag and looked at the pattern of the carpet between his feet. 'I'll make you a proposition,' he said without looking up. 'We'll forget all about it. Neither you nor I will mention this to anyone. You won't speak of it to Sophie, and I won't tell my wife.' He looked up. Vavra stood in front of him, visibly moved. He gave Sellmann his hand.

'Give my regards to the ladies.'

II

Games

WHEN KATHARINA RETURNED from her visit to the anthropological museum, Sellmann was in bed with a temperature. The doctor diagnosed tonsilitis, not serious, but still . . . Late in the evening Sophie put through a long-distance call to Berlin. When it came through, Sellmann put his dressing gown round his shoulders and went to the telephone. He spoke for a long time with Frenzel. Sophie brought a chair, but he waved her away crossly. Telephoning had exhausted him. He became dizzy, called his wife, Hanka, his daughters, but nobody heard him. He held on to the candle bracket beside the mirror and wrenched it off as he fell.

The mountain-cock shoot with Amery had to be abandoned and the trip to Vienna postponed.

The following day Christine met Amery for lunch on the top floor of the Pelican restaurant. The place always reminded Amery of the first-class dining-room of a transatlantic liner, for the waiters wore white jackets with gilt buttons, and the way they pushed the hors d'oeuvre wagons between the tables made him think that the ship was rolling. The walls were covered with sea-green material, and one expected the hoot of a fog horn with the roast beef.

Christine spent too much time apologising for her father's illness. One sentence would have been enough, but she spoke of it for so long that Amery might have begun to doubt the reality of the indisposition. But he did not. He had always tried not to think of anything that would only deepen his uncertainty. To consider whether a woman was speaking the truth appeared to him as much a waste of time as to seek proof of the existence of God simply because one is a free-thinker. He could not remember ever asking Christine where she had been the night before.

He had originally met her at the main post office, at the telegram counter. The post office employee had, for some reason, refused to explain in German a mistake Christine had made in filling out a Czech form. Amery had helped her, then he had walked beside her down the steps to the exit. Christine had thanked him, then hesitated outside, wondering which way to turn. It was windy and sleeting, and they had looked at each other through the rain in a rather embarrassed way. Amery had opened his large, black umbrella, and while he had held it over her fur cap he had introduced himself and asked her to have tea with him. They sat in the hall of the Palace Hotel, and when Christine mentioned that her parents had stayed there when they had come to take Heinrich to the eye clinic two years before, it became clear to Amery that Christine was not a tourist, but actually lived in Prague. He asked her to dine with him at the Pelican, and over dessert had gone into the attack.

'To your apartment?' Christine had tilted up her chin and laughed. Afterwards she had been astonished how lightly he had taken his defeat. After a quarter of an hour she could scarcely believe that he had made such a suggestion. She agreed to see him again, and now, three months later, she sat opposite him at the Pelican and this time it was she who wanted to see his apartment. Amery had never repeated his invitation, since he had expected just such a turn of events.

61

Christine sat in one of his leather-covered tubular steel chairs and let her long white arms dangle over the sides as if the time for self-control had passed. She looked around her as if to decide whether she should move in. The living-room windows had light coloured linen curtains and looked out on to the river. The carpet was reed green and ran from the window to the tall book-cases full of books which were not in alphabetical or subject order, but arranged according to the colour of their binding. The bands of colour started with a red block in the middle, then became wider and wider towards the ends as they turned to blue, green and yellow.

On the walls hung paintings which Amery had bought at exhibitions: a female nude painted in the manner of an old master but with the left leg ending in an artillery grenade; a landscape where the trees stood upside down, their roots in the clouds; and 'the crooked village', a cross-section showing the interior of peasant huts which were built at such an angle on the slope of a mountain that the inhabitants slid from the chairs, and the soup poured out of the plates. A strange collection for a businessman, thought Christine, and Amery was not sure himself whether he wanted to keep them or give them away. He had bought them more for the sake of making himself agreeable than because he liked them. The firm received invitations to 'private views', since they donated large sums to art societies. There were always painters in desperate straits to pay the rent, glad enough to make original drawings which could be transferred on to a dinner service. Besides, he met on such occasions long-legged self-indulgent young ladies who were ready for a casual adventure.

Though Christine kept saying how much she admired the apartment, she did not in fact find it easy to like it. She sat in the quivering chair, and while Amery began to talk about their coming visit to his father, she picked up his table lighter and looked at her face in the glass table top. Why doesn't he try to kiss me? she thought, watching her blond hair swing beside her eyes. Am I too boring, too sad, too smooth, too cold? Why is he going to marry me? Because I threw his straw hat into the river? Does he suddenly feel that everything is over, because he has asked me?

Christine had no idea how embarrassed Amery would have been had she really asked him. Since he had declared himself at the tram stop opposite the Café Slavia, he had known that he had set off an inevitable course of action which led, that same afternoon to 'I want you to be my wife', and went on like a train on a slope, without brakes, ending inevitably at the altar of the Tyne

Church. Why should he marry her? Did he love her? But he knew that this was chiefly a matter of mood, of opportunities made and occasions arranged, and he had enjoyed playing a game with her and himself, making it difficult for her to say no.

Jan Amery had, in some ways, a tendency to 'be on the other side of the barricades', as his father expressed it. He hated anything fanciful like people calling President Masaryk 'the younger brother of Christ', or calling Prague Castle 'the new Jerusalem'; he detested *The Good Soldier Schweik*. He went to Mass every Sunday, to confession twice a year, and to communion on the main holidays. If someone had asked him if he believed in God, he would have answered as badly and baldly as he would have the question if and how he loved Christine Sellmann: 'yes', and 'very much'. But though people were glad enough to overlook his brusqueness as long as the china business prospered, and quite happy to disregard his piety as long as he didn't enter a monastery, there'd be no end of gossip over his marriage to Christine. One could marry a Czech dancer, if necessary even a divorced one, a Jewess, any foreigner, a Hungarian or Pole, in certain cases (especially when financially advantageous) even a Slovak, but one could not marry a German. Had the number of German employees in the post office, the state railways, and the army been drastically reduced only to bring in German personnel by way of the family?

Amery looked forward to the scandal he would cause. He sometimes wondered whether the prospect of going against society didn't, more than anything, add spice to the thought of his marriage with Christine. When Christine had asked him whether she should learn Czech, he had pretended surprise and said, 'Whatever for?' and he had seen in her face that she was grateful.

Yes, he loved Christine, and 'very much', though not ecstatically. She was tall, but small enough to lean her head against his shoulder. She had thick, light hair with a maize-coloured streak over her right temple. Her long eyelashes framed grey eyes, unusual in blondes, and she could change her expression, by lowering her lids, from indifference to admiration, from flattery to displeasure. Amery enjoyed the mechanics of such changes. That wasn't a gift one was born with, it argued training, a predominance of head over heart. To reverse this condition even for some hours would make his earlier experiences with women seem insignificant. He wanted to see her eyes dissolve. He wanted to hear her cry out in his arms. But he also longed for her face at the breakfast table, very cool and indifferent, as if nothing had happened. Yes, he loved her. And very much. He especially loved her formality, the feeling she gave of being totally under control, and he loved it particularly because he knew the time would come when she would break the bounds which she seemed to have fixed for herself. He had had a glimpse of this when she had taken his hat off his head in the middle of the street and thrown it in the river and he had been overwhelmed.

Christine sipped at her glass and smiled at Amery. He had been talking about their visit to his father for the last fifteen minutes, but she knew that he had been thinking of other things. She was afraid he'd not been thinking of her, and she suddenly went and sat next to him.

'What is it?' she asked.

'I love you.'

'Very much?'

'Very much.'

'Good,' she said and got up. 'Where is your bedroom?'

He showed her the tall, white-painted door.

'May I go in?'

'Of course.'

She took her handbag and went into the bedroom, locking the door after her. Amery was non-plussed. Had the time come? Strangely enough what came into his mind was not what might be in store for him, but that he had made an appointment for five o'clock with a photographer in his office. Though the business they had to discuss, the layout of a publicity prospectus for the autumn trade fair, could have waited until another day, it seemed to him improper to keep someone with whom he had an appointment waiting. He did not look at his watch. He did not want to know that it was barely three. Also he could hardly take up the telephone and ask somebody to put the photographer off until six or seven, for Christine might hear the conversation and consider it tactless or even insulting to set such a limit. Nor could he say to her when she called him, 'one moment, dearest, while I cancel a conference!' After what had gone before, Christine was bound to expect an impatient lover. Manoeuvres were at an end now. A beautiful war had broken out. But Amery felt himself not altogether mobilised. The declaration had been too unexpected.

He heard the key turn and the door opened a crack. Amery, who had been standing near the table with the telephone, stayed where he was. Christine's voice was soft but determined. 'Please draw the curtains,' she said, and he did so.

'Please sit down,' she said. 'On the couch, and look at the wall.'

Ah, a surprise, he thought, and felt, as he turned his face to the wall, an agreeable warmth in his stomach. He almost laughed. He heard the door open and one or two soft steps as if she was walking in stockinged feet.

'May I turn round?' he asked.

'No, not yet.'

She had spoken this in a louder voice and all in one word. Amery heard a sound as if something heavy and soft had dropped on to the floor. The scent of heliotrope drifted across, mild and sweet, like the memory of vanilla pudding, then Christine said, 'Jan?'

When Amery turned, all he could see was her left foot without shoe or stocking. The two big easy chairs behind the glass table obstructed his view. Nor was it very light in the room now that the curtains were drawn. Amery got up and walked around the table and chairs. Christine lay on the carpet, her right leg bent up, her hands under her head, her hair spread out, eyes closed, completely naked. On the white skin below her breasts there were pink marks, and across her hips a tight elastic had left a lightly perforated imprint. What confused Amery most were the blond tufts in her armpits. Without a thought he sank to his knees and rested his arms on the carpet which looked dark now, almost sea-green. He wanted to lean forward to kiss Christine, but she opened her eyes and said, 'Go and sit in that chair and look at me. You're just to look at me. Take your time, smoke a cigarette if you feel like it. I don't want you to touch me. I just want you to see me.'

Amery couldn't speak. He got up, turned a chair round and lit a cigarette.

'Why are you doing this?' he finally said in a voice that seemed strange to him.

Christine closed her eyes and smiled.

'Why?' Amery asked again.

'Because I love you,' she said hardly moving her lips. 'So that you know what is waiting for you.'

Amery said something.

'You've got to speak German.'

'I said that you don't love me,' Amery said softly in his usual voice.

'What more can I do for you?' Christine asked.

'Be more friendly,' Amery said and stubbed out his cigarette.

Christine smiled again.

'More tender,' said Amery.

'Hanka can do that,' Christine said, stretching out her right leg and bending her left.

'Who is Hanka?' He had quite forgotten.

'Our maid,' said Christine. 'Take her then.'

Amery slid from his chair. Christine took her hands from under her head, propped herself on her elbows, and laughed into his face. Amery slapped her across the mouth with the flat of his hand. She continued to laugh and he slapped her again. She threw her arms around his neck, kissed him with bleeding lips, and pulled him down with her. 'Take her then,' she whispered.

At half past four he accompanied her to the tram stop. They kissed. Behind the window of the tram Christine held a handkerchief to her mouth and never left him with her eyes while the tram was stationary, but did not turn round once it was in motion. Amery wanted to whistle for a taxi but couldn't. He ran all the way to Amery & Herschel. He was very much in love. But he couldn't whistle with his swollen lips. Nor could he sing, for though he had never worn uniform, had been exempt from military service for health reasons, his way of life had forbidden such public exuberance.

The suggested prospectus the photographer showed him was awful. Amery, who found it difficult to feel disappointed, looked silently at the paste-ups and shook his head.

'I know exactly what the trouble is,' said the photographer and took the sketches back. 'Next week, Herr Direktor, I'll show you something that'll really surprise you.'

No, Amery thought when he was alone, nothing will ever surprise me again. He looked out of the window at the crowds below. They had not changed in the last three hours or the last three centuries. He was amazed. He sat down at his desk and felt his lips with his finger. The swelling had gone down. He tried to whistle, yes, that was all right again. He telephoned his father. Friday about six would suit him, Amery senior said. He would invite Aunt Marketa. Did the young lady speak Czech?

'No,' said Amery. French? 'Yes,' all right then, goodbye.

Afterwards he telephoned the Sellmann apartment.

'Yes?' asked a young voice.

'Who is that please?'

'The maid.'

'Hanka?' he asked and noticed that he was blushing.

'*Ano*,' she said.

'Could you ask Fräulein Christine to come to the telephone if it isn't inconvenient?' Amery asked in German.

'She isn't at home,' replied Hanka.

'Please tell her that I shall telephone again in the course of the evening.'

'I'll tell her, Herr Amery,' said Hanka, again in Czech.

For a moment the receiver hummed, and he thought he could still hear Hanka's breathing. He put the receiver back and suddenly remembered that, having telephoned the Sellmanns, he should have enquired after Dr. Sellmann's health. He wrote a note, rang for a messenger, and asked him to take it and a bunch of flowers to Bubenech. It worried him that Christine, having said goodbye to him an hour and a half ago, had not yet arrived home. He would have liked to have telephoned the police or the tram depot to find out whether there had been an accident. He thought for a moment that he would have to kill himself if anything had happened to Christine, but then laughed aloud at himself and decided that he must go and eat. And indeed, when he left a few minutes later he was so hungry that he kept looking at a sailor who was walking beside him and devouring a hot sausage. Yes, that was it. No lobster or crab, nothing gratiné, garnie or flambé, no little pastry or little roll – something large and filling and porcine. He turned into a pork-butcher's which was almost empty and where a sweet, fat smell wafted out of a wooden vat, a smell such as he remembered from pig-killing feasts in winter. He went up to the fat butcher who hooked a large piece of freshly-cooked pork out of the broth with a wooden fork and flung it on the scales. Half a pound.

'All right?'

'Yes please,' said Amery.

The salesgirl picked up the meat in a piece of paper and waited until Amery had paid for the meat, horseradish and a salt stick. He went across the shop to a ledge, helped himself to a knife and fork, and began to eat. When he had eaten half the portion he began to feel new life spreading through his very bones, explosive and challenging, and when he had finished all the meat he looked dreamily at the fatty paper and the remains of the salt stick.

'Good, eh?' he heard the butcher say and nodded in agreement, then went out into the street and to the station where he dialled the Sellmann telephone number.

Katharina answered, and he asked her to fetch Christine.

Christine laughed.

'Where were you?' he repeated.

'Wherever should I have been?'

'I rang an hour ago, and Hanka said you weren't home.'

'Hanka?'

'Yes.'

Christine laughed. 'That wasn't Hanka, that was Sophie.'

'Why did she pretend to be Hanka?'

'Because she enjoys it.'

'And you were at home!'

'No,' Christine said. 'Father asks me to thank you for the flowers.'

'Where were you then?'

'I went to buy something.'

'What?'

Christine didn't reply immediately.

'What did you buy?'

'Witch hazel. You put some on a piece of cloth and press it on a swelling, if you have a swelling. I just walked up and down for an hour between the Belvedere and the cadet school with a piece of cloth against my mouth. Under the chestnuts. You know where I mean?'

'Yes,' said Amery softly.

'That's where I was.'

'I love you,' Amery said. 'Very much.'

'I love you too,' whispered Christine.

They arranged to meet on Friday to go and see Amery's father. When Amery left the station it was already much darker. There was a palpable disparity between his mood and the mouse-grey colours of the evening. He went into a bar and redressed the balance with a large glass of rum. When he walked into Wenceslas Square, the sky had turned a deep blue, and from the red beak of the stork above the lingerie store the great white electric cotton balls fell one by one.

12

The Silver Cow

BOHUSLAV AMERY POSSESSED a certain likeness to a long-dead actor who had made a name for himself as a comedian in the last century. His son maintained that he was the absolute image of this Kaschka. His portrait, cut out of a newspaper, had been put under plate-glass, and Bohuslav Amery made a habit of looking at Kaschka's picture as into a mirror. Though he did not like comparing himself to a clown, there was certainly a great resemblance, and it had become more obvious with the years. Like Kaschka Amery senior wore his long parting on the left, his eyebrows were broad and arched above dark eyes, and two deep folds ran from the tear-ducts to the chin. Above the serious mouth sat the same bulbous nose, and Kaschka's ear – in the picture only one was visible – had the same in-turned, knobbly rim and round lobe. But this would have meant little if there had not also been a striking similarity of expression. Both faces, the living and the dead, seemed to say, 'We know what's going on. You won't put anything over on us.'

Amery senior nodded appreciatively when he read that Kaschka had said, 'What, they say I acted naturally? If nature were only half so clever!'

At home he wore the same kind of shirt as the actor, with stand-up collar and a dicky round his neck, and over the double-breasted waistcoat a jacket with brown velvet binding, and when he wore this costume and looked at the picture of his *doppelgänger* he was happy to think that his own curtain would soon fall, and that he might meet the comedian in the next world where there was time for long conversations, half an eternity if necessary.

Bohuslav Amery took great, and especially financially important decisions after thorough preliminary work, and always only after he had slept on them. Decisions of a minor kind often depended on a sort of divine judgment. A window blowing shut, a pencil breaking, or a knife lying on its back, took on special significance. He did not, for example, own a domestic animal because a fortune-teller had told him to beware of dogs. But if she had warned him against a new glazing process or the signing of a contract with a Swiss firm, he would have laughed at her. Oracles were only valid in the undergrowth of private matters, not in the high forest of finance.

But the union of his son with Christine Sellmann reached from root to topmost branch, and when Bohuslav Amery, before his siesta on Friday, kicked his slippers from his feet and they landed perfectly parallel, lined up with the bed-side mat, this good omen alone could not set his mind at rest.

His researches into the personal history of Dr. Sellmann had not at first revealed anything of special interest. That a Catholic should work in a Jewish bank did not seem strange, and that Herr von Lilienthal should employ a German to keep an eye on what went on in the Reich argued for his business sense and the size of the firm. But why – and at this point Bohuslav found himself stopped short – why did Dr. Sellmann see so little of his compatriots? One could understand that he did not go to the emigré cafés. But why did no one know him at the Deutsche Haus or at the Society of German Nationals? The German beerhouse was just around the corner from the Böhmische Landesbank. Was he a stay-at-home who hardly left his family? Not at all. According to reports, he was neither unsociable nor a misogynist. He went to race-meetings and to the football club, had a box at the theatre, entertained guests, and had a good relationship with Eugen Lustig. But Jan had reported that apart from him, only the 'nordic' Vavra and a young Slovak had been asked to tea. Why this preference for things Slav? And for what reason had Sellmann given up his position in Germany? How could the Saxonia let such a man go? Had they suddenly not needed him? Was he too old, too headstrong, too narrow? But then Lustig would not have engaged him.

No, Amery had to ask his question the other way : who gained from the transaction? Sellmann? That was likely, but one did not know how. So it must be Lustig. But not just he, for otherwise Berlin would not have let a capable director go. But how could both Lustig and the Saxonia capitalise on the same man? To this there were only two answers. Either the interests of the Böhmische Landesbank and the Saxonia were temporarily the same, or Dr. Sellmann was not one man but two. If the first answer was the correct one, Sellmann would surely only have come to Prague for a limited period, and not moved here bag and baggage. If the second were true he must be either mad or a crook. Schizophrenia seemed ruled out. What remained? No, he must not allow Jan to marry this young lady. Amery senior turned on his side. The decision was made. He went to sleep. When he got up after an hour, his housekeeper told him that Frau Farel had arrived and awaited him in the small drawing-room.

Frau Farel, his dead wife's sister, was a tall, very slim lady with ice-grey artistically arranged hair, a wrinkled face with hardly any cheeks, and friendly brown eyes. Her straight black dress fell from her neck down past her knees without encountering a single bulge or bump. Long before the war, a doctor had suggested she drink Pilsner beer if she wanted to do something against her extreme thinness. The beer had no effect, but she continued to drink it for thirty years, about four pints a day in small sips. She lived on a widow's pension and regular contributions from her brother-in-law. She only visited him when invited, and on such occasions carried a little paper bag of violet lozenges, because she knew that he did not like the slight smell of beer which clung to her. Her restraint had retained for her both authority and respect. He valued her society, sometimes longed for it, and many times he reinforced the recommendations of his fortune-teller by seeking Marketa Farel's advice.

'I don't know, I'm against it,' he said when he had sat down by her.

'Has your witch forbidden it?' asked Marketa and bared her white teeth.

'I haven't seen her for three months.'

His sister-in-law offered him a lozenge.

'No, thank you,' he growled, so she helped herself.

'What have you got against it?' she asked and pushed the sweet against her cheek to make a bulge.

'They're not our kind of people.'

'Do you know them?'

'No. But I've enough experience.'

'Why did you invite the young lady then?'

'I've only realised an hour ago that it is all wrong.'

'A rather recent experience.'

Bohuslav Amery shrugged his shoulders. 'But in time.'

'How can you tell whether a man and a woman are suited to each other?'

'That is my son's problem.'

'Nevertheless,' Frau Farel said, 'you presumably haven't invited me to see whether this young lady understands anything about your business. I remember how surprised my sister was when she heard that you owned a china-shop.'

At the word 'china-shop' Amery raised his eyebrows, but then he smiled.

'That can't be the trouble,' Marketa went on. 'You are bothered by the fact that he should have chosen a German girl. I must tell you, Bohuslav, that I would, in your place, accept even a Chinese.'

'What makes you say that?'

'So that he finally settles down. These affairs of his . . .'

Amery interrupted her by getting up and asking, 'Would you like a beer, Marketa?'

'Very much,' she said, and while he went to the door she took the lozenge out of her mouth and put it back into the paper bag.

'You'll have to have a good look at the girl,' Amery said when the housekeeper had left. Frau Farel took a tiny sip and rinsed her teeth. 'You'll do that, won't you?'

Marketa nodded and took a larger mouthful and noticed that Amery sat down to one side so that she should not breathe on him. 'We're going to speak French with her,' he said.

'*A quoi bon?*' asked Marketa. 'Do you want to find out whether she got good marks at school? You'll just torment her.'

'I can't bear to hear German spoken.'

'May I come back again to an earlier point?' Marketa said. 'When you married my sister – how did you know that she was the right one?'

Amery shook his head. 'I've never bothered about outward appearances,' he said.

'I know that,' acknowledged Marketa. 'What was it then?'

'One recognises the right woman by the fact that in her presence one is a real man,' Amery said and felt that he had spoken the truth.

'How beautiful,' said Marketa. 'If I hadn't drunk some beer, I'd have given you a kiss for it, Bohoush.'

Amery, taken aback, drew his chin into his collar and looked at his sister-in-law. A kiss? And 'Bohoush'? Was she drunk? He would have liked to have crawled into his suit, hands, head and feet, like a tortoise.

Until the arrival of Jan and Christine he spoke only in monosyllables. When the bell rang, Marketa put another lozenge into her mouth and Amery was astonished to see how her tongue distended her cheek. Horrible woman!

Tea was served in the large drawing-room where a collection of hand-painted earthenware and china plates covered three walls. Between the windows hung a view of the Castle, almost unrecognisable in the bad light, and obscured by the gathered fold of the curtains. Frau Farel waited to be introduced, her hands folded over her stomach.

Christine wore no make-up. Her dress was coffee brown with long, tight sleeves. The material made her skin and hair glow. Her only jewelry was a bracelet of Bohemian garnets on her left wrist. She carried a small dark leather handbag.

Jan introduced her to his aunt.

'*Je suis enchantée, Mademoiselle,*' said Frau Farel, and bit on her lozenge.

She imagined she could feel excitement in Christine's cool hand. Not a bad sign, Marketa thought. Christine looked questioningly at the plates on the walls, and Amery senior showed her his show-pieces. At the same time Marketa whispered to her nephew, 'A beauty.'

'Do you really think so?' asked Jan. 'Do tell her.'

The housekeeper brought the tea. They sat down. Bohuslav poured some cream into Christine's cup from a little silver cow.

'How pretty,' said Christine, and took the toy from the old gentleman.

'From the Launa collection,' he explained. 'An isolated piece.'

'I thought as much,' Christine said.

'Why?'

'As far as I know, Monsieur Launa's collection was mainly of goblets.'

'That's true,' said Amery senior, astonished.

'Mostly of the seventeenth century, with coats of arms, flowers and scenes from the Bible.'

'Quite right,' said Amery and couldn't think of anything more to say.

Aunt Marketa took over the conversation by asking where Christine and her parents lived.

'Bubenech? That's that village, isn't it? It wasn't incorporated until after the war. The capital of a republic always wants to be bigger than that of a monarchy.' They went on to speak of Prague, and she admired Christine's knowledge of the city.

'I owe that to my younger brother,' Christine replied. 'I take him into town and describe what he doesn't see.'

'*Comment?*' asked Bohuslav, surprised.

'Oh, I thought Jan had told you,' said Christine. 'Heinrich is blind. That is, he was blind. He's now had an operation on one eye. That's really why we've come to live in Prague.' Christine smiled, but when she found that neither Frau Farel nor Amery senior had understood her, she blushed.

'My parents had tried everything, in Berlin and Leipzig, but no surgeon would risk an operation. Only here in Prague . . .' she lowered her eyes and took up her cup.

'And he's better now?' asked Frau Farel almost in entreaty. Amery shook his head as if such a question was improper.

'I don't know quite how to explain,' Christine replied. 'Last week my sister Sophie brought him a bunch of . . .' she could not remember the French word for poppies and admitted it.

'Do speak German,' Amery senior begged, speaking German himself.

'Sophie brought him some poppies, and of course they withered after a few days and he said, "Why didn't you ever tell me?" but we didn't know what he meant. He touched the poppy stalks and the petals dropped. "Why didn't you ever tell me that everything gets spoilt," he said. "The plaster is flaking off on the house next door, everything becomes grey and dirty, the pages of a book, the table-cloths. There are stains everywhere. I didn't know that." I tried to explain to him that everything has to wear out to make way for new things. "I don't want anything new," he said. "I want everything to stay the same." Now he often sits in his room in the evening without turning on the light.'

Christine was silent and nobody spoke.

'I'm sorry,' she said after a while.

'Would you pass me the cow, please?' Amery asked his son. He tipped the remainder of the cream into his cup, rinsed out the four-legged silver jug with some tea, and said, 'There are, thank God, a few things that don't wear out and are more durable than man. This toy has lasted through generations. Take it back to your brother. Perhaps it'll make him like the world a little better.'

Bohuslav Amery put the silver cow next to Christine's plate.

'I can't accept that,' said Christine.

'Not you, but your brother.'

'Then I must thank you for my brother,' Christine said, got up, and kissed Amery lightly on the cheek. She wanted to sit down again immediately, but Amery held her by the arm and, pointing to his left cheek said, 'This side too, please.'

The ice was broken. But Aunt Marketa still held back. That her brother-in-law should allow himself to be kissed twice by someone he didn't even know, while the mere thought of a kiss from her had made him want to pull his head into his collar seemed to her outrageous. Well, he had invited her to put the unknown girl under the magnifying glass, and that's what she was doing. It did not escape her that everything that Christine said was meant for one person only: Bohuslav. Even when she addressed a word to Frau Farel she immediately glanced at him again. Jan Amery seemed to be made of air. He sat at the table like someone who has shuffled the cards and dealt them, but isn't allowed to play himself, and Aunt Marketa had the impression that he was pleased that it should be so. Why did this Fräulein Christine never look at her lover as if she were in love with him, or if not that, at least in a friendly or interested way? If Jan spoke, which he scarcely did, Aunt Marketa felt that Christine only listened to him because it was good manners to allow other people to finish talking, but that she was already opening her mouth to say something quickly, in case he said something silly. One might have thought it was she who had taken Jan to visit relations, and not the other way round.

No wonder then that Bohuslav used the occasion of having such an audience to bring out all the old stories and jokes that had failed to make the family laugh these twenty years.

Christine laughed, of course, and bent back her head just far enough to show off the beautiful arc of her neck. She is cold, Marketa thought, and clever. Only cold women are really clever. The others get entangled in their temperament. But she's out of luck. I'm cold too. One shouldn't tell a personal story like that of her brother, because it leaves other people no way out. They are made to feel sorry, whether they want to or not, and that is ill-bred. I never tell people how Captain Farel was shot in the back by the Serbs when he tried to swim across the Drina, and certainly not the first time I'm their guest. One keeps that sort of thing to oneself. Bohuslav – whom I shall never call Bohoush again because he crawled inside his shirt-cuffs from fright – Bohuslav is a fool. So is his son, but there are excuses for him. He blows out his nostrils when she moves her shoulders. That means he hasn't had enough of her yet.

When Jan and Christine got up to leave, Amery looked at his sister-in-law, but she indicated that she was staying.

'Why didn't you tell her?' Jan asked softly when he said good-bye to his aunt.

'What?'

'That she's beautiful.'

'She'll hear it often enough from you,' she said and held out her cheek to him.

When Bohuslav Amery came back from the hall, he found Frau Farel in the small drawing-room with another glass of beer.

'I hate tea,' she said and laid her arm along the side of the sofa with finality, as if she was determined to stay for hours.

'I'm a little tired,' said Amery without sitting down.

'Your face is red. You should sit down.'

He growled and sat down in an armchair.

'Well, when is the engagement to be?'

'Perhaps soon,' Amery said and smiled.

'May I ask you something?'

'Please do.'

'Why were you so affable to her right from the start?'

Amery nodded as if he had expected this question.

'That was a ruse.'

'Indeed,' said Frau Farel. She could see that he was lying. 'And what did you hope to achieve?'

'I wanted to give her a sense of security,' Amery replied, thinking this a good argument in retrospect. 'She might have made a mistake.'

'Well? And did she make one?'

'No,' said Amery, and he smiled again, deepening the two folds in his face. 'None.'

'I want to tell you something, Bohuslav,' said Frau Farel. 'This girl is dangerous.'

'I know it,' Amery said and continued to smile.

'But not in the way you mean,' scolded Frau Farel and put down her glass with a thump. 'This Fräulein Sellmann is unscrupulous, false and hard-hearted. And worse: she is cold. I wish to God the same could be said of your beer.'

Frau Farel realised that she had gone too far.

Bohuslav Amery stood up and said, 'In any case, my dear Marketa, I'm grateful to you for having come to see me.'

There was nothing for her to do but leave. Amery took her to the door of the apartment and kissed her hand. Then he went into his study, sat down at his desk, and looked for a long time at the picture of his double under the plate-glass.

13

Lift Up Your Hearts But Keep Your Feet On The Ground

IN SEPTEMBER, AT the engagement party for Jan and Christine, Jan's father proposed a toast in German. He ended with the words: 'My name is Bohuslav. That means, more or less, "God be praised". I praise God that I was allowed to live to see this day.' Then he kissed the engaged couple and gave Christine a necklace with a blue-flashing diamond.

They had kept the celebration small. After all, it wasn't a wedding. Only Uncle Wilhelm from the Wildfowler had made the journey from out of town.

Sellmann tapped on his glass and embarked on one of his reflective speeches which gave his daughters the horrors. Only Betty settled herself comfortably as in a church pew before the sermon, and looked thoughtfully at the flower decorations of white and red roses.

On and on he went, from St. Anthony of Padua (with reference to his own Christian name) to the importance of self-imposed tests, the meaning of waiting and maturing, until he seemed to notice that he had been speaking for too long, for suddenly he took up his glass as if he hoped this would help him to a quick conclusion. The opposite was the case. While everyone except Betty made ready to toast the happy pair, Sellmann went on to mention Florence Nightingale, Habeas Corpus, the sinking of the *Titanic*, until he seemed to be speaking mostly to himself. It became quite painful, and there was nothing for him to do but make an end with 'However that might be', – Sellmann cleared his throat, which some of his audience took to mean that he was deeply moved – 'You know what I wish you!'

When the glasses had once more been filled, everyone was astonished to see Wilhelm Sintenis, Frau Sellmann's brother, getting to his feet. This was quite unexpected, for he had only been asked because nobody had thought he would come. Now he stood up, his hands folded over his black jacket, and Betty expected the worst. She hoped that he would at least not demonstrate how to smoke cigarillos the wrong way round, the burning end in the mouth!

'My friends,' he said, 'I don't, strictly speaking, really fit in here at all. I'm a sworn bachelor. But that is the very reason why I've come to your engagement party, which'll let me off coming to the wedding. For I am more interested in beginnings than in ends. The fathers of the happy couple have spoken, in moving words, mainly about themselves. I understand that. What else should one speak about on such an occasion. So I'll do the same. I'll tell you about love. Don't be afraid, Betty! Not about my own. And you needn't be afraid that I'll get up and dance on the table. I know how to behave in polite society.'

'But Wilhelm!' Frau Sellmann exclaimed.

'I'm talking about love, a great love at a time when hobble skirts were in fashion. You'll remember, my dear lady,' he turned to Aunt Marketa. 'Below the knee skirts got so narrow that the girls were only able to mince along. But they danced like mad nevertheless. Well, it was Sunday and the band was playing, when

77

a young man we hadn't seen before came to the Wildfowler, a young man in a blue double-breasted suit.

'The pavilion beyond the pond was lit up with carbide lamps and was reflected in the water. 'Twas a fine evening, Betty, wasn't it?'

'Yes,' said Frau Sellmann and lowered her head.

'The new young man with the gold spectacles didn't dance. Not because the girls didn't want to. No, no, no. They couldn't crane their necks far enough, and the mothers began to fuss. They could just smell that he was single and grand and maybe high-born, and even with a bit of money in the background. They couldn't stop looking at him. Right?' he asked Betty, but she just nodded.

'But the young man looked only in one direction. And who stood there?' Sintenis paused, and then said amongst general laughter, 'I did.

'But I wasn't alone. Betty and I stood by the table with the glasses under the chestnut tree. Because we had to keep our eye on things. Sometimes we had some long-fingered customers, you'll know what I mean. Suddenly the young man got up and came over and asked Betty, "From whom do I ask permission to dance with you?" And she said, "My brother." That was me, no more than a snotty-nosed youngster in those days, but I said, "I don't mind," and off they went to the dance floor and started to dance, he in his blue suit, and she in a white dress, a waltz and another and another. Well, you could soon see what was in the wind, but things didn't go quite as fast or as simply as nowadays. Every Sunday Dr. Sellmann came to the Wildfowler, and when he finally asked my sister when she'd introduce him to her father, she said ...' he looked across at Frau Sellmann, 'Well, Betty, what did you say?'

'Soon.'

'Soon,' Sintenis repeated. 'But then you said, "When the chickens fly south in the autumn", that's what you said. Because you were a girl with rather a prickly manner.'

'Yes,' said Frau Sellmann.

'But in the autumn you had your wedding.' He paused for a long time and shut his eyes. 'I wish you a love as great and as simple,' he finally said to Jan and Christine, 'and that it lasts as long. My toast is: to love!'

Christine fell around his neck and cried.

'*That* is a man,' Aunt Marketa said to Bohuslav Amery. He nodded.

Jan was a little embarrassed when he thanked Sintenis. But embarrassment suited him, and in Sophie's eyes he looked like Herr von Sternberg again.

Next morning the engagement was announced in most of the Czech and German papers, and cards and flowers came from Lustig, Professor Kulik, Vavra, Fräulein Kalman and Karol. Two days later Uncle Wilhelm said goodbye, and life went on as before, except that the Sellmanns now had an engaged daughter in the house.

At the beginning of October, Jan Amery renewed his invitation to go on a shoot, and Sellmann went with him to the Böhmerwald, accompanied by Christine and Katharina.

'I'm bound to shoot a twelve-pointer stag,' Katharina called out of the window of the car.

Every free afternoon Sophie went to Fräulein Kalman's to study, with her teacher and Pavel Sixta, the songs she was to sing at a concert in November. They soon had difficulties with the texts, for Fräulein Kalman thought the poems Sixta had chosen stilted and overblown. An attempt to use German verses foundered on his lack of an ear for the language. He kept putting the emphasis on the wrong syllables, and Fräulein Kalman constantly brought this up against him.

Finally they decided on a Czech cycle of Italian folksongs by Jan Neruda.

'That's international,' Fräulein Kalman said. 'A German singer performing the Czech version of Italian folksongs.' When she got home at night, Sophie was determined to become a professional singer, and since she slept in Heinrich's room while Katharina was away, she told him about it, and Heinrich became very enthusiastic. 'The moment I've had my second operation I'll learn to play the piano and accompany you.'

Since the summer holidays, she went to Vavra only once a week. The 'nordic' Professor seemed to have become old and slovenly in the course of a few months. Sometimes he had not shaved or wore no collar. He began to keep strictly to the length of each lesson, finishing off promptly when the bell of St. Ludmilla struck the hour. The texts he gave Sophie to translate were shorter and seemed chosen at random.

The night Sellmann was due back from the trip to the Böhmerwald, she arrived home from her lesson to find her father's and Amery's coats hanging in the cloakroom. Hanka was just coming out of the kitchen carrying the tray with the punch-bowl and glasses, and the smell of the Loden coats and the steam from the punch mingled in the corridor. Sophie heard Katharina's voice through the open door and went in.

They all sat round the table, still in grey hunting jackets, and gave Sophie a great welcome. Sellmann embraced her and would have liked to have pulled her on to his knees but had to let her go to greet Amery and her sisters. Jan kissed her hand. His blond, stiff hair, which shone as if it were wet, was suspended for a moment before her face, then she laid her face against Christine and Katharina's red cheeks. The redhead had been interrupted by Sophie's arrival in her description of how they had caught trout and baked them with caraway seeds and scrambled egg in a cake tin, and how they had all drunk beer with the dish. Then they all toasted the twelve-pointer stag Sellmann had shot, whose antlers would arrive the following week after the necessary treatment. Jan Amery hardly spoke, but only smiled and nodded now and then when Sellmann or Katharina looked at him as if they needed confirmation from somebody who knew all about it. Christine was very quiet. Sophie realised that she would have liked to have gone to change, to get rid of the smell of wood and fire, fish and game.

'It was really rather boring,' she said to Sophie when they were in bed around midnight. 'We had to cook, wash up, and see to the fire, and we slept on wooden bunks. I think the stag that Papa shot had been tied to a tree, otherwise he wouldn't have hit it.'

'Were you there?' asked Sophie.

'No,' said Christine. 'Four o'clock in the morning is too early for me to go into the forest, and anyway, I had a headache.'

Christine threw aside the bedclothes and lifted her outstretched legs in the air. Her nightdress slid on to her stomach and revealed her white thighs. Then she straddled her legs as wide as they would go, and after a while moved them together again, slow and trembling.

'For the stomach,' she said, groaning. 'I saw it in an illustrated paper. Do you want to have a go?'

'I haven't got a stomach,' said Sophie.

'Perhaps there's an exercise for the bosom,' Christine said before lifting up her legs once more. 'Or haven't you got a bosom?'

Sophie turned to the wall without replying.

'By the way, he has got a very smart gamekeeper,' Christine said, continuing her exercises.

'Who?'

'My bridegroom.'

'And did you stay in bed so late for the gamekeeper?'

'Oh no,' Christine laughed and snorted. 'He'd be much more in your line. He only speaks Czech, or pretends he only speaks Czech. Also he had to guide the gentlemen. He came and chopped wood and took his shirt off.'

'For your sake.'

'He simply got hot,' Christine said and put her legs down and cracked the joints of her toes.

'Have you finished?' asked Sophie.

'You'll soon be rid of me.'

'When are you going to get married?'

'In May,' Christine said. 'If it were up to Jan, we'd get married tomorrow. But Papa thinks one should test each other for six months.'

'And if it were up to you?'

Christine stretched out her legs once more. 'I think Jan has passed his test already. He is very good. He gets an A with a star.'

Dr. Sellmann enjoyed his return from his expedition more than from longer business trips. On those occasions he exchanged, so he said himself, green plush for red plush; this evening he crawled from a lair under the sky into a carpeted and down-upholstered eight-room cave.

'Don't exaggerate so,' Betty said, smiling. She took his head on to her shoulder and stuck her nose into his hair. Sellmann wished for nothing but that this contentment should last a few weeks, perhaps until Christmas, or until the hare-shoot in the winter to which his future son-in-law had invited him. A family where the parents loved each other, and the daughters married for love *and* money seemed to him a paradise on earth. Next morning the dream was shattered.

At breakfast Katharina told them that Karol's father had made his first speech in Parliament. She didn't know, of course, which party he belonged to. Sellmann's suspicion was soon confirmed: Dr. Djudko was a representative of the Communists. Sellmann decided to take immediate action. He knew that Karol, after graduating from school, was due to go to the law school of Prague University against his father's wishes, for he had wanted him to study in Vienna.

Sellmann telephoned Dr. Djudko's home and spoke to Karol's mother, who told him in a querulous, but possibly just sleepy voice that her son would not be home until almost noon. Since

Frau Djudko spoke hardly any German, they spoke French. It seemed to Sellmann that it took her a long time to find a piece of paper and pencil to make a note of the number of the Böhmische Landesbank. From the way she spelled out his name he deduced that it meant nothing to her, which in a way put his mind at rest, but also displeased him.

Karol telephoned soon after twelve o'clock.

'I want to see you,' Sellmann said, and was surprised to find that his voice trembled.

'Has something happened?'

'That depends what you mean.'

'To Fräulein Katharina?' asked Karol.

'Where are you?' Sellmann asked without answering Karol's question.

'Here, in the bank.'

'Are you speaking on a house telephone?'

'Yes,' Karol said meekly.

Sellmann considered this an impropriety.

'Come up,' he said. The thought that one of the counter clerks might have heard this impudent young whipper-snapper asking if something had happened to his, Sellmann's, daughter, filled him with rage. He asked his secretary to keep the young man in the waiting-room until he called. Then he pulled down a small wash-basin from the wall, and washed his hands in cold water. Some minutes later he asked Karol to come in. The boy wanted to apologise, but Sellmann would not let him.

'That is a question of taste.'

'I was afraid . . .' Karol tried again, but Sellmann cut him short.

'How do you feel here?'

Karol blushed. 'I don't understand . . . do you mean in Prague?'

'No, in this building.'

Karol lowered his eyes and laid his hands on his knees. 'I feel fine, Herr Doktor.'

'Really?'

'Yes,' said Karol. 'I don't suppose you asked me to come and see you to enquire how I liked it in a bank.'

'Why not?' asked Sellmann, taking Karol's quiet insistence for impudence and boastfulness. 'Why should I not discuss such a thing with an acquaintance of my daughter's?'

'I don't know,' Karol said, looking up at him. 'You're probably right.'

Karol's easy compliance provoked Sellmann, since he now had to attack into a void, a risk in conversation as well as in war.

Karol looked like a Roman, or a dancer, or a young herdsman from a Slovak goat-village who'd been dressed up in English suiting. It was Sellmann's deep-seated opinion that a person could not be at one and the same time healthy and intelligent, well-built and clever, apple-cheeked and distinguished. This Karol seemed a monster to him. Had Sellmann been in his place, he would have learned to sing or tap-dance, or play on a comb. One couldn't believe anything that a man with such a face said. He belonged in a variety show, or the life-class of an art school, not in an office or the auditorium of a university.

'I have a request to make,' Sellmann said at last. 'No doubt you can guess what it is.'

No, Karol couldn't think what it was.

'I want you to break off your acquaintance with my daughter.'

Now it was out. Not perhaps very impressively, but at least in a stern and final manner. Karol suddenly put his hands on the arms of the chair as if he wanted to get up and leave. But then he smiled.

'What do you think so funny?' asked Sellmann.

'Nothing, Herr Doktor,' Karol said. 'On the contrary. I'm just wondering why you should ask me. Wouldn't it be simpler if you asked Katharina?'

'I'll do that too,' said Sellmann and noticed how awkward he was in dealing with those of his daughters' admirers whom he wanted to get rid of.

'It would be easier for me if Katharina told me.'

'She will, she will.' Sellmann nodded.

'Will she also tell me the reason why we mustn't see each other again?'

'She'll write to you about everything,' said Sellmann and rose so formally that Karol could not but get up as well.

'May I ask one more question?' asked Karol. 'Is your decision purely and simply because of me, or are other people involved?'

'I have nothing against you personally,' said Sellmann.

'Thank you,' said Karol. He bowed, and went out without taking any notice of Sellmann's slightly outstretched hand.

That day the postman brought a little parcel which was addressed to Mademoiselle Katharina Sellmann. The sender was a firm in Annemasse, a name which meant nothing to the rest of the family. When Katharina came home at noon, the packet lay beside her soup plate, and they all noticed her embarrassment with pleasure. She hurried with her meal, went into her room, and soon after Sophie and Christine heard the bathroom door being bolted.

'Soap,' Sophie guessed.

'Or a love potion,' said Christine, 'for the handsome boy from Bratislava. She never stopped talking about him at Dubislav. She probably finds him too shy.'

They heard Katharina come out of the bathroom, go into her room, and when she was on her way back to the bathroom, Christine had her eye to the keyhole.

'She's carrying a thick book,' she whispered. 'I don't know what it is. Perhaps the Bible.'

Katharina had fetched the French-German dictionary from her room, for her French wasn't quite good enough for the directions of use for the *rectificateur* which she had ordered from a business called '*Le beau nez*'. Half an hour later she sat on the side of the bath, the strings of the 'nose corrector' tied firmly behind her head, and felt a pleasant prickling under the apparatus which she thought was the beginning of the desired shrinking. 'I'll do it,' she kept saying to herself, and though the instructions counselled use for only a short time to begin with, she left it on until the evening. When she took it off in the end, the *rectificateur* had dug two vertical red furrows. She shut herself up in her room, and did not appear at the evening meal. When Frau Sellmann went to fetch Heinrich, Katharina held her hands in front of her nose but did not cry.

When Sellmann came home that night he was in a bad mood. He felt wounded by the conclusion of his interview with Karol, and in the course of the afternoon he had been called in to see Herr von Lilienthal who had made, to Sellmann's mind, a malicious enquiry about Sellmann's recent stag hunt. On his drive home, the car had slid on a curve on the wet road, and Sellmann had hit his forehead against the hard rim of the window, whereupon he had had an unpleasant quarrel with his chauffeur.

The supper, his favourite dumplings, should have made him feel better, but Katharina's refusal to come to the table made him suspicious, cross, and took away his appetite. When he asked whether she had left the house in the afternoon, or whether anyone had telephoned, he was assured that there had been no messages. But that was no alibi. Karol could have met Katharina after school, since he had left the bank in good time.

After supper, having refused the pear dessert, he said to Betty, 'I expect Katharina in my study in half an hour.'

She appeared right on time and held a handkerchief to her nose. Sellmann thought she wanted to blow her nose and gave her time for this. He left his Van-de-Velde desk and walked to the door, then turned and sat down in an easy chair. He had become calmer. He wanted to be gentle. Katharina took the handkerchief from her face, and let him see her blood-suffused nose.

'My God,' Sellmann exclaimed. 'Who's done that to you?'

'You,' Katharina said. 'You and your wife. You've brought me into the world with this horrible nose, and I've got to live with it.'

He put his arm around her shoulder, and decided to put off what he had meant to say, but Katharina asked, 'What did you want to tell me?'

'We'll leave it till tomorrow.'

'Is it about Karol?'

'Yes.'

'Has something happened?'

Sellman shook his head and stood up.

'You haven't seen him since we got back from our trip?'

'No,' Katharina replied.

'I don't want you to see him again.'

'Why not?' asked Katharina.

'If it's important to you, I'll arrange for you to meet once more. Apart from that I demand your word of honour that this affair is at an end.'

'But why?' asked Katharina.

'I cannot allow you to be friendly with the son of a Communist.'

'Is Dr. Djudko a Communist?'

'Yes.'

'But Karol . . .' Katharina began, 'he's nothing. I mean, he has no definite views.'

'That makes it worse. Do you want to see him again?'

'No,' Katharina said. She had turned very pale. Only the thick, bloodshot nose glowed in her face. She got up and left the room without turning round. Sellmann had to admire her composure. Lectures in history obviously paid off. One went to bed with one's tears, not into the streets.

But some time later Katharina came back.

'I've thought about it,' she said and sat down opposite her father. 'I want to see Karol once more.'

'As you like,' Sellmann said, a little disappointed.

'But I want to ask a favour.'

'I'm listening.'

'I want Karol to come here.'

'Why not?'

'That isn't all,' said Katharina. 'I want you to be there when we . . .'

'What?'

'When we say goodbye.'

'What do you hope to gain by that?'

Katharina did not seem prepared for this question.

'It's better that way,' she said on the spur of the moment, and since such a statement, spoken by a woman, always sounded more plausible to Sellmann than any logical explanation, he suddenly felt himself that it was only right, indeed 'better' that he should comply with her request. Once Katharina had left the room, he began to think that it had been a mistake. But he had given his word, and there was nothing he could do.

Strangely enough they were able to keep their project secret. Neither Betty nor the girls knew about it. Frau Sellmann was busy taking Heinrich to the eye-clinic for examinations and to prepare him for his operation. Christine had, without telling Jan, but with her parents' consent, started a course in book-keeping in the German business college, and Sophie stood every afternoon beside Fräulein Kalman's piano and sang, 'Whom do I love? Ah, I have inscribed his name in my heart', into Sixta's ear and he nodded, beat time, and corrected her. The twelve-tone line of the first verse had a leap from 'F' to 'F-sharp' which demanded courage and close attention, if she was not to land on the straight octave.

Thus they were all busy and Karol and Katharina's last meeting remained unnoticed. Katharina waited until her nose was less swollen, then fixed a day when the family was engaged, informed her father at breakfast, and asked Karol, from a public telephone, to come to Bubenech at four in the afternoon.

Though the outcome was never in question, the meeting between Sellmann and Karol had something of the breathless formality of a duel. Karol wore a light-grey linen suit under his black raincoat, Katharina a dark green high-necked dress, Sellmann a double-breasted suit in herringbone tweed. Sellmann rose from his desk when Katharina and Karol came in.

'Katja has asked me to be present,' he said.

'I know,' said Karol. She had told him on the telephone.

'Would you like something to drink?'

'No, thank you.'

Karol was extremely pale. Katharina had pulled her hair back and secured it with a comb at the nape of her neck. She held her hands behind her back as if she were about to recite a poem.

Sellmann would have liked to lighten the atmosphere with a joke, but after one look at Karol's sad eyes, he lost all desire for pleasantries. He offered them seats and went to sit behind his desk, but Katharina said, 'Come and sit with us, Papa.'

'Now children, let's come to the point,' he said when they had taken some minutes to settle down. 'You know that I . . .'

'I want to say something,' Katharina interrupted.

'Please.'

'I want to tell you something,' she said to Karol. 'We have never discussed it, but I don't want you to leave here without knowing it. I don't know what you feel about it,' she went on, her eyes fixed on him. 'In January I shall be seventeen. Then there are only four more years until I am of age. You understand what I mean?'

'Yes,' answered Karol.

'I can't promise to become prettier in that time. I can only . . .'

'Please don't,' Karol said softly.

'No, I wanted to say something else. I promise you that no other man . . .'

'I won't go on listening to this,' Sellmann said. He was furious, took off his glasses and put them in his breast pocket. He wasn't surprised that Katja was in love with this Slovak, but he suddenly felt like a voyeur who, after looking through the keyhole, is asked into the room so that he can continue to watch the love-making. He took off his glasses because he believed, like many short-sighted people, that he wouldn't be able to hear so well without them.

'My father would have reacted in just the same way,' Karol comforted Katharina.

'One point at least on which we agree,' Sellmann grumbled.

'No, there are two points,' Karol said to Sellmann. 'He has forbidden me to see your daughter.'

'Oh, suddenly?'

'Yes,' Karol said and looked at Katharina. 'I'd asked him what he thought of the idea of Katja and I marrying.'

'Have you gone stark raving mad?' Sellmann roared, took his glasses and looked through them first at Karol, then at the door.

'That's more or less what my father said.'

'Well, we're in complete agreement then. Anything else?'

When Karol spoke of marriage, Katharina blushed bright red. Not in her wildest dreams had she expected such a development.

'No,' she now said and got up to end the conversation as quickly as possible. Every word could only do damage. She switched on the standard lamp and for the last time took in Karol's white face, pale lips and dark eyes. Then she turned and went blindly out. When the door closed, Sellmann rang for Hanka, but she did not hear the bell, and he was obliged to show Karol into the hall himself. Karol put his raincoat over his arm, bowed without a word and left.

That night Sellmann lay awake for a long time although he had taken a sleeping pill. While Betty lay quietly snoring beside him, he thought of a proposal Lustig had made him a few days after Christine's engagement, a proposal well-wrapped up, yet distinct enough to be made out under the wrapping. This was, indeed, the second point that he had wished to make on the occasion when Sellmann had visited him, and their conversation had been interrupted by Victor. It was Victor who had been the subject of the suggestion, Victor who, at that time, had still lived in Vienna where the Sellmann family were about to travel, but who, since then, had come to live in his father's house. After having to leave the Vienna clinic, Victor had been sent to live with relations, but this arrangement had foundered on their greed, for they had tried to defraud Lustig by making his son sign legal papers, as well as trying to make Victor marry their own daughter by accusing him of making her pregnant.

Now Victor lived at home, and after Christine's engagement Lustig had asked Sellmann whether it might not be possible 'to bring the children together occasionally, before,' and these were his words, 'all your young ladies are married.' Sellmann had felt flattered, and had accepted in his daughter's name. But during this night after the parting between Karol and Katharina he suddenly saw Lustig's invitation in a different light. Lustig's relations had made a cardinal error by trying to rush into an advantageous position. Patience and perseverance were needed if one wanted to be on the spot when real money was at stake. Nor could one hope to cheat the wealthiest man in Bohemia, do business behind his back, or plan to pinch his son from under his nose as if he were a piece of boundary meadow which accidentally got ploughed up with the neighbouring field.

Sophie, Heinrich, and most of all Katharina, would go to the Lustig mansion on Sunday to have tea with Victor. After he had made his decision, Sellmann fell asleep.

14

The Elopement

HEINRICH'S RIGHT EYE was to be operated on at the end of November, and Sophie's concert had to be postponed until December 14th. It had been thought that all that was necessary was to change the date on the invitation cards, but Sixta found that the hall at the Education Institute was already booked for that night. They could not sing Czech songs at the German Casino, nor had Sixta any success with any of the other concert halls he approached.

'It must be my face,' he said sadly.

Fräulein Kalman wondered whether she should approach the director of the National Theatre, 'my bosom-enemy', to ask for the small ballet room, then had the idea that the Italian legation might make a room available since they were singing Italian songs. But before anything could be decided Jan Amery appeared one afternoon at Fräulein Kalman's, to everyone's surprise but with a matter of fact air, and offered to hire a room in the Prague Municipal House. He said he had heard of Sixta and Sophie's problem from Christine and was ready to take them at once to see the room and arrange everything. Sixta's objection that it would be too expensive was countered by an offer by Amery to advance the rent until 'the composer and singer' could repay him.

'Well, don't just stand there,' roared Fräulein Kalman at the bewildered Sixta. 'Run along! And take the Smetana room if you are sure of your music and Sophie's voice.'

The three of them set off in the rain, and as they passed the National Theatre, Amery, putting his hand under Sophie's elbow, asked, 'And when are you going to sing here?'

'When Pavel's first opera is produced,' she said, fast as a flash, and turned to Sixta, disengaging her arm from Amery's hand.

'Are you working on an opera?' Amery asked, and saw the rapt look of gratitude on Sixta's face.

'No,' he said and felt that the reply was too short and too timid. He tried to find something to add but could think of nothing. He disliked Amery's assured and indolent manner. He was put out, almost embittered, by the fact that Sophie's future brother-in-law had succeeded where he, despite all importuning and begging cap in hand, had failed. He was afraid of making himself ridiculous in front of this man of the world by his faulty pronunciation, and as they walked along, he felt the water from the puddles seeping into his right shoe. That silenced him for good.

The Municipal House, with its glass cupola and its frontage on to four streets, was filled from cellar to roof with restaurants, cafés, club rooms, conference rooms and concert halls.

Amery had obviously expected his offer to be accepted, for an official was waiting for them. The room that he offered them seemed ideal in size and furnishing. About fifty chairs stood in a half circle before a platform. Amery looked at Sophie who nodded, smiling. Sixta, on the other hand, as if to prove the seriousness of the undertaking, went to the black grand piano and asked to try the acoustics. He took no notice when he was told that concerts had been held here for twenty years without a single complaint, but asked Sophie to sing. She gave Amery her coat, climbed on to the platform, while Amery and the official sat down in the third row. Sixta opened the lid and told Sophie to sing, 'Give me your heart', the tenth song in the programme.

'Remember to sing *piano* when you come to "when I die",' he reminded her, 'and sing the end *fortissimo*.' He gave her the score and raised the piano stool a little.

Even the prelude bewildered the official who turned to his neighbour as if to beg for help. But Amery kept his eyes on the platform, and as Sophie began to sing, the scent of an unknown perfume rose from her damp coat. He tasted in his thoughts the necks and ears of former girlfriends, but could not think what it could be.

He found the text of the song vulgar in an old-fashioned way, at times even absurd, and Sophie's voice occasionally struck him as squeaky, but he found this moving rather than annoying. Sixta's composition seemed to him extravagant owing to a lack, rather than an abundance, of ideas. That a young man should write such music because he was in love with a singer seemed to him extraordinary. Only towards the end of the song did he seem to have allowed his heart to overcome the twelve-tone hurdle, and Sophie sang radiantly, accompanied by strong chords, 'I'll cut on your heart to boast of you to the dead!' Bohemian-Italian love-frenzy in unexpected F-sharp out of the mouth of a German banker's daughter who would soon be his sister-in-law – he was amused, and applauded.

'Could you hear well?' Sixta asked from the platform.

'Magnificently,' Amery called back and nodded encouragingly to the official. It was all settled. As he helped Sophie into her coat, he asked her for the name of her scent.

'But I haven't got any,' she said and turned, laughing. Amery looked at the little gap between her teeth and shook his head.

'Then somebody has tipped some into your coat.'

Sophie held the right armhole against her nose and said, 'I'm sorry, I can only smell mothballs.'

Two weeks later Amery sat next to Christine in the first row of the recital room. The seat on his left was empty. Katharina had telephoned around noon from the house of a schoolfriend to say that she would come straight from town. On any other day her parents would have insisted that she come home for dinner, but on this December day there was only one subject of conversation: the resignation of the President of the Republic. Sellmann had brought the special edition with the announcement from the office at lunchtime, and towards evening he telephoned twice to Berlin.

Sophie was worried whether anybody would still be interested in her concert, and her father too only pretended confidence to comfort her. This made their surprise all the greater when they found the room almost completely full. But when Sellmann exchanged a few words with Professor Kulik and Herr von Lilienthal in the cloakroom, he became conscious of the fact that they had not come so much for Sophie's sake, or for the sake of the Neruda songs, but to exchange opinions with a few like-minded people about the immediate future. The men greeted each other with unusual seriousness, bent quickly over the ladies' hands, stuck the programme in the pocket of their dinner jackets, and, walking up the broad marble stairs, began to discuss the possible successor to the President.

Sellmann was pleased to see Eugen Lustig amongst the guests. He waited at the end of his row to catch his eye, and bowed briefly. Amery senior appeared with Frau Farel. Near them sat Professor Vavra next to Fräulein Kalman. On the left side of the room sat the professors of the Conservatoire and their ladies, and behind them the students in tight, dark suits and spotted bow-ties, determined to cheer Sixta's first public appearance to the echo.

Sophie wore a long, black, tightly-fitting dress. At her teacher's

91

insistence she had pinned a light-coloured cloth rose to the V-neck.

'I know,' Fräulein Kalman had said, 'a cheap effect, but Pavel's music is so damn highbrow, a bit of kitsch won't come amiss. Also you look so ravishing like this, that nobody'll notice the botched notes.'

Sixta had borrowed evening dress, shirt and patent-leather shoes. In the afternoon he had given himself a herbal compress which had turned his face the colour of a Red Indian.

Christine had asked Sophie for a translation of the texts, but Sellmann and Betty understood nothing at all. But perhaps because of this they were very conscious of the friendly attention given to their daughter, the quiet, mounting good-will which suddenly changed to true enthusiasm, so that Sophie, and this had not been expected, had to repeat the fifth song. The applause dispelled the undefinable odour of an amateur entertainment, and Fräulein Kalman began to breathe the attenuated air of the zenith of success.

During the interval there was a cold buffet, and while Lustig took Betty Sellmann aside, Sellmann exchanged a few words with Aunt Marketa, and her question, whether Katharina had stayed at home to look after Heinrich, made him think that he might telephone home to hear what was going on. It took him some time to get away and to ask his way to the telephone. When he found it in the basement it was in use, and when it was finally free he had no change. In the hope that Katharina might have arrived in the meantime, he took the elevator upstairs and arrived just in time for the second part of the programme. On Katharina's chair lay a bouquet which Amery had brought in at the end of the interval to give to Sophie after the last song. The empty chair with the bouquet appeared to Sellmann a bad omen.

The recital continued with the song Amery had heard when they had tried the acoustics. But Sophie's voice now sounded strong even in the soft passages, and after the surprising harmonic conclusion, the audience demanded a repetition. Sellmann looked at his watch. He saw that it was a quarter to ten, and however little he begrudged Sophie this evening, he wished it were over.

'Did you telephone?' Betty whispered.

Sellmann was unable to answer since Sixta already had his hands on the keys. He shook his head and realised by the way Betty settled her shoulders that she shared his worries.

When the song cycle was over at about ten thirty, Amery, Jarmila and an unknown girl went on to the platform and gave

Sophie and Sixta their flowers. An encore was called for, and Sophie sang, tenderly and beautifully 'Heidenröslein'. She sang the folksong version and sang it like a child, Amery's bouquet in her arms. Sixta accompanied her so quietly that one could hardly hear the piano. Fräulein Kalman cried and made sure that she was seen to cry. Betty too had tears in her eyes, and for a second put her hand on the sleeve of Sellmann's dinner jacket. While they were still applauding, Lustig went to the front and kissed Sophie's hand.

'That's as good as a medal,' Sellmann heard someone say.

But then something unfortunate occurred. A fellow student of Sixta's, a little fellow with a striped tie, forced his way to the grand piano and roared a long sentence of which Sellman only understood 'Republic' and 'Masaryk', and before the audience had got over its surprise, he sat down at the piano and began to sing the national anthem, helped by some voices in the back rows. There was nothing to do but stand up, though among Sellmann's acquaintances only Frau Farel was pleased with the patriotic demonstration. To Amery senior's astonishment, she even hummed part of the melody.

It was half past eleven when the Sellmanns arrived home. Katharina was not there. They woke the maid, but Hanka had thought that Katharina had joined her parents at the concert. Betty took a blanket into the drawing-room and sent everybody else to bed.

At about the same time, Karol and Katharina put a thick fur rug over their bed in Amery's hunting lodge and watched as the fire slowly died down. At midnight they listened to the last radio news, but nobody seemed to be looking for them.

Instead of going to school that morning, Katharina had gone to the University, but had found at the faculty of law that Karol would not be arriving until about ten o'clock. She waited about for a while, took her history book and her pencil case out of her school bag, and tipped the rest of her books into a refuse bin. She went to the station and bought two tickets to Strakonice, and copied the times of departure and the names of the stations where they had to change into her history book. On the way back to the University she took all her money out of her post office savings book and bought, apart from underwear, an umbrella, two tooth-brushes and some soap. With this new luggage she suddenly felt free and unimpeded. The fact that Karol did not yet know of her project and might have scruples, appeared to her, as she pressed the two railway tickets into her palms, of no consequence.

Katharina's plan was simple because it had a single goal, and clever because she had taken the frame of mind of her pursuers into account. In his Italian campaign, Napoleon had taken into account the lack of vision of the Austrian generals. And though it was not a question of Mantua and Marengo, but of Dubislav, a hamlet in the Böhmerwald, Katharina too felt quite like a commander-in-chief with her eye on victory. She expected her parents to look for her in Prague, in Germany or in Slovakia, but they would not think her so bold as to hide herself in Amery's hunting lodge.

She waited for Karol at the entrance to the University, put the new umbrella in his hand and took his arm.

'I'm abducting you,' she said. 'Do you want to offer resistance?'

'On the contrary,' said Karol, smiling. 'My right foot is already in the carriage.'

'Don't you want to know where we are going?'

'We are moving in a north-westerly direction,' Karol said and looked across at the astronomical clock on the town hall. 'But perhaps we could just stay long enough to listen to the carillon.'

'You'll need stout shoes,' Katharina said imperturbably, 'and your razor. I've already bought a toothbrush.' She took the tickets out of her pocket and pressed them into his hand. 'From Strakonice it's only thirty kilometres. Do you feel up to that?'

Karol put the tickets in his coat and nodded.

'We can't take the train until the afternoon,' Katharina said. 'I've got to ring up at home and put my . . .' she was about to say 'my parents', but couldn't, '. . . my people off with a fib so that we have a better start. It'll be an advantage if they don't start looking for us until tomorrow. Tomorrow is Sunday. There'll be practically nothing they can do until Monday.'

Karol thought that Katharina would probably like him to express his agreement, but could find nothing suitable to say. Then the thought struck him, with the force of an electric shock, that Katharina wanted them both to commit suicide.

'Are you feeling ill?' she asked immediately.

'No, no,' he said. 'I'm just so pleased.'

But then, why all these preparations, he wondered. And why not here? Why take a razor and stout shoes? He began to feel better.

'Go back to your apartment now,' Katharina suggested. 'Tell them that you haven't got a lecture, but that you're going on an excursion with friends. Not to expect you until late evening. Please remember that we will need some money. Can you shoot?'

'Yes,' said Karol and turned pale.

'Then we can get a hare in the forest,' said Katharina. 'Do you like to eat it "Polish" or roasted with cranberries?'

'Polish,' Karol said and shut the umbrella because the rain had stopped.

'Don't bring a big case,' Katharina warned, and they arranged to meet at twelve o'clock at the station.

Karol took a taxi. His knees shook, and when he got out and paid, a ten krone note fell on to the pavement. He did not dare pick it up for fear of fainting.

At home he was told that his mother had gone into town, and saw the cook's face as through a black fog. He ran into his room and threw himself on to his bed without taking off his coat, and he remained there for a quarter of an hour in mortal fear. Then he wrote a letter to his parents and put it in his pocket. He packed what he needed and took all the money he could find in the apartment. When he searched his father's desk he found a black-covered notebook. He opened it and read the first sentence, 'It is nowhere more important to break faith than in the case of treaties signed in blood.' He underlined this in red and felt better. It fortified him greatly to think that treachery could be a programme. Karol tore up the letter to his parents and threw the pieces down the lavatory. He told the cook not to wait for him with the evening meal. He gave no reason. He was not in the mood for trifles.

Exactly at noon he went into the waiting-room of the station, but Katharina was not there. He sat down at a table and ordered Slivovitz. He was startled when she put her hand on his shoulder. She had telephoned her parents. An hour later they sat in the train, packed tightly between workers and market women, most of whom soon got out. When the last passenger had gone, Karol sat down opposite Katharina by the window. Until then they had hardly spoken to each other. At the next station two young, buxom women got in and unwrapped their sandwiches. They began to speak in loud voices while Karol and Katharina spoke quietly in German.

The country beyond the window looked uneven and knobbly. The hills followed each other like great old moss-covered elephant rumps, with room only for a village in between, a saw mill or a gravel pit. Everywhere things opened up, a stream, a valley, a field of winter wheat, but before Katharina could look properly

95

the country closed in again. The fields hardly ever ascended gently, but came and went fast on the sides of the hills. The mast of a power-line on a height vanished to the south-west in the pale light of the wintry sun above the leafless apple trees beside a long, straight road.

When Katharina looked in the other direction, she saw that both the women were licking their thick red lips and heard one say to the other, 'Now I'll just eat that handsome boy in the corner, then I'll have had enough for today.'

Karol pressed his forehead against the window pane and looked out.

'Why don't you ask him,' the other suggested and laughed.

Katharina had understood the simple Czech quite well and expected Karol to rebuke them. But he did not move.

'He looks like an Italian,' one of them said, and the other gave a coarse answer of which Katharina only understood little. They both laughed and scratched themselves. Karol turned slowly and said something in which there were expressions Katharina had only seen on the walls of the school toilets but had never heard. The two women stuck their sandwich papers into their pockets and went into the corridor.

'Please forgive me,' Karol apologised.

'I don't know enough Czech, thank God,' Katharina said.

At the next station the women passed by on the platform, and one of them stuck out her tongue at them.

At Pisek they had to wait for an hour and wanted to shop for groceries, but the shops were shut. They bought some cold sausages at the station buffet, a bottle of rum and some bread. The train to Strakonice only warmed up halfway there, but then became so hot they had to take off their coats. Karol laid an arm around Katharina's shoulder, but though they were tired, they did not want to go to sleep. She leaned her head against his chest and felt the rough edge of his collar. Karol's arm began to get stiff, but he could not bear to move away from the scent that rose from Katharina's hair.

When they got out at Strakonice it was dark. It had also begun to rain again, in cold, flaky drops which stuck for a while to their chins and noses. An elderly man asked Karol whether they were looking for an inn. Karol shook his head. The man repeated his question in German, and Katharina said that they needed a vehicle to take them to Dubislav.

'That's a good step,' the old man replied, 'but nothing is impossible in this world.' After a pause he continued, 'Tomorrow is

96

the second Sunday in Advent. Father Christmas will soon be here.'

Karol took a fifty krone note out of his pocket. The old man took it and clicked his tongue to call his horse. Out of the darkness a kind of hackney coach appeared, drawn by a single horse. The old man waited until the coupé stood in front of them, opened the door to let them both climb in, then climbed on to the box. The leather smelled musty. Their breath dimmed the panes and made the houses they jolted past nothing but passing shadows. Only occasionally did light from a street lamp fall on the four white hands and two dark cases. Neither of them knew where they were going. It was unlikely that the old man would take them to Dubislav, but the journey seemed endless. They finally stopped in front of a house where the ground-floor windows were all lit up.

'Perhaps it's an inn,' Katharina said, but before Karol could reply, the old man was back again.

'He has a visitor. We have to try somewhere else.'

It was almost seven oclock when they stopped again. Katharina put her bag down to rub her hands together, for they were stiff with cold. Karol unbuttoned his coat and jacket, took her hands and pushed them under his arms. He tried to kiss her and touched her nose with his lips.

'What are you doing,' she said angrily.

'I wanted to kiss you.'

'Don't you know where my mouth is?'

'I can't find it,' Karol said and leaned forward, but Katharina took her hands out of his jacket and crawled into the corner, then suddenly threw herself on to his lap and sobbed so heartbreakingly that Karol wondered whether he shouldn't make it easier for her by starting to talk about going back.

Then they heard an ear-splitting noise, the door opened, and the old man stuck his head inside and called something. But he had to get in and close the door before they could understand him. He had got hold of a man with a motorbike, 'a Harley-Davidson with sidecar'. Because it was dark he asked for two hundred krone, but promised to get them there in half an hour. Karol gave the old man the money, and when he saw him hesitate, added another fifty.

The motorcyclist, sitting on the heavy machine, wore a leather jacket and turned on the headlight. Karol put the bags into the side-car, helped Katharina into the low seat and secured the sailcloth cover. He tried to say something to the driver, but he only nodded and put on his goggles. Karol clambered on to the pillion, and before he could turn to the old man he had to hold tight, for they were off.

The road, as far as it could be seen, led through hilly country. When they went uphill, Karol pressed himself against the back of the driver. Downhill he lifted his feet to keep them out of the huge puddles through which the bike splashed when they came to the valleys. They drove through several villages without losing speed, past glaring white house-walls and flickering fences, and saw, as they flew past, the warm windows of an inn. Karol shut his eyes against the lashing rain. Presently he got used to the noise of the engine and could differentiate between the shrill screech of second, the whine of third, and the growl of fourth gear, and he suddenly heard a voice singing, the wind tearing the melody away. He laid his head on the driver's shoulder and looked in the direction of the voice. Katharina was leaning forward against the windscreen and turned, feeling Karol's eyes on her, and he saw the white patch of her face.

When they passed the sign saying Dubislav, Katharina pointed to the right, and they stopped behind the village. While they took out their bags the driver held his wristwatch near the headlamp and said in Czech, 'Twenty-eight minutes. Bad time. But with this rain . . .' then turned his machine and drove away.

Half an hour later they reached the hunting lodge. Katharina put her bag down by the door and went into the toolshed to fetch the key. Cold air struck them as they entered the hall. Katharina searched for a torch in the dark, and, when she had found it, shone it on Karol.

'Welcome,' she said and then pointed the light at the fuse box so that he could turn on the electricity.

The house had three rooms and kitchen and bathroom downstairs, and four guest-rooms upstairs. Karol and Katharina decided to use only the big room with the fireplace, since it would be the quickest to heat. They hung their wet coats from the horns of the hunting trophies and put on the warm slippers belonging to the house, then walked about the place as if it belonged to them. Since it would have been difficult to move the heavy beds, Karol made a fire and then collected mattresses from the bedrooms and put them between the fireplace and the gun cabinets, then piled pillows and featherbeds, which Katharina had covered in clean linen when she had left in October, over the easy chairs so that they should get thoroughly warm and aired. When she came in with a tray of sausages and grog, Karol squatted on the floor looking at a map of the district on which Amery's hunting lodge was marked by a cross. Katharina put down the tray and kneeled down. She was wearing a man's sweater and had turned up the long sleeves. Karol leaned over the tray and tried to kiss her, but she pushed herself right back and he had to let her go.

'But back there . . .' he said in apology.

'Now we are here,' she interrupted him.

'I don't see the difference.'

'Don't talk like that,' she said and took her glass of grog in her hands.

'Frankly I don't understand you,' Karol said and smiled. 'Have you abducted me to ask me history dates?'

'Why not?'

'We could have done that in Prague.'

Katharina nodded and bit into her sausage. While Karol continued to expand this idea, as if he were speaking in general rather than about the two of them, she ate and kept quiet. At first she was embarrassed by the free and easy way in which he spoke about the last weeks, but the longer she listened the more she perceived that it was all swagger, so that she was so moved she was hard put to it not to fall around his neck. She began to see the advantage of letting him talk until he was too exhausted to oppose her own opinions. She did not love him less than before, but there was a new ingredient in her love for which the word 'pity' seemed wrong, since it would have seemed to diminish him. It seemed to her as if too much had been expected of Karol, not only today, in their flight, but also the other day during their meeting with her father. Nevertheless he had said straight out that he wanted to marry her. But that had merely led to secret meetings in Prague, in a park or on a tram. He had talked about his lectures while she had expected him to give her a revolver or a bottle of sleeping pills, or two tickets for the Holland-America Line. Now she felt that she must not press him to be more determined and courageous than was in his nature. He might well fail some harder tests, and it seemed important to her not to take his poses too seriously, to allow him some leeway so as to love him not only today or tomorrow, but for ever.

When she put her glass on the tray she noticed how quickly her hands got cold again. She was not surprised, for she knew the same feeling when playing chess or bridge. The blood went to the head, hands and feet froze. But now she learned that a woman is never more cool and calculating than when she has to deny a man, so as to keep him.

She let Karol finish and didn't mind that his voice became loud, and that he crumpled the map of Southern Bohemia between his knees. When she asked him for a cigarette, she noticed that his hand was quite steady.

'I absolutely agree with you,' she said and paused so that Karol thought she had finished. When she continued, he felt as tricked and provoked as his grandfather when, during a visit to the Vienna Philharmonic, he had applauded loud and long after the first movement of a Mozart symphony. 'We didn't have to come here to do what you were talking about. There are plenty of hotels in Prague where you could have taken me. No, Karol, don't misunderstand me. I'm grateful that you didn't try. But you mustn't take the easy way out now. Or rather: we mustn't. We must not be weak. If our ...' she avoided the word 'flight', thinking it too petty, 'If our journey has any meaning, then it is to show that we are the stronger.'

Katharina was listening to herself. She was quoting from a pious and unblemished novel which she had never read, but which she knew by heart. She felt ashamed when Karol asked seriously, 'Stronger than who?'

'Than my parents and yours. Don't you think that we'll have the advantage if we ...' she had to escape once more into the novel, '... if we can stand before them without lowering our eyes?'

Karol frowned, and Katharina knew right inside her stomach that she would be delivered up to him if he just said, 'Don't talk such nonsense.'

'I see it differently,' he said, so that she could feel either disappointed or fortified.

'You'd better eat something,' she said and held out the plate with the sausages which were now cold.

'Why?' he asked. 'Wouldn't it be best if we simply starved ourselves to death?'

Katharina laughed. She had won. 'No, I still need you.'

Karol looked at her as if he hadn't understood properly.

'I need you,' she repeated, 'for a very long time.'

Towards midnight they aired the room, put a bearskin over the mattresses and listened to the final news. The reader repeated the announcement of Masaryk's resignation and read extracts from European evening papers. For the south and west of the Republic he forecast the first snow, and the roads and railways would be hampered by snowdrifts. The broadcast ended with the harp-motif from *Ma Vlast*.

15

Happy Bird

ON SUNDAY, AFTER Mass, Frau Sellmann and Christine went to see Heinrich in the clinic. Sellmann telephoned the schoolfriend from whose house Katharina was supposed to have called. He heard that his daughter had not even been at school, let alone at her friend's house. They looked in her room to see whether any clothes were missing, but Sophie found everything in its place, and Hanka even brought the red toothbrush with 'K' scratched on it from the bathroom. Sellmann put it in his pocket as if he had found a first important clue. He had, in fact, no idea what to do next. When Betty and Christine returned, it was decided to make enquiries at the police. When Sophie finally tracked down the official who dealt with accidents, he told her that none of his reports could be in any way connected with Katharina, but that he would not get notification of accidents that occurred during the previous night for another two hours. He asked her to telephone again at two o'clock. During lunch Betty cried, and Sellmann ate his leek soup as if it were cod liver oil.

'We must send Wilhelm a telegram,' Betty said. 'Perhaps she has gone to him.'

'Without a passport?' asked Christine.

'Could she be with your friend Jarmila?' Frau Sellmann asked Sophie and smiled as if Katharina had already been found. Sophie shook her head but telephoned the Mangl estate. Katharina was not there.

'Perhaps Herr Lustig knows something,' Betty said, but no one replied. They continued to sit at table, looking at their half-empty plates.

'May I make a suggestion?' asked Christine in an impatient tone of voice.

'Do,' said Sellmann, knowing what was to come, and glad that Christine would be the one to bring it up.

'I can't telephone the gentleman,' he said when Christine had spoken.

'Then I'll do it,' said Betty. 'Find the number, Sophie.'

Sellmann persuaded her to wait until they had been in touch with the police again. But before they could do this the telephone rang. It was Dr. Djudko.

Sellmann composed himself and took up the receiver. Representative Djudko sounded relaxed, amiable, and very Viennese. He wanted to ascertain whether the Sellmanns too were missing a child. If so, he was quite ready to do without the help of the police, for he did not expect the deserters to hold out long in this weather. Also, knowing the Czech authorities, he thought that the less they pressed for action, the more success they would have. In any case, he thought it impossible to alert all the policemen in the country, and was quite ready to sit back, do nothing and await developments.

Sellmann replied in a determined but courteous voice that there was a difference between a young man of twenty and a girl of sixteen staying away overnight. If Katharina had not returned by next morning he felt he must ask the police to start a search. He considered it an advantage that Djudko's son was with her, since two people would be easier to find than one.

'I can neither advise you, nor dictate your actions,' Djudko said. 'If Karol is behind this, they have probably gone to Slovakia.'

'That's what I think.'

'Give me time until this evening, Herr Doktor, and I'll phone Bratislava and call you back.'

There was no news from the police accident department. The afternoon dragged into evening. When Sellmann spoke to Djudko again he sensed that the other man had become worried. There had been no news of Karol when he had spoken to the Slovak relations. They arranged to get in touch again in the morning and Sellmann gave Djudko his office number.

Next morning, on his way to the bank, Sellmann read the critique of Sophie's concert in the paper. After a few cutting remarks about the Neruda texts, the reviewer wrote:

The surprise of the evening was without doubt Fräulein Sophie Sellmann. Almost too assured and perfect for an amateur, she commanded the enchanting technique of *riforzamento* (a technique lost by our professional singers through constant *forte* singing) to such an extent, that the audience was carried into veritable storms of enthusiasm. One would like to hear her sing some German Lieder.

He called Pavel Sixta's compositions 'academic and half-baked'. He advised the composer to throw off the fetters of the twelve-tone system and to venture on a larger project with more spirit and courage.

Sellmann nodded, pleased, folded the paper and left the car. His secretary told him that his wife had asked him to telephone her immediately, and he heard from her that the police had found several of Katharina's schoolbooks in a dustbin. It took Betty some time before she managed to tell him that if he wanted more information he would have to go to police headquarters.

Sellmann arranged to meet Dr. Djudko, and when he reached the building Djudko was already there. He closed his umbrella to take off his hat and shake Sellmann's hand. Somewhat irritated by the bourgeois habits of the Communist representative, Sellmann wanted to go straight in, but Dr. Djudko opened the umbrella once more and, putting half of it over Sellmann, asked for a word in private.

'In everything that we do now,' he began and paused to give Sellmann time to realise their common interest, 'I would ask you to take into account that neither of us will benefit from a scandal.'

Sellmann allowed Karol's father to finish speaking, studying his angular, almost square face in which the mouth, the brows and the lines of the forehead were perfectly symmetrical. A man without a future, he thought, but then remembered that Djudko had been elected to Parliament.

'There are people who'd like to injure me,' the lawyer ended, 'and I can imagine, my dear Doktor, that not everybody in Prague is your friend.'

'I'm searching for my daughter,' Sellmann said.

'As you feel,' said Djudko, and they went into the building.

The police commissioner who spread out Katharina's books, told them where and when they had been found. Dr. Djudko translated for Sellmann. He pointed to the place on a map of the city.

'Only a few steps from the Faculty of Law,' Djudko said.

'How can I institute a search?' asked Sellmann.

'I can do that,' the Commissioner said in German. 'But it would help if we had a photograph of your daughter.' Sellmann promised to bring the picture himself that afternoon, and left with Dr. Djudko.

When he got home for the midday meal, he told Betty that he had persuaded Djudko that a search should be instituted, but he did not tell her that, over a cup of coffee, he had offered to leave Djudko's name out of the affair, only to find him suddenly soft and fatherly.

They found a picture of Katharina which had been taken the year before at the seaside. Her round hat sat so far back that the rim stood out like a halo. This left the face free, which appeared to Sellmann 'very suitable for the purpose'. He put the picture in his pocket and was grateful to Sophie for speaking about Sixta and the reviews.

Sixta had appeared in the morning with all the newspapers, his arms full of hot-house lilac. He had immediately taken up the idea of a larger work and had brought a list of historical themes for Sophie to choose from.

'Will it be an opera?' Sellmann asked, and Sophie told them of some of Sixta's hare-brained schemes. They were amused, and Hanka was astonished to hear them laugh on such a day. But that changed soon enough.

Heinrich, who had already asked for his younger sister in the clinic, was to come home in the middle of the week. Frau Sellmann had told him that Katharina had gone to the mountains with her class, and that she would be back for Christmas. But this not only made it impossible to speak of her in his presence, but it also set a definite term to her absence. Betty noticed how he looked for a postcard from his favourite sister every morning.

On the Friday, Sellmann and Djudko were asked to call at police headquarters. There was nothing to report, the commissioner told them, except for a statement of dubious worth made by two women who thought they had seen the fugitives in the train at Pisek. But their reputation was so bad that the police had little faith in this lead.

Sellmann returned to his office and continued to wonder whether the investigations the commissioner had promised would lead to anything, then asked himself whether Karol and Katharina could really have been seen in a train to Pisek. Where was this Pisek anyway? He asked his secretary for a map and followed the line of the railway south. Pisek lay on the Otava. The name was familiar. He remembered driving along the river on his way to Amery's hunting lodge.

Sellmann leaned back slowly in his chair and contemplated what he had just found out. He could not believe his discovery. Now that the difficulties and worries of the past week could be forgotten, it seemed to him almost unpleasant to have suddenly arrived at his goal. The result seemed to have been reached without effort; he found this suspect since it resembled chance. He laid his paper knife along the railway line to Pisek, extended the trip to Strakonice, then laid a matchstick along the last few kilometres to Dubislav. He had arrived. And, taking a leaf out of Lustig's book, he took out his handkerchief and blew his nose noisily and with feeling.

Jan Amery, who had been put in the picture by Christine earlier in the week, sent a telegram to his gamekeeper asking him to telephone. The man, Hanusch, rang back at noon but did not know whether there was anyone at the hunting lodge, since the previous week he had spent 'from morning till night' putting up snow fences. Four young deer had died in a snowdrift, and he was not sure whether he would be able to reach all the feeding places before the weather got worse. If he, Amery, wanted to come, Hanusch would send a sledge to Strakonice. He promised to investigate and phone back the same day.

To save time, Amery had given him the Sellmanns' phone number, and he went to Bubenech towards evening to be here for the phone call. As always when he went to visit them, he brought flowers for Betty and a present for Heinrich. He had to explain its English name, 'Happy Bird', to the eleven-year-old boy. It was a small bird balanced on a cross-bar, its lower part made of a glass bulb covered in feathers. When its head got wet, a violet-coloured liquid mounted into its neck, until it became so top-heavy that its beak dipped down into the glass of water over which it was perched. This made the violet liquid go back into the bottom, and the game began all over again. Betty, Christine and Sophie loved it, let alone Heinrich, and when Sellmann came home, Amery told him how he had seen the 'Happy Bird' at the Brussels World Fair.

As Betty called them to the table, the telephone rang. Sellmann watched Amery as he spoke with the gamekeeper. First he laughed, then he frowned, his voice became sharper, then he was silent while the receiver quacked. Finally he turned to Sellmann and asked him if he were ready to take a night or early-morning train to the Böhmerwald.

'Of course,' Sellmann said and felt how his heart contracted.

'He's looking up trains,' Amery said to Sellmann in German, then ended the call and went with Sellmann into his study.

'Something strange has happened,' Amery said and remained

standing. 'Hanusch went to the hunting lodge this afternoon. About forty metres from the door somebody fired at him.'

'That means Katharina isn't there,' Sellmann said.

'I'm afraid it doesn't,' said Amery. 'Hanusch recognised her: the girl with the red hair who was there in October.'

Sellmann sat down. 'What have you arranged?'

'A horse-sleigh will meet us at Strakonice station.'

16

I Love Me

THE MORNING AFTER their first night at the hunting lodge, Karol and Katharina opened the windows, draped eiderdowns around their shoulders, and looked to see if the weather forecast had been accurate. The valley was white. For some time they heard nothing but the noise the electric pump made in the cellar, then gradually the church bell from Dubislav, hesitantly and quietly, as if it had to thaw out on the way, calling to Mass. Karol lit the fire and Katharina brewed tea and put the rum bottle beside the teapot. They found it difficult to talk. They looked for sentences as if they were searching for Easter eggs they wished neither to find nor eat. What they had to say to each other could not be easily expressed in words. But if they couldn't get themselves sorted out, Karol felt that other people must suffer. He took an axe from the fireplace and broke open Amery's gun cabinet. It held two double-barrelled guns, two repeater rifles, and one automatic rifle with telescopic sight.

'Didn't you say something about Polish hare?' he asked and took out a rifle, took off the safety catch, and looked through the barrel.

'Yes,' she said and looked at him rapturously.

He put the rifle back and opened the drawer at the bottom of the cupboard. When he held the packets of ammunition in his hand he had to sit down. He suddenly appeared to himself so daring that his knees trembled. So as to hide his weakness from

106

Katharina who had come to stand by him, he explained to her the difference between the various bullets, coarse and fine shot, and showed her how to load.

'How do you know all that?' she asked.

'Oh, I went shooting with my grandfather.'

'And did you hit anything?'

'Of course.'

'Bears?'

'Not bears, but wolves.'

'Where was that?'

'In Eastern Carpathia.'

'Would you take me one day?' she asked and put her hand on his shoulder.

'Oh, you know,' Karol said and pushed the splinters of the door under the cupboard with his foot, 'that's not really suitable for women.'

'Do you think I'd be afraid?'

'No . . .' Karol said looking up at her, 'but I'd be afraid for you.'

'What's this?' asked Katharina and took out a small pipe that looked like the mouthpiece of a hookah.

'It's used to attract roebuck,' Karol said, put the instrument to his lips and blew.

'And they're taken in by it?'

'It depends on the season and the state of their feelings.'

She took her hand from his shoulder. However much she had been impressed by the wolves, she didn't want to go back on yesterday's resolution.

Towards noon they started to go through the house. Upstairs they found nothing but laundry and bed-linen. In the downstairs room that Amery used they found, apart from some clothes which would fit Karol, books, magazines, a wind-up gramophone and some records. It was only when they went into the cellar that they found anything to eat and drink. Karol broke the padlock of the door with the axe he had used on the gun cabinet. In a six-foot-high rack lay stored some hundreds of bottles of wine, also a few packets of biscuits, and three deer hams, dried hard and covered in muslin.

'They'll keep us going until the spring,' Karol said.

They took a day's ration upstairs, ate their midday meal in the big room, and drank a bottle of wine. Katharina, who was not used to drinking wine, let herself sink back after the last swallow, and went to sleep. Karol covered her up, cleared up the dishes and closed the window shutters. When she woke the fire was out;

Karol's watch said half past six. Opening the shutters and looking out didn't tell them whether it was morning or night, it would be dark in either case. Karol wanted to turn on the radio, but Katharina stopped him.

'Why should we need to know?' she said.

'It'll be better if we sleep in the daytime,' Karol said, 'so that nobody sees the smoke.'

Katharina did not contradict him. Her plan had only gone this far. There was nothing beyond. Now everything was up to Karol, and he seemed to be settling down as if they might well wait for the first violets. She would gladly have talked to him, but he sat by the fire, read the magazines and drank. She wondered what Christine or Sophie might have done in her place, but she did not spend much time on these thoughts. Instead she pushed herself out of bed with her elbows and heels. If, as she thought, it was now Monday morning, Fräulein Anglade, her biology teacher, would be stepping up to the blackboard and going over the metamorphosis of the chrysalis into the butterfly. The fact that there were still lessons, breaks, homework, outings and holidays, confirmed Katharina's fear that life would go on in the same old way after her death. Only Karol's laugh brought her back to the present. He'd read a joke and translated it for her.

Thus the second day passed with eating, drinking, making the fire and reading. Karol kept to their agreement and moved Katharina's mattress so far from his own that even in his sleep he would not touch her.

On the third day he told her how, as a boy, he had spent his holidays in the country with his grandfather, a Hungarian officer who had been dismissed from the Army in disgrace, but had married a rich wife. He owned an estate beside the Danube and taught his grandson how to talk to horses.

'He read me a fable by La Fontaine, the story about the horse and the wolf. I used to sit in the stables at night and wait for the animals to talk to each other. When he saw how sad I was because they didn't speak, he taught me how to talk to them.'

'And how did he do that?' asked Katharina and allowed Karol to put his hand first on her shoulder, then on her neck, and finally on her face. She closed her eyes and heard him say something that she took to be Hungarian.

'What does that mean?' she asked when he took his hand away.

'I'll tell you later,' he said and smiled, then told her how frightened he had been when his father came to visit them in the country. Dr. Djudko had had the habit of threatening his son:

'One of these days I'll eat you'. Karol had thought that he would start with his toes, fingers or ears, since, when his parents were expected on a visit, these parts of his anatomy were given a special wash.

Katharina had lain down in front of the fireplace, and now she turned one way or the other, according to whether the fire seemed too hot or the room too cold.

'Who do you expect will find us?' Karol asked after a while.

'My sisters,' she answered promptly.

'Why do you think that?'

'Because my sisters have imagination,' Katharina said, 'and because they are jealous. They envy my being alone with you, they are jealous because I . . .'

'Go on,' urged Karol.

'Because we have the courage to break the rules. Christine in particular must be furious.'

'Pity she can't see us here,' Karol mocked.

'What do you mean?' Katharina asked and sat up.

'Their minds would soon be set at rest.'

'I don't know why you've got to bring that up again.'

'Oh, it just came to me,' Karol said, excused himself, and went to fetch a bottle of wine.

'All right,' Katharina said when he sat down beside her. 'You can have it.'

'What?'

'Me,' she said and made a face as if she were about to be slaughtered.

'Do you really love me?'

She nodded with her eyes shut.

'Why don't you tell me then?'

'Is that part of it?'

'Yes.'

'I love you.'

Karol drank a mouthful of wine and leaned down to her.

'Say it more affectionately.'

Katharina opened her eyes wide and said reproachfully, 'Why are you being so particular?'

'Am I?' he asked.

'Have you had lots of women?'

'No,' he said, 'thirty at the most.'

She pushed her fists against Karol's chest, but he took her shoulders and drew her to him. She opened her mouth because she was getting no air and felt Karol's tongue between her teeth. I

109

could bite it off, she thought, but then she suddenly wanted to know whether one really felt as if one was swimming in warm, bubbling water when one was kissed, as Sophie had said. She didn't notice anything like that, so Sophie had lied. Katharina was like a great balloon covered in gooseflesh, blown up tight, and the higher she went the more she feared she'd burst. She felt as if she were doing some acrobatic trick, and when Karol let her go for a moment she thought she was going backwards on a tottering slack wire, and was glad when he took her in his arms again. She heard him move the tray with the clinking spoons, and her arms slid past his neck. She thought she would break in half when he put his hands around her waist, but he only lifted her to make them both fall back. Her arms still around his neck, she turned towards the carpet and, as if she had to hold on to him, she took his chin in her mouth.

When Karol lifted her pullover she felt so alone and betrayed under the sweaty knitted material that she held the seam tightly over her breast. She thought, if indeed thought was still possible, that he would tear her hands away. Instead he laid his lips on her stomach and said something that she could not understand. It tickled. She pulled the sweater off her face. Karol followed her sleeves with his lips as far as the tips of her fingers, undressed and lay down beside her. He turned her on to her stomach, kissed her between the shoulder blades, and when she turned over, laughing, took her ear between his teeth. She snapped at him, lost all moderation, gave him a bite instead of a kiss, stroked his back with her outspread fingers and trembled when his short nails pressed into her skin. When he laid his head between her legs, she sat up with a jerk, about to take hold of his hair, but then fell back hard. When he moved up on her she looked past him at the panelled ceiling, and while her hips responded unconsciously, her eyes filled with tears.

When she got up to go and have a bath, Karol sat naked in front of the fireplace and put wood on the embers.

'Don't turn round!' Katharina said, and after a while she returned in a long, blue bathrobe. Karol had tidied up the mattresses and made the beds. Katharina sat down in the easy chair opposite him and tucked her feet under the robe.

'Aren't you cold?' she asked.

'I shan't get dressed again while we are here,' Karol said.

'I bled,' she said.

He bent over and drew her right foot from under the bathrobe and kissed the cold toes. She drank a sip of wine and looked down at him through her glass.

'I'm hungry,' she said. 'There's some salami left in the larder, will you fetch it? But put something on!' As he went out, he scooped up a sheepskin and wrapped it around his body.

'You said something to me,' she said later with her mouth full.

'I did?' asked Karol and brushed the ash from his cigarette.

'Was it in Slovak?'

'No.'

'Hungarian?'

'Yes,' he replied and blew smoke into her hair.

'Tell me what it was,' she begged and turned her head so as to look at him above her knees.

He stubbed out his cigarette, put his mouth to her ear and said, 'Little horse.'

'What?'

'Little horse,' Karol repeated.

'You said "little horse" to me?'

'Yes, "come my little horse".'

'Say it again, but like last time.'

He said it again in Hungarian.

'No, here,' Katharina said, slid from the chair and pulled his head towards her. 'Lie on top of me and say it again.'

He lay down on top of her and said it again.

Later they collected all the eiderdowns they could find and remained on the mattresses without knowing that three days went by. They only opened the windows when it was dark outdoors.

Karol often went to have a bath, and when he returned he stretched himself out and turned his face to the wall. Katharina wanted to talk with him and looked for something to say. Finally she said, 'God made the night for the trees, so that they get a bit of quiet and can talk to each other. Don't you think that is true?'

'Yes,' Karol grumbled, 'but I'm not a tree.'

'Do you mean you don't want to talk to me?' she said and threw herself on him and smelled his breath. 'You've been drinking wine.'

'I'm no tree,' Karol said and smiled with glassy eyes, 'but I've got to be watered now and again.'

Katharina found a dozen empty bottles under the bath tub. She went down to the cellar, took the axe with which Karol had broken the lock, and began to smash the bottles on the shelves. When a glass splinter cut the back of her left hand she let the axe fall, licked the blood, and watched the wine run on to the floor.

'That'll do,' Karol said behind her. 'I won't drink any more.'

He took her into the kitchen, bandaged her hand, and wanted to comfort her, but she knew by his awkward movements, his silly laughter and the way he frowned and screwed up his eyes, that he was not yet sober. He had not shaved, his hair stood on end, and there were dark rings under his eyes. He seemed so changed that she believed for a moment that she had set off with a stranger, yesterday – or whenever it had been – outside the University. She thanked him for the bandage and ran on shaky legs back to their room to start the fire. When he wanted to help her she sent him back to bed and he obeyed like someone who lies down to die because the doctor says so. Katharina continued to sit by the fire.

'What year did Maria Theresa die?' she asked Karol when he opened his eyes.

'Seventeen hundred and eighty,' he replied, but could not remember in which year Cromwell had become Lord Protector. He went to the bathroom to shave. Katharina remained where she was. She felt the muslin bandage on her hand and sniffed the iodine-soaked gauze. She put her dirty nails, which smelled of resin and ashes, in front of her eyes and held her breath to retain the acidulous scent. I ought to be disgusting to myself, she thought, instead I like myself. She took off her sweater and lifted her elbows. I can smell myself. She began to kiss her arms.

'What are you doing?' asked Karol from the door.

'I love me,' she said and blushed to her shoulders.

'I want to explain something to you,' Karol said, drying his face.

'Oh, there's plenty of time,' she whispered.

'I've discovered something that is at least as important as Haeckel's bio-genetic law.'

'Really?' asked Katharina and took a piece of skin from her right arm between her teeth. 'Why don't you come over here.'

'No, wait. I must explain it to you.' He sat down in an armchair and crossed his legs. 'There are fundamentally five stages in the history of man.' He counted them on his fingers, 'Prehistoric society, feudalism, democracy, dictatorship and socialism. Now, if one were to associate some fundamental characteristic state of mind with each of these stages, and if one succeeded in showing that each corresponded with the various stages of man's life, one could postulate that man does not simply recapitulate the stages of life biologically, but that each living person repeats what mankind has anticipated in its history.'

'That's marvellous,' said Katharina sitting up.

112

'I call it the socio-genetic law,' Karol said modestly and looked down at his hands.

'They'll give you the Nobel Prize for it,' exclaimed Katharina.

Karol waved a denial. 'That's not what I'm after,' he said. 'The important thing now is to define the fundamental states of mind of each stage accurately.'

'Could you do that lying down?' Katharina asked, and pressed herself against him when he stretched out beside her.

'Hate belongs to prehistoric society,' Karol explained, 'but so does the wish to submit oneself. Feudalism stands for respect but also for contempt. Democracy goes with envy.'

'Quite right,' said Katharina unbuttoning his pyjamas.

'But to hide the envy there is charity, soup kitchens, the dole. Fear goes with dictatorship. But fear is not possible without the pleasure in being oppressed.'

'And then?' Katharina asked. 'What's the next thing?'

'Socialism,' said Karol and held on to her hand.

'And what belongs to socialism?'

'Love.'

'I like socialism.'

'It won't work today,' Karol said.

'Why not?'

'I can't.'

'But I can,' said Katharina.

'I believe you, but that won't help.'

'We should at least try,' Katharina whispered.

'Your hands are too cold,' Karol said after a while. She turned her back on him.

'How can such a thing happen?' she asked and felt Karol shrug his shoulders. 'Is it the wine?'

'My grandfather drank three litres a day, and yet half the village was pregnant by him.'

'I'll just have to try a bit harder. You'll have to think of some definite thing. What are you thinking of?'

'Of my grandfather,' Karol said. 'But it doesn't help.'

'How long can this go on for?'

'I don't know. It's the first time I've experienced it.'

'You'll have to think of something that excites you. What excites you?'

'I don't know.'

'You mustn't think of your socio-genetic law.'

'No.'

'Shall I tell you a story?'

'I think that would make it worse.'

Katharina sat up and looked at her clothes. 'I'll get dressed,' she said.

'Why?'

'Then you can undress me.'

'Stay here,' Karol said and held her when she wanted to get up.

'It's only an experiment,' she said, but Karol would not let her go. 'You're so strong.'

'I lack albumen.'

'What's that?'

'I need milk.'

'Did your grandfather drink milk?'

'No. He ate fish. Oysters in Vienna, catfish at home.'

'But how can I get hold of catfish?' Katharina got up, but forced Karol to stay in bed.

'I'm not ill,' he defended himself.

'You are, in fact, very ill,' Katharina contradicted and pressed him back into the cushions. She warmed up some biscuits on the electric plate and put slices of deer ham on them, and served warm red wine with it. While he ate she got a German book out of Amery's room and read to him.

' "The true general must be a person of character in the fullest and most noble sense of the word; he must believe in his star, and never doubt his own strength." '

'That sounds good,' Karol said and wanted to know the title of the book.

'*Paul von Hindenburg, the man, statesman and general,*' Katharina told him. ' "Where difficulties abound," ' she continued to read, ' "strong demands, and the strong will of the leader call forth the power of the weak better than words of comfort and promises of better times to come." '

'That's good,' Karol repeated, 'very good.' But it didn't help.

Next morning Katharina squatted about two hundred metres below the house in a small snowdrift and pulled a line across the stream, not allowing the artificial fly to drop in the water, but flicking it over the water the way she had seen Amery do two months ago.

The cold of the last few days had not been severe enough to freeze the stream, but in some places the snow had been blown into wide drifts, arching out over the water, so that it looked as if it were only a step from one bank to the other. The last of the night's mist still floated amongst the spruces and seemed to pull the edges of the valley up towards the sky. But when a mild, moss-scented wind sprang up, the illusion soon vanished; objects stood out once more and Katharina's red hair blew from her forehead. She felt hot and pulled the line in to go further along the stream. Now and again she looked up at the house. When she was about to cast again she looked down and saw the snow dark at her feet and she thought she would fall in. She stuck the end of the fishing-rod in the hard trodden snow, but the bamboo gave her little support, and she had to straddle her legs until she reached safe, hard snow again.

Karol reproached her, but she only looked at him in silent anger because she had not caught anything. In the afternoon she stood by the stream once more, a linen bag over her shoulder and a net in her left hand, but evening came so quickly that she had trouble finding her tracks back to the house.

Karol slept, and she thought for the first time that so much tiredness could perhaps be explained not by exhaustion, but by his Slovak-Hungarian-Macedonian, therefore at least partly Balkan, origin. When he began to speak of his socio-genetic law in the night she yawned and turned on her side.

Next day, Friday, was clear, and above the two white hills which closed the valley to the east, the sky was lavender blue. They won't find us, thought Katharina, they'll never find us, or not until spring. Karol put his hand on the nape of her neck, but she stepped away from the window and went into the kitchen to change the bandage on her hand. She heard him wind up the gramophone and slammed the door shut.

In the afternoon she walked down to her fishing place. It was so warm that she took off her gloves and cap. Close to the bank she saw a trout, small as a school ruler. She bent down, and at the same moment Karol called her. To spite him she looked in the opposite direction, only to hear a coarser echo of her name. Hanusch, Amery's gamekeeper, stepped from the shadow of the woods and approached her slowly across the snow. She recognised him and ran quickly back to the house without turning round. Karol was waiting by the door.

'That's it, then,' he said.

Katharina pushed him aside and ran into the big room.

'Take a gun and load it,' she said. 'Do what I say,' she exclaimed when Karol hesitated.

'Who is it?' he asked as he fitted the magazine. And when she did not explain, 'Are you going to shoot at him?'

'What else?' she said, and took the gun from him.

'But it isn't his fault,' Karol said, and looked out where the powerful figure of Hanusch had come within fifty metres.

'Stand still,' he called in Czech.

'You're a coward,' Katharina said through her teeth and took aim.

'Fräulein!' Hanusch called in German.

Katharina released the safety catch.

'Go away,' Karol roared. 'Quick, run.'

Hanusch took off his hat and waved. 'We know each other.'

Katharina pulled the trigger without aiming. Karol tore the gun away from her.

'Go away,' he called and fired the remaining bullets into the snow. After the second shot Hanusch understood. He turned and ran, hat in hand, down the valley, and seemed to accelerate the closer he came to the edge of the forest.

When he had gone, Katharina tried to explain that she had only fired to stop Hanusch from coming into the house. Karol nodded, but did not believe her, then closed the window. After a while he realised that it was really a warning shot, even, when he had thought it out to the end, a 'decoy shot'. For if they had welcomed Hanusch, given him a glass of wine and told him that they were having a few days' holiday in the hunting lodge, he'd probably have been good-natured enough not to betray them. Now he could only go to the police or the telephone.

Karol noticed that Katharina was clearing up the room. She took the beds and cushions away, fetched the broom and dustpan, brushed the floor and dusted the shelves, the gun cupboard, the lamps and the mantelpiece.

'Are you glad?' he asked. She blushed as if to prove it.

'You've got funny ideas!' she said and took the dishes out.

'I don't think there's any sense in lying down,' Karol said when he was helping wash up in the kitchen.

'Let's take it in turn, every three hours,' Katharina proposed. 'They'll need lights if they come in the night. We'll see them before they see us.'

She made a bed for Karol in one of the upstairs rooms and took the first watch, put two chairs in front of the fireplace so that the fire didn't impede the view outside, and put on her coat. When she could not hear Karol moving about upstairs any more she opened the cupboard silently and took out the long gun which she had used in the afternoon. She leaned it on the window-sill and propped her head beside it in such a way that the butt stuck out far beyond her shoulder.

'Great moments,' Uncle Wilhelm had once said, 'make one want to sing or make water.' For three hours she felt like singing.

At nine o'clock she woke Karol, lay down in the bed, and heard him put the gun back in the cabinet. When she turned on her side, she remembered that she hadn't prayed for a long time. She folded her hands and was surprised to think how easily she had gone to sleep all week. She smiled, stretched until her knees cracked, and unfolded her hands. That she didn't need what children needed any more seemed to her proof enough that she had grown up.

Karol decided not to wake Katharina. But when she came downstairs at midnight, he was glad to be relieved. He kissed her neck in the dark, and smelled the warmth of the bed in her open collar. He put his hands on her back, but she whispered, 'Go, lie down.' He went upstairs, took a chair to the bedroom window and looked out over the valley, one storey above Katharina. He tried, but could not sleep, and because he thought sleeplessness a weakness, he decided consciously to stay awake. But towards three o'clock, when he was due to relieve Katharina, he went to sleep. She heard his snores, went upstairs, toppled him from the chair into bed, and covered him up. Then she took the gun out of the cabinet once more, sat down at her place and waited for the sun to rise.

The gentlemen who left the train at Strakonice had become somewhat better acquainted during their journey. As far back as Radotin, Amery had offered his companions a drop of Slivovitz, but Djudko resisted as far as Karlstejn, and Sellmann did not relent before they had left Tetin. The dark monotony beyond the window hardly provided subjects for conversation; they were thrown back on their night-thoughts, for it was difficult to sleep in such company. So, a little sip to warm you up! As they unbuttoned their furs so they unbuttoned their thoughts, and at Pisek Amery's silver hip-flask was empty. When they changed trains, Dr. Djudko made a snowball with his bare hands and threw it at the nearest lampstand.

'Goal,' cried Sellmann.

Unfortunately it was impossible to get the flask refilled at this early hour, but Hanusch had put a litre of gin in the straw of the sleigh, so one could continue as one had begun. Sellmann and Djudko had tacitly agreed not to discuss the reason for their excursion, and since Amery took care not to ask any questions, they looked much like three drinking companions who'd been

117

left over from yesterday's Prague Christmas fair, and were drinking their way towards an early pint in the Böhmerwald.

In fact neither Sellmann nor Djudko knew what to do once they were face to face with Katharina and Karol. One could simply have boxed their ears and put them in the sleigh in the ordinary way but this was impossible in Amery's presence as future son- and brother-in-law. There was also the long journey back, the two changes of train, and the inevitable parting. What made them even more thoughtful was the probability that Katharina and Karol would welcome them with a double salvo from shotguns. So, have another drop, Herr Doktor! To your good health! The sun rose in its usual laborious way behind the mountains, and after each hill they slipped once more into deepest night. It took the whole of the bottle before they finally got onto the road to Dubislav.

Hanusch was waiting for them outside his house, repeated what he had said on the telephone, and asked them in for a bite to eat. But Sellmann wanted to get on. Hanusch took over the reins and they drove on until they reached a path that would take them to Amery's land. Sellmann was glad Amery sent his gamekeeper back once he had put them on the path to the house.

They walked in single file, the hems of their furs trailing in the snow. Since the path climbed, and the snow sometimes came up to their knees, Djudko had to ask for a rest after a time. They stood under a tree and smoked their cigars.

'My question may seem strange to you,' Amery said as they smoked. 'Do you believe that facts justify anything?'

'No,' said Sellmann and Djudko with one voice.

'I'm glad you're so much in agreement.'

'I don't know exactly what moved you to this question, dear friend,' Sellmann said, 'but at best the opposite is really true: facts need justification.'

'It is a pleasure to be in agreement with you,' Djudko said and bowed to Sellmann, puffing at his cigar. 'But I tell you, there are facts that one gets rid of quite simply before they embarrass one into the necessity of seeking justification for them. Perhaps that sounds immoral, but it is really only what nature does everywhere. What can't succeed is simply eliminated.'

'Marvellous,' Amery exclaimed. 'Your son will shoot at you.'

'Please, Jan,' Sellmann said. 'Don't tempt fate . . .'

They tramped on. Sellmann did not want to come to any arrangement with Djudko about their immediate actions. He saw no reason for such intimacy, but as they stepped out of the forest and came within sight of the house he allowed the other man to speak some words of consolation. They had children who had formed some sort of relationship. Bad, but possible to repair, possible even to reverse as the lawyer had said. They had drunk Slivovitz together, later gin – superfluously. That was enough.

They found them asleep with the door unlocked, Karol in bed, Katharina at the window, the unloaded gun in her arms. When, an hour later, they set out for Dubislav, Amery and Katharina walked far in advance, behind them came Djudko and Karol, and Sellmann, who for some reason had taken Katharina's school bag, made up the rear. There had been no tears. They had spoken to each other like two rival climbing parties who had met on the summit of a high mountain, agreeing on the route for the descent. Though he was unhurt, Amery's gamekeeper would receive a considerable sum as compensation. Karol would not return to Prague but travel to Bratislava where he would spend Christmas with his grandparents and then continue his studies in Vienna. Katharina was to accept an invitation to spend a year on a farm in Bavaria, whose owner Sellmann had known in the war. Sellmann started to write a letter to him on the train, while Dr. Djudko, in another compartment, wondered whether he would have to inform the chairman of his party of the events of the past days.

The only one who simply travelled home seemed to be Jan Amery. He looked at his face mirrored in the window behind which the snowy landscape went by and thought, 'One ought to invent a mirror which doesn't reverse the sides of the face but shows us as we really are. My right eye ought to be my right eye.'

Book Two

I

Venetian Lace

THE CANNON OF the artillery barracks of San Giorgio Maggiore fired
its noon salute over Venice and the lagoon. It was May. Jan and
Christine were staying at the Grand Hotel d'Italie Bauer-Grünwald, between the Campo S. Moise and the Grand Canal.

The wedding had been impressive. Betty and Aunt Marketa
had cried. Sophie had lost her voice during the solo in the
'Laudate Dominum', and a chorister had had to take her place.
Heinrich had been unable to take his eyes off Christine's veil and
dress. Katharina had sent a telegram to say she had missed her
connection in Munich. Dr. Sellmann had made one of his dreaded
speeches, and the chaplain of the Tyne Church had got drunk to
stupefaction with a china manufacturer from Falkenau.

All business matters had already been settled in March. They
had been mostly on the side of the groom, for in comparison with
his wealth, what his bride brought him looked, she said herself,
more like a little present than a dowry. In a legal settlement,
Amery had made over to his son Jan his entire property including
all land and shares in other enterprises. Apart from some gifts,
charitable bequests and other obligations which the elder Amery
had taken on through the years, often only sealed with a handshake but had always honoured, the settlement contained only
two liabilities: one to Bohuslav, the other to his sister-in-
law. So as to meet the expected inflation, Jan guaranteed his
father no fixed monthly sum, but the salary of a secretary of the
Ministry of Justice, and Frau Farel the income of a county court
judge, both to the end of their lives.

The day before the wedding, Jan had taken Christine to the
Tyne Church. Christine followed Jan into the bare and cold nave.
If it had been up to her, she would have been married in St Jacob,
two hundred yards away. Maria Tyne seemed to her so Protestant.
But the choice was not hers.

Jan looked at the ceiling and said, 'That's baroque. The original roof was made of wood. It was about to be replaced in 1437, but they needed the beams to build fifty gallows, and after that it took them twenty years to get enough for a new roof.'

Christine laughed. For some time now she had laughed at anything she did not understand, and to her surprise this had given her a reputation not for being superficial and stupid, but for being witty and cunning. She knew that she was being tested, but she laughed at every test.

At dinner, her neighbours were often good-looking young merchants or lawyers, first generation inhabitants of Prague, who had been taught not to lose their equanimity. But their ears turned red when the fiancée of the china millionaire laughed when they spoke about the raising of the income tax, and some were afraid of this German Fräulein who would not even take the occupation of the Rhineland, the anti-comintern pact, or the Olympic Games seriously.

'She was nice,' a china manufacturer described a conversation with Christine (it was the same man who got so frightfully drunk at the wedding). 'At first she was really nice. Then she lifted up her chin and looked at me fixedly with such ice-cold eyes, my dear boy, I thought I was about to be shot. The sweat began to run down me. And then she suddenly laughed at me.'

'That's Prussia for you,' Jan explained. 'But don't you find her ravishing?'

Christine would gladly have put her cards on the table, but after each of her appearances Jan thanked her with such passion, that she found it easier to lie and to love, rather than to confess and possibly to be left high and dry. But she underestimated him. If Jan had known that her attitude was less nature than conscious effort, he would probably have loved Christine, instead of feeling he must conquer her again and again, as on that first afternoon when she had taken his hat off his head. He liked people who did not remain static, and he admired the audacity of those who lived far beyond their limits and who mistook imagination for perfection.

Venice was the perfect stopping-off place for driving a woman to extremity, and this seemed more important to Jan than simply making Christine happy. He liked this concept very much, especially since he thought it his own. In reality he had read it in a book the previous winter. To read good books and not only to remember them, but also to become so like them that after a while he had the courage to imagine them his own invention, was one of his most brilliant talents.

To go to extremes, wherever they led, even to the point of extinction. But what was this extremity? Perennial lust, or something philosophical? Neither really suited the yellow-grey bedroom of the Bauer-Grünwald, with its view to the south and east.

'No, it must not be something active, some incident or happening, but a thing yet to be attained, don't you think?'

Christine nodded and lifted a silver spoon with honey-yellow melon pieces to her lips. (Amery had begun to develop his theory in the Taverna de Fenice.) She wore a white silk dress with blueberry-coloured stripes, which was too thin for the time of year. Her neck rose out of the collar between bluish veins and supported the pale face with the heart-shaped painted lips in the half-shadow by the window.

'As children we know happiness, because we are still like animals. Our golden age ends with our first deceit. Lying proves that we see through the world and accept its rules, and our judgments, based on that experience prove us right in future. Very reasonable, but also very boring, and people who manage, through naïvety, deeper insight, or financial independence to turn their backs on the rules, do so with the greatest pleasure. But is that the extremity I'm speaking of?

'No. That is boorishness, cynicism or politics. It's a pretence at wildness and still calculated. Does one have to be morally irresponsible if one wants the extreme? The saints are beyond expediency. Who would equate St. Francis with the calculus? The extreme is total lack of objectivity, the purest, most passionate interest.

'But what must we do to reach this extremity? No, the question should be: how should we be? And this means knowing what we are.

'My examples come from my own department. They are the cheese bell and the chamber pot. Excuse me! One stinks from below, the other from above. *Je vais quitter cet image!* What I mean is: those who shut themselves off from things from above are no better off than those who close up towards things from below. A bad example. I'll now give you one without smells.'

Jan took his arms from the table to allow the waiter to serve the coffee.

'Man as a dragnet! What do you think of that?'

Christine lowered her chin and smiled.

'You understand. It is a happy philosophy. To be open in both directions. Not to feel the difference between inside and outside. To keep the shape,' Jan lifted his voice, 'Indeed, to find the shape while speeding along. To be inflated with the catch of life. After that death is only to change one's element, to fall on the deck, taut and heavy. But until then, one's belly trailing on the sand-banks and on the summits of the ocean highlands, to fill oneself with the wrecks and watery corpses, with mussels and monsters, with stars and serpents and life-belts and letters in bottles, to let the small fish escape through the mesh so that they can grow up and swim into our jaws again . . .' He looked at her, more exhausted than enquiring.

'Yes, I like that,' Christine said. 'But I have an appointment at the hairdresser's at half past two.'

Jan leaned over, kissed her right hand above the knuckles and whispered, 'You've understood me!'

He accompanied her part of the way, then went to the bank to cash a letter of credit. Then he returned to the hotel and tried, while he changed his shirt and tie, to complete his theory. But he discovered that a thought, lately still so fresh, lively and in working order, sometimes wilts away quickly when the thinker is on his own. It did not help him to lie down on the sofa. The stucco rosettes remained silent, so did the filigree pendants of the chandelier. A scent of heliotrope stood in the open door of the bedroom and came in with a puff of wind which made the shutters tremble.

Jan kept his eyes on the Salviati chandelier, and as all theories evaporated, real happiness came to him from memory. For, coming from Vienna nine years ago, he had visited Murano and had worked in the Salviati workshops for a month without pay, so as to add to his knowledge of lead-free Bohemian crystal, that of the treatment of Venetian glass. At the same time he had learned a great many new techniques. He had lived on Murano, but had, at the insistence of the director of the Salviati works, visited Venice after the first week, to see the world of the Murano school at the Accademia. Whether he had lingered too long on his way to the bridge over the Grand Canal, or whether it was a public holiday – he only remembered that he had stood before the locked doors, though the shadow of the Minerva and the lion above the entrance had not yet reached the water. He remembered that he had spent part of the evening opposite the Giardino Reale where ten, fifteen or more boats lay, decorated with red, green and yellow lanterns, and he could still recall the serenade to the sound of which one of the boats had pushed on to the white path of the moon. But what he remembered totally was the narrow face of a sixteen-year-old girl. Her name had been Jane Osgood, and she had stood beside him that afternoon at the closed doors of the Accademia.

Amery got up, took a light coat and went downstairs. He left his key, and when the receptionist confirmed his reservations for a box at the theatre, he thanked him in English, to the man's surprise. Then he took a gondola to the Punta della Salute, stepped on to the point, and looked at the basin of San Marco. The vaporetti rubbed themselves against the floating landing places, and made the iron beaks of the gondolas dance up and down between the larch posts like the heads of imprisoned polar-bears. Further away, a heavy cruiser of the Zara class had made fast. It lay motionless on the water, a grey flat-iron mounted with guns, untouched by the city and lagoon steamers which passed well below its superstructure.

What had changed? Everything was in its place as it had been nine years ago: the Piazzetta, the Palace of the Doges, the spires and cupolas. Only it had been night then, *una notte di luna*, mandolins, funiculi, funicula – and love had popped up like a jack-in-the-box. 'It's a dream,' Jane Osgood had whispered. Had it been a dream? Every morning after her bath, she had rubbed herself with a white powder which smelled of talcum.

'You smell like a new glove,' he had told her.

'Well, pull me on,' had been her reply. 'You are the best hand I know.'

He had loved Venice very much then, because he had loved Jane Osgood very much. Did he not love Christine? Did one need to be in love to love this city? He was annoyed with himself for coming here to test a platitude. He put up his coat collar and walked along the Zattere. When Jane Osgood was pleased, she put her heel on his foot. She was going to marry a tobacco planter and visit Jan in Prague with their children. But she had only sent him a picture postcard from Richmond, Virginia, and inked a gondola into the James River. How many children had she had in the meantime?

He walked on, but when he got to the Accademia it was closed. How could it have been otherwise, for it was past five o'clock and nobody who resembled Jane Osgood stood in front of the door.

After saying goodbye to Amery, Christine had not immediately gone to the hairdresser, but had sat down at a café table and ordered ice-cream. She knew that it was absurd to sit in this windy

127

spot and eat an ice, but she had more than half an hour before her appointment, half an hour out of which she had cheated her husband.

It was cool and one look at the passers-by was enough to confirm that she was cold. People wore woollen coats, even pullovers, and the children chasing the pigeons wore long brown stockings. Despite this she ordered nut, pistachio and vanilla, and folded the hem of her gaberdine coat under her knees.

Amery's way of talking as if he were in a seminar on a question of happiness of the upper middle classes had made Christine angry. She did not yet suspect that a man with nothing to do was at times inclined to question the world to such an extent that there was no answer but the invention of a radical rule of life. Nor could she imagine Amery abandoning his new-found truth equally quickly. She was twenty-two and on her first honeymoon. So she took her husband at his word, though not literally. Man as a cheesebell? Nice!

But what did it mean, 'living like a dragnet?' Jan had been excited. She had known it by the way he jerked his shoulders. A year ago she had thought that the armholes of his jackets were too tight. Now she knew that it was a nervous tic which did not come on often, but always when he tried to be ruthless. Christine felt that she had to adjust to something that she did not understand, not because it was beyond her, but because it left her cold. To speak of happiness seemed to her superfluous. One only spoke of shoes if they hurt.

A gust of wind went through the square, lifted the pigeons and took a few hats along. Christine crossed her legs, tucked the skirts of her coat around her and stuck the spoon into the greenish ice-cream. When she leaned forward she felt a stab of pain in her lower abdomen. She let go the spoon, bent over her knees and noticed that she was too weak to lean back. She thought of knitting needles pushed slowly through her groin. Picturing the pain helped. The tablecloth with its chrome clamps reappeared and immediately after the bowl with the tricolour scoops, and when she sat back at last she was already opening her handbag to look in the mirror.

She was, of course, pale, and her nose a little peaked. But there, it wasn't the end of the world. Her lips seemed without feeling and furry as after a tooth anaesthetic. But hadn't she got through it bravely? She realised that she couldn't even suffer without being proud of it. This bothered her for a while, until it came to her to blame Amery for it. Thank God I'm not pregnant, she thought. If it were a child, I'd break. We'd rather wait a few years.

When Christine returned to the hotel, Amery sat in their room reading the *Corriere della Serra*. He heard her step, did not put down the paper, but told her what he had just been reading.

'Imagine, in Rome a tramp went into a men's shop and asked for a tie. When the salesman asked what colour, he said, "to match my socks, please!" He was barefoot!'

Amery laughed, put the newspaper on the table, and looked around for Christine. She was behind the open wardrobe door, hanging up her coat.

'What do you think of that?'

'Funny,' she replied, closed the cupboard and turned around. 'And what do you think of me?'

Only when he'd said 'marvellous' at random did he notice the change. Christine's hair wasn't blonde and piled on top any more. It was chestnut brown and puffed up, and it stood out from her temples with curled ends. As if to give him no time to get over his surprise, she jumped on to his lap and whispered something incomprehensible. A bush of hair was pressed into his face, and under its scent it smelled of burning and verdigris. He pushed his nose against her ear, but didn't know whether he should kiss it or say something into it.

'Isn't that a great deal?' he heard her ask.

'Oh yes,' he replied.

'It isn't quite the extreme yet,' she continued. Her tone alarmed him since the pitch was that which precedes confessions. He didn't feel in the mood for that sort of thing. He therefore kissed her ear and muttered, 'You kept me waiting a long time. But it was worth it.'

'Wasn't it,' she said and made as if to get up.

Though his thighs hurt because Christine was pressing her knees into his muscles, he held her tight. He knew that she liked to have the width of a table between two points of view. If she had to explain something, she preferred to do it in a restaurant.

'It shines,' he said and looked at her hair.

'It'll go better with the colour scheme of the bedroom,' she said and felt his grasp slacken.

'How do you mean?' he asked foolishly.

She repeated it, slipped from his lap, let herself fall into the other armchair and laughed. Amery realised that he had just declined an invitation.

129

'One can always wash it out,' he heard Christine say. 'Or I'll buy a blonde wig.'

'And if I say that I like it?'

'Then I just don't believe you.'

'Tina,' Amery begged and would have added something more, but she suddenly sat up and tipped so far over that he thought she would hit her forehead on the edge of the table. He got up and stood beside her and put his hand on her shoulder.

'I really like your hairstyle,' he said seriously, but she shook her head so energetically that he was amused.

'Please leave me alone for a bit,' she whispered.

'All right,' he said. 'I'll get dressed for dinner.'

When Christine heard the bedroom door close she leaned back groaning and wiped the sweat out of her eyebrows. Then she pushed herself upright and, with shaky steps, went to the bathroom.

Later at dinner she drank a great deal of wine and asked Amery to hire a gondola. He asked for the awning to be put up, and they sailed through the canals until midnight.

Next morning there were letters from Prague on the breakfast tray. Frau Sellmann wrote full of gaiety and exuberance, as if she had to prove that she remembered her own honeymoon very well. But she expressed some worry in the postscript. 'Sophie,' she had written in the margin in steep letters, 'Sophie cannot add her love to this letter since she has just gone to see Professor Ruschka (supposedly an authority). She will probably have to give up her singing completely for the time being. She sends you her best love.'

Christine gave Amery the letter and crawled under his arm while he read.

'How can one suddenly lose one's voice?'

'I expect she has nodes on her vocal chords. It often happens to beginners if they strain their voice.'

'I'd love to know how you know that,' said Christine, 'But I shan't ask.'

'Thank you,' said Amery and opened a business letter with his egg spoon.

'Perhaps she needs a man.'

'I don't think so,' said Amery. 'Sophie is one of those people who can't do two things at once. When she is singing, she sings. I've sometimes felt that she has difficulties talking at table, because when she is eating she can do nothing but eat.'

'You are right. She is inhibited when there are guests. She gets on best with Hanka. But you'll be nice to her anyway, won't you.'

130

Amery nodded, his mouth full.

Christine wondered whether she should reply to her mother's letter. But why? She wasn't, after all, 'dear little Tina' any more. She was a married woman. As soon as she had her own household she'd have to make this change clear to her parents. She regretted that Amery had not rented a house but only an apartment, though a very smart one. She would fix a visiting day for the family, perhaps the second Sunday of the month. That would be enough. Christine breathed so deeply that Amery turned to her with a questioning look.

'Everything is all right,' she said and smiled.

During the next few days they saw all the sights of Venice that were considered worth seeing, and reserved tickets to see *La Bohème* at the Teatro Fenice. When, on the morning of the performance, Christine looked for a dress, she found, though she had brought two ankle-length evening gowns for the trip, nothing suitable. It was no more than she had expected. Indeed she wasn't *looking* in the true sense of the word, but just making sure that she had nothing, but absolutely nothing to wear.

When she allowed the hangers to scrape across the metal rod for a third time, Amery became aware of it, and asked what was the matter. Christine apologised for not having thought of her dress for the opera before, and begged Amery so earnestly to go to the Teatro Fenice without her, that he was determined to buy her a new dress. Christine knew where this dress was. She had already had it altered to fit her. But instead of taking Amery to the salon in question, she first took him to various shops where she tried on quite unsuitable models which she returned to the saleswoman with a smile of regret. This took a great deal of time, and Amery grew visibly tired. When, towards one o'clock, he asked her if she wasn't hungry, she took his arm without a word, and they went back towards their hotel. A few yards from the Bauer-Grünwald Christine suddenly stopped and looked into a shop window.

'Why don't you try it on?' Amery begged her and held the door open. The dress in which Christine stepped out of the changing-room a few minutes later was of white Venetian lace.

'A *point-de-rose* piece,' the manageress said rolling her eyes. The shoulders and the high collar, as well as the clinging sleeves, were unlined to allow the skin to show through the relief-like flower pattern. From the breast to the hem the lace was lined with white satin.

'My God,' sighed Amery. 'And we've gone past it all this time.'

131

'It goes very well with my hair, doesn't it?' asked Christine, lifted her hands to her red-brown curls and turned to show Amery the back décolletage. It reached from the narrow collar to the waist, and resembled the outline of a leaf, through the middle of which ran the soft shadow of her spine. Amery was enchanted and made no bones about it.

'I don't want you to buy it,' Christine said quietly. The manageress vanished.

'Why not?' asked Amery.

'There are so many noughts on the label.'

Amery stepped towards the table where two little cardboard labels lay, and read the amount on the first.

'Please,' he said and smiled.

'That's just for the shoes,' Christine said and took her lip between her teeth.

He took up the second label and kept it in his hand.

'No,' Christine said.

The sum corresponded to the aunual earnings of one of his managers.

'*Punto a rilievo*,' Amery read aloud and looked at Christine. 'How nice it sounds.'

She put her hand on one of the dress stands as if she needed to hold on to something.

'Signora,' Amery called, and the manageress tore open the curtain of the changing-room to help Christine get dressed.

The performance at the Teatro Fenice started late as is customary. For a quarter of an hour the Amerys moved between dresses, furs, uniforms and dinner jackets through the foyer, and Christine enjoyed not having to greet anyone but being admired by everybody. She had bought a bordeaux-red lipstick that afternoon, and its colour matched her hair so perfectly in the dim light of the electric candles that her pale face looked as if it had been cut out of a Renaissance painting. When the crowd was so dense that her lace sleeves were in danger of being torn, Amery and Christine went to their seats, and the bell rang at the same moment.

Christine felt the eyes of the gentlemen and the opera glasses of the ladies trained on their box, and she was annoyed when Amery moved his seat closer to her. As the centre of such uninhibited interest, she preferred to be on her own.

'Do they always start so late?'

'No,' Amery said, 'only tonight.'

She wanted his next reply to be flattering and asked, 'Why?'

'Because of you,' he said promptly. 'So that everybody can look at you.'

She put her programme in front of her face and whispered, 'But I want only you to see me.'

'Let's go then,' Amery said, and made as if to get up. Christine smiled and pressed him back. The lights went out. *La Bohème* had begun.

During the interval Christine got up, but her knees gave way at that moment, and she stretched out her hand as if she wanted to pick up something from the floor. Amery bent to anticipate her.

'It'll pass in a moment,' she groaned.

'Do you feel ill? Shall I fetch a doctor?' he asked and felt for her shoulders.

'No.'

While they heard the sound of closing doors and the coughing and talking of the audience, they squatted opposite each other, and Amery remembered a sensation he had almost forgotten since his schooldays. It was pity. He felt the folds of his patent-leather shoes press into his feet but did not alter his position as if the small discomfort helped him to share Christine's pain.

After a few minutes she got up and sat in her seat. 'I'm sorry,' she said. He wanted to ask her a question, but she anticipated him and confessed that she had had previous attacks.

'Perhaps it is a child,' he said and looked into her eyes.

She shrugged her shoulders, more from tiredness than in agreement. He kissed her hands.

'We'll go home. On the night train.'

'But I want to see the rest of the performance.'

'It isn't good for you now,' he contradicted, but they remained to the end, and, while the dying Mimi repeated the beginning of Rodolfo's aria from Act One, Christine dabbed the sweat from her forehead. Next day they went back to Prague.

2

Pseudologia Phantastica

WHILE CHRISTINE WAS away, the weather turned warm in Prague, and on clear days one had a foretaste of summer. It was such a day when Sophie sat on the terrace of the Lustig mansion, above the acacia in bloom, with Victor, Heinrich and Jarmila. She had insisted that her friend came with them, and Jarmila had been a tremendous success. After tea they played Happy Families and only said goodbye when it got dark. Under the eyes of the valet, Victor accompanied the young ladies as far as the stairs and called after them how much, oh, how very much, he had enjoyed their company.

When Sophie was alone she sat down at the grand piano, pressed the forte pedal, struck a few keys and listened to the vibrations. Then she went around the room feeling the curtains and cushions as if she expected to find the sound again in the folds and materials. Sometimes she took off her shoes and brushed the carpet with her bare feet until she finally went back to her room like a sleep-walker.

She had not sung since Christine's wedding. She did not try, even when Pavel Sixta asked her. He had written her a new long song, but she forgot its title the same day. Sixta did not hold it against her, but accompanied her to Professor Ruschka who could find nothing wrong apart from slightly swollen tonsils. He gave Sophie a tin box of sweets to suck, and explained fairly harshly that any further consultation was a pure waste of money.

Sophie shook her head and remained silent when she joined Sixta in the corridor of the clinic. Before they reached the street, she said, 'Laryngospasm, probably,' through her teeth.

'What is that?' he asked, but she did not reply.

That evening he looked it up in his dictionary of foreign words. But its explanation didn't mean anything to him. A few days later he borrowed a medical dictionary from a friend and found that the symptoms were whistling breath, anxiety, blue discolouration of the nails and lips. On his way home he would have liked to have cried. Instead, a largo theme came into his mind, and he wrote it down on a cigarette packet. But soon after he was so ashamed that Sophie's illness should be an occasion for a work of art, that he put the cigarettes into his jacket pocket and threw the packet away. In the afternoon he used the theme for a funeral march and orchestrated it for wind instruments. He determined to tear it up, but Fräulein Kalman, when he visited her towards evening, opposed this so energetically that he was content to roll up the sheets and hide them in his bookshelves.

Sophie said nothing to her parents about 'laryngospasm'. During the evening meal she told them that the complaint would get better, but that she should not sing for some weeks. She showed them the yellow sweets, and the Sellmanns were glad they had been let off so lightly.

Jarmila, on the other hand, who was in the country, was alarmed by a letter full of dark hints, and Sophie spoke in a whisper when she saw her teacher. She was often in town, wandering about and standing at the tram stop where she had first seen Jan Amery. When she walked home in the dark she lit two cigarettes and held one at arm's length so as to make people coming towards her believe that someone was with her. Sixta had listened several times to stories of her being followed by a man in white gaiters, but when he offered to see her home, she refused. 'Perhaps we shan't meet again,' she said and patted his coat sleeve. Once he tried to follow her secretly, but she noticed him and got off at the next stop, making him jump from the tram.

When he confessed that he had originally wanted to become, not a composer but a poet, she teased him mercilessly, and she told endless, unlikely stories, allowing her imagination free rein.

But it was neither Sixta nor the 'nordic' Vavra who got to the root of the change in Sophie, but Frau Farel, Amery's aunt. From the first she had been infatuated with the dark Sellmann daughter. Sophie's trusting and spirited, but sometimes rash and capricious behaviour appealed to her own nature, however much she hid it behind the manner of the widow of a cavalry captain. At Christmas she had given her a stole she had crocheted herself. While the honeymoon couple were still away she invited the 'little niece', as she liked to call her, to her house. After taking Sophie to her tram stop in the evening, she visited a schoolfriend of her husband's who had been, until recently, a specialist in nervous complaints. Dr. Kavalár was a bachelor and lived on the second floor of an apartment house. He offered Marketa a cool glass of beer, and after a few courtesies listened to her for a quarter of an hour.

'Good,' he then said. 'Would you like another glass?'

Marketa refused, so as not to give him the opportunity for digression.

'We have a name for it, of course,' he explained. 'But . . .'

'I'd like to know it,' Frau Farel said.

'Pseudologia phantastica,' Dr. Kavalár said. 'Delbrück has described it. It occurs mostly in small children and hysterical personalities. They think up stories and believe them the more they tell them. Fundamentally none of us is free of it. It is a kind of revenge against those who don't think us grown up enough to hear the whole truth. A reaction against our feeling of inferiority, if you want to call it that. Those who have a gift for acting – take Herr Hitler – can convince not only themselves, but others. Is the young lady closely related?'

'Not at all,' Marketa lied.

'I'll have a look at her, if you like.'

'I wouldn't like to bother you.'

'From what you have told me, I would guess her to be a person with more than average imagination. She could even be a confidence trickster.'

'That's out of the question,' said Marketa categorically.

'Would you consider it possible that her stories are a compensation for some disappointment?'

'Yes, that could be.'

'How old is she?'

'Twenty.'

'Then it is obvious,' Dr. Kavalár exclaimed. 'Find her a man, one that suits her, and you'll see.'

'I'll have another beer now,' said Marketa.

When she got home she sat by her stove and considered. It's obvious, she concluded, and since her self-respect demanded that she pretend to be a little more magnanimous than she really was, she decided to offer Christine her friendship and confidence, before a catastrophe occurred. The young people weren't expected back from Italy until the middle of the following month, and she thought she had time to go to visit a cousin in the country.

On the 15th June, St. Vitus's day, she was at her brother-in-law's, as usual on that holiday. When he asked her, with some reproach in his voice, why she had not yet called on his daughter-in-law, she heard to her surprise that Jan and Christine had been in their new apartment for more than two weeks.

'Tina is having to stay in bed a bit,' said Bohuslav.

Marketa cut her visit short. She had a project but no plan, and if she hoped for some success she would have to find a favourable moment. When she rang the bell at the young Amery's and was invited in not by the maid but by Sophie, she was afraid the game was already lost.

Sophie kissed Aunt Marketa on both cheeks, took her coat, and led her into the drawing-room. 'We mustn't talk too loud,' she said. 'Tina is asleep.'

'Isn't there a maid?' asked Marketa.

'It's her day off.'

'On a Monday?'

'It's because it is a holiday, St. Vitus',' Sophie explained. 'But I can make coffee.'

'No, don't bother,' said Marketa. 'Since when do you use make-up?'

'I've only been trying Tina's lipstick,' Sohpie replied without blushing and showed Frau Farel into an armchair. 'She bought it in Venice to match her new hair. Oh, you don't know about that,' she chattered on, 'but now her fair hair is growing in again.'

'That isn't why she's in bed,' Marketa grumbled and settled herself in her chair.

'Oh no,' Sophie sighed and turned her head to the window.

'Tell me.'

Sophie looked at Frau Farel, and all the excitement of the past weeks was wiped away. Calmly she put her hands in her lap and nodded before beginning to speak, as if to confirm that all she had to tell was the sad truth. The child is really rather like an angel, Marketa thought, and, so as not to be over-impressed, she pulled the hem of her skirt about her ankles.

'It's a . . . Shall I explain it to you?'

'I beg you,' Marketa said.

'It is salpingitis, an inflammation of the Fallopian tubes. You know what that means?'

'Yes,' said Marketa not quite firmly, but distinctly enough to be spared the details. She had grown up in the belief that a woman of a certain class did not somehow possess all these unmentionable parts, and she was surprised to find herself hearing such a word without feeling ill.

'She is in pain and has a temperature,' Sophie said. 'It was quite high last night.'

'Were you here?'

'I'm always here,' Sophie replied. 'Tina does not want a nurse

137

and the maid has enough to do running the household. Sometimes I stay the night.' She smiled. 'I'm the only one of us three who hasn't learnt anything. You think I can sing? That's all over. I change compresses and don't want to do anything else.'

'And Jan?'

'Jan?' Sophie asked and put her hand to her throat to adjust her necklace. 'He looks after his business and is glad I am here.'

'Perhaps we can take it in turn a bit?' Marketa suggested, expecting Sophie's refusal.

'Oh that is kind of you! Let's ask Tina when she wakes up.'

While Sophie went into the kitchen to make coffee, Frau Farel wondered whether she had been mistaken. No, no, she stuck to her suspicion. She got up and went into the corridor. She had looked over the apartment two months before, and knew her way. She even knew that the walls of the bedroom were covered in sea-green silk. 'It's more like a place to swim in,' she had said to Bohuslav.

She knocked softly and when there was no reply, opened the door. Sophie was sitting on Christine's bed and putting a compress on her forehead. She smiled at Frau Farel and said, 'Tina has just woken up.'

And you heard that all the way from the kitchen, thought Marketa and went up to the bed. Christine wanted to sit up, but Marketa pushed her gently back. She did not expect Sophie to leave the room, but the familiar way in which she sat down on the other bed annoyed her. Christine took the compress from her forehead, smiled an exhausted smile, and left the conversation to Frau Farel and her sister. After a few minutes she said, 'Do drink your coffee here with me, won't you.'

When Sophie had left the room, Marketa bent over Christine and wiped her face. 'I want to confess something,' she said quickly as if there were no time to lose. 'I was against your marrying Jan, but today, my dear, I'm glad that you belong to us. Not because it is a *fait accompli*, but because I like you. I want to beg your pardon for mistrusting you. I want to help you. To be precise I want to do all the things that your sister is doing for you. Please don't refuse! I'm an old woman. I know about sickness. Farel had haemorrhoids. He wore rubber pants in bed. You're the first person I've told that to. Also he was a drunk. Please think about it.'

'We'll ask Jan,' whispered Christine.

'No, you've got to want it,' Marketa said. 'I don't know how to prove to you that I really mean it. Would you like me to give you my diamond earrings? I know that you like them though they are not as valuable as they look, and your husband could buy you better ones. I'll bring them.'

Christine moved her head weakly.

'I have a little garden, which even your father-in-law doesn't know about. There's only a summer-house and a few wild cherries and elder. It's a bit windy up there, but there's a lovely view of the castle. Would you like it?'

'No,' Christine said in a loud voice, but with the same breath, 'but come and stay with me, Aunt Marketa.'

By the time Sophie came in with the coffee, everything seemed to be fixed, but Marketa thought it advisable to obtain Jan's consent.

The time until he came home passed quickly, especially since the doctor dropped in, and after the examination he sat down in the drawing-room while Sophie went to the chemist's to get the prescription. Dr. Jedlitschka, a bald and therefore rather older-seeming man in his forties, was at first very reserved, but when Frau Farel explained her relationship with his patient he made no secret of his worries. Like most doctors, he did not explain the technical terms he used, but Marketa understood enough to realise that it was not just a question of an inflammation, but that there was also a psychological disturbance which might transfer itself to the vasomotor sphere and cause the muscles to become rigid.

'My God,' she said, and refilled his sherry glass.

'If I may advise something,' Dr. Jedlitschka said and sipped at his drink. 'It would be either making her immediate environment more stable, or changing it.'

'You are a good doctor,' replied Frau Farel. 'I'm for a stabilisation.'

When she took him to the door, Sophie appeared with the medicine, and soon after Marketa heard Jan's voice in the hall. He immediately went to see his wife, and when he entered the drawing-room kissed Marketa's hand, then sat down opposite her on the sofa under the 'crooked village', right in line with the very picture which, because of the banality of its glaring colours, always made her look the other way. The parchment shade of the standard lamp made his blond hair look silver grey. It suited him, she thought, and she had to keep herself from stroking his temples. He wore a business suit of dark worsted.

'Why don't you change your clothes and make yourself comfortable,' she asked.

'I've still got to take Sophie home. Do you want to spend tonight here? No? Then I'll send a car for you tomorrow. About eleven. Does that suit you?'

'The question is, does it suit you, Jan?'

He looked past her with his mouth half open, like a schoolboy suddenly confronted with an exam. 'I can't tell you how glad I am,' he said softly.

'What is the matter with you, Jan?'

'I don't know,' he said quickly as if he had expected the question. 'I sometimes feel as if I were mad. I know what you want to say: we are all more or less mad. But I'm not talking about our way of life, of our culture. For while we can hear the cracklings and rustlings, we're still pretty solidly upright.' He laughed, but Marketa took good care not to interrupt. 'It isn't pessimism, you understand. I know where I belong. I'm not even questioning the sense, or the permanence of such unspeakable things as immunisation, artificial honey, bakelite. No, I tell you, Aunt Marketa, it isn't that. I feel something in myself like a roaring in my ears. As if I had a conch-shell in my head instead of a brain.

'I realise I'm speaking too fluently for you to take me seriously. That's due to business, and dealing with wholesalers and middlemen. Or perhaps it's my education – or Vienna. I have the same difficulty when I go to confession. The prior at Strahov thinks I confess my sins too elegantly to be really repentant. He just lacks the courage to tell me so. Should I stutter or babble before anyone believes me?'

'You're overworked.'

'There's no such thing. If one works too hard one is tired.'

'Perhaps you should forget everything that you've been taught,' Marketa advised. 'Your attitudes, your manners, all the varnish you've been covered with to make you look the same as lawyers, bankers or ambassadors. I think your wife would be pleased.'

'The theory of happiness,' Jan said under his breath.

'What do you mean?'

'Nothing.'

'You are hiding something?'

'I'm not sure that you can bear it,' Jan said. 'I . . . I believe, I . . .' he began.

'Ah, you're stuttering,' Marketa said with a desperate smile.

Jan pulled himself together and said, 'I don't believe I can really love.'

Marketa gave him time to continue, but after a while she was

140

sure that there was no more to come. She felt relieved but also cheated.

'Oh, my dear boy,' she said.

'Would you like a beer?' Jan asked coldly.

'Don't be hurt,' Marketa begged. 'We'll have time enough to talk of it in the next few days. But one thing now: If you can speak like that of not being able to love, you're on the way to learning. Yes, please let me have a glass of beer and then take me part of the way when you drive Sophie home.'

An hour later Marketa got out of the car near her apartment, and Amery drove on with Sophie.

'We might go for a bit of a walk,' Sophie said. Amery stopped the car but did not cut the engine. 'I'd just like to go down the stairs once and come up again. I've been imprisoned in your apartment for a fortnight, and it's so warm tonight.' She wound down the window as if to prove it.

'The maid won't be home before ten, and Tina is alone.'

'She's asleep,' Sophie said.

'I'm sorry. Not today.'

'Drive on then,' Sophie burst out. 'Go on, drive quickly.'

'Have I offended you?'

'No, drive, drive!' she exclaimed and left the window open while he went on.

'It isn't good for your throat,' he warned her but she took no notice.

Outside her house she gave him her hand and said, 'Goodbye Herr von Sternberg.'

Amery had meant to thank her for her help, but was taken aback by this form of address.

'What does that mean?' he asked without letting go her hand.

'But you're Herr von Sternberg.'

'I don't know enough about the gentleman to know whether to say, "I'm not, thank God", or "unfortunately not".'

'You'll know one day,' Sophie said and showed the gap between her teeth.

'Herr von Sternberg?' Amery asked and felt the roaring in his ears.

'Only you don't know it yet,' said Sophie, took her hand away, and went quickly towards the illuminated entrance of the house.

3

Fräulein Siebenschein

THE PRESIDENTIAL CHANCERY sent Herr Jan Amery an unexpected invitation to the State Reception on 28th October. He explained this to himself by the fact that he had, in the summer, been voted deputy chairman of the Chamber of Commerce. From a personal point of view he thought it boring, and from the point of view of the business it seemed senseless to stand around amongst people to whom he was so indifferent that he wasn't even sorry for them. But Bohuslav Amery, who'd avoided such honours himself in his day, persuaded him to accept. Under the prevailing conditions, he said, smiling, it would be good for the business to be represented not just at motor-races and the produce exchange, but also at Government banquets.

When Christine heard that she would be introduced to the President on the following Wednesday, she clapped her hands with pleasure. Her condition had improved since the summer; the attacks had not only become less painful but also less frequent, and Aunt Marketa arranged the daily routine so imperceptibly, that Amery was hardly conscious of it. In July, Christine had gone for a first drive, but in the heat of August a slight relapse had made it impossible for them to consider going away.

But now, in October, even Dr. Jedlitschka had no objections to Christine going to the reception. Since she would have to walk from the car to the second courtyard of the castle, he asked that she should wear warm underwear, angora wool if possible. Her black satin dress was delivered punctually on the 27th October, but towards evening she was suddenly in such acute pain that the doctor had to be called. Her temperature rose to over a hundred, and Dr. Jedlitschka suggested to Amery that the time had come when her treatment should be continued in hospital. The reception at the castle wasn't, of course, even mentioned.

Amery was completely bewildered when, during the afternoon

142

of the 28th Sophie appeared and announced that she would accompany him in her sister's place. She said that Christine had telephoned her that morning and asked it as a favour. While Jan was still trying to explain to her that this time it was not just a short attack, but that the symptoms pointed to a really serious condition which might place her in danger of her life, the maid came and asked them to come to the bedroom.

Aunt Marketa had gone home to see whether she had any mail. Christine was on her own. Her temperature had dropped. It appeared that Sophie had indeed told the truth, but Amery's distress increased rather than diminished when his sister-in-law now refused to accompany him as loudly as his wife demanded it, and for the first time since his school years he had the feeling that other people were making decisions about him, as if he were a puppet to be moved about. He sat thinking about it for a moment, but by the time he got up Sophie had already put on her sister's black evening dress and stood, still protesting, in front of the mirror. Christine asked Jan to call the sewing woman, and he succeeded in persuading her to come straight away.

During the afternoon he heard Christine and Sophie say again and again that everything was being done for his sake, but he did not believe it. Something inexplicable was happening before his very eyes, something so unlikely that he felt he must have been suddenly transported to another planet. He found it difficult to understand why Aunt Marketa, who came back early that evening, should be so pleased that Sophie had 'so kindly stepped into the breach'. And when his father telephoned later to thank Sophie for her assistance, he thought seriously that he was surrounded by a lot of madmen. He nevertheless shaved, put on his dinner jacket, and said goodbye to Christine and Frau Farel as if he had changed his mind, and drove off to an occasion which everybody except he obviously thought of as a great piece of luck.

Sophie straightened her dress and got into the car. She did not seem to care what kind of impression she made on Amery. Perhaps he expected her to be sorry for her frivolity, or even to suggest at the last minute that they should give up the reception and return home. She didn't do so. All she wanted was, for his sake, to look out of the window with a tired and bored expression like all the ladies who were being driven to the castle at this moment by their husbands or lovers.

In the summer she had spent two months on a farm in Silesia with her mother and Heinrich, in a green and faultless world where the creaking of a door-hinge was mistaken for the call of a blackbird, and where early apples falling on the roof of the veranda made one think visitors had arrived.

She had tried to understand herself, and nobody had disturbed her. At first she had cried a lot, especially at night, but one Sunday she had found the expression 'toll of tears' in a book. She had run into the nearby forest and climbed on to a high observation platform and thought about it until dark. Were tears really the toll you paid to enter another country? Were fear and pain just the toll-booth? Why did her father grind his teeth every time one of the war songs was played on the radio? And why did her mother leave the room whenever Sophie sang one of the songs from her own childhood home? Did tears help one over the next bridge where a new country lay, fresh as after a summer storm? The sky light and wide, the roofs red, the trees pure, the people as on the first day? 'And God saw everything that he had made, and behold, it was very good.' Had good come into the world like that, and was evil only an invention which one carried inadvertently through one's life? Why should there then be rules? Why not kill, commit adultery, lie? The heathens, Paul said, were a law unto themselves, and only through the law did they come to know their sins. Where was that other country where a different law-giver went up the mountain to speak with God? She wished he would come down with a different tablet in his hands. It would be as if she herself had suddenly stepped out of the shadow, as if she had burnt her bridges at last. Her heart leapt almost as if it had stopped beating. But it went on beating, and because it would have to stop one day, it enjoyed the present moment.

For a few days she still walked about as if she were asleep, but slowly she began to feel that she had both feet on the ground. She became softer, more indulgent, and joined her mother on her walks. Her distance from reality diminished.

Amery parked the car and helped Sophie to get out. A double line of young soldiers in Italian, Russian and French Legion uniforms pointed the direction to the Spanish Hall, and in front of its entrance civilian doormen took the invitation cards.

In front of the curtained windows stood a cold buffet which, with its red,white and blue hydrangeas, somehow gave the impression of a lying-in-state; as if, at the playing of the national anthem, the white folding doors would open to allow the catafalque of smoked ham, trout, game pies, stuffed eggs and cubes of cheese to be consumed in flames.

Either the guests under the low-hanging chandeliers and in front of the huge mirrors were used to these decorations, or were so impressed by their own splendour or the magnificence of the renovated hall that their faces showed nothing but a readiness to be affable to everybody. Amery greeted acquaintances and was greeted in turn, but before anything could be said, the middle doors swung open and the President entered, followed by the President of the council and some members of the cabinet. His entrance might have remained unnoticed, he was so short, if the orchestra had not struck up the national anthem. Sophie did not manage to catch a glimpse of him while he spoke. Instead she saw a man who so resembled her language teacher that she thought for some time it was Vavra himself. He must have felt her eyes on him, for after the cheering had died down he came over, accompanied by a waiter, handed her and Amery a glass of champagne and introduced himself as the 'roman' brother of the 'nordic' Vavra. He was larger than the translator of the *Edda*, had broad, powerful shoulders, but was as ready to talk as his brother. Amery had no objection when Vavra asked whether he might take Sophie to the buffet, and vanished with her in the crowd. The silent drive to the castle and the sight of this patriotic assembly had not improved his mood. When he therefore saw a fellow student from his days in Vienna he beckoned for a couple of glasses of champagne and joined him.

'Don't take anything you hear literally,' the 'roman' Vavra said when he had helped Sophie to saddle of venison and cranberries. 'Three-quarters of what is said here is in any case superfluous.'

When Sophie had finished and put down her plate, Vavra took her to one of the groups which stood like small impenetrable circles about the room, but which opened up when he appeared.

'When I came back from Vladivostock,' a white-haired man with a sonorous voice was saying, 'I asked my wife, "and what have you been doing all through the war?" – "We've been making *buchty*," she said, "We've been making cottage-cheese *buchty*".'

'A former legionnaire,' Vavra whispered.

'Then I went to see a witch,' the white-haired gentleman continued. 'First I had to drink some coffee, good coffee, mind you, and had to turn the cup upside down. In the meantime she read my hand. "You will receive high office," she said. "Well, I'm president of the health insurance company. Then she turned the cup over, and I read – as truly as I stand here – nine letters in the coffee grounds. I don't know to this day what they meant!' He looked around him, and everybody laughed. 'I told Masaryk about it, but he didn't know either,' he cried and lifted his glass. 'Long live the Republic!'

Vavra drew Sophie away, feeling her embarrassment. 'Would you like something more to eat?'

'No, thank you.'

'Would you like to meet the clergy?'

'Yes, everybody,' Sophie said. 'How is it that everyone here knows you?' she asked as they moved to the corner near the orchestra.

'I don't know,' said Vavra, smiling, then introduced Sophie to the clerical gentlemen, and, after a moment, took part in their conversation as if he himself had started it and decided on the subject. His fluent way of talking about matters that were not necessarily new to him, but were unexpected, bewildered Sophie.

'One should only forgive the stronger, only the stronger,' he exclaimed and put his arm round the thin back of a clergyman. 'The Elbe is after all a tributary of the Vltava. Oughtn't we to be pleased if the sons of the Vltava return to their native river?' He held out his glass to Sophie, and she was obliged to clink glasses with him and the others. When she looked round for a tray, she saw a small gentleman behind her whose face seemed familiar.

'I'm afraid I'm not the waiter,' he joked, took her glass and handed it to an officer. 'I've been listening a bit. I know it's rude, but I don't like to leave the supervision of the most beautiful ladies to the secret service, but prefer to do a bit of it myself.'

'Herr President,' Sophie whispered and wondered for a moment whether she should drop a curtsey or put out her hand. But the 'roman' Vavra came to her aid, introduced Sophie and explained that she was taking the place of her sister who was ill.

'Where is this Herr Amery?' asked the President. 'Since we buy our crockery from him, he might say "good evening" to us.'

'Come with me,' Sophie begged, 'and we'll both go and look for him.'

The President made the same kind of face that Charlie Chaplin makes when a dog, a friend or a girl runs away from him. His lips smiled, but his eyes looked sad and pinched. He stood in front of Sophie like a good-natured and reliable head gardener who can not remember the name of a shrub that he himself planted last autumn. He pulled down his eyebrows and blinked in a way drunks do to clear their sight. Then he said with some charm, 'My dear lady, let us seek your husband.'

'My brother-in-law,' Sophie corrected and remained on his left side.

'You don't come from Prague?'

'No. I'm German.'

'From the Reich?'

'Is that so bad?'

'I hope nobody takes a photograph of us,' said the President.

'Surely nothing can happen to you?'

'Not to me,' he smiled. 'But over there, in front of the mirror, Colonel Tschunke is looking at us.'

'I'm afraid I don't understand anything to do with soldiers,' Sophie said.

'He is the German military attaché,' the President explained. 'When I was your age, young ladies were only interested in uniforms. We civilians without tassels and cockades had little luck. Today it seems to be different.' He gave Sophie a teasing look. 'Today one throws oneself into the arms of the Church.'

'That was just by chance,' Sophie said against her will, as if she had to apologise for being found amongst the clergy.

'There he is,' Sophie said, balancing on her toes. 'My brother-in-law,' she added.

It was by now about an hour since the President's address, but Amery was still with his Viennese student friend, a certain Danesch who had become an adviser on social questions to the President. Neither Amery nor Danesch were surprised that they differed in their views on almost everything, but their mutual respect was elastic enough to make it possible for them to talk to each other in that quick-witted and ironical way, which depends on showing the superiority of one's point of view by mocking it.

Amery had not known, or had forgotten, that Danesch was a tippler and known as such to all the waiters who were ready at hand with fresh supplies. Conscious that their conversation needed a great deal of champagne, they emptied a dozen or so glasses. After the third glass, Amery noticed that he didn't sip any more, but drank a glass down in one draught. At first this annoyed him, but when he found how cleverly he enticed Danesch into new feints and lunges by pretending to be helpless himself, he found pleasure in it, and drank some more. By and by he began to feel that not only Danesch but most of the guests around him made him want to rejoice. He was, of course, too disciplined, or not yet drunk enough, to act out of character, but he did feel that he would have to risk doing something daring soon, if only so as not to end the evening in the same mood as the one in which he had begun it. When Danesch whispered that the President was coming towards them, Amery saw no reason to change his attitude. Only when he heard Sophie's voice did he turn round.

'You see,' Sophie smiled. 'Now I can introduce you.'

147

Amery made a bow but kept his glass in his right hand until the Head of State, after a glance at Danesch, held out his hand. The President seemed to have a good memory, for he asked in a friendly, almost concerned manner after Amery senior.

'Thank you, he is well,' Jan replied politely but not very courteously.

'He must be in his seventies . . .' said the President.

'Yes, in his seventies,' Jan said and took his white handkerchief out of his breast pocket and handed it to Sophie. 'I can see you are sweating,' he said.

'Well, I'm very glad,' the President said in a loud voice as if the very loudness could make one forget Amery's gaucherie. 'I'm very glad.'

Amery saw Sophie's embarrassment and scolded her, 'Do wipe your forehead at least.'

'Is it really so hot here?' the President asked and looked at his adjutant.

'Oh yes,' said Amery. 'It is very hot here, Herr President. I need a little refreshment.' He took his glass and held it high as if to prove to everyone that it was filled to the brim. With his thumb and forefinger he opened his breast pocket and poured the champagne into his dinner jacket.

'Hmmm,' the President grumbled without losing his composure. 'I hope our champagne is so good that it won't leave any stains.'

'As excellent as your mayonnaise,' said Amery. 'A little while ago I saw General Syrový put a lobster sandwich in his trouser pocket. So your mayonnaise must be first class.'

'It isn't true,' Danesch intervened. 'You didn't see anything like that at all.'

Amery laughed. 'Of course it isn't true. But it would fit in well, wouldn't it?'

The President turned to Sophie and said in German, 'My respects, dear lady.' His escort stepped aside to let him through. My God, what he hadn't been through at receptions, here, in Paris, in Bucharest, in Moscow! Without saying another word to Amery, he went away, taking the 'roman' Vavra with him.

Amery wanted to apologise to Danesch, but Danesch had vanished. There was suddenly a lot of room around him and his sister-in-law. 'I am quite wet,' he whispered as if only Sophie should know about it. He put down his glass and pressed his hand to his heart as if he were wounded.

'Why ever did you do it?' Sophie asked between laughter and tears, but looked at him as if he had received a decoration.

It suddenly occurred to him. 'Because I love you,' he said and put his hand to his forehead.

Sophie put the white handkerchief back into his breast pocket. 'Come along then,' she said, took his arm and led him away.

While they were waiting for their coats, Amery said, 'I hope he doesn't think I have something against him.'

Sophie stood in front of the mirror and put her hands to her hair.

'I must go back,' Amery said without moving. 'I must explain to him that I'm simply indifferent to him.'

Sophie smiled between her naked arms.

'Otherwise I'd have thrown the champagne in his face,' he said and put his arms around her.

'Do you know Charvat Lane?' Sophie asked.

'Yes.'

'That's where we are going.'

'Aha,' Amery said and would have asked something more, but at this moment a lieutenant who had gone to collect their coats returned and would not be dissuaded from accompanying them out of the castle.

'Are you coming along from a sense of vigilance or friendliness?' Amery asked and put his top hat on.

'It's my first day here,' said the lieutenant. 'I wouldn't like to make a mistake.'

'The fireworks begin in an hour,' he said when they arrived at the gate. 'You ought to watch them.'

'Perhaps next year,' Amery growled and put his hand to the brim of his hat.

'Olga Siebenschein,' Sophie said in the car, mentioned the house number and put her head in his lap.

When they arrived at Charvat Lane, Sophie had a house-key. She preceded Amery to the fourth floor and unlocked a door which had a visiting card saying 'Olga Siebenschein, stud. phil.' pinned to it. There was no hall, and the room itself was hardly wider than a corridor, leading towards a glass door on to a wooden balcony overlooking the backyards of other alleys. The unmade bed, the faded curtains, the linoleum full of holes and the iron sink, made him remember a hotel room to which a girl journalist had taken him in the last year of the war.

'Where is this Fräulein Siebenschein?' asked Amery and hung his top hat on the towel rail.

'Here,' said Sophie and dropped a curtsey.

With the same gesture as in the cloakroom of the castle, Sophie put her hands in her hair, then stepped out of her shoes, and asked, without looking at Amery, 'Will you turn out the light?'

Amery heard the sound of a zip in the dark, then the click of a hook, and an elastic snapped against a chair. Sophie undressed with a lack of embarrassment as if she were climbing out of a sweaty tennis dress to go and take a shower. But she breathed in a different way. Breathing in, she gasped as if she had a cold, breathing out she seemed to have enough air for two.

'It's cold here,' she said and suddenly flung herself around Amery's neck.

In the apartment next door somebody clapped their hands as if they had seen her leap; or it might have been someone having their face slapped.

'I love you too,' Sophie whispered like a belated reply to Amery's confession in the Spanish Hall. She clasped her arms around his neck and her legs around his hips.

Next door a falsetto voice began to sing the Hussite battle hymn, 'Ye warriors of God and his commandments...' but stopped after the first line.

Amery searched for Sophie's mouth, grasped her thighs, and, without letting go of her, went to the window. She took his lips between her teeth, turned against his chest and began to moan.

The tenor next door started to sing again, but in a lower key and as if he had left out several verses.

'Come on,' Sophie begged and pressed her wet forehead against Amery's chin, 'or I'll jump out of the window.' She leaned back, lifted herself up for a moment and then slid very slowly down his body until she was so full of a tearing and itching pain that she became rigid.

The tenor stopped singing, began to swear, and seemed to be trying to break up a chair. After this a short polyphonic squeaking sounded as if he had pulled at a concertina or had thrown it aside.

Sophie began to move, pushing away from him and then, after a trembling pause, returning.

'I can't stand it,' she said and Amery kissed her.

'Is it right like this?' she asked into his mouth.

He nodded.

'Is it nice for you?'

'Yes,' he said and pressed her against the door frame.

'Or would you rather..?' but she couldn't go on, for he pushed her against the wall behind which the tenor seemed to have decided once and for all to demolish his apartment. Suddenly she rose up so high that she seemed to want to fly away, and Amery had trouble holding her. Then she sighed and hung around him like dead, though she was still moving her body without knowing. Next door wood cracked, glass splintered. In between there were cries of, 'When I catch you, I'll strangle you with my braces, serpent! But if there's a God in heaven, one day you'll come and eat out of my hand.'

Amery felt Sophie's silent laughter under his hands.

'And do you know what I'll say to you then . . .' cried the tenor, but did not give himself an answer for a reddish glow ran suddenly over the wall, followed by blue and white. Sophie lifted her head and pressed herself against Amery. He carried her to the bed and lay down beside her.

They heard their neighbour go on to the wooden balcony and bellow, 'That's what those rogues throw good money away for!' But he had hardly said it when the last rocket exploded. He trampled about for a while as if he expected an encore, then shouted, 'Those buggers don't even manage a proper fireworks display.'

Sophie pressed her mouth into Amery's shoulder, choking with laughter, and drummed on the bed with her calves. 'He rented me the room,' she whispered into Amery's ear and inundated his neck with kisses. 'He thinks I study psychology because I bargained with him for such a long time.'

Their neighbour slammed the glass door into his room and fell, to judge by the noise, full length on the floor. Sophie laughed, but took the corner of the pillow into her mouth so as not to hurt Amery.

'What are you thinking about?' he asked her hoarsely and had to clear his throat. Sophie would have answered, but the tenor began to snore.

'We've got to look for another room,' Amery said.

'No,' Sophie said. 'Please don't let's. It's my room. Also he's never at home in the afternoon. In any case we can only meet in the afternoons. Today is an exception, because it's a holiday.'

151

4

Tuesdays and Fridays

THE DAY AFTER the reception Sophie announced during the evening meal that she would start her singing lessons again, but asked her father to pay Fräulein Kalman double the amount in the future, so that she could have four lessons a week.

'It is simply madness to have missed so much,' she explained. Sellmann nodded, but warned her not to overdo the singing.

Fräulein Kalman looked doubtful when she heard that the lessons would be paid for even if Sophie did not come regularly for her instruction.

'So he's married,' she said straight out.

'Who?' asked Sophie.

'I didn't fall on my head as a baby,' Fräulein Kalman spat, got up and hobbled round the grand piano in her brown ski-ing trousers. 'There are wives, you know, to whom one does too much honour by deceiving them.'

Sophie nodded without thinking.

'They sit on their husbands, they drive them to the pubs, the monasteries and the madhouses. But what is worse is that men get a taste for their own wives the moment they take a mistress.'

'Who says he's married?' Sophie asked.

'What else? Emigrant? Communist? Jew? Spanish? All those things at once?'

'Russian,' Sophie whispered.

'That's a relief,' said Fräulein Kalman, 'Then it'll soon be over. He'll love you for a month, then he'll beat you for four weeks, then he'll get drunk, leave without paying his hotel bill and send you a post card from Nice. My God, how relieved I am. I thought it was something serious. But don't start smoking. Those Russian cigarettes are too strong. I once had a lover, Count Dudinzev, who could play the Imperial Russian anthem on the piano with his penis. Well, let's leave that. So, Tuesdays and Fridays. Lord almighty! But today is Tuesday! Well, well, well, my dear. Have salt together and be at peace with one another as they say in St. Petersburg, and think of your voice.'

Sophie ran to Charvat Lane where Amery had been waiting half an hour. The place had the advantage of being only a few minutes from both Fräulein Kalman's 'studio' and Jan's business. The disadvantage, that it was only a quarter of an hour from the Amery apartment, was balanced by an escape route through a passage way, and the proximity of the tram stop.

Sophie now led a double life, and was surprised that she appeared to be the same person to her parents, brother, sisters and acquaintances. When she travelled home by tram on Tuesdays and Fridays, she changed from the alluring Olga Siebenschein into a peevish young lady who feared secretly that the conductor might make her pay a second fare since she had changed into another person.

When Katharina returned from her year on the farm and wanted to tell her how she had met Karol on the Austrian border, Sophie would not even let her finish speaking. The thought that there could be something comparable between other couples seemed unbearable, and even to listen to such things appeared like treason. She had not taken Jan for a lover because she found him more handsome, more clever, or more manly than other men, or because she had seen him at the tram stop opposite the Café Slavia a year and a half ago, but because he belonged to her from the beginning, from long before she or he had even existed.

As a schoolgirl she had often wondered whether her soul had been put in her head or her heart. Since she had begun meeting Jan in Charvat Lane she knew that her soul was in the whole of her body. Her conscience was neither good nor bad. Instead, she felt for the first time that she was herself from head to foot, because she had given herself without reserve.

She was glad that she and Jan lived in a city in which many people were in hiding. Small towns were glad to welcome the victorious, but losers were given little sanctuary. In the cities happiness was still a business, secrets were hatched before everyone's eyes, and conspiracies were the more successful the more their bloody aims were advertised. Not even the weather was the same all over one big city. Sellmann had once told them how he had sat on a windless hotel balcony in Paddington reading the paper, while a storm, twenty kilometres away but still in London, took the roofs off several houses.

She met Sixta more often in the following weeks, went to the theatre and concerts with him, invited him home where he played to her mother, and even took him to Christine's where he was given a confection made of biscuits and chocolate, and lukewarm café-au-lait to drink. Sophie did not speak, except to start sentences for Sixta to finish, and Christine and Aunt Marketa noticed that she occasionally put her hand under the sleeve of his jacket. After the third cup he felt ill, but Frau Farel poured him another with loving care, and with the help of God he not only drank it but explained to the ladies the themes of the outer movements of Dvorak's first symphony, the première of which he had just witnessed, and finally played a nocturne and mazurka by Chopin.

Frau Farel sat watching Sophie who stood by the piano stool and turned the pages. She wore a grey woollen blouse cut in military style which was emphasised by an olive green tie. Her heavy skirt fell to the top of her black lace-up boots, and Aunt Marketa wondered how men could find this ensemble attractive. Well, love, and that was what it was all about after all, had strange ways, and if this boy with the thick dark hair and the soft lips liked these galoshes, Sophie had, of course, no choice.

At Sophie's suggestion, Christine asked Herr Sixta for Christmas Day, and after he had drunk a sherry on top of the café-au-lait, he bowed to Frau Amery but did not dare kiss her hand since he could not remember whether it was all right to touch the fingers of a lady's hand with his lips. 'No,' Sophie told him firmly on the stairs, and put her totally confused and sweating friend into a tram.

Since it was nothing more interesting than a Thursday, she wandered about the town until it was time to join her father for their journey home, but was told at the bank that he had already gone, then looked into the windows of Amery & Herschel where, between fir branches, two pyramids of whitish green tea-sets stood, and bought an evening paper before getting into the tram. She read the report of the Crystal Palace fire, how three hundred and fifty fire engines had been called out, and how they had tried to save the manuscript of a composition by Handel from the flames. It was some time before she realised that the tram had stopped before reaching the Stephanik Bridge. She turned to the women's page, and, while reading about the new tunic dresses and the dangers of the new fashions for the fuller figure, she heard more and more often the word 'accident', and without taking her eyes off the paper, she began to believe that something had happened to her father. Christine's luke-warm coffee, Sixta's helpless face, the bland information of the bank cashier that her father had already left for home, and the burning down of the Crystal Palace in London all made it likely that Sellmann and his chauffeur had drowned in the Vltava, and Sophie wondered, with a promptness which appalled her, whether she might wear a black tunic dress at the funeral.

'Is he here?' she asked Hanka when she got home.

'Yes, and they're all eating already.'

Sophie washed her hands in the bathroom, looked guiltily at her father's shaving-strop next to his shaving mirror. 'Forgive me,' she said and ran along the corridor and called, 'It really isn't my fault,' while closing the door of the dining-room behind her. Then she saw Amery sitting beside her mother. He took his napkin from his lap, got up and shook her hand.

'Whose fault was it then?' he asked, smiling.

'Somebody got run over,' Sophie whispered and sat down on the empty chair between Sellmann and Heinrich. 'The tram had to wait for the ambulance.'

'Tell us about it later,' said Frau Sellmann who did not like catastrophes discussed at table.

Sophie only looked far enough from her plate to keep Amery's right hand in sight. At first it lay still, then took up the stem of the wine glass, then turned slowly like a beautiful brown five-footed animal on its back to show its rosy, warm, dry underside. At this movement Sophie felt herself go liquid from the ribs down, but had to laugh since she immediately thought of a description of what she felt. 'I'm turning into jam,' she thought.

'I don't know whether one could say that,' she heard Amery say to her father. 'But at any rate, there is the Marseillaise!'

He doesn't notice me at all, Sophie thought. He comes here without warning me, and now pretends I'm not here. That is very suspicious, and what does 'Marseillaise' mean?

While Hanka changed the plates she looked up and ran so blindly into Amery's glance that her eyes hurt.

'How exactly do you mean?' Betty asked her son-in-law.

'Well . . .' Amery began but seemed to have forgotten what they had been talking about.

Sellmann hastened to his aid with, ' "Oh God, our help in ages past," for example.'

'Oh, I see,' said Frau Sellmann and pressed her chin into her neck.

'Or "They shall not pass",' Katharina said.

'Exactly,' confirmed Amery and tried to take the bowl of pudding from Frau Sellmann.

'Or "Ye warriors of God and his commandments",' Sophie suggested.

'I'll hold it for you,' Betty said and gave Amery the spoon.

'What kind of a song is that?' asked Sellmann.

'That's the song of the Hussites when they went into battle against the Crusaders,' Heinrich explained and began to sing the anthem in Czech.

Amery pushed the spoon into the pudding, lifted it over the rim of the bowl and looked at Sophie for a second. She sat, pale and with her eyes lowered, between Sellmann and her warbling brother.

'Doesn't he sing nicely?' Betty asked.

'Very,' Amery said but couldn't stop the spoon striking the edge of his plate and upsetting the pudding all over the tablecloth.

'That'll do, Heini,' Sellmann said.

'It takes at least a quarter of an hour if one sings it slowly,' Heinrich said.

'Exactly,' Sellmann replied. 'It would take rather too long just now. Jan and I have to talk. So we'll put off that pleasure.'

Amery apologised to his mother-in-law for the stain on the tablecloth, thanked her for a second helping, and watched as Sophie helped herself and her brother. When she began to eat she pushed her lips forward and looked at him coldly across the table as if she were sitting opposite an importunate stranger in the tram. Soon after, the gentlemen went into Sellmann's study and Jan left the house after midnight.

On the following day Sophie went into town and walked about until it was time to go to Charvat Lane. She always had gooseflesh when she mounted the creaking old stairs, and she could tell the floors by their different smells. From washing-up water and wine sediment she went up to floor polish, then into tripe soup, followed by cat dirt, and lastly to small beer tempered by a tinge of gherkin and a pinch of cigar ash. If she opened the door on to the balcony, a south wind would waft clouds of soot from the chimneys. Frau Sellmann had already complained one evening, 'Sophie, you smell of soot. Perhaps you shouldn't sit down in the tram.'

Amery arrived punctually. When he left Sophie two hours later, she sat once more in the same position as when he had arrived: her feet side by side, her back pressed against the back of the white wickerwork chair, her hands on her knees and her chin above her right shoulder. Thus she had looked when he arrived,

156

and in the same way she thought about him for half an hour after he had left. She searched for her place in Amery's account of affairs, and was excited by it in a way for which she could find no expression.

He had spoken very openly, at great length, and had gone into some of the detail so deeply that he sometimes seemed to quite vanish in it. At first he had only wanted to explain to her how it had come about that he had suddenly been a visitor at Bubenech: business obligations, our firm and the Böhmische Landesbank. But then he had thought about it again, exhibiting all the outward signs of reflection, looked up, looked down, looked into himself, and suddenly began to speak of a purchase which would make it necessary for him to travel to Falkenau the following week. Then he interrupted himself again, and finally got into such a tangle that he realised that if he was to explain at all, he would have to explain properly.

Jan's father had heard in a round-about way that the Government was about to help workers in the Sudentenland by channelling Government commissions in that direction. In August, during a visit to the region, the President had said, 'I feel at home here, as if I were in Prague.' That was no rock to build a business on, but still pretty friendly. Yet Jan had hesitated when a Falkenau china manufacturer had made him an interesting business proposition in that very part of Czechoslovakia. Then Sellmann too had suddenly spoken of the plan for the rehabilitation of the Sudetenland. An official of the Berlin Labour Ministry had assured him, after talking with the Czechoslovak foreign minister, that there would be neither war nor civil war. The Reich would take a strong line with the German-Bohemian nationalists if a treaty was agreed upon which, apart from settling the language question and the representation of the German section in public office, also undertook to provide economic help.

In mid-September Amery had acquired a spinning mill and a small knitwear factory through his business friend from Falkenau, the same one who had got so drunk at Amery's wedding in May. When he told his father about it, Amery senior went into a frenzy, 'My God, how could you change your line! What were you doing, getting into the rag-trade?' Jan defended himself with the argument that the Government would hardly order fine china cups or pastry forks for the army, but would need uniforms and underwear.

But he himself, in the meantime, had doubts, for he had bought without first looking. The Falkenau china friend, a certain Uhl, had sent him, apart from photographs and plans, a legal survey which constituted the basis for the negotiations with the authorised agent of the owner in Prague, and also helped towards obtaining credit from the Böhmische Landesbank. It appeared thorough and conclusive, laid bare without prevarications all turn-over, debit and profit figures. The only thing wrong with this legal opinion was that all statements except for the name of the street where the factory was supposed to be, were false.

Amery's representative, when he returned from Falkenau two days before the Presidential reception to which Amery had gone with Sophie, jokingly suggested that Amery should quickly take out insurance against fire, and added, 'a pyromaniac could easily be found in that region'. At the same time there was a rumour that the President, when shown a photograph of a march of the Sudeten German nationalists, had given it as his opinion that the Reich would only take the Germans if they brought their land and their industries. 'Since we won't let them do that, they stay here and make trouble.'

Amery tried to get to the root of the matter. The surveyor, a former public prosecutor, suddenly disappeared. A search for him showed that he had followed the former owner of the plant to the Reich. Amery now made enquiries of the Falkenau china manufacturer, but friend Uhl pretended deafness. When they met in Prague he simply asked why Amery had not looked at the enterprise before the purchase, and could not remember ever having urged the swift conclusion of the agreement. As a china manufacturer he knew little in any case about spinning mills. A few days later Uhl's firm apprised Amery & Herschel that they would not renew their contract which was due to expire at the end of the year. Jan heard through his manager that soon afterwards Uhl had signed a long-term contract with their German competitors in Prague, and there could now be no doubt that he had been thoroughly taken in.

Jan decided to confess his debacle to Herr von Lilienthal, the director of the Böhmische Landesbank. But first he wanted to tell his father-in-law. Since he had taken it for granted that the Government would enquire into the circumstances of the new owner, the plant in Falkenau had been bought not in his own name, but in the name of his German wife. The neglected spinning mill and the mismanaged knitwear factory belonged to Christine, and for this reason Amery had paid his unexpected visit at Bubenech the night before.

Sophie was silent for a long time before she asked, 'What did my father say?'

'He is thinking of a transfer of the mortgage to our Prague business.'

'Why don't you go to court?'

'Against whom? Uhl will maintain that he himself was deceived. The surveyor is an immigrant in the Reich. The Germans won't hand him over even if we offer them a dozen Berlin Communists in exchange. Also, Christine would have to be a witness in a law suit. I can imagine Lustig's and Lilienthal's reactions if the newspapers said that one of their employees was trying to buy factories in Bohemia with the help of his daughter. Lustig would have no more use for a German known to be involved in failed speculations.'

Sophie had moved to the window and was looking into the courtyard.

'Why didn't you go to Falkenau yourself in the first place?' she had asked and known the answer in advance.

'Because of you.'

She breathed against the cold window pane and passed her thumb across the misted glass.

'I simply cannot manage to leave you for a whole week,' she heard, but so quietly she thought Amery had gone to the door. She turned and saw him sitting at the table as previously.

'Are you afraid?'

'No,' he said, 'but I'm crazy. I'm going to modernise the factory. Tomorrow I'm meeting an engineer, perhaps I'll make him my manager at Falkenau. But first I need money. And I can only get money through Lustig. Or do you think we'd better shoot ourselves?'

'There's plenty of time for that,' Sophie had said, laughing.

When she was alone she sat down in the armchair and pressed herself against the creaking back and collected herself, hands, feet, heart, eyes, and mouth, until she was sure she hadn't lost anything.

She kept thinking of a contradiction, and the more she wanted to get away from it the more she thought of it. Why did Jan want to give the impression that he had failed to go to Falkenau for her sake, when he had closed the deal in September while she was still away on holiday? She couldn't understand why he should say that he had spent months waiting for her in Prague, for she'd been back more than a week before they had met at dinner, and a fortnight later he had resisted her offer to come to the reception

159

with him. Had he said, 'Because of you' in the way in which old married people sometimes tell each other that they love one another so that everything is all right and they can go to sleep? It didn't make any sense.

Of one thing she was sure. That she did not want to be in the right against Amery, even if he insisted to the end of his days that he had stayed in Prague for her sake when she had been far away. No, she must live on neither memories nor hopes, for everything she did she had to do for the present moment.

At the tram stop, on her way home, she thought: it's raining. People are sheltering under umbrellas and have turned up their collars. But I shan't be taken in. It is too dark to see the clouds. Perhaps it is really raining, but as long as the clouds are hidden in the darkness I shan't believe in the rain.

5

Why so sad, dear lady?

ON SUNDAY SOPHIE went to see Jarmila to borrow money. She gave her so much that there was enough to pay the rent for the room in Charvat Lane until March. When Sophie offered an IOU, Jarmila looked at her threateningly from her blue, close-set eyes and growled in the old, monosyllabic common language, 'Frinz'.

She'd managed to have an affair – 'but just a one-act play, not a drama', as she admitted laughingly – with a supposedly West Indian construction engineer who had explained to her the use of Trinidad asphalt for road surfaces, and subsequently had taken her to a hotel where he was unable to pay for the room as he was out of work. Nor had he ever been in the Caribbean, but had worked in a local hat factory.

'He spoke beautifully of Trinidad, just as if he'd been there. As a farewell present I bought him a pair of patent-leather shoes. His eyes almost fell out of his head, and he wanted to know my address "to thank me for them". But I remained adamant. But what does it all add up to?'

On Monday, Sophie visited Vavra. The warm cordiality of earlier conversations was missing. Both talked as if they wanted to save themselves from having to listen. Vavra spoke of a newly-discovered Celtic settlement. Sophie spoke of Silesia where she had spent the summer. Then he told her of a manometer which he used to check his blood pressure every day, and Sophie spoke of her sister's year on a farm. After an hour they were silent and exhausted and Sophie felt as if she had, out of boredom and a love of gossip, confessed to a fellow passenger a few abominations for which she would be ashamed to the end of her days. Vavra's belt and braces, about which she had laughed tears a year ago, now seemed embarrassing and when he turned his face towards the lamp she saw with horror a long white hair in his left nostril. Only when they said goodbye did she realise that he had been speaking German with her all the time.

On Tuesday at four she rang the bell at Fräulein Kalman's, but had to wait half an hour before the lame singer groaned her way up the stairs.

'My God, where were you?' Sophie asked anxiously.

'At the orthopaedic surgeon's,' she carolled in falsetto up the stairwell. She smelled of alcohol.

'Supposing my mother had telephoned?'

'Then nobody would have answered,' she sang, unlocking the door without taking the keys from her neck. 'It's better for nobody to be here than for me to have to account for you not being here!'

With Sophie's help she took off her opossum coat, put it to dry over a chair and flung herself panting on the green settee. 'What ought I to say if somebody did call? Or is Ivan already in Nice?'

Sophie shook her head.

'What are you doing here then? Are you ill? Alora, I know the answer in advance: he's tied up with business.'

Although Sophie was sure that Fräulein Kalman did not suspect anything, her gibes annoyed her. She would have loved to have said Amery's name aloud. She imagined the appalled face of her teacher and longed for a person who would know only so much of her secret as she herself would tell, and yet would support her as if he knew everything. But there was someone, of course, to whom she could turn, and she didn't have far to go.

'Bye-bye,' Fräulein Kalman waved from the settee, and asked her to shut the door carefully.

Sophie ran to the Charles Bridge as if she had an appointment. Under the portico of the church of St. Salvador she waited until the lamplighter had lit the gas jets in the square and on the bridge. Now the city's towers were swallowed up behind the yellow-blue light of the street lamps, and the paving stones between the tram lines gleamed like broken ice after the first frost.

Perhaps I could tell Aunt Marketa, she thought, but the danger of being first questioned and then laughed at was too great.

A dozen light-coloured headscarves, floating independently above black jackets and coats, hung above the benches of the nave. His face to the altar and his knees on the hassock of a lectern, a priest prayed between two candles. Sophie dipped her fingers in the holy water and crossed herself. The rosary would last at least another quarter of an hour. That was more than enough. She looked at the ceiling, but the painting of the four quarters of the world was dissolved in darkness. She went on tiptoe to the confessional with the figure of the apostle Simon. She remembered that he was the patron saint of wood cutters because the heathens had sawn him into pieces. She slipped behind the curtain.

'Blessed be Jesus Christ,' she said quietly and repeated the greeting after a while.

'For ever and ever, amen,' answered a very high voice which took all her courage away.

'Well?' asked the priest who seemed to think it was taking too long. Sophie heard a dull thud as if a book had been shut.

'May I tell you something, Reverend Father?' she asked, whispering.

'A little louder, please.'

'I don't know how to start,' she said and brought her mouth nearer to the grating.

'Are you a Catholic?'

'Yes.'

'When did you last confess?'

'Before Easter.'

'Did you perform the penance?'

'Yes.'

'Well then,' said the effeminate voice, and the wooden bench creaked as if it too wanted to say, well then, let's get on with it!

'I love a man,' Sophie said quickly and took a deep breath. 'He is married to my sister. Since May. But I've loved him longer than that. Two years already.' She paused. 'That's what I wanted to tell you. Please excuse me for troubling you.'

'Have you shown him your attachment?' Sophie heard as she took her right knee from the board.

'Yes.'

'In what way?'

162

Sophie did not reply.

'Have you told him?'

'Yes.'

'And then?'

'Everything, Your Reverence.'

'Look, my child, this is neither a police court nor a complaints department, but a church. You've come of your own free will to confess your sins to our Saviour. Or ought I to ask?' He took Sophie's silence for agreement. 'Have you given yourself to this man?'

'Yes.'

'And now you repent?'

'I'm sorry,' Sophie replied, 'but I've only told you because there is nobody else I can tell.'

'If you don't repent, I will have to refuse you absolution.'

'I know,' Sophie whispered and got up. 'But I feel better in spite of that.'

'Why not come and see me in the presbytery,' he called as if he could hold her back.

'Yes, thank you, perhaps.'

She kneeled in an empty pew to join the last part of the rosary, but kept an eye on the confessional. When the Salve Regina began, a small, bespectacled man of about thirty stepped out from under the apostle Simon and blinked in the candlelight. His white surplice made him look more portly than he probably was. He pressed a newspaper covered book against his stole. He stood by a pillar near Sophie and joined the chanting high and loud for a verse, until he ran out of breath. He did not look at Sophie but vanished into the sacristy. On the confessional she read his name: Chaplain F. Svoboda. She went back to Bubenech relieved and calm.

Sixta, who visited her on the Thursday, was surprised at how patiently she listened to his account of the Spanish Civil War. He spread a plan cut from a newspaper on the grand piano and showed her the positions of generals Miaja and Mola with the blade of his pocket knife. He regretted that he could not go to fight himself because he had to take his master-class exams at the Conservatoire in May. Sophie comforted him with the prospect of a long war. He looked at her firmly and sadly until he blushed. Then he put the knife and the newspaper in his pocket and opened the piano lid. When Katharina joined them later, in a green winter dirndl with a very tight bodice and white, puffed sleeves, he stopped playing and once more brought out the map

163

of the Spanish front. To Sophie's surprise, her sister took her stand with the Republican side. Sixta was pleased.

'They're pulling down the churches,' Katharina said softly, looking at the door. 'That's how freedom begins.'

'Pavel has just composed a psalm,' Sophie said.

'How can you waste your time like that,' asked Katharina. 'If I were a man I'd be in Spain.'

Sixta looked silently at the map, took his knife out of his pocket and snapped it open.

'You're right,' he said. 'I'm not a man.'

'And where is Karol?' asked Sophie to help out Sixta.

'He's collecting money for a relief fund,' said Katharina and felt how unconvincing her answer was. 'He's got to pass his exam first, after all.'

Sophie took Sixta as far as Bubenech market. He offered to fetch her from Fräulein Kalman's next day, but she used an appointment with Jarmila as an excuse. 'We'll meet on Christmas Day,' she said.

'May one kiss a lady's glove?' he asked.

'One may,' she said and smiled.

Her mood changed suddenly the following night. She tipped out of half-sleep into a bottomless pit, not landing on her familiar pillow, but plunging into a world of moving lights, soldiers, fleeting sunlight on helmets, swords, spears and crossbows. A wind moved the chequered flags and made the grey water foam, but then snow began to fall and veiled the view. Sophie got out of bed without turning on the light, opened the curtains and looked into the garden. The snow fell as in a children's story, in big flakes, vertically, softly and without ceasing. She opened the window and stretched out her hand, but the eaves stuck so far out above her that the snow missed her hand. Only towards morning did she go to sleep.

When Frau Sellmann closed her door after lunch, Sophie put on a broad, tobacco-coloured hat and tied a veil under her chin. She wore a brown winter coat with a flat, broad fur collar. He won't come, she said to herself in the tram. Six days are long enough to make a man forget everything. Perhaps Amery had even forgotten the address. Perhaps he'd go to the house next door, surprised when the key didn't fit. Perhaps he was afraid to see her again, since she would seem strange and changed after a week. Or he had realised on his trip that she had a gap between her front teeth, hips which were too broad, calves which were too thin, and hair on her shins. Perhaps he had decided in the meantime that she was too stupid, too silly, too superficial, too impetuous, too impatient, too unrestrained, too mad. Perhaps he wanted to put an end to it before she became a burden to him. Perhaps he had an appointment this afternoon with a banker who would help him out of his Falkenau difficulty, and couldn't put it off. Perhaps he had been arrested because he had poured champagne into his dinner jacket. Perhaps he had committed suicide. Perhaps he was lying dead, his eyes open, in his office, and nobody dared break down the door.

Sophie got off the tram before her stop and began to walk. An elderly dandy accosted her, 'Why so sad, my dear lady?'

'Because it is snowing,' Sophie said.

Until a quarter to four she stood opposite Amery & Herschel and watched the door. Then she ran to Charvat Lane. When she turned the key she felt giddy. She opened the door and closed her eyes.

'I've been waiting an hour,' said Amery. She threw herself into his arms.

'Why are you crying?' he asked and pulled the veil up over her nose.

She trembled. Because I love you, she wanted to say.

'Because it is snowing,' she said.

6

Blackmail

AMERY TOOK THE elevator to his office, hung up his coat and shook the wet out of his hair before sitting down at his desk. Under the green desk lamp lay a folder of letters to be signed with a note, 'Immediate Attention', but he did not open it. He rubbed his damp hands on his trousers. In a few minutes Christine or Aunt Marketa would ring to ask when he would be home. When the telephone rang he picked up the receiver and asked, 'Well?'

'I'll be with you in two minutes,' he heard a man's voice say, and all he knew was that he had never previously heard it on the telephone. Before he could ask for his caller's name, he had hung up. Amery opened the folder and signed a letter without reading it. He thought of asking the door-keeper not to let anyone in, but then appeared to himself cowardly and absurd. When there was a knock at the door he put the top on his fountain pen and only turned when his visitor entered. It was Sixta.

He took off his rain-soaked beret and knocked it against his long coat as if he did not expect Amery to shake hands with him. He wiped his dishevelled hair from his forehead and smiled.

'What can I do for you?' asked Amery.

'I'd like to take my coat off, if you don't mind,' Sixta said. 'It's warm in here.'

He was wearing a rather tight grey jacket above brown knickerbockers. Amery offered him a chair.

'I followed you,' Sixta said and drew his eyebrows together as if to prove how difficult this had been. 'From Charvat Lane to here.'

'I suspected as much,' Amery said against his will and too quickly.

'Aha,' said Sixta and crossed his legs. 'But you didn't turn round.'

'I could smell you.'

Sixta laughed. 'Perhaps you can guess why I've come.'

'You need money.'

Sixta blushed like a girl. 'I've never done this before,' he said. 'But I see no other way. Your wife was kind enough to invite me for Christmas. Unfortunately I can hardly come in these clothes.'

Amery nodded, took out his wallet, and put some notes on the table. Sixta puckered his brow and looked at the money.

'Too little?' Amery asked.

'Oh no,' Sixta assured him and put the money away. Then he looked at his dirty shoes for a long time. 'It is strange – but I have confidence in you, though I don't specially like you. Do you feel the same?'

'Approximately.'

'That's good,' said Sixta. 'If I liked you, I'd have inhibitions. But the way things are between us, I feel quite free when I talk to you. Fundamentally we're both nothing special. We won't change the world, you and I. We'll go into history like Boleslav the Forgotten. Sixta the Forgotten. Amery the Forgotten.' He laughed as if he had told a joke that needed helping along. 'It hurts me. That is stupid, but what can I do? You've come to terms with it because you are older. I believe I'm at least unusual because I realise that I am average.'

The telephone rang, and while Amery said that they should not wait dinner for him, Sixta helped himself to a cigarette out of Amery's box.

166

'You didn't explain to your wife why you'll be late,' Sixta said when Amery had finished. 'Don't you ever, or did you not want to tell her lies in front of me?'

'It was my aunt,' Amery said as if he wanted to apologise.

'Why don't you throw me out for my insolence?'

'Why?' asked Amery. 'You amuse me. I've finished all my business, why shouldn't we talk for a bit?'

Sixta nodded. 'Do you like music?'

'Only Gershwin,' Amery said to annoy him.

'During the holidays in Budweis, I composed the ninety-eighth psalm for soprano, mixed choir, and large orchestra. In D-major. Do you know the ninety-eighth psalm?' He looked at Amery wide-eyed, beat three-quarter time on the table, and sang, 'Let the floods clap their hands, let the hills be joyful together . . . That's a piece out of the middle. A commonplace.'

'Yesterday they emptied the suggestion-box at the Conservatoire. We were told we could put suggestions and complaints in it without having to sign them. A very good arrangement. The letters were read out. One of them said, "I am unhappy, what shall I do?" Isn't that screamingly funny?'

'Did you write it?'

Sixta laughed and shook his head. Amery looked at him.

'Do feel free to look at me,' Sixta said.

Amery contemplated the soft, clear face which still gave the impression of being half hidden in a photographic developing solution. But one could not really take exception to Sixta. He had a large forehead above flat, dark eyebrows, the nose sat between high, fleshy cheekbones which lengthened the head; the full lower lip would in time change from sulking to sensuality, the chin seemed a trifle long but well defined. What was missing in this face? I see him, Amery thought, but do I see him as he really is? Does he imagine that he has great promise but that it is too indefinite and tentative ever to be realised? Why does his expression change from confusion to obstinacy?

'Yes, I'm ugly,' Sixta said, 'But I don't care. On the contrary, it keeps me going. You know that a man is grown up only when he has come to terms with his face. I've done so. I'm at home with my ugliness and with my bad health. Did you feel the wind when you crossed the square just now? You don't even wear a hat. I've caught cold, but I don't mind. I'm fine when I'm ill. I lie in bed and think about more things than the whole theological faculty. Have you ever asked yourself why all the fish – and not only one male and one female in Noah's ark – lived through the flood, and

167

why the fish became a secret sign? I've racked my brains over it through the whole of a pleurisy two years ago. Not because I am devout. My parents are Protestants. The Catholics have the upper hand because we have to believe things we cannot see. But that is our strength.'

Sixta took out a checkered handkerchief and wiped his forehead.

'Would you like something to drink?' asked Amery.

'No, thank you. I shan't keep you long now. In May I shall finish at the Conservatoire. I could marry into a bakery at Wittingau. The girl is nineteen. She is fair-haired and has eyes like ponds. When I took her into my arms for the first time I felt like a newly-discovered continent, like an Indian who had dreamt all his life of Columbus – and suddenly he's there.'

'Very nice for you,' Amery said.

'Also she doesn't ask me to paint half the country red and white.'

'Who?' asked Amery, puzzled.

'This girl. Helena Kantor. Has your wife never asked you to do impossible things?'

'Not that I know of.'

'But they are sisters,' Sixta exclaimed. 'Sisters have much in common. It's all so ridiculous. And so that you may understand me, I'll tell you that there is nothing I fear so much as ridicule. I love Sophie, you understand, but it makes me seem ridiculous. I phoned her from the station when I got back to Prague from my holidays, although I'd sworn throughout the whole journey that I'd never see her again. But her father said she was still in Silesia. I took it as a judgment of God and moved into the suburbs, but I didn't bring myself to the point of throwing her photo away . . .' he cleared his throat and took a cigarette out of the box. Amery lit it for him.

'Since she came back I see Sophie almost every day except Tuesdays and Fridays when she's busy.' He smiled. 'She's singing again.' He stubbed out the cigarette with such determination that Amery was ready for a new outburst. 'I've been wondering whether to go to Spain,' Sixta said instead.

'To the Civil War?' Amery asked. 'In your place I'd marry the girl from Wittingau instead.'

'Yes,' said Sixta and got up. 'Give my compliments to your wife, please. If she agrees, I'd like to play a few improvisations on Bohemian folk songs at Christmas.'

'She'll be enchanted,' Amery said and watched as his visitor put his wet coat over his shoulders. 'I hope you have some Aspirin at home.'

'Thank you,' said Sixta.

Amery accompanied him to the elevator. When Sixta's face vanished under the floor he regretted that he had not given him more money, and going back into his room he felt that he envied that 'baby-face' something. He opened the folder with the 'Immediate Attention' note and put his name under a letter and blotted it. When he looked at it again, he saw that instead of Amery he had written 'Sixta'. He tore off the bottom quarter of the page, folded it, and put it in his wallet like a receipt.

7

The White Mountain

CHRISTMAS DAY PASSED quickly. Because of Heinrich, who expected an additional present when visiting 'Uncle' Jan, and who had been urging their departure since lunch, the Sellmanns appeared at the Amery flat earlier than arranged. Bohuslav Amery and Sixta arrived punctually at four and were embraced and kissed in the corridor by Aunt Marketa, which almost took their breath away.

Sophie took Sixta to the table under the Christmas tree and insisted that he open his present immediately. She whispered that it was she who had chosen the propelling pencil and fountain pen with the gold nib.

They drank coffee round the oval table, and Aunt Marketa arranged it so that Sixta should sit beside Sophie. Heinrich put his present, a microscope with an eyepiece specially made for his vision, by his plate, waited until the cake was cut, then helped himself to a variety of crumbs to put under the lens.

At first the talk was about the Christmas Masses at the various churches they had attended, then passed on to the subject of the moment, the abdication of Edward VIII and his probable marriage to Mrs Wallis Simpson. While Frau Sellman and Aunt

169

Marketa condemned this step, and Sellmann joined them 'for family and state reasons', Christine maintained that the English king had acted correctly. Betty was shocked.

'Not to leave the woman what loves him in the lurch,' Amery senior joked in country dialect in defence of his daughter-in-law. They all laughed.

Later they watched Heinrich who, in the meantime, had taken to dipping his crumbs into coffee and cream before examining them. Frau Sellmann wanted to stop him, but Bohuslav Amery prevailed upon her to leave the boy in peace. Sixta felt that he had not been asked just to play the piano, but also to take part in the conversation. Now and again he sat up straight, but every time he thought of a suitable remark, Sophie put a piece of cake on his plate, and when he had taken a bite it was once again too late.

Christine asked for the light to be turned off. Heinrich protested, but when the candles had been lit and Sixta had sat down at the piano, he quietened down and began to eat.

Sixta improvised on the themes of two Bohemian carols, 'Jesus Christ was born today', and 'Come let us go to Bethlehem', treating them first as *ricercares*, turning them into waltz rhythm, then swung into a military march in which the themes were just decorations, until he finally ended with a solemn and festive chorale.

There was applause. Sellmann even pressed his hand, but the enthusiasm was forced, for Christine and Aunt Marketa had left the room while Sixta was playing.

'My wife isn't well,' Amery explained. Betty also went out. Those left behind tried to disregard the incident, but when, after a quarter of an hour, Frau Sellmann asked for the doctor to be called, everybody decided to leave. Christine was taken to a clinic for observation.

Until the end of January, Sophie and Jan met twice a week in Charvat Lane. Sophie lived so much from Tuesday to Friday to Tuesday, that the intervals seemed to her like a bad copy of the real world. On the first Tuesday in February she found a letter from Amery in the room. He wrote that he would not be able to see her before the 12th. The Falkenau project, the preparations for the trade fair in March, and the Chamber of Commerce would keep him away. She tore up the sheet, then fitted it together again, read it through once more, put the pieces into her coat pocket and threw them down a drain on her way home. On the Friday she might have told her mother that her singing lesson was cancelled, but it was Amery's birthday on 11th February, and Sophie went in search of a present. For an hour she looked into the shop windows around Wenceslas Square, then she saw a carved gold frame in a window. When she bought it, the manager asked whether it was a horizontal or vertical painting.

'Vertical,' Sophie said, 'But I only want to frame a piece of glass.'

'Pardon?'

'It isn't a picture, just a window pane.'

An empty frame without canvas or cardboard, paper or mount, and yet glass in it? Sophie realised that the manager thought her mad, but she could not very well tell him that she wanted to frame the right hand pane of the balcony door, because every Tuesday and Friday she looked through this window while waiting for Amery.

A workman came with her to Charvat Lane and installed the frame. How long would it take Jan to understand the present?

Sellmann invited his son-in-law to Bubenech to celebrate his birthday, but Amery excused himself, since he wanted to spend the evening with Christine in the hospital. The next afternoon Sophie presented him with the empty picture. Amery put his face close to the gilt-framed pane and easily found the explanation, looking out of the window at the wooden balcony.

'The glass is brown from your eyes,' he said.

Soon after her husband's birthday, Christine was examined by the head of the clinic. By profession more interested in the scientific exposition of the fertility cycle than in questions of pathology, and in his practice less in organic symptoms than the total picture of the patient, the professor learned more about Frau Amery's illness by simply listening to her, than from all the X-rays, temperature charts and haemoglobin levels. Christine asked what medicines or cures he recommended.

'A child wouldn't be a bad thing,' he said.

'I had thought of a cure at Franzensbad,' Christine said and put her hand to her hair. 'Or are there objections?'

He shook his head.

'My husband has a lot of business in Falkenau. That's nearby. He could visit me at weekends. When can I go?'

He shrugged his shoulders. 'As soon as you can walk about again.'

She gave him her hand and thanked him quickly so as to be alone.

At the beginning of March she went to Franzensbad. Amery

171

was to visit her later, 'As soon as I've got settled in.' When she had been away a week he received an 'Aerial View of Franzensbad', inviting him for the weekend, and the same evening Frau Sellmann telephoned him to confirm that Sophie and Katharina should go with him if he agreed, for Christine had invited her sisters to visit her. Amery arranged for them all to fly to Marienbad on the Friday, and to hire a car there for the remainder of the journey.

On that Friday afternoon it occurred to Sellmann that Sophie had probably forgotten to let her teacher know that she would not be coming for her lesson. He closed a letter to Frenzel which was to go to Berlin by courier, looked at his desk clock, and found that it was already a quarter past four, too late for a cancellation, but still in time for an apology. Fräulein Kalman answered immediately, and before Sellmann could explain the reason for his call, she said that she was sorry Sophie could not come to the phone since she was very kindly doing an errand for her which she, Fräulein Kalman, had put off for some time because of her bad hip. She couldn't really say when Sophie would be back, since she would be giving the little packet to the caretaker to save herself the stairs. She would make up for the lost time next week, and Dr. Sellmann must on no account think that he was wasting her fee.

Since Sellmann did not believe that anybody could be in two places at the same time, he knew that Sophie could not be in Franzensbad and doing errands for Fräulein Kalman. He telephoned to find out whether the trio had landed safely, but said nothing to Betty.

On the Sunday Sellmann went to the aerodrome to collect the travellers. The girls' faces were white and they wanted to walk about a bit before getting into another vehicle. They left their luggage and went ahead. Sellmann put his left hand under his son-in-law's arm and asked him about Franzensbad and Christine's health. When the girls had recovered he drove into town, delivered Amery at his home and wondered during the rest of the trip whether he should ask Sophie about Fräulein Kalman's strange message. He was certain that a man must be involved. It could not be Sixta since Sophie met him as much as she liked. No, he'd put off speaking about it. If Sophie was warned by Fräulein Kalman, she would tell him of her own accord.

But nothing was said during the following week, and on that Friday at a quarter to four, Sellmann sat in a taxi near Bubenech market and saw Sophie get into the tram. She wore a bright red beret. At the Powder Tower she changed trams. When she got out, Sellmann watched her through the rear window of the taxi and felt ashamed. Suddenly she vanished. Sellmann had discussed this contingency with the driver. He jumped out of the taxi and ran after her through a passageway. When he emerged into Charvat Lane, he saw the red beret above the black hair twenty yards in front of him. He allowed the distance to increase without losing sight of Sophie. She slipped into the door of a house. Sellmann went on, made a mental note of the number, turned into another street, then returned, sweating, to the corner of Charvat Lane, not hunter but as if hunted now.

He saw his son-in-law approach, hid behind a transformer box and read some hand-written notices in a shop window. Amery went into the same entrance as Sophie. Sellmann followed. The dark hall was silent and smelled of gas like the fields of Flanders in 1915. The stairs creaked. Amery was probably taking them two steps at a time. Then the sound of a key, a door, both very high above.

Sellmann went into a bar and ordered a rum and beer. The rum tasted as if it had been watered, but the Pilsner beer foamed bitter and tasty. I'd rather admit to being a sinner than a fool, he thought. It's in my character.

When he paid his bill he counted the money in his wallet. He'd let the bank and Betty know later. He asked the waiting taxi driver if he would drive him to Franzensbad, and arranged to pay his overnight expenses and return trip. On the way he wondered whether he should not make a detour to Bubenech, but the rum and beer gave him courage as far as the White Mountain. There he suddenly asked the driver to stop, but could only get rid of him by paying (though they'd only come ten kilometres) four times the tariff.

Sellmann entered the walled game-park through the wrought-iron gates. He had been here with Sophie the previous year, visiting the 'Stern' castle. Then the limes had been in flower, and nuts like green figs had hung from the chestnuts. Now the lilac was budding, and blue crocuses showed amongst dark leaves. The unmistakable smell of decay rose from the borders of the lawns, perennial, sweet and ordinary. Sellmann felt seasick and sat down on a bench in the avenue leading to the castle. He imagined that he was sitting on a bench overlooking the sea, and after a time the Good Lord came over the water, not Christ, but I-am-who-I-am Himself, and not alone but in the company of two gentlemen who looked like Eugen Lustig and Bohuslav Amery. They were wearing the same dust-grey coats as Sellmann, and smoked the same cigars.

'What's the trouble then?' asked the Good Lord. Amery senior wiped the sweat from the inside rim of his hat, and Lustig blew his nose as if he were moved.

'The children,' Sellmann said.

'Yes, the children,' all three replied and sighed. They sat down.

'Your daughter?' the Good Lord asked.

'And my son,' said Amery.

'The longer one looks at a thing, the funnier it is. Precision makes everything ridiculous.'

'But there are laws, and conscience,' Sellmann protested. 'I was an officer.'

'Don't get excited,' Lustig said. 'I've known for the last year that you work for the Saxonia bank. Your reports go to the Reich by courier every Friday. You might have let me into the secret. But I'm not angry with you. What can one do in these times when the body is a pleasure and the soul a burden? There is a middle way between righteousness and sin. So you can expect a sentence half-way between reward and punishment.'

'St. Augustine said that,' the Good Lord remarked as if he wanted to defer the decision.

'How do you know about it?' Sellmann asked Lustig.

'From the secret service,' the banker replied. 'You've nothing to fear, but they'll take their revenge when the time comes.'

Sellmann looked at Amery, who was the only one sitting on his right.

'Just as well you didn't go to Franzensbad,' the old china manufacturer said. 'At best it would only have led to a scandal. And to what purpose? Little loves last three months, big loves half a year.'

'Love never ceases,' corrected the Good Lord, but Bohuslav continued to speak to Sellmann.

'There are people who think one is mature when one begins to look for excuses for one's father's life. I sometimes wonder whether it would not have been better if Jan had drunk himself into a stupor instead of selling glasses and coffee cups. You see I'm asking for forgiveness for my son. I am a man with a thin skin. I went to Plovdiv, Cracow and Paris. Back home I asked myself: is that all? Where were the flying ponds, the trees which bore fruit four times a year, the leaping automobiles, the legless wonders? I always thought that life went on outside.'

'He who is wise sits by the window and knows the whole world,' the Good Lord said.

'Exactly,' confirmed Amery senior. 'And that is why I want Jan to remain with Christine. Pythagoras sacrificed a hundred oxen when he discovered his theorem. I gave her a silver cow the first time she visited me.'

Lustig said, 'Sophie could marry my Victor.'

'I've already thought of that,' Sellmann said, 'but there'll be difficulties.'

'We'll naturalise her,' said Lustig, 'and I'll present her with a hotel to give her something to do.'

The Good Lord got up and cracked his knee joints. 'It's getting cool,' he said. 'I'll have to make the sun go down, otherwise the Americans will get worried.' He lifted his hat and bowed to Sellmann. 'I hope you're feeling better now, dear sir. Believe me, only those who don't know where they are going will get to the Promised Land. Goodbye!' He turned and went down the avenue. Lustig and Amery got up too.

'He's got too much on his mind today,' Lustig excused the Good Lord.

Lustig went away, and Amery said quietly, 'You simply didn't see anything in Charvat Lane. In a couple of weeks it'll all be over in any case. Shall we have a bet on it?' He went after Lustig and when he caught up with him they both began to run after the Good Lord.

Sellmann went to a tourist pavilion, ordered a taxi, and returned to Bubenech. Neither Betty nor the children noticed anything. But during supper he dropped his fishknife on his lap and gave Sophie such an embittered look as if she had tried to murder him.

Sellmann's look reminded Sophie of Christine's eyes in Franzensbad the previous Saturday. Amery and Katharina had gone out, and the two sisters were sitting in the reading-room in plush armchairs with quilted backs. Beside Christine in her Wedgwood blue dress with light grey mink trimmings, Sophie felt like a poor relation with whom one put up for a while as companion, before despatching her back to her attic or for a walk. She wondered why Christine spent so much money on shoes, hats, and furs, and had rented a whole suite in the hotel, when Amery didn't know how to pay the Falkenau debts.

The only other person in the reading room was an elderly lady, a Hungarian or Romanian Jewess. She sat at a desk, licked stamps and stuck them on picture postcards, hammering them secure with her small fist. Nothing else but the humming of the elevator could be heard. Suddenly Sophie felt a kick on her shin and turned. Christine pointed her chin at the illustrated papers she had discarded on the floor. When Sophie hesitantly bent down to them, she met the cold, indignant Sellmann look. Blind with hate she bent down, collected the illustrated pages and laid them on the table.

'*Merci*,' said Christine, and the lady behind them again hammered with her rosy palm on the desk.

'Who'll drink a glass of beer with me?' asked Sellmann.

'Me,' said Heinrich and Katharina as one.

'Shall I order some tea?' Christine had asked at Franzensbad.

'No, thank you,' Sophie said now as last week.

The following Tuesday she found a letter from Amery in Charvat Lane.

Beloved, [he wrote], I shan't be with you today. When you read this, I shall be on my way to Franzensbad. Something has happened that Christine didn't want to tell me on the phone. She asked me to come very urgently, and you know why I cannot refuse, though I am up to my neck in work. She even cried, which is unusual. Perhaps it is only a mood, or she is so bored she wants to talk to somebody. But perhaps she really feels so ill that it is better for me to go and comfort her rather than have her turn up in Prague suddenly. The only thing I ask from you is patience which nobody needs more than I. Please expect me on Thursday since you won't be able to go to singing lesson on Good Friday. At Easter I'll ask you all to come on an excursion, then we'll at least see each other. All planes are grounded because of the weather, that's why I am taking the train. I am too tired to drive. I didn't sleep at all last night. I hardly recognise my own writing. But I love you, Jan.

Sophie went to the window. The word excursion had made her think of the Wildfowler, the tea-garden and the swing. Five years ago she had worn a dress embroidered with asters, and Heinrich had upset his raspberry juice over it. Uncle Wilhelm had balanced a glass of beer on his stomach and they had eaten sugared strawberries. She would have liked to have gone to see Sixta, Jarmila, Vavra and Fräulein Kalman, but she felt that once one has said goodbye to everybody, one is unlikely ever to go away. What would Uncle Wilhelm have advised? 'Don't make a fool of yourself, keep calm.'

On Thursday it rained, and Frau Sellmann made Sophie wear

galoshes. Soon after three she was in Charvat Lane with wet shoulders and hem. Amery's jacket hung over the back of a chair. Quietly she took off the galoshes and shoes.

'I'm not asleep,' he said from the bed. She lay down beside him. He kissed her as tenderly as if he were afraid of hurting her, and put his arm under her neck. His hand shook. 'We're going to Franzensbad in an hour,' he said. 'My car is round the corner. Christine has shown me a letter. It arrived from Prague on Monday, unsigned. I know who sent it.' He lifted his left hand, and smilingly looked at his injured knuckles. 'I've already dealt with that. There's no more danger from that quarter.

'We'll drive there now, and you'll explain that it is all nonsense. But we'll have to move from here. She knows this address, the floor, even the name under which you rented this room. She knows when we meet. Don't be afraid. I've admitted nothing. I laughed at her. She pretended to be very jealous, but one cannot take her feelings any more seriously than her illnesses. If you manage to convince her, she'll go to Capri or Sorrento in April, and the summer will be ours. I'll rent an apartment so that we can at last get out of this hole, and we'll furnish it to our taste. If you like we'll have a bath put in as large as a double bed. Perhaps you'd like a Chinese room? I know just the man to supply it. What do you think?'

'Yes,' said Sophie.

'Are you crying?'

'No.'

He stroked her throat and unbuttoned her dress.

When they left the house it was still raining. For the first time they went along Charvat Lane together.

'We'll have coffee outside town somewhere,' Amery said. 'We'll let your parents know once we're under way,' he called above the roof of the car as he was unlocking the door. Sophie smiled and nodded. Today it is raining, she thought. I can see the clouds.

8

Maundy Thursday

AT DUSK ON Maundy Thursday, halfway between Mies and Pilsen, a house painter called Bartosch noticed a car lying on its side about twenty metres from the road. He stopped his three-wheel delivery van near a tree which showed the scars of the impact of the car, went along the wheel-marks down the slope, and walked across the muddy field. After a few steps he came upon the motionless body of a young woman. She was wearing a grey raincoat and on her feet were black galoshes. Blood flowed from her split lip and ran, mixed with rain, from her chin to the collar of her coat. When he wiped the wet hair from her face, the skin from the hairline to the parting turned back. He took hold of the hair and pressed the skin back in its place.

Since the woman remained silent and without motion, he took her to be dead and went towards the car. It carried the Prague symbol under its spare wheel. Behind the shattered windscreen, Bartosch saw a man whose body lay diagonally across the seat. The housepainter wondered whether he should inform the police or whether he should try to get the man, who seemed unhurt but unconscious, out of the wreck and take him to the nearest hospital. He went to his three-wheeler and collected a linoleum knife and a tarpaulin which, on his way back, he spread over the woman. He cut the sunroof open, and with some difficulty extricated the driver. He broke the driving-mirror off and pressed it against the man's mouth and nose. He tossed the mirror back into the wreck, then went to stand in the middle of the road.

The driver of a lorry promised to notify the police, and Bartosch went once more down the slope because he had left his linoleum knife by the car. He wondered whether it would not be better to make himself scarce, but he would have to take the tarpaulin since it had his name on it. When he took it off, the young woman moved her head, and blood bubbled from her mouth. He put his

178

arm under her neck to save her from suffocating, and held his hat over her face against the rain until the ambulance arrived. Bartosch listened in silence to the reproaches of the ambulance men, gave the police his name and address, rolled up his tarpaulin and drove away after a last look at the two stretchers.

Apart from a travelling bag, the only thing found in the car was a gilt wooden frame in which there were some glass splinters, but no sign of a painting or photograph. The identity of the driver was found in his jacket, and the details were reported to Prague but could not be passed on, since there was no reply from the Amery apartment. Only towards morning, when a sergeant went through the list of accidents, did he make the connection between Amery's name and the china business.

Amery senior went to Bubenech. Hanka took his hat and coat and showed him into the drawing-room. The two folds from his tear-ducts to his lips divided his face. When he noticed that his chin was trembling, he pushed the knuckles of his left hand under his lower jaw, and clenched his teeth.

When Sellmann came in, bringing with his Good Friday shirt a little light into the room, Amery said, as if to himself, 'They've had an accident.'

'Pardon?'

'Jan and Sophie.' He let go of Sellmann's fingers and grasped the back of a chair. Sellmann jerked his head as if he wanted to shake the words out of his ears.

'You'll have to let Christine know,' Amery said slowly because he found it a strain to speak German.

Sellmann sat down on the sofa beside Amery and felt like an old man whose memory was so bad that he could not even regret the things he had failed to do. Amery told him what he knew. A quarter of an hour later Sellmann telephoned Christine, and gave her the name of the hospital in Pilsen. Towards noon he and Amery senior were in an express train, and Sellmann told him how Jan had unexpectedly telephoned the previous day to tell him and Betty that he and Sophie were driving to Franzensbad. Amery was silent, looked out of the window, but listened.

'They must have been in a hurry,' he said. 'Otherwise they'd at least have taken a suitcase.'

The doctor in Pilsen first told his visitors of Sophie's condition. When he had put stitches in her scalp, her tongue and her lips, she had regained consciousness for a few minutes. Though there might be concussion, a vascular rupture was ruled out. The X-ray showed a diagonal fracture of her right shin which had to be operated on. He personally thought it likely that the young lady had bitten her tongue at the sudden impact, and had then been thrown out of the car. 'A month or two,' he answered Sellmann's question of how long she would have to be in hospital. 'It'll depend on how the leg heals.'

Amery asked after Jan. 'A fracture at the base of the skull,' the doctor said. 'His wife is with him.' He gave directions to have the gentlemen taken to the patients. A sister in a white headband, starched veil and white cuffs preceded them.

They entered a white-tiled room. Christine sat at the head of a wheeled stretcher and did not look up. Her smooth, black shawl caught the light from the high slits of windows and shone on her arms. Amery's steps became shorter the nearer he came to his unconscious son. The white-clad sister stayed by his side as if she were afraid he might fall.

'Tina,' he said, but she did not move.

He leaned forward and kissed Jan on the lips.

Sellmann nodded to the sister and was taken to Sophie. She lay in a single room with the blinds half drawn. The bandage round her head reached down to her eyes, the ends of stitches stuck out of her lower lip, and her leg hung from a sling. The sister left, and after a while another one came in, in the same habit but younger than the first, and smart like the cook in a parsonage. She introduced herself as Sophie's nurse, Sister Arsenia.

'You can call me Seni,' she added when she noticed Sellmann's frown.

'Who is your patron saint?'

'St. Arsenius, the abbot,' she said and blushed under her veil.

Sellmann gave her a thousand krone bill and asked her to have a Mass said for the recovery of his daughter. She thanked him and set a chair for him near the bed. After a while Amery senior came in. Climbing the stairs had made him hot, and he wiped his forehead before looking at Sophie.

'Christine is with the police,' he said. 'She's looking after everything. I offered . . .' He went to the window and looked through the chinks of the venetian blind. 'But she wants to arrange everything herself. She wants them to bring Jan to Prague.' Only when he turned from the window did he seem to notice the nurse. 'Are you Czech?' he said.

'No,' Arsenia replied.

'Christine expects us at four at the Grand Hotel,' he said to Sellmann.

They said goodbye to the sister, and Sellman told her that his

180

wife would soon be coming, settled some formalities and went to have a light meal. The unexpected journey with its shocks, the festive Good Friday atmosphere of the industrial town, and the quick meal put them into a mood which made them long for a siesta rather than the tea-room of a hotel, and without saying so to each other, each was amazed how helplessly he had to obey the summons of a daughter and daughter-in-law.

Christine eluded Sellmann's embrace by taking his hand in both of hers.

'You've been to see Sophie?' he asked.

'No,' she said fixing him with her blue eyes, and continued, sitting down, 'I shan't be going to see her.' She spoke in a whisper and asked the waiter for coffee. Then she turned to her father-in-law. 'I take it you're going back to Prague today?'

Amery senior nodded irresolutely.

'Would you tell Herr Vejvoda that I expect him tomorrow around three o'clock at our apartment?'

'As far as business is concerned, I'm at your disposal,' replied Amery.

'I'll manage all right,' Christine said.

Bohuslav put her hand to his lips. 'I have a daughter,' he said to Sellmann and didn't know what to do with his face.

Their farewells were loving. Christine took her father and Amery part of the way to the station, then went to the evening Mass at St. Bartholomew's. At the hotel she looked through Jan's bag, hung the jacket he had worn in the accident over the back of a chair, and ordered a light, meatless meal with beer. Afterwards she felt tired, slept for half an hour, then got up again to go on with Jan's bag. She held one shoe in her hand and stroked it for a long time, until she realised that she was sad without being dejected. I'm imitating the motions of a woman who has lost her husband, she thought, and threw the shoe on the floor. When she put Jan's trousers away, his bunch of keys fell out. 'That's all I need!' she said aloud as if complaining at accidentally finding the keys. But she had a look at them all the same. Between the saw-edged apartment keys and those to the office, hung a finger-long key rubbed shiny with use. She detached it from the ring and put it in her bag.

That Saturday afternoon she received the business manager in her apartment. Herr Vejvoda's skull was shaved to the eyebrows. Though Christine did not notice the difference, his expression oscillated between solemn dignity and controlled horror during the whole of their conversation. There was cause for both. Christine announced that while her husband was in hospital she would want to acquire a complete knowledge of the business, and would use Amery's office twice a week, she thought perhaps Tuesdays and Fridays, for this purpose. Only then could she decide whether everything should go on as before. She thought that the success of the Falkenau project had proved that investment in other spheres of business was not as dangerous as had been feared by Amery senior. She wanted to use this occasion to point out that questions or advice from Amery senior should be neither answered nor taken into consideration without first getting her own permission, this in even the most unimportant matters. Since she could not speak Czech, important agreements and correspondence should be translated for her. If this was too much for the personnel employed at the moment, an experienced interpreter should be hired to help her. She was especially anxious that her arrangements should be implemented not timidly, but ruthlessly. 'I'm young,' she said, 'but I know what I want, and soon you'll know it too. There must be no difference between your interests and mine.'

'If I've understood you correctly,' Herr Vejvoda said, 'you won't be continuing with your cure.'

'You've understood me correctly.'

'I'll be at your disposal over Easter Sunday, of course,' he said, and they both got up.

'You are my only support,' she replied and accompanied him to the door of the drawing-room where he bowed once more.

Alone again, she went to her bedroom to comb her hair. When Frau Sellmann telephoned, the maid said that madam had gone into town. But Christine did not go to Charvat Lane until dusk. She found the house and went in, determined to turn back as soon as she had seen the name on the door.

In the corridors, the Easter cakes wafted warm aniseed smells through key holes and door cracks, covering all other smells, even the floor polish, with the scent of vanilla. Christine bent down in front of the narrow doors and read the unpronounceable names, breathed through her nose, and felt envy for Sophie's excursion into the life of simple people. When she finally came to the white card with 'Olga Siebenschein, stud. phil.', the stair light went out. She took Jan's key and pushed it blindly into the lock.

A dim bulb behind fake alabaster. A grey towel beside the iron sink. A cover thrown hastily over the bed, and on the sideboard a cheap bowl with hair pins and a letter. No carpet, but linoleum full of holes. An empty cupboard with see-sawing clothes-hangers. So that was happiness, the extreme. This was where one lived like a dragnet with the catch of life, full of wrecks and monsters, watery corpses and letters in bottles?

When Christine wanted to lean her forehead against the windowpane of the balcony, she noticed that the glass was missing. She turned and took the letter out of the bowl on the sideboard. 'Beloved,' she read in Jan's fluent writing, 'I shan't be with you today. When you read this . . .' Christine sat down on the table under the dim light, '. . . up to my neck in work. She even cried . . .' Christine smiled, '. . . that it is better for me to go and comfort her rather than have her turn up in Prague suddenly.'

There was a knock at the door. Christine folded the sheet, put it in her coat pocket and slid from the table.

'Yes?' she asked after a time.

A big man of about fifty in a blue and white striped open shirt came in. He stuck his left thumb behind his braces when he saw a stranger, and addressed her in Czech.

'I'm her sister,' Christine replied without having understood.

'Where is Fräulein Siebenscheinová?'

'She won't be coming again.'

'And why didn't she give notice on the 15th as arranged?'

'I'm giving notice,' Christine said.

'Popischil,' the landlord introduced himself. 'But who's going to pay for the window?'

'I am,' said Christine and took out her purse.

'And the rent for April?'

'That too,' replied Christine.

Popischil named the amount and received the money. 'I hope it isn't anything serious.'

'Appendicitis.'

'That isn't dangerous,' Popischil comforted her. 'Perhaps sometime in the future madam might use the room herself? We're in the centre of the town here, and it's not expensive.'

Christine looked into his moist eyes.

'There are all sorts of situations in one's life,' Popischil continued. 'And life is short and full of shit like a baby's shirt, if you'll forgive the expression.'

'Yes,' said Christine.

'I'll replace the glass immediately,' Popischil crowed. 'I'm like the three holy Indian monkeys. I don't see, I don't hear, and I don't say anything. Now and again I sing a bit, because I was in the army when I was a young man. But all you have to do is knock on the wall, and I stop automatically.'

'I'll think about it.'

9

The Gilt Frame

WHEN SIXTA HAD begun his studies, he had conquered the city like an heiress whom he wanted to keep for himself at all cost. When his parents visited him for the first time, he had gone up to the castle with them and had gestured towards the horizon as if to say. 'One day it'll all belong to me.'

Then there were times when he felt that he could not stay one hour more in Prague. On certain days in July the water ran from the street cleaners' watering cans in dusty drops in the gutters, and in November, when it had rained cats and dogs for a week, the dampness crept into the lungs, and the wind in January cut off one's breath. At that time he missed Southern Bohemia so much that he often walked out into the country to see the great expanse of the sky. But because the city was only kind to those it liked, he kept quiet about what he really thought, and after two years his relations with this big town were rather like those one has with a girl one is too lazy or too vain to marry, but who is too beautiful and passionate to be left behind.

At the beginning of the winter semester he had moved into a district which was called – though not officially – the 'vale of tears'. Like the bobbin of a sewing machine, it fitted between the Bottich an industrial waterway, and the railway line to Pilsen, below smoking factory chimneys. The straight, treeless streets bore the names of long-dead princes, but were bordered by black tenements. Sixta did not mind this. As long as people left him in peace he enjoyed the neighbourhood, and when he sat at the piano at the open window on a warm afternoon he felt like a missionary in a small, hopeless district.

Sixta had been fortunate. He lived with a solid, elderly married couple whose son had been sentenced to thirty months in prison for robbery. His landlord told him straight away that while he was with them, they would treat him like their own child. Two tram lines ran under his window, but since it only took him a quarter of an hour to walk to the Conservatoire, he saved the fare and bought cigarettes instead. When he moved his piano in January and found a loaded Mannlicher gun under the floor, he was already so used to the district that he was only amazed at the innocence of the police. He returned the weapon to its hiding place, trod down the floorboards, pushed the bedpost over it, and slept like someone who has power over power, peacefully and deeply.

He had planned to visit his parents in Budweis for Easter, but something happened on the morning of Maundy Thursday which forced him to stay in Prague. He had heard his landlord and land-lady go out, and when the bell rang several times, Sixta did not go to the door. He finally looked out of the window and saw Jan Amery leave the house.

'I'm sorry,' he called down, 'I heard you too late.'

Amery looked up through the rain and nodded when he made out Sixta's face.

'Are you alone?' he asked when they went upstairs.

'Yes,' Sixta said, took him to his room and apologised for the general untidiness. Amery did not reply. He took off his coat, folded it and put it on a music stand.

'Don't bother,' he said, shaking his head, when Sixta offered him a chair. 'Contrary to our agreement, you have written a letter to my wife. You were, of course, too cowardly to sign your name. So what do you expect?'

Before Sixta could reply, Amery smashed his left fist into his nose. The pain brought tears to Sixta's eyes. He was suddenly blinded, staggered, and felt the second blow to his chin. His knees gave under him. Amery took hold of the front of his shirt and hauled him up. His blows went to the forehead, the mouth and right ear.

'Please,' Sixta whispered.

'No,' said Amery, hit him in the neck with his fist and finally kicked him in the stomach, which made Sixta fall first forward, then back, taking the piano stool with him.

Amery unfolded his coat and put it over his arm. Sixta heard him slam the door of the room, and he felt the noise in his head like a last blow. He stretched out his hand to the bedpost, but did not have the strength to move it. When he heard his landlord

185

return, he got up and silently turned the key in the lock. He tried for a time to see his face in the glass of a small portrait of Dvorak above the piano, then he picked up the piano stool, sat down, and put his face on the cool key-board. When he got up the keys were covered in blood from 'b' to 'f'.

'Would you like to eat with us?' his landlady asked from the corridor.

'No thank you,' he called back, 'I've already been asked out.'

He wiped his lips with a dampened handkerchief and lay down on the bed. I'll kill him, he thought. Then I'll take a train to the frontier and make my way into Poland and then by boat to Portugal and on to Madrid. But I must dispatch him with the first shot to save ammunition. He got up, moved the bed quietly, took the gun from its hiding place and put it into his coat pocket.

Afraid that he might change his mind, he ran out of the house and took a tram into town. He sent a telegram to his parents, bought a ticket at the station, and went to Amery & Herschel where he was told that the boss wasn't in. He went to the Amery apartment, and outside the door took hold of the gun with his right hand while he rang the bell. The maid, who remembered him from his visit at Christmas, could tell him no more than that her employer had left the house a quarter of an hour before. Where had he been going? She didn't know. When would he be back? She shrugged her shoulders.

There were a hundred thousand places where Amery might be. It was senseless to look for him. Sixta stood in the centre of the town, equidistant from the Amery business and apartment, and rehearsed in his mind every occasion he had met the man. He had often been envious of him, but only today had he been weak enough to hate him. When he had met Bohuslav Amery after the concert, he had understood that the superiority of these men did not rest only in their possessions. They simply always said what they meant, and the way they listened provoked good ideas. They were interested in things that were quite unconnected with them, and touched anything personal very cursorily. To *be* more rather than to *have* more, seemed to be their motto. One wasn't superior because one knew from which glass to drink one's red wine, but because one overlooked it when someone drank out of the finger bowl, and ate the slice of lemon. One was well-bred if one did the right thing spontaneously.

Sixta rubbed his raw chin against the coarse material of his coat collar to stoke his anger. Why had Amery acted like a mad-man? he asked despite his resolve. His wife had had an anonymous letter. What had Sixta to do with that pale lady? He was as indifferent to her as to the statues in the square. But why had Amery thought with such certainty that he and no one else had written to her?

The more Sixta thought about it, the more ridiculous it seemed to him to be waiting with a gun for a man who'd obviously made a mistake when he had beaten him up.

At five o'clock he telephoned the Sellmann apartment, and while the maid fetched Fräulein Katharina, Sixta remembered that he had not eaten since breakfast. Katharina told him, without being asked, that her sister had gone to Franzensbad with Amery. Today? Yes, a little while ago. Sixta wished her a happy Easter and went to the station to get his money back on his unused ticket. But it didn't go very far. He ate two fish sandwiches at a snack bar in Wenceslas Square, and drank away the rest between evening and morning.

He slept through Good Friday and went to the Turkish baths on the Saturday. The swelling on his face had taken on a greenish-yellow tinge. On the way home he stood for a moment amongst the crowd reading the newspaper on a wall. The report of the accident near Pilsen carried a photograph of Amery. Sixta bought the paper. Not a word about Sophie, so she too must be alive. But he had to be sure. He was told that she lay, badly injured, in a Pilsen hospital, and he gave Katharina his address in case he was wanted. Then he went home but could not stay in his room. He walked about the city until late at night, and occasionally thought he saw Amery's back as on that winter evening when he had followed him from Charvat Lane. Towards ten o'clock he rang the bell at Fräulein Kalman's. Since she only read the papers after a première, she knew nothing. After Sixta had told her everything, she was silent for a long time. Then she said, 'I'm a complete idiot.'

'You know who wrote the letter?'

'Yes.'

'Do I know him?'

'Yes,' said Fräulein Kalman and shook herself.

'Tell me.'

'No. You're in love with her, aren't you? Do at least nod, my angel. Why didn't you take her? Why just look at her with tragic eyes? A woman wants to be conquered with orchids and Chanel. If you haven't the cash, daisies and soap will do, and if you're completely bankrupt you should take her swimming.'

'I'll visit her in Pilsen.'

187

'With your battered face? And she's lying there with broken bones. Do you want to feel her pulse?'

Sixta got up, but she pushed him back on to the sofa. 'Do you have your fare?'

He shook his head.

'I'll give it to you. But don't leave me. Tomorrow I want you and Vavra to come and have dinner with me. I'll send out for something. Do you like lamb cutlets and green beans? Well, he can laugh again! Ah, you're a grand chap.'

Sixta was afraid she would embrace him. He didn't get away until midnight.

The following days he passed in a state between sleeping and waking. When a letter from Christine arrived on the Monday he hid it away. He did not want to think of anything that was happening outside his room. Only three days later did he take up Frau Amery's invitation to call on her.

'You must tell me all about yourself,' Christine said, and put her hands behind her head so that her wide sleeves slid to her elbows. Then she took a hair clip out of her hair, put it between her teeth and put it back without embarrassment after she had arranged her coiffure. Christine asked after his origins, parents, friends, and he spoke as freely as if he had been waiting for this opportunity for a long time. She urged him on, fluttering her eyelids, but when he stopped he noticed that she had not been listening. She got up and said, as she left the room, 'Don't get up. I want to show you something.' She came back carrying an empty gilt frame and leaned it against the big table.

'You no doubt know what it is?'

'A picture frame,' Sixta said.

'Is that all?' she asked and sat down by him again.

'I don't understand,' Sixta said naïvely.

'It was found in the car,' said Christine. 'I'd like to know what it's all about.'

'I'm sorry, but . . .'

'How much?' Christine interrupted. 'What'll it cost?'

'A frame like that?' Sixta shrugged his shoulders.

Christine laughed. 'You're more cold-blooded than I thought. How much do you want? A thousand, two, five thousand?'

Sixta shook his head.

'Ten thousand? Please think it over straight away.'

'I think I'd better leave,' Sixta said. 'You ought to rest. You are tired. You've been ill.'

'I'm well,' she said imperiously. 'I've always been well. You wrote me a letter to Franzensbad.'

'No,' he said and repeated it energetically when he saw her unbelieving expression.

'Why are you getting excited then?'

'I know nothing about a letter. I don't know what this frame means.'

'And Charvat Lane doesn't mean anything to you?'

'No.'

'Twenty thousand.'

Sixta lost his nerve. 'No,' he roared, stood up, and made the cups jingle. He felt this was not the way to leave a lady, but he could not bring out another German word.

'That's all right,' Christine said, and her right arm sketched a gesture halfway between warding him off and waving.

Sixta went to the door, and when he closed it behind him it was as quietly as if he were leaving a symphony concert in the middle of the second movement.

10

The Little Miracle

WHEN SOPHIE MOVED her tongue, the ends of the catgut seam ached. When she turned her head the room went with it. She saw a rosy and a wrinkled woman's face, and the face of a man with a small white moustache, and she recognised the faces when she saw them again. She saw her right leg suspended above the bed, and felt a pull in her thigh. When she put her hands up to her hair, she felt a bandage. The doctor and the sisters introduced themselves: Dr. Budin, the Menjou, Sister Flora, the wrinkled face, Sister Arsenia, the rosy one. She should drink something, then she might go back to sleep. While Sister Flora went out, Dr. Budin asked a few questions which Sophie answered by lifting her right hand – yes – or the left – no. Sister Flora brought the feeding cup, and the lukewarm beef-tea burnt in the wound, but

189

Sophie said no when the doctor asked whether it hurt to swallow. As soon as the sister bent down to get the bedpan out of the bedside table, he left the room.

On Easter morning a bird trilled outside Sophie's window until the noise of a dustbin lid chased it away. A steam locomotive whistled far away. Rubber wheels slid over the linoleum, the cold glass of the thermometer was pushed under her arm, water ran into an enamel basin, a sponge touched her eyes, mouth and hands. Sister Arsenia changed the bedlinen, lifting Sophie on to clean sheets, telling her about Easter at home where her parents and eight brothers and sisters lived. Her father worked for the railways, the brothers in workshops and weaving mills, two were out of work, the youngest still at school, the sisters were married in the village except for Brigitte who had been sickly from childhood, but was the gayest. Later she put a bunch of flowers on the window sill and asked whether Sophie wanted anything else. No, she answered with her left hand.

Frau Sellmann and Katharina arrived in the afternoon. Even without their helpless way of talking Sophie would have realised that they knew the truth. She only remembered a giddy jolt before she lost consciousness on the Pilsen road. Fortunately her mother and sister had to catch the evening train.

During the following nights she felt her crumpled nightdress between her shoulder blades. When sweat made her breasts stick to her ribs, she threw off the covers and rubbed her foot so long on the sheet that the skin on her heel burned. She longed for a sound, for some other reason for her sleeplessness. Looking for a word that would make her sleep, she sometimes thought she had it on the tip of her tongue but could not speak it because she had bitten her tongue. I am not silent, I am dumb. To be silent means not to want to speak, to be dumb, not to be able to.

When Sister Arsenia stayed with her, Sophie went to sleep after breakfast, and no one woke her for the doctor's rounds. Though the youngest of all the nurses, Sister Arsenia enjoyed an authority over the doctors and patients which was the more effective since Arsenia did not know about it, and nobody thought of telling her.

On Wednesday she brought Sophie a pencil and paper, 'In case you want anything.'

Sophie wrote, 'What were you thinking when you were telling me about your sister Brigitte?' And when she noticed that Arsenia didn't want to answer, she wrote 'Please' in capitals.

'Do you know the game "I spy with my little eye"?' Arsenia

190

asked and blushed when Sophie nodded. 'It's a very vulgar game. We used to play it together, and I used to give her the clock, the ironing board, or the money-box to guess. When it was Brigitte's turn she always used to catch me out. Once I'd already guessed that it was on my head and black. My eyes? No. My hair? No. I had to give up. The dirt in my ears, she told me. But you mustn't laugh, Fräulein, it'll hurt your mouth.'

On Thursday Sixta stood by the door in a light-coloured jacket and chequered knickerbockers. He put his dusty shoes down very carefully as he walked towards Sophie's bed.

'Are you better?'

Sophie nodded.

'When will you get out?'

Sophie shrugged her shoulders and pointed to a chair.

'Aren't you allowed to speak?'

She shook her head with difficulty, and he looked as disappointed as if he had come to Pilsen to be entertained by Sophie. She held out the cardboard plate of chocolate eggs her mother had brought her. He took one and peeled off the green tinfoil while Sophie wrote down for him what it meant when she lifted her right or left hand. Sixta read her explanation and nodded and tried to find questions that could be answered so unequivocally, but apart from a few commonplaces which he preferred to keep to himself, nothing occurred to him. At last he said, 'I've travelled here on a platform ticket. I had to be careful at every station not to get into the same carriage as the inspector. I was almost caught once. My clothes are too noticeable. So I went on foot the last lap. I wanted to steal some flowers for you, but there were too many people in the parks.

'I worry about you,' Sophie wrote.

'Because of the return journey?' Sixta asked. 'Don't let that worry you. I know a bassoon player who comes from here, and he's travelled to Prague for years without a ticket. He's told me how to get through the barrier. He's a joke. When he hears a certain piece of music he has to take a drink. I'll whistle it for you. It isn't even for bassoon, but from Brahms D-major violin concerto.'

'Do eat your chocolate,' Sophie wrote.

'Oh yes,' he said and put the whole egg in his mouth, then went to wash his hands.

'What are you working on?' he read when he sat down again.

'I'm not working on anything,' he replied. 'I'd like to explain why, but I'd better wait until you are back in Prague. I read a lot, especially modern poetry.'

191

Sophie held her piece of paper out to him. 'I shan't be going back to Prague,' she had written.

'But where will you go?'

Sophie shrugged her shoulders, and while she thought where she might go, tears came to her eyes.

'What is the matter with you? Your voice? Your larynx? You aren't forgetting our project? The opera?' He noticed that Sophie wanted to reply, and stopped speaking. She wrote, 'I shall have a scar,' and pointed to the bandage on her head.

'A scar?' asked Sixta, 'Why not comb your hair into a fringe?'

Sophie lifted her left arm. No, he didn't understand. He didn't know what everybody else knew. He had come to see her because he respected her, or liked her, or loved her, but what she had meant to convey by mentioning the scar was something that he had not understood. He remained until Sister Flora came in and told him in Czech and German that he would really have to go.

When Sophie learned to speak again, at first with a very Icelandic aspirated 'T', which would have delighted Vavra, they also took the stitches out of the wound on her head. Before they put a light gauze bandage on it, she saw in the mirror a reddish line, about the length of a finger and just at the hairline, which ended in two jagged red lines.

'It won't show at all,' the doctor said.

'I don't care,' said Sophie, but was immediately sorry, for she had to listen to a lecture on prospects and confidence, etc. But when the leg had been X-rayed, the doctor wasn't quite so self-assured. Thinking that Sophie couldn't understand him, he asked, in Czech, for heavier weights, and gave Sister Arsenia a thorough dressing down for allegedly going to sleep instead of watching the pressure and stress. After this, Sophie detested him, not because he had had heavier weights put on her leg, but because he had treated Arsenia like a dog. Later that spring when the bone had to be rebroken, she even suspected him of being in cahoots with her father.

Sellmann visited Sophie on the second Sunday in May. His expression, even at the door, was of a man who was determined to carry through his intention, without knowing, for the time being, how to begin. When he bent over her, she smelled the fresh scent of lavender.

He told her of the burning of the Hindenburg at Lakehurst three days before.

'You really must order a daily paper.' He sighed and smiled. 'I hope you're impressed by my suit. I'm not just wearing it because of the heat. I'm staying the night here and going on to Falkenau tomorrow. Christine wanted me to look at the business there. It is incredible how it is running.'

'Badly?' asked Sophie.

'On the contrary, splendidly!'

'There were difficulties at first . . .'

'Chickenfeed,' said Sellmann, 'A firm like Amery & Herschel can manage that sort of thing. Since January we've been making a profit.'

'I thought the factory was going to be demolished.'

'What are you thinking of!' Sellmann exclaimed. 'Jan bought a few machines and put a new manager in. Do you think he'd put his money into a lame duck affair? He's much too fly for that.' He was silent as if to allow a minute for memories. Sophie was amazed by the unaccustomed jargon: 'chickenfeed', 'lame duck', 'fly', she'd never heard her father use such expressions, yet they somehow suited him, and this amazed her most of all.

'We have to discuss something,' he said at last. 'We don't want to talk of what is past, though the present is part of the past as well as the future. What's going to become of you after what has happened? There are people in Prague who know all about it, especially Bohuslav Amery and Frau Farel. That couldn't be helped, and they have no reason to go around talking about it. I don't want to speak about the hell your mother has been through. Only someone with children can understand that. Perhaps you'll think "hell" too strong a word, but I tell you . . .' Sellmann stopped and didn't tell her after all.

'No,' he continued, 'we're really speaking about someone whose happiness has been completely shattered, and though I usually regret all violence because I consider it a sign of weakness, I can understand Christine when she insists that you do not return to Prague. We have thought a great deal about your future, and we want you to think seriously about our suggestion.'

'Who is "we"?' Sophie asked.

'Your mother and I,' Sellmann replied. 'It occurs to me that you did not want to finish your schooling in a foreign country. So we thought you should go to Zerbst, live with Uncle Wilhelm, and take your final exams. The headmaster is a relation of Mama's. Please don't say anything. After the finals comes your year's labour service. I'd be glad if you didn't try to avoid it. I don't have to explain to you why. And then . . ? I'm old fashioned. I believe marriage is still the best profession for a woman.'

Sophie thought, for fifteen years I sat on your lap every evening and pressed a kiss on your scratchy chin, and when I told you that your beard prickled, you promised me a husband who'd shave twice a day.

'What do you think?' asked Sellmann.

'I'll think about it.'

'You have time, but you have no other choice,' Sellmann said in a low voice. 'I'm sorry.'

'I'd like you to go to St. Salvador in Prague,' Sophie asked. 'You know where it is? Good. Ask for Father Svoboda. I confessed to him in December, but he doesn't know my name. Would you give him his fare and ask him to come and see me?'

Sellmann promised, feeling ashamed and moved. After another quarter of an hour he went to see the Sister and heard that Sophie's shin would have to be broken again, because the bone had grown together badly.

After his return from Falkenau, Sellmann visited Svoboda. He produced Sophie's request rather like someone ordering the *specialité de la maison* in a strange restaurant because everything else is 'off'. Either through indolence, or to banish any suspicion of a breach of the secret of the confessional, the corpulent young chaplain said he remembered nothing of Sophie's confession, and his remark, that he spent six hours a week in the confessional, made Sellmann think him vain. When he had explained Sophie's circumstances, and suggested a date at the end of May, Svoboda even asked whether there were no priests in Pilsen. If the matter had been one concerning only himself, Sellmann would have walked out. But he was here for Sophie's sake. And even leaving aside the possibility that she might take more kindly to his own suggestions concerning her future if he managed to get Svoboda to visit her in Pilsen, he now felt that he simply had to get his own way with the priest. This was the kind of duel where he chose the weapons, and he chose the most unerringly successful. He not only paid for the railway ticket and expenses, but donated a sum for the poor of the parish, which it would have been sacrilegious to refuse. He wished the chaplain a good trip, and did not realise until a month later how he had defeated his own object.

Sophie confessed unreservedly and received absolution, the communion for the sick, and blessing. Then Svoboda put the leather case in which he had brought the sacrament away, kissed the stole and folded it.

'I'll be back in an hour,' he assured her and returned punctually to the minute. Although he moved his chair some distance, it did not escape Sophie that he had smoked and drunk beer.

'I want to enter a convent,' she said bluntly.

'I've seen that coming,' Svoboda answered in a sing-song voice and put the back of his hand to his mouth as if he wanted to belch. 'It is understandable in your position. But wait until you can walk again.'

'I'm serious about it,' said Sophie and leaned on her elbow.

Svoboda smiled. 'Perhaps yes, perhaps no.' He put his right index finger against the red, pearl-onion size point of his nose, then pushed it to the bridge of his spectacles. 'We believe what we believe,' he said. 'But sometimes it is only a pious mood. A cup of coffee too many and you feel deeply affected. A rainy Sunday, and eternity seems close. I don't want to dissuade you, you understand! But you mustn't persuade yourself either. When I was nineteen, I wanted to join the Benedictines at Strahov and become a librarian, because I was afraid to live amongst people. You are afraid, because your family have left you alone and you are in pain.' Svoboda stretched out his legs and crossed his high, black lace-up boots. 'You are forgetting that God loves you especially when you are suffering. A human being without God is not only Godless but inhuman. He has lost himself when he loses God.'

The subject of the convent seemed finished for Svoboda. He talked about his mother. Was he not ridiculous, a thirty-year-old bachelor, inclined to corpulence, who forgave sins and talked about all living creatures having to be saved because they had been expelled from paradise with Adam?

It had been agreed between Sophie and Arsenia that she should go to the Sisters of Mercy. After Sixta's visit, Sophie had thought of nothing else. When Sellmann suggested that she should go to Zerbst, she was already sure. But only at Whitsun, while Arsenia was on night duty, had she found the courage to speak of it. Arsenia had stood by the bed and held Sophie's hand, and they had cried like two girls in love with the same man, and both determined to give him up. Then Arsenia had opened the window and knelt down before the crucifix and had said the Lord's Prayer and the Ave Maria, and Sophie had said it after her, and had folded her hands so tightly that the knuckles showed through the skin. Then Arsenia had sat down by her and they had smiled at each other like two little saints who had succeeded in performing their first miracle.

The following night Arsenia had tiptoed behind the folding screen as if she would leave it up to Sophie to be silent and forget, or to speak and remember.

'I'll do it,' Sophie had said, and the Sister had crept back like a shadow.

'I've prayed for you all day. Go to sleep now.' And Sophie had gone to sleep as if she had arrived at the end of a long, happy journey, in a cool bed, under a safe roof.

Now she said to Svoboda, 'Please explain to my parents that I want to join the Sisters of Mercy.'

'Don't start with that all over again,' Svoboda sighed and struck the back of his hand against his knee. 'Are you of age?'

'I'll be twenty-one in July.'

He nodded. 'So why the Sisters of Mercy? There are I don't know how many orders for women. Allegedly only the Holy Ghost can count them. So why the Sisters of Mercy?' Svoboda grasped the seat of his chair between his thighs and moved closer to Sophie. 'I'll tell you. You want to make your novitiate nearby and eventually work here as a nurse, to be near your friend.'

'You've been listening to us,' Sophie said.

Svoboda smiled. 'No. But while I ate a sausage and drank a glass of beer just now I wondered why you sent off Sister Arsenia so coldly when I first came into your room. I said to myself, "Frantischku, you may have only got a 'satisfactory' in psychology, but you can well see that those two girls have been together for three months and didn't want to admit in your presence that they've got fond of one another. Why?" Well, now I know.'

'You mean I'm too weak?' Sophie asked.

'Weak . . .' the chaplain said. 'That's one of those words. One could also say you're too strong. Why do you want to enter the Order?'

'I don't want to. He wants it.'

'The Sisters of Mercy of the Slovak Province have their mother house by the Danube, in Bucovice. It's no more than a gipsy village. I'll tell you right off. I know the Superior in Bratislava. Shall I talk to him?'

'Yes,' said Sophie.

'There might be difficulties because of your nationality,' Svoboda said. 'When are you coming to Prague?'

'At the end of June, when my sister has left.'

'I'll have spoken to your parents by then,' said Svoboda. 'Or do you want a bit more time?'

Sophie shook her head and held out her hand to him. She wanted to thank him but could not find any words. She had arranged with Arsenia to call her the moment the chaplain had gone, but half an hour passed before she rang the bell.

A fortnight later she made her first attempts at walking between Katharina and Arsenia. She hobbled around the pansy beds, and Katharina told her that a priest had come to Bubenech and talked to their parents until midnight.

'I think they wanted to make their will.'

Sophie put her arm around her sister's hip and smiled. 'You need a lawyer for that, not a priest. They've been discussing my going to Bucovice. That's a convent near Bratislava.'

'Will you visit Karol?' Katharina asked as casually as possible.

'No,' Sophie said and explained to her why not.

'Why are you crying?' Arsenia asked when Katharina wiped her eyes with her sleeve. 'Is there anything more beautiful?'

'Of course there is,' Katharina scolded and stuck her large nose into a small handkerchief. 'You're not serious?'

'Yes, I am,' smiled Sophie.

In the last week of June, her father fetched her in the car. He had already written that he consented in principle, but on the condition that, should the Sellmanns return to Germany – and this was very possible in the current uncertain state of affairs – she would arrange to be transferred to a German province of her choice. She promised. He pushed the glass division aside, and said to the chauffeur, 'A little more slowly, Herr Schwarz.' He pointed to the hops in bloom beside the road, 'Pretty, aren't they?' Sophie nodded and leaned against him. He cleared his throat. 'I must tell you that I have the greatest respect for your resolve, the very greatest respect, little one.' His shoulders trembled and his breathing was short and fluttering. 'I want you to pray for me very often, you understand. I need it a great deal, my child. More than you think.'

During the next two weeks all the formalities were taken care of with the help of Svoboda: birth certificate, certificate of baptism and vaccination, health and school reports, and in some unexplained way Svoboda even managed to entice the Superior of the Sisters of Mercy to Prague to look at the future postulant himself. He was a man to Sellmann's taste, pious but not bigoted, frugal but no teetotaller, witty but not a joker. They agreed on the amount of the dowry and fixed the 15th September as the day for Sophie's arrival. Before he left, the Superior spent half an hour alone with Sophie, gave her a copy of the rules of the order, and wished her a happy 'last holiday'.

When the schools closed, Katharina and Heinrich joined Sophie and Jarmila on the Mangl estate, and the weeks passed quickly. Even Sixta's unexpected visit seemed to all, except Sophie, like no more than an additional distraction, though Herr Mangl wondered later why the young composer had run away without asking for a carriage to take him to the station.

Perspiring and sunburnt, Sixta appeared in the courtyard one Sunday morning, but had to wait until the family with their guests and retainers returned from church, when he was asked to join them at lunch. It did not occur to anybody that he ate a lot so as to talk little, for Herr Mangl entertained the company with anecdotes about Bismarck. Then Heinrich said Grace.

They dispersed through the house, slept on ottomans, or swung in hammocks, and Sophie walked with Sixta through the maple avenue. She wore a pearl-grey silk dress with a white collar, and had pinned up her hair because of the heat. Sixta took off his jacket, rolled up his sleeves to the elbows, and unobtrusively pushed his shirt into his trousers. At the end of the avenue they turned back without a word. Important words hung in the air, both felt it, but they were not easy to seize.

'You know that I'm going away?' asked Sophie.

'Katharina has told me.'

Sixta hung his jacket around him as if he needed padded shoulders for what he had to say. He was very pale.

'I want to marry you, Sophie,' he said. 'I've been to Budweis and have talked to my parents. We could live with them for the time being. I saw the headmaster of the grammar school. I can have a post as music teacher.'

Sixta went on talking, louder as his hopes grew smaller, until he suddenly stopped in the middle of a sentence because he realised that he had not mentioned that he loved her. He saw in Sophie's eyes that it was too late. When he said it nonetheless, it sounded like a birthday greeting.

'Yes,' Sophie said. 'I like you very much too, and I'll never forget you. You'll stay for coffee?'

Sixta was so confused that he felt cold. He lifted his arm to grasp her shoulder, but at that moment she turned and smiled. 'Do you sometimes think of our concert?' she asked, and quoted the review. ' "The surprise was doubtless Fräulein Sophie Sellmann." '

Sixta knew that he had lost.

'I've learned the review by heart,' she said. 'I can still recite it. That insolent fellow calling your music academic!'

'And half-baked,' Sixta added.

'But you didn't mind?'

'Oh yes I did. I wanted to commit suicide.'

'Really?' Sophie suddenly had tears in her eyes.

'But I couldn't make up my mind whether I should jump into the river or out of the window.'

They went along the avenue to the house, but when Sophie was about to step out of the sun, he stopped her. 'I want to ask you something. No, I'm not starting that again. It is ... Perhaps we won't meet again for a long time, and I'd very much like to know something.'

Sophie hesitated.

'On the day of your accident ...'

She lowered her head and went on walking in the shade beside him.

'Maundy Thursday. Yes?' he continued. 'Herr Amery came in the morning and insisted I had written his wife an anonymous letter. Madness. But before I could explain ...'

'Yes?' Sophie asked.

'I don't hold it against him, that would be silly. But – why did he beat me up?'

'I wrote the letter,' Sophie said and stood still. 'I did it,' she repeated. 'But I didn't tell him until we had gone past Pilsen. I'm sorry. Shall we go into the house?'

Sixta understood, and the blood shot into his face. He accompanied Sophie to the house door and gave her his hand.

'Goodbye,' he said and could say no more. Then he ran along the hot towpath to the nearest town.

In September, while Frau Sellmann and Hanka were packing, Sophie visited the 'nordic' Vavra. The elevator sighed when it stopped at the fourth floor. She rang the bell. The professor appeared old and slovenly. For the first time she saw the grey hairs on his chest through the open shirt.

'You're going to Slovakia?' he exclaimed. 'Why not go straight amongst the Hottentots?' He jumped up, threw up his arms, stomped across the room, and crowed in an unintelligible singsong. 'You know what that is? That is Slovak culture. You can't do this to me, Sophie!' When he realised there was nothing he could do, he said, 'All right. In six months you'll come back to Prague, lousy, dirty and with bad manners. But please, at least keep your language pure. Don't get used to that dialect. It's only an invention anyway. We should have given the whole herd of goats to the Hungarians. Instead, they are now our brothers. Fine brothers! Gipsies!

'I want to show you something,' he continued, getting up and taking a wooden box with thick metal fastenings out of his desk. He extracted a stiff, green piece of paper and gave it to Sophie.

'What is it?'

'My life insurance. Read it.'

The sum mentioned in case of death was half a million krone.

'That's a lot of money,' she said and tried to give him back the document.

'Go on reading,' Vavra urged her.

The policy was dated 17th July 1935. I was nineteen that day, she thought. A coincidence, but then suddenly saw her name.

'Forget it,' Vavra said, taking the sheet. 'I know it is childish. I won't die so soon, and if I kill myself the money won't be paid out in any case. But even if you are a rich woman then, take it and use it for whatever you want.' He put the paper back and shut the box into the desk.

'I didn't show you this rubbish to . . .' he smiled. 'If this has been your last visit to me, all right. Nothing is changed for me. That's all I wanted to say. But be specially careful in future of the durative and perfective verb forms. In Slavic languages everything depends on the verb!'

There weren't many people travelling first class to Bratislava. Hanka sat in a second-class compartment with the cases, because there was no third class in the express train. During the journey through the Bohemian hills, Sellmann spoke of Betty, Eugen Lustig, Frenzel and himself. The sky above the stationary white September clouds, the smooth stubble fields, and the unchanging meadows made one think of eternity. 'He has made all nature beautiful,' Sellmann said, and Sophie nodded as if she knew of whom he was speaking.

In Brno, Sellmann beckoned the newspaper vendor who passed a black-bordered special edition through the window.

II

The Revolution Knows no Homeland

IN FRONT OF Bratislava station the flags were at half-mast. In the windows of the Bata shoe shop stood photographs of the old President, bordered in crêpe. Even the Mother Superior in Bucovice thought the state was dead because Masaryk had died. On the return journey, Sellmann paid a supplement so that the maid could sit in his carriage. Hanka cried, Sellmann did not know whether it was because of Sophie or for Masaryk, or because she was travelling for the first time in an upholstered carriage. He didn't want to ask, and when she was still sobbing into her handkerchief halfway home, he went and stood in the corridor.

The day the President's body was taken from the castle to the station – the gun-carriage escorted across Wenceslas Square by a Czech, a Slovak, a German, a Hungarian, a Polish and a Ruthenian soldier – Sellmann saw Herr von Lilienthal, the director of the Böhmische Landesbank, kneeling in the gutter beside a peasant. He thought it an exaggerated gesture, but it gave him food for thought.

Lustig too, when he visited him the following week, seemed worried. 'I think we are in for a bad spell, possibly even bankruptcy. Masaryk was always good for an international loan. He made Austria small and Bohemia big. Masaryk was a fox, but Beneš is a rabbit who thinks he's a tiger.'

Sellmann waited for the arrival of Frenzel of the Saxonia before asking for his transfer to the Reich.

'We have never needed you so badly in Prague as now,' Frenzel said when he arrived in December. His wife was with him. Sellmann thought of her shaved armpits on the Binz promenade, but now she wore a high-necked suit. Instead of going to the opera for which Sellmann had reserved tickets, they went to a cabaret, for Frenzel had forgotten his dinner jacket. After the second glass, he lapsed into a manner which disturbed Sellmann. He trumpeted exclamation marks after every sentence, and his questions took agreement so much for granted that no replies were expected. If Sellmann tried to speak, he said, 'I know just what you mean.' This certainty, and the irony he displayed made Sellmann sure by midnight that he had missed his chance of being asked to return.

After Frenzel's departure, Sellmann decided on a step which at first brought him doubt, then admiration, and finally a fortune. He advised Lustig to sell his mines in the west of the country *en bloc* to the Czech Gewerbebank, the competitor of the Böhmische Landesbank. Though Lustig understood the point of this plan, he first asked Herr von Lilienthal's opinion. That man was speechless. It was agreed that the project should be kept secret for the time being. In March prices were discussed, but the Gewerbebank was deterred by Lustig's demands which were not only three hundred per cent of the nominal value of the mining shares, but also transfer of all the money into pound sterling. It was not until July that the agreement was signed with all Lustig's stipulations accepted, because the Gewerbebank wanted to assure themselves of the North Bohemian districts before a German consortium could steal a march on it. The whole amount was paid into a London bank.

The deal, which had been celebrated in the financial press in the summer as a stroke of genius on the part of the Gewerbebank, was, by autumn, shown to have been a mistake. The Sudeten mines bought by the Gewerbebank fell into German hands by virtue of the Munich agreement.

Sellmann divided the commission he received from Lustig into three parts. He used one part to buy shares in an armament factory. With the second part he bought a piece of land beside the Sázava, and with the last third he bought a Mortlake tapestry, a silver everlasting calendar by the Augsburg Master Thelott, and a solid gold monstrance of the Battle of Lepanto with the sea-battle against the Turks in cloisonné enamel. The apartment in Bubenech was completely repapered, claret coloured wallpaper for the dining-room, pale green for the drawing-room, and blue with white lilac boughs for the bedroom. Katharina was left in charge of the redecorating while her parents and Heinrich went to stay with Christine, and Sellmann did not notice until they moved back that the bedroom wallpaper had been put on upside down. The white lilac did not point towards the ceiling, but slid down to the floor. Since Betty did not notice the mistake there was no need to rectify it. To reproach Katharina seemed useless. She would only have laughed. She had become impudent since passing her final exams. Let the lilac fall down. The important thing was that the ceiling stayed up.

Katharina had signed on for a course in history and philosophy at the University. After a few lectures in the latter subject she was convinced that each philosopher worried at the theories of his predecessors like a dog, until he had sniffed out a new solution, the lifespan of which depended on the ability of his successor to do likewise. Katharina came to the conclusion that it was just as well to *have* a philosophy before studying it.

In November a fellow student lent her the Bhagavad Ghita. Katharina put the poem, swollen into a thick volume by a fore-word, translation, commentary, index and leather cover, into her school bag, and when, that afternoon, a fight developed between Czech and German students, she threw it at a policeman. When her particulars had been examined, the commissioner explained to her that the police had turned out to protect the German students. All they asked of her was an apology before sending her home. But Katharina insisted on her right to defend herself, and even the warning that the sergeant who would hear her case was a one-time legionnaire who had walked thousands of kilometres through Siberia without changing his socks, could not stop her. She was sentenced to a fine of three hundred krone.

When she left the room, she saw a young man in the corridor being led along by two policemen. His forehead was cut, the blood ran over his closed eyes, and he was panting like a dog. Only after he had vanished into the court room did she realise that it was Karol. She ran to the door, but was not allowed in. When she started to scream, she was put out into the street. She was surprised that all the people in the police station thought it quite natural that someone who had been hurt should have to see a magistrate before seeing a doctor.

She wondered why all Karol's letters, which she collected once a week at the main post office, should be date-stamped in Bratislava if Karol was in Prague. Two days after she had seen him she received a letter in which he wrote that he had been on a boating trip on the Danube. She was not jealous enough, or too intelligent, to wonder whether he was unfaithful to her. She would have put up with the thought that he had fallen for some Slovak female, but that he should be arrested in Prague while letting her believe that he was rowing on the Danube in November, hurt her.

She'd have to do something. She telephoned the Djudko apartment, but got no reply. On Monday she went to the University, but Karol was not registered. Since she did not trust her own Czech, she asked Frau Farel for help.

Aunt Marketa, on the telephone to the commissioner, pretended to be the cousin of the Minister of the Interior.

'Compliments, my dear lady,' he replied coldly.

'I hear you have a nephew of mine in custody,' she said. She mentioned his name and after a pause was told that her information was correct.

'I want him to be treated as severely as possible, without consideration for his family connections,' she said.

'Certainly,' said the commissioner. 'But we shan't have much opportunity, since he will be released on 15th December.'

'What a pity,' Aunt Marketa sighed. 'But please tell me the exact time, so that he doesn't escape me.'

Katharina fell round Frau Farel's neck, kissed her, thanked her, and ran to the hairdresser's.

Waiting on Monday morning in front of the main police station, she wore her hair pinned up, with a fringe over her forehead. Karol left the building with a man the same age. They turned up their collars to the rim of their caps, and stuck their hands into their pockets. Karol hesitated when he recognised Katharina, then said goodbye to his companion and joined her.

'I've just reported to the police,' he said. 'I arrived from Bratislava an hour ago.'

Katharina admired the composure with which he deceived her.

Last time they had met it had been at a railway station in August. Karol had arrived by train from Prague, Katharina by bicycle from the Mangl estate. All day they had looked for a place to be alone. On the banks of the Vltava excursion steamers passed with passengers whose binoculars were trained on anything that moved. Among the hops it was damp, in the fields the grain was being harvested, in the castle park children were collecting chestnuts, and Karol did not have enough money to take a room in an inn. Since Katharina had lost the chain and padlock of her bicycle on the way, they had to take it with them everywhere, and this had been particularly annoying for them. Karol's train back was due just before ten thirty, and at nine thirty it was still not dark. Karol took the spanner out of the bicycle's repair kit and removed the saddle. He put it under his arm, and they pushed their way into a toolshed which smelled of tar-paper, lubricating oil and potato sacks.

Karol caught his train to Prague, but Katharina had to ride the eight kilometres standing up, because there had not been time enough for Karol to fix the saddle back on.

Now they took the tram to the Djudko apartment. He made love to her hastily, ate one of the sandwiches they had bought, and spoke with his mouth full. He had changed. Instead of cufflinks he wore buttoned cuffs, instead of a waistcoat, a sleeveless jumper, instead of braces, a leather belt. He blew his nose in a blue-chequered handkerchief and cleaned his nails with a penknife. Two years ago in Amery's hunting lodge he would have wanted to go back to Prague if he had forgotten his nail file. Now and again he went to the door as if to make sure no one was listening. Katharina envied him his secret, which she thought must be an adventure. She told him where and when she had seen him a fortnight before.

'A traffic accident,' he lied, but when she reached for her coat, he took hold of her and confessed.

Since the beginning of October he had been handing over coded messages which his father had sent him through a man in Nusle to various people in Prague. Katharina's letters had arrived with them in a special envelope, and Karol's replies had taken the reverse route.

She was disappointed. Expressions like 'illegal' or 'conspiracy'

204

did not impress her, because Karol said them in such an indifferent tone. Only 'bourgeoisie' lay heavy on his lips. She would have brushed her fringe from her forehead if she had been certain it would let her out of that category.

'I made a mistake,' he said. 'I shouldn't have taken part in that demonstration.'

She told him of her own arrest.

'It's different for you,' he said and brushed her fringe from her forehead.

'I'll cut it off,' she promised.

'Perhaps it would be better.'

'Then I can join you?'

'That isn't only up to me,' Karol replied.

'I'll go today and see the man in Nusle,' she said and did not allow Karol to interrupt. 'You are being watched. Do you want to give the whole game away? Nobody knows me.' She got up and lifted her chin in a threatening gesture. She felt that a strand of her hair had escaped and pulled out the combs, and her red mane fell over her neck and shoulders as if she had taken off a bathing cap. She had given birth to her courage and Karol sat by like a man who had fathered a mammoth. When he had given her the Nusle address, they arranged a meeting place for afterwards.

'I'll give you a box of chocolates,' she said. 'The letters will be inside. You'll kiss me, and I'll wish you a happy birthday.' There was no holding her. She went to Nusle, collected the mail and bought a box of chocolates. Despite the rain she sat down on a bench and ate half of them, then emptied the rest into a waste basket. She wondered where she should put the letters, which she now had between her skin and her girdle, into the box, and decided to go into a bar. A few dozen men sat before their glasses of beer and smoked cigarettes or ate potato-pancakes. A ventilator roared on the opposite wall, but it was impossible to tell whether it sucked the air away or blew it in, for the cloud of cigarette smoke, beer fumes and baking-grease hung motionless above the tables, and only the waiters, passing with their trays of beer, made little eddies of air which collapsed immediately when the white jackets vanished through the flap of the counter.

Katharina sat down at a table and received half a litre of beer without asking for it.

'A *placičky*,' murmured the waiter. Katharina nodded because she was too nervous to understand. She then realised that she had ordered three small potato-pancakes. I mustn't make a fuss here, she thought. I must eat at least one pancake and drink half the beer, though I'm full of chocolates. She took off her right glove and put a paper napkin round the pancake and bit into the brown crust. She breathed for a long time over the hot bite, until it occurred to her to cool it with beer. At a neighbouring table two men lifted their glasses to her. Katharina took another sip. One of them was in railwaymen's uniform. She ate her pancake slowly and looked away from them. The time had come, she thought, her hand on the empty chocolate box.

When she came back from the toilet, a glass of rum stood beside her beer.

'Your health,' cried the railway man, and lifted his own glass.

She drank to him, emptying the rum at one draft. It burnt her tongue and her throat. Why am I doing all this, if not for them? She ate her pancakes and drank her beer, and when the waiter brought the next half she asked for the bill. The railway man wanted to pay for the beer, but she refused. He went up to her table, very tall and blond, with broad shoulders.

'Give me a chocolate to remember you by,' he asked her. 'I love nougat.'

'I'm sorry,' Katharina stammered in Czech, 'but the box is empty.'

The roilwayman turned to his friend, 'A German,' he jeered. 'She goes to the lavatory and stuffs herself with chocolates, and I buy her a rum!'

Katharina got up, put the chocolate box with the letters under her arm, and went to the door.

'Heil Hitler,' the railwayman roared after her.

Katharina took the tram and noticed, when she got off, that she was not quite steady on her feet. When she and Karol both said, 'Happy birthday' she burst out laughing.

'You've got everything mixed up again.'

'Give here,' he said.

'Only after a kiss,' she demanded, and held on to the lapels of his coat while hiding the box behind her back.

'You're drunk.'

'Because it's your birthday,' she whispered and stood on tiptoe.

Karol kissed her and reached for the box. When he had it in his hand he tore himself away and ran off without a word. When she saw a newspaper seller nearby grin, she put out her tongue at him. Then she suddenly felt sick. She leaned against a shop window until her fury overcame her weakness. Before going home she bought a box of Christmas cards.

After supper she took Heinrich's printing set and on each card with its stylised fir-branch and red candle, she printed, THE COMMUNIST PARTY IS ALIVE, AND WILL CONTINUE TO

FIGHT. Signed, THE ILLEGAL COMMITTEE. The Czech text was correct except for the word 'illegal' which Katharina did not know was spelled with a single 'l' in Czech. She licked all sixty envelopes and put them under her bed. Next morning she copied the names and addresses of manufacturers, bankers, businessmen, judges and politicians from the telephone book, and posted the cards. She read all the papers, and on Friday she found a paragraph headed 'Happy Christmas'. It read:

If the German Communists who have fled from the frontier regions think they can disturb the stability of our Republic in this way, they are mistaken. In view of these happy greetings it is difficult to know whom to congratulate, the Communist Party for having such an illegal committee (with two 'ls', of course!), or the Czech Republic for having such feeble enemies.

Katharina locked herself in her room and cried.

On the Monday she went to Nusle again and collected the post from Bratislava. Her contact wanted to know where the replies were, but she did not know. From a phone box she called Karol and said, 'I've been to Nusle'.

'Wrong number,' he said and put the receiver down. She took a taxi and met him coming downstairs. He wore a black coat, a grey Homburg, kid gloves, and a white muffler. He gave her the key to the flat.

He was back after two hours. 'It makes no sense dressing up like a worker,' he explained his different clothes. 'A masquerade!'

'Where were you?' Katharina asked.

'I went to see an editor. His name is Sputa. He's mad about revolutions as long as he hasn't got to take part in them. He sends greetings telegrams to Spain when the Republicans shoot down a few planes. I'm to write reviews for him to be signed with his name. He doesn't mind that I know nothing about the theatre. One doesn't have to be a chicken to know an egg is rotten, he says.'

Katharina gave Karol the letters she had brought. He tore them up.

'The fellow in Nusle is a police spy,' he grumbled.

She told him of her mishap with the Christmas cards and showed him the newspaper cutting.

'All the better if they think us stupid,' he said. 'That'll make them arrogant. By the way, we're counting on you. I'm not allowed to tell you any more. You'll get your instructions from me, but you'll have to think about it carefully. I don't want to deceive you.

We've got to know who visits your father from the Reich. He won't tell you what he talks about with these people, but he corresponds with them privately.'

Karol gave her the names of several Slovak politicians and Katharina repeated them.

'Did you think I'd give you a gun?' he let fly at her. 'Or do you have a bad conscience because you're going to spy on your father?'

'And if I don't agree?'

Karol moved to the window and looked out. 'Then we won't be able to meet again.'

'Do you want to see me again?'

'I'd cut off my left hand for your sake,' he said into the curtain, and seemed to mean it. Katharina laughed, but on her way home in the cold tram, between wet coats and dripping umbrellas, she suddenly felt so moved by his words that she broke out in a sweat.

On Tuesday, when Betty and Heinrich had gone to do the last bit of Christmas shopping, Katharina sat down at the Van-de-Velde desk. On top of it, on the right, stood the everlasting calendar of the Master Thelott, on the green, leather-bound blotter lay a fountain pen which was never used since it was a present from a former German Chancellor. Sellmann hated keys. They made a mess of ones pockets. Even presents weren't locked away but had always been put in the large linen cupboard. 'If you have to take a look: help yourselves. Spoil your own surprise.'

Katharina rummaged amongst passports, birth certificates and receipts and found her school report from the fifth form. She found a bundle of letters in a lower drawer, but only read the beginning of the first. 'Zerbst, August 18, 1912. My beloved Anton. Today is Wednesday, the day of the civil servants. You'll know the sequence by now. I'll have to wait four more nights for you ...' She felt ashamed, but she went on searching. In a box she found photographs which had not been put into the family album. There was her father as an officer at the front, with helmet, moustache, and puttees, as a boy in a velvet suit, his left arm on a balustrade, as a sultan, dressed up for carnival, a strange lady on his lap. She discovered foreign notes and coins, receipts for payments and for the rent; lottery tickets, a rusty hunting knife, and a bottle of sleeping tablets, but she did not find the names Karol had mentioned. She leaned back and looked at the Mortlake tapestry. Leander, in a fluttering cloak, held Hero's hand, above them flew Cupid, his bow poised, in the background a temple-frieze of crooked Corinthian pillars. It seemed that her father knew nothing of these men.

12

Excuse Me!

WHEN SLOVAKIA GAVE up its southern territories and a third of its population to Hungary, Sellmann, though occasionally worried about Sophie's safety, was not really concerned. True, there was a sugar factory which the Saxonia had bought in the spring from a Paris bank, but from the point of view of general finance, Slovakian autonomy did not affect him.

In October he went to Berlin with Herr von Lilienthal to offer those branches of the Böhmische Landesbank which were in the occupied zones to the Saxonia. The Saxonia acquired the North Bohemian establishments, but took over parts of the business in cash, paid for the real estate at a very low rate of exchange, and refused the Jewish creditors and debtors, who were liable for the recently-introduced levies in the Reich, a right to emigrate to Prague. This resulted in a debit balance for the Böhmische Landesbank of more than a hundred million krone which was adjusted by the sale of Czech industrial shares. At the same time the Saxonia bought the mines which Lustig had earlier sold to the Gewerbebank, and celebrated the settlement with a breakfast at Schramota's. At the end of the meal, Frenzel assured Sellmann that he would soon receive the directorship of the new Sudeten Coal Mining company.

The Böhmische Landesbank was now in difficulties, and when, in February, Sellmann suggested a rescue operation, Frenzel told him that the Prague establishment was a lost cause. The bank was to a large extent dependent on Jews who wanted to draw out their deposits and emigrate. A vast new credit would be needed, and the Jews on the board of directors, on the management committee, and in general personnel would have to receive pensions.

'No, my dear fellow,' said Frenzel when they parted. 'Time'll put it right. *Tempora mutantur*. I've never been able to stand that lily-livered Lilienthal in any case. Pearls in his tie and shit in his pants. A Yid right out of the book. But, of course, just between

ourselves. You're his employee, loyal to the death, that goes without saying.'

In March Sellmann was in Berlin again, took a room at the
Adlon, and heard from his room waiter that the President of the
Czech Republic had also arrived at the hotel. Wednesday's papers
brought the announcement that 'Dr. Hacha had put the destiny of
the Czech people into the hands of the Führer of the German
Reich.'

In the express to Prague five days later, Sellmann ordered the
second menu: marrow dumplings, goose with red cabbage, peach
Melba, and drank a bottle of Beaujolais 1935. He read *Le Roman
d'un Tricheur* by Sacha Guitry. When he bought a German paper
before the frontier, it contained the declaration of independence
of Slovakia and Carpatho-Russia, and the name of the Protector of
Bohemia and Moravia. Konstantin, Freiherr von Neurath. It gave
him hope, and Sophie seemed safe.

The following week Herr von Lilienthal and another fifteen
Jews resigned from the Board of Directors of the Böhmische
Landesbank. Seventeen new members were co-opted, including
four representatives of the Saxonia. The new Board of Directors
elected Dr. Anton Sellmann as its chairman.

Coming out of the bank one Saturday in May, Sellmann was
accosted by 'Herr Croissant', Eugen Lustig's valet. Rohlik did not
wear the black suit which had made him look so elongated. In a
brown jacket he looked like an actor who had always played
officers, but had, for this afternoon, taken a civilian part. He
brought greetings from Lustig, and asked for a meeting.

'Not right now,' he said when Sellmann pointed to his car. 'If I
might collect you towards nine o'clock from Bubenech in a hire-
car?'

Sellmann understood and held out his hand, but the valet only
bowed, and went off with stiff strides as if he were carrying a
dripping candelabra.

That evening he was half an hour late, opened the back of the
car for Sellmann and sat in front. In the city he paid the taxi and
walked behind Sellmann through unknown streets. Sellmann felt
pleased to be going in the right direction without a word being
exchanged. When they stood in front of a small hotel, he believed
he had found it by himself.

Two German sergeant-majors sat in the hall, their caps beside
their glasses of champagne. Rohlik raised his right arm, but Sellmann only nodded. They found the stairs behind a velvet curtain.
On the second floor they met a naked guest who asked for the
toilet. Behind a door a woman laughed and a man's voice roared.

On the third floor the valet knocked on a door. Though they heard the key turn in the lock, Rohlik waited a moment before opening the door. He had given Lustig time to sit down again, for when they entered, he was seated on the sofa, and got up to greet his guest. The room was no larger than a bathroom, but Lustig moved around in it as between marble and oleanders.

'You'll take a drop?' he said, and gave Sellmann some port. 'Sometimes it's a bit noisy here, but in stormy times there's only one safe place: the eye of the typhoon.' His hand shook when he lifted his glass, but he put it to his lips without spilling a drop.

The wallpaper burst at the seams, the weak ceiling light threw shadows without outlines. Sellmann did not want to offer Lustig empty phrases. He outlined the situation of the bank as well as his own, and emphasised that he had succeeded in obtaining a lump sum settlement for their dismissed Jewish colleagues.

'Very noble,' said Lustig and stuck a finger into his waistcoat to stop his hand shaking. 'I'm astonished by the chivalry of your fellow-countrymen. I don't suppose you know that I was a soldier in the old army? A captain in the reserve. It is pretty bizarre to be dislodged by this Herr Hitler, a lance-corporal.'

'I want to confess something to you,' Sellmann said and heard sounds like people slapping each other from downstairs.

Lustig smiled, and Sellmann noticed only now that he was wearing small rimless spectacles with a narrow gold bridge, instead of his pince-nez.

'I've deceived you.'

'Oh well,' Lustig said. 'How else would you have got the idea that I should sell my mines to Gewerbebank!'

'No, from the beginning,' Sellmann disclosed and took a cigar.

'I've read the dossier of the secret service,' said Lustig and stroked the plush back of the sofa. 'Also your personal mail as far as it was important. They wanted to arrest you, but I was able to show them that it was advantageous to leave you alone and be in the picture, rather than to imprison you and be in the dark ourselves. It wasn't always easy, but in the end it was worth it for both sides. I just thought we'd have a bit more time.'

Sellmann put out his cigar and laid it on the side of the ashtray.

'Look,' said Lustig. 'A man who is innocent at fifty is either an imbecile or he's been asleep all his life. Someone like you who comes from the provinces and has to make a career can't afford detours. You're not smoking?'

'No, thank you.'

'We meet for the last time today, Dr. Sellmann. I have a request which concerns my son. Victor lives with my sister, but eventually she herself will be in danger. Take Victor to Vienna when you can. I've written down the address on a piece of paper. It's in this envelope.' Lustig took a thick envelope out of his jacket and gave it to Sellmann.

'What's inside?' asked Sellmann.

Lustig smiled. 'The cheapest thing on earth.'

Sellmann took out the visiting card and put the envelope full of money beside the ashtray.

Lustig put his white, blue-veined hands on the table. That was, Sellmann knew from many conferences, the sign for departure.

'No, wait,' Lustig said. 'I must tell you one thing more. Long before the war I was in Scheveningen with my wife. You know it? Do you remember the refuse bins on the promenade? One put one's foot on a lever, and the lid opened. Very hygienic. One day I saw a dark gentleman from the Dutch East Indies go to one of these bins. He picked up the lid with one hand, and the bin tipped forward and all the papers fell out. He jumped back and said, "Oh, excuse me!" He had not seen through the mechanism. "That's what has happened to me. I beg you to forgive me, Doktor Sellmann.'

'You make me feel ashamed,' said Sellmann, almost in tears. 'I've never known a greater man than you.'

Lustig sent greetings to Frau Sellmann, the daughters, and Heinrich, especially to Heinrich. Then he rang for the valet.

On Tuesday evening Sellmann and Betty went to Christine's. Since she did not use the dining-room any more, she had made it into a second drawing-room so that the guests could move about three rooms, counting the music room. Frau Amery's 'day' had soon become known amongst the administration of the Protectorate and amongst the officers. One stood about on Aubusson carpets or sat in baroque chairs, spoke, after a concert, about Cocteau, Bergengruen, Eisenstein and Ernst Jünger, put one's hand out for a crystal goblet from the tray of a passing waiter, and left around midnight for the barracks out of town or a hotel in the city. Unlike similar evenings in Hanover, Mainz or Dortmund, these hours left the participants with the pleasant feeling that they had been living in the past without having to reproach themselves for having left the present. Sellmann entered into conversation with the adjutant of the Reichsprotector, and asked for an audience with his master. The following day he was given an appointment.

Freiherr von Neurath received the head of the Böhmische Landesbank by reviving common memories. They had both been admirers of the opera singer Max Hansen. When Sellmann produced his request to allow Eugen Lustig to emigrate, the Reichsprotector was surprised.

'The Gestapo has been looking for him for eight weeks – and you know where he's hiding?'

Sellmann explained the catastrophic results that Lustig's arrest would have for foreign business of both the Böhmische Landesbank and the Saxonia.

'You exaggerate,' von Neurath reprimanded, as if they were still talking about the opera. 'But you're entitled to do so. But remember what Count Eulenburg said, "A discussion between two reigning gentlemen is only blessed if they speak of nothing but the weather!" Where are you going this summer?'

'To the Danube,' Sellmann said and turned pale.

'I love the Danube,' said Freiherr von Neurath. 'As a young man I went duck shooting there.' A yellow signal began to blink on his telephone. He took off the receiver and laid it on his desk. 'I will ask the Czech Ministry of the Interior for a passport for Herr Lustig,' he said. 'Please give my adjutant his address.' The Reichsprotector got up, and Sellmann shook hands with him. He felt that it was hopeless to ask for a passport for Victor too.

A week later, Herr Croissant appeared at Bubenech with a bouquet of yellow roses. Betty took him into the drawing-room and asked whether Lustig had left.

'Yes, madam,' he said and pointed to an envelope pinned to the tissue paper. While Betty read the letter he seemed to imitate one of his employer's gestures. He took a large white handkerchief out of his breast pocket and blew his nose.

In pointed and rather ink-stained letters, Lustig had written, 'My dear lady, I hope you will forgive me for not coming to see you before my departure for London. This little bunch of flowers is to remind you of our first meeting.'

13

Lasciate mi morire

IN OCTOBER, AFTER his return from a convalescent home in the Beskyd mountains, Amery gave the impression of a man who, though he had been told to take things easy, seemed determined to take up his life where he had left it at the time of the accident. His business associates could well understand that he should give up the post of deputy chairman of the Chamber of Commerce, for his own business had to come first. But during the winter it became more and more noticeable that his early resolution diminished, he refused to see people not only at home but at the office. After a while, the switchboard operator connected his calls with the manager, and if a representative wanted an appointment, Vejvoda suggested he see either himself or Christine. That went against all accepted custom.

The evening of his return to their apartment, Christine had wished to make it easy for them to talk things over, and welcomed him in a friendly manner. She even drank the sour Melnik wine for his sake. Silence, or recriminations would have relieved her. Instead, Amery chatted in such a way that she began to realise that no obstacle is harder to overcome than a pleasantly spoken, incontrovertible sentence. After an hour she interrupted him to say that she had paid Herr Popischil the rent that was due for the room in Charvat Lane. But this did not disconcert him. Without a smile he asked her whether she wanted to continue to look after his business, for he was very pleased with everything she had done.

Christine felt that she had been praised for a success that was due more to her obstinacy than her judgment. For the last six months she had repulsed her father-in-law's attempts to meddle, had listened to no one except Vejvoda, and sent two or three of her decisions to Jan in the convalescent home. He had acknowledged them merely with picture postcards. Jan's compliment now suddenly put a different complexion on what she had thought of as indifference. She wondered whether she should throw herself into his arms to make, if words would not do it, a clean sweep of things. But while she was still considering, Amery rang for the maid and asked her to make up a bed for him in the larger of the two guest-rooms. He gave no reason for this arrangement, and eventually Christine came to terms with the fact that Jan lived like a bachelor in their apartment.

He appeared once or twice at Amery & Herschel, and at business friends' and paid duty visits at Sellmanns', his father's and Aunt Marketa's, without asking them back. In the meantime he replaced the double bed in the spare-room with a divan no wider than a cot. He pushed an easy chair from the drawing-room under the standard lamp, hung up the old bookshelves in which he kept

214

his books according to their colours, as he had done before his marriage.

When the maid called him to meals he changed his clothes, went into the dining-room, pushed Christine's chair in, and asked about the china patterns of the current season, the Bubenech family, or what was on at the theatre. When Christine suggested an excursion or a visit, he nodded seriously and encouraged her so comprehensively as to the places to go and the people to see, that by the end of it he could not only put his knife and fork on his empty plate, but also give up all claim to participation.

From the beginning of December he even ordered the barber to the house, thus doing away with the last reason for leaving the apartment. He had few needs. A messenger brought papers and cigarettes, also books and records which he ordered from catalogues.

In hospital, when he had heard his heartbeat between two periods of unconsciousness, he had been too weak to wish for anything but the end of pain. Later, in the convalescent home, when he heard from his father how strenuously they had concealed the whole affair, he suspected that his and Sophie's death would have been a chance to escape ridicule, and he also wondered whether the accident had been brought about by chance, or by a frivolous, almost arbitrary mistake. For after Sophie's confession that she had herself written the letter to her sister, he had let go of the steering-wheel for a moment, and the car had suddenly struck something hard. Amery did not remember being startled, nor did he remember making a decision, and the idea that he had tried to commit suicide seemed absurd to him. Only when he heard that Sophie had entered a Slovak convent did this thought pursue him again. Wrapped in blankets, facing a golden forest where a pair of buzzards flew above paper kites, he admitted to himself not only that he had done everything wrong, but that, with a new start, he was about to make the same mistakes.

Back home it was May before he finally went outdoors again. In the parks the lilac was in bloom, the windows of the Czech High School shimmered in the grey façade, and the double row of acacias was green. Amery forgot why he felt himself to be between so many temptations, took off his hat, and was surprised when a passer-by responded with a similar gesture.

'Hitler in Rome – Pius XII leaves the Holy City' he read on a newspaper stand, and the difference it made, reading news between his own four walls and here in the street, confused him even more.

When he received his call-up papers, he sent his old certificate of exemption, but had to go for a medical where he was declared unfit for military service. At the beginning of July he asked Christine during lunch whether she would buy a car for him, a roadster if possible, he didn't mind what make. He wanted to go to Dubislav for the summer. She smiled, pulled at the lobe of her ear, and asked how long he would be away.

'Until it starts to snow,' Amery said, pushed his fork under a potato and felt that Christine expected him to say something more. When I've swallowed this, I'll suggest she goes to Nice for her holidays, he thought.

'I'm going to Garmisch,' Christine said.

'That's better than Nice, of course,' Amery said, still chewing.

'Nice!' she exclaimed, 'In August! With my skin!'

Amey looked across the table and studied her throat. He was amazed to think that Christine had a skin which, more likely than not, stretched from her finger and toe nails to her hair, and which, because it was white, must not be exposed to the sun. He suddenly noticed how her throat blushed under his eyes right to the collar bone. He looked higher up. He had not been mistaken. Only her nose remained white for a while, like a small iceberg in a sea of tomato soup. So it was Garmisch and a lover, or something? My God, she might have been prepared for this moment! Green, he said, to calm her, green would be the colour he'd like best for the bodywork. But it didn't help. Her nose too turned red. Amery continued to eat. When the maid came to serve the dessert, Christine was once again as pale as her napkin.

The headlights of the Walter coupé were painted over in blue paint like the street-lamps in the town, to comply with the black-out regulations. War might start overnight.

'Perhaps it's quite a good idea for you to be in Germany for the next few weeks,' Amery said when they said goodbye.

'That's what I think,' said Christine and gave him her hand.

She's a bit like a horse, Amery thought while descending the stairs. One can see by her eyes that she would like to lift up her forefeet and smash your skull, but insteads she sticks her teeth into her nosebag and snorts.

In Dubislav he heard from his gamekeeper's mother that Hanusch and his wife had gone to the shooting lodge to tidy up and light the fire. So Christine had let them know that he was coming. Amery turned on to the path between the two hills, and heard the stones drum against the bottom of the car. Hanusch and his wife stood outside the door to take the luggage, and for the first time since Amery had employed him, Hanusch addressed him in German. When Amery asked why, Hanusch said, 'Because we are Germans.'

'I didn't know,' Amery said to Frau Hanusch.

'Oh yes. Now we're getting anatomy!'

'Autonomy,' her husband corrected her and put Amery's trunk on his shoulder.

Amery asked them to bring him food every three days as on earlier visits, milk, eggs, bread and meat, but when he saw the massive man and his dainty wife walk down the path to Dubislav, he was sorry that he hadn't said a conciliatory word. He promised himself to make up for it later, but on the Tuesday when Hanusch called at the house he was out walking, and later, in August, he forgot about it.

In the dog days the forest hummed. When Amery clambered up to a hide, the bark crumbled under his fingers. The fir trees shed their needles. The puddles dried out until the mud cracked. The flies left the dead frogs to buzz around his perspiring neck. In the county town nearby, where Amery ate on Sundays, the people stood about in the market-place after church and looked at the fenced-in piece of lawn in which the first mushrooms usually grew at this time of year, but this year there was only dry grass. The women from the cottages in their black national costume, white kerchiefs knotted under their chins, and the townswomen in dark dresses and beige hats with the brims turned up on the left side like former colonial troops, stayed in the shade of the lime trees and glanced across at the men who took their cigarettes out of their mouths to spit, pushed their hats to the backs of their necks, and looked at the sky as if they were expecting rain. When the local policeman came by they bent down to tie their shoes, or turned to read the names of the dead on the war memorial, so as not to have to acknowledge the Czech sergeant.

In spite of the heat, Amery went everywhere on foot. At home he threw himself on his bed, pressed his face into the pillow, headaches making him moan, his shoulder jerking as it used to do. In the evenings he went downstairs, wound up the gramophone, and put on a record of Gigli.

That lunchtime at the Swan, one of the young holiday makers had rubbed her naked foot against the leg of a table for so long, that the same cold eddies had formed around her and Amery as when Christine had first visited him in his bachelor apartment, a whirlpool of greed instead of desire, panting and rapturous. The girl's husband put his pint down hard on the table, then clinked his wedding ring against the glass. Her toes had hesitatingly made their way back into the high-heeled sandals, and the fingers which closed the buckle seemed to repeat a well-remembered movement. Memory crawled over him like insects. A marriage was a marriage. *'Lasciate mi morire'*, sang the Italian. The pitch seemed a little low, but then perhaps the turntable didn't go round fast enough.

At the end of August, Hanusch offered to buy the shooting lodge and woods. Both his breast pockets were full of cigars as if he were making the round of the woodmen's cottages before Christmas. He smelled of schnapps and spoke German. On his left lapel he wore a badge which Amery did not recognise in the light of the open fire. He did not want to refuse immediately.

'Have you got so much money?'

'The Czechs are selling their land cheaply,' he said, and lit his cigar from the fire.

'How's that?'

'Because of Lord Runciman, Tschaimberlain's mediator. Don't you listen to the radio?'

'I haven't turned it on since I came.'

'It would be in your own interest,' Hanusch advised, and named a ridiculous price. 'As a basis for negotiation,' he added because Amery smiled. 'Or do you think you'll get compensation when we join the Reich?'

Amery shrugged his shoulders and got up. It took the game-keeper some time to realise that the conversation was over. He looked at his cigar as if considering throwing it into the fire, but then decided to smoke it on his way home, and, knowing that Amery was watching him, wrote glowing noughts into the darkness.

A few days later a letter from Vejvoda arrived. He asked, in Christine's absence, whether it might not be advisable to sell the Falkenau factory since it 'lay in a district the ownership of which even local patriotic businessmen did not feel was guaranteed for all time'. Amery, who made the messenger wait, wrote under Vejvoda's signature, 'I am no patriot. I'm keeping the factory.' He addressed the envelope and stamped it, and sent the messenger back with the letter and a tip.

I ought to go to Prague, he said to himself while walking through the rain-soaked forest in September. But who needs, who expects me? Christine, my employees, Sellmann, Aunt Marketa or my patriotic business friends? Only his father could claim the right to speak to him. He sat amongst his faience and played rummy with his housekeeper. He didn't write letters any more. Whoever telephoned him heard the same helpless question, 'How can I be of service to you, dear sir?'

It was about twelve kilometres from Dubislav to the Bavarian frontier. On clear nights one could see the fires on the German hills. When the north wind finally cleared the sky, Amery drove to Javornik. In the smoky, crowded inn he asked the landlord, who had always bought his game from Amery's woods, to give him the key to the tower on top of the hill.

'There's already somebody up there,' was the answer.

The tower stood on a wooded, cone-shaped hill a quarter of an hour from the village. As he approached, Amery heard some men talking in the broad dialect of the region. They fell silent the moment they saw him, and when he asked about the key they went to stand in front of the entrance.

'The tower is occupied,' a German suddenly said behind him.

'Pity,' Amery said to the stranger and felt his hands grow cold and numb. 'I wanted to look at the fires.'

'Sorry,' a voice called out of the darkness. 'Perhaps some other time.'

The man behind him stood aside, and Amery went away.

When he opened the door of his house he noticed that it had been double-locked which was not his habit. He stood in the hall for a while and listened to the well-known noises of the house. He flung the door to the main room open and turned on the light. It smelled of cold smoke as always when he had forgotten to empty the ashtray. He lit the fire, wound up the gramophone, and put the needle into the groove of the start of the second movement of the Dvorak cello concerto. Later he checked all the upstairs rooms, but found nothing suspicious, but after he had turned the record over he suddenly saw a splintered piece of wood by the gun cabinet, the same piece which had been planed, lacquered and refitted after Karol had broken open the cupboard. Amery put his hand in the opening and the door swung back. It was empty of guns and ammunition and even the cleaning rods were missing. Professionals.

Next morning Amery drove to the county town. The police station gave the impression of a beleaguered fortress. He had to show his documents to the sentinels at the entrance, and again to the duty officer in the guard room. Amery told his story and was then taken to the sergeant's office where he told it again. Under the window stood a light machine gun, and on the table lay a gun belt with a gun in the unbuttoned holster. In the corner, next to the filing cabinet, stood four rifles crossed like a tepee.

The sergeant nodded and opened a drawer of his desk, and Amery expected him to take down his statement. Instead he took out a brown medicine bottle and counted fifteen drops on to a lump of sugar which he held in a tin spoon.

'To keep me calm,' he said and wiped his mouth with his sleeve. 'Would you like some?'

'No, thank you,' Amery said.

'We'll pursue the matter in due course,' the sergeant announced and pressed the cork back into the bottle.

'I have a definite suspicion,' Amery said.

'German or Czech.'

'German,' Amery replied. 'It is a question of a man whom I . . .'

'That's bad,' the sergeant interrupted. 'At the moment it would be madness. I can't order the search of a German's house.'

'And if they should shoot you with my guns?'

'I'll die of heart failure. Anyway, our boys are lying in the woods. They'll soon see to things with a few fowling-pieces. Or the English will come. We're not alone in the world. By the way, why have you not been called up, Herr Amery?' he suddenly asked. 'Is your year not due yet?'

'I am ill.'

'Heart?'

Amery tapped his right index finger against his forehead.

'That's dangerous too,' the sergeant agreed and put out his hand towards the holster. 'I'll come and see you in the next few days to see whether there are any clues. Until then you must not touch the cupboard. You promise?'

'No,' said Amery.

'Oughtn't you to go and see a doctor?'

Amery went past the sentinels and walked across the slippery cobbles to his car. When he drove through Dubislav, Hanusch stood by his door and took off his hat to him.

On the Monday a police car brought the sergeant with the heart condition and two young policemen who stood on the meadow before the house and made water.

'The radio,' the sergeant called, short of breath and without greeting.

'Are these your finger-print experts?' asked Amery.

'Don't let's have any of your jokes,' he shouted at Amery. 'You'll be liable to criminal proceedings.'

'How?'

'Tonight Hitler speaks over all German radio stations.'

'But I am Czech,' Amery contradicted.

'I had to give up my radio as well,' the sergeant whispered. 'Before the law all men are equal. Well, get on with it, boys,' he said to his men. 'You haven't come here just to piss. Where is the radio?'

'On the chest of drawers,' Amery said, and the policemen vanished into the house.

The sergeant mopped his brow with a large chequered handkerchief. One of the policemen roared, 'The gramophone too?'

'No,' the sergeant called and shook his head, smiling, as if to say, that's the type one has to deal with! Then he said, 'Sometimes one longs for death, and then one is sorry again that one has to die.'

'Yes,' Amery said.

That night a noise at the front door woke him. It was not Frau Hanusch's double knock but a modest, almost respectful rap. Amery went into the hall, turned on the light, and drew his loden coat over his pyjamas. Outside it mizzled with rain.

'Who is it?'

'Schramek,' was the answer, 'From Dubislav, the basket maker. Could I disturb you for a moment?'

'Are you alone?'

'To be sure,' the unknown replied, and he could be heard scraping his shoes on the cement step. When Amery opened the door he climbed out of his rubber boots, took off his hat and stood in thick black wool socks on the doorstep, a small, thin and pale man around fifty.

'I really don't want to trouble you,' he said when Amery asked him to come in, and would 'on no account' sit down.

'What can I do for you?' asked Amery and remembered his own father.

'I expect you've already packed,' Schramek said without looking around him.

'No?' Amery asked.

'Oh,' said Schramek and sighed. 'If you're staying . . .' he put his right foot on his left and scratched his toes. 'Well, you have this nice house and the land. We'd thought you might take us as far as Mirotice. It's on your way. My wife has relations in Ostrovec. Perhaps I can make a new start there. We'd have to take my tools and the beds. There are only the two of us. My daughter is married, but our relationship with our son-in-law is a bit difficult. I'd not like to be a burden to him. It is better to stand on one's own feet. Or do you think the Wehrmacht will march straight on?

221

General Syrový said on the radio that new frontiers would be fixed, but a fortnight ago he still wanted to defend the old ones, and now the Germans are down the road. Tomorrow it'll be our turn. They're already sewing flags in the village to welcome them.'

'Do at least sit down,' Amery said.

Schramek unbuttoned his coat and hung the coat-tails over the arms of the chair when he sat down. He looked like a great, grey bird that has been half drowned and half plucked.

'In times of change like these, one's liable to get hurt,' he said. 'And sometimes only because one had a fight years ago with some snotnosed boy who's now grown up. Hoffmann, also a Czech, just jumped on his motor bike when he heard that we're to get over our disappointment and pain so that the nation can take courage again. But he's got a brother in Kolín with a repair shop.'

Amery lit a cigarette, and while he smoked in silence he looked again and again at the thick black home-knitted socks.

'Would you help me pack?' he finally asked.

'Of course,' Schramek exclaimed and was immediately on his feet.

'No,' Amery said. 'Go into the kitchen. On the top shelf there is a bottle of turpentine. Clean the colour off the headlights.'

Schramek ran into the corridor and found the right door. From his window Amery, who was changing his clothes, saw Schramek in the light of the outside lamp stand barefoot in front of the car, wiping the headlights with his socks. At midnight they drove to Dubislav.

'I'll stay in the car,' Amery said in front of the basket maker's house. 'Bring everything you have.'

After Schramek had got out he heard steps which stopped beside the open side-window.

'Good evening, Hanusch,' Amery said.

'Off to Prague?'

'Yes.'

'I've got the contract here, if you'd care to . . .'

'I've thought about it,' Amery said. 'I'm giving the house to my wife. She's German.'

Hanusch bent down to look into Amery's face.

'But what I wanted to ask you is that I've cut a lot of grass and have had to leave it. Please make sure that it is cleared away. So that the meadow doesn't spoil.'

'All right,' Hanusch replied and stood up.

'And when you put the guns back, make sure you put them back in the right order. The key is on the back wall.'

Hanusch put his hands against the roof of the car as if he had decided to overturn it. But at that moment Frau Schramek appeared with featherbeds over her arms.

'Excuse me,' she said, and Amery opened the door for her against Hanusch's chest. The gamekeeper watched for a while as the basket maker's tools, saucepans, sieves and cake-tins were stowed away in the back of the car. Then he turned and went away.

When Amery wanted to turn into the main road to Strakonice, an army captain forced him to stop. A column of grey tanks rattled past, followed by lorries full of infantry soldiers.

Amery got out and asked the captain whether this was the last division.

'Yes, the last,' the captain said. His chin trembled, and he suddenly sobbed like a child. He straightened his back, but a second bout of weeping made him bend forward so far that his cap fell into the mud, and it looked as if he were bowing to the withdrawing soldiers. Amery picked up the cap and held it out to him. On the captain's face rain and tears intermingled. The face reminded Amery of Sixta, of the winter evening when he had thought he was being blackmailed, of the mixture of despair and obstinacy, and the wet, incredulous eyes in the 'vale of tears'.

'Thank you,' said the captain. 'Go with God.'

'Now the cock ought to crow,' Amery said.

'How?' asked the captain. 'What do you mean?'

But Amery was already on his way back to his car.

Since he could not overtake the slow military transport it was daylight before they got to Strakonice. On the road to Pisek the clouds tore apart. The wind blew the morning mist and the poplar leaves towards the east. Women in blue skirts, with large baskets hanging from their arms, followed behind the potato-diggers across the fields. Schramek and his wife had gone to sleep and woke up only at Ostrovec when Amery asked them where their relations lived.

Amery arrived in Prague about ten in the morning. After his sleepless night he got his second wind as he unlocked the door to the apartment and asked through the half-open door whether his wife had had breakfast. When he got no reply he pushed the door open.

'It isn't my fault,' a strange maid said in German, pressing her back against the dresser. Amery learnt that she had been hired two weeks before because her predecessor hadn't wanted to work for Christine any more, and that his wife was already at work. He gave her the key, and she brought his case from the car.

When they had lunch together, Christine insisted that Amery had changed. Lightly and cursorily she told him about Garmisch, her parents, and the business. Stocks would last until Christmas. After that they might have to import china, change to ceramics, or enlarge their cutlery division. She had made enquiries in all three directions, so that he need not worry. If necessary, there'd still be Falkenau.

'It was a good idea of yours to buy the factory in my name,' said Christine. 'A good idea,' she repeated while she took a piece of pear from her fruit salad. 'You sometimes have good ideas.'

If she says 'good idea' once more, Amery thought, I'll stuff so many pears into her throat that she suffocates.

'How do you like the new maid?' asked Christine and licked her lips.

'Nice,' Amery replied.

'You see, I have good ideas too sometimes,' Christine said and got up. 'I'm afraid I've got to go back to the shop. But Marianne makes excellent coffee.'

Amery declined the coffee, went into his room and lay down on his bed without taking off his jacket. He spent the evening with his father, and heard the latest joke from the housekeeper.

'For three hundred years we suffered under Austrian rule. Because of its exceptional success, the performance will now be repeated.'

When he got home, the maid told him that his wife was with her parents in Bubenech. Amery took the opportunity to explain to Marianne his daily routine, and what her duties would be.

'You don't go out at all, sir?'

'No,' he assured her, but added, when he saw her amazed expression, 'Perhaps in the spring.'

'Very good,' she said, and stifled her laughter.

Book Three

I

The Convent

BELOW BRATISLAVA, HIDDEN by dams and thick woods, the Small Danube leaves the Large Danube and does not rejoin it until it has taken on several tributaries and produced countless side-streams. In the north-west corner of the island formed by the two rivers lay the Provincial House of the Sisters of Mercy. It was a large, two-storey building. In summer, damp, warm air blew up from the Danube and warped the window frames, blew mildew on the tracts, pressed on heart and temples, and made phlox and rosemary flourish. In winter the snow piled up as high as the top of the iron fence.

The windows of the refectory, the library and the chapel were at the front. Two wings joined the main building containing the hospital and the school, the cells of the Sisters, the dormitories of the novices and the guest bedrooms. Beyond the gatehouse was the room for visitors, the office of the Sister Bursar, and a roomy kitchen which supplied the refectory on the floor above by a food elevator. The church, a fourteenth century Gothic building with a Romanesque core, was reached through a doubly-secured corridor. It stood on the edge of the vegetable garden, with its main doors facing on to the main street of the village. The high altar showed Christ on the cross with two Sisters of Mercy at his feet, the left-hand Sister supporting an invalid, the one on the right teaching a boy to pray.

In the hospital they treated only abscesses, appendix, broken bones, toothache, burns, marsh-fever, dislocated joints and alcohol poisoning after the big holidays. Dr. Packa sent more difficult cases to the Bratislava hospitals, unless the patients preferred to die more cheaply and comfortably in their own beds. Lessons in the two-class school were from seven o'clock until eleven, and when the pupils didn't have to help with the harvest they came back in the afternoon to learn to knit, weave, make lace, sew and do pottery. Of the forty-two nuns, sixteen worked in the hospital, three in the school, and four in the kitchen. The rest were postulants and novices, the Mother Superior, the Novice Mistress, the Sister Bursar and the Portress. Two Sisters prayed day and night in the small choir.

The Mother Superior, Mother M. Regina, was a lean, friendly woman in her fifties. Modesta, the oldest of the sisters, called 'the owl' because of her half-closed eyes, believed in the influence of the moon on the soul, alarmed the novices with dark prophecies when the conjunctions were unfavourable, and did not eat in the refectory on such days, but demanded that whoever was serving at table leave the meal outside her door. The Novice Mistress, Kasimira, frequently quarrelled with her on the subject, and swore by all that is holy that Mother Modesta was a gipsy and read the cards in her cell.

Sister Blanka had the most admirers. She was the head Sister of the hospital and a Slovak, a big, round woman with a broad red face, and she saved the day by just entering a room. Dr. Packa said, 'She is worth more than injections and tablets, and a better diagnostician than I to boot.' The younger girls were sorry that they saw her only at meals and at prayers but hardly ever during their recreation; Sister Blanka worked like a horse.

Most of the convent Sisters did their duty unobtrusively and modestly. Sophie found it difficult at first to tell the faces apart. 'I feel as if I were in China,' she confessed to Sister Kasimira. But during the first winter she learned to distinguish between the Sisters, knew one by her rustling walk, another by her voice, a third because she was always late for morning prayers. By the following summer she knew all the names in alphabetical order.

The convent day began, by Sellmann standards, in the middle of the night. Whatever time of year, a wooden rattle woke them at five o'clock. With the other postulants Sophie, in a long black dress, walked into the main chapel, her rosary between her fingers, and knelt in the first pew. After a communal prayer, the Mother Superior read a devotional text. At half past five Herr Dubravec appeared and celebrated Mass. When the priest had pronounced the blessing, the kitchen Sisters left the chapel while the others sang one or two verses of a hymn. After Herr Dubravec had left, the others followed in order of seniority, after an interval of meditation which was ended at a signal from the Mother Superior. For breakfast there was malt coffee and milk, bread, butter and honey.

Until the midday prayers the postulants worked, and this would have been no trouble if Mother Modesta had not come along to remind the girls that they were not cleaning the lavatories for the sake of cleanliness, nor weeding the beds for the sake of the vegetables, but to prove their submission.

After lunch the postulants and the novices took their recreation in the craftroom, or, if the weather was fine, in the garden. They were allowed to talk together, walk up and down, mend their clothes, read, or write to relations on their name-day. Newspapers, magazines or books (apart from the New Testament, devotional literature, and the Legends of the Saints) were not available. Sister Kasimira had the key to the library.

Sophie made friends with a girl called Hanna with whom she could speak Czech. Apart from that the liturgy was in Latin, the convent language was German, and the village people spoke Slovak. After this free time, more work was done; after supper there was another hour of recreation, and then evening prayers. After nine o'clock everyone except the Sisters who worked in the hospital were in bed.

After a few weeks Sophie felt that she could live in Bucovice because nobody asked her why she lived there. The day was as long as eternity, but eternity was only a day before God. There was no doubt: the bucket was a bucket, the broom a broom. In the confessional Herr Dubravec held a white silk handkerchief in front of his face and fumigated the cells at Epiphany. In February, after Candlemas, the May children were baptised. The lid of the manure pit screeched over its cement frame: that meant it was spring. On Ascension Day the blossoms fell from the cherry trees and cucumber and lettuces were planted out. The Mother Superior and four Sisters made a pilgrimage: that was summer. When the maize was yellow as egg yolks and polished like the beads of a rosary it was autumn. On All Souls the last starlings left. After Martinmas the featherbed of the convent priest was filled with new down. On the day of the Annunciation, a drunken bricklayer climbed to the roof of the church, hung on to the cross on top, and shouted into the convent yard, 'I'll fuck you all till the feathers fly.' Mother Regina locked the postulants and novices in the library until Police Sergeant Illin announced that the good-for-nothing had fallen off the roof and broken his neck. The Superior came for a visit of inspection, looked at the books with the Sister Bursar, gave the episcopal blessing, and tasted the wine used at Mass with the Mother Superior. A year had passed and Sophie had told Hanna no more than that she had two sisters in Prague and a brother who had had an eye operation. Sometimes she thought of Amery, prayed for him, and spoke his name as if she read it in a card-index or on a signpost. She felt that she would be lost if she allowed herself to remember. In the convent there was only one man, and he hung from the cross on every wall.

When the Novice Mistress came to tell her in September that her family were in the visiting-room, she wanted to hide. Then she followed Sister Kasimira to the gatehouse, embraced her mother, father, Katharina and Heinrich. Betty cried, Sellmann spoke of the Bratislava trade fair. Katharina asked whether Sophie could go to the cinema once a month. Sophie wanted to tell them how pleased she was to see them, but could not say a word.

The visitors' room was painted white from wainscot to ceiling. A water-colour of Kaschau Cathedral, painted from a photograph, hung on the wall. They sat on leather chairs around a high table covered in a lace cloth.

'You're content here?' Betty asked.

'Yes, very,' Sophie said. She felt like a fish that has been enticed to the glass wall of the aquarium. Two or three strokes of her fins, and she could vanish behind some stones or water-plants. She passed her hand over her forehead.

'One can hardly see the scar,' Katharina said.

'Tomorrow we are going to Theben Castle and the grave of Rabbi Nathan,' Heinrich said.

'Chatan,' Sellmann corrected. 'Chatan Sopher, the wonder-Rabbi from Frankfurt.' He was about to add something, but was silent when Sister Kasimira cleared her throat.

Betty suddenly moved her chair close and put her arm around Sophie's shoulder. She did not say anything. Sophie felt the warmth penetrate her skin through her mother's suit and her own dress, and this was the happiest memory of her visit.

As she walked along the corridor on her own to fetch her apron, she met Sister Modesta.

'Your parents?'

Sophie nodded.

Sister Modesta opened her eyes wide. The pupils were black, and the green irises were speckled in yellow.

'Those who think too much get pimples,' she said and lowered her lids.

'I'll remember.'

Sister Modesta put her mouth close to Sophie's ear. 'I'm going to die next week,' she whispered. 'Nobody suspects. They'll be surprised. You're a good child. But don't you believe that every-thing is behind you. The best is still to come. Life, you understand? Life. I know everything. I've cast your horoscope. Half cancer, half leo, a good mixture. Think of me when you push your first baby through the streets. Give me your left hand.'

Sister Modesta stepped under the high window with Sophie, looked at the folds between the line of the heart and the little finger, and pushed the edge of the hand under her nose. When Sister Kasimira appeared at the end of the corridor she let go of Sophie's hand and vanished into her cell.

'Your family is talking with the Mother Superior,' Sister Kasimira said. 'Would you like to go and rest a little?'

Sister Modesta died on the 11th September. The local people took the washing off the lines, chased the chickens into the coops and the children into the house, for the local gipsies came to Bucovice, tied their horses to the fences and stood around the grave. The men pressed their hats against their jackets and the women sobbed.

'So I was right all the time,' Sister Kasimira said.

In June of the following year, Sophie was told by the Mother Superior that Sister Kasimira's quarterly report was so favourable that nothing now stood in the way of her admission to the novitiate. She therefore asked whether she might let His Eminence the Lord Archbishop know that Sophie was ready to take the veil. Sophie, who was on her knees, said, 'Yes, Reverend Mother, I beg you, and may God reward you.'

Mother Regina was visibly touched. She raised Sophie up and made her sit on a stool. 'I've been keeping a letter for some time,' she said and went to her desk. 'I want to give it to you today. It contains nothing objectionable, but I wanted to wait until you had made your decision. The sender is Herr Pavel Sixta.'

'Please burn the letter,' Sophie said.

'No,' Mother Regina said, and gave her the open envelope. 'If I were you, I'd send Herr Sixta my condolences. We have a condolence-form for that.'

Sophie read Sixta's letter in the lavatory until she knew it by heart. Then she tore it up.

'Dear Fräulein Sophie,' he had written on the 12th January, 1939.

Perhaps you have heard from your parents that I am working as music teacher at the Budweis Grammar School. When the news of the capitulation came through the loudspeakers of Wenceslas Square, I didn't want to remain in Prague. Since the day before yesterday I have an added sorrow. My father is dead. My mother and I were with him in his last hours. He had cancer of the gall-bladder and was conscious to the last. When I asked him if he was in pain he nodded, but refused another morphine injection. He said something that to my mind is quite extraordinary. I hope that it does not offend your religious feelings if I repeat it. He said, "For a man like me, dying is the only occasion for showing one's courage." He worked for the same firm for forty years, first as messenger, then in book-keeping, and finally as chief cashier. He wasn't able to take part in the war because of his poor health. His name was Vaclav, Wenceslas. His name-day is on the 28th September. Perhaps you would pray for him? As far as I know, the rules of your order forbid a reciprocal correspondence, but the Reverend Mother Superior may allow me to write to you occasionally. Budweis is a small town, and it would be a solace to me. I want to assure you that I would make no unseemly (I found this word in the dictionary and hope it is the right one!) use of such permission.

A few days later, walking in the garden, Sophie asked Hanna, 'What sort of a capitulation was there last year?'

'No idea,' her friend replied and held her face up to the sun.

It had been arranged that the postulants would become novices, and the novices take their first vows on the Feast of the Assumption of the Blessed Virgin during High Mass. The week before there were thunderstorms by day and night, and the Mother Superior ordered prayers against storms to be said at each Mass. The lightning lit up the dormitory and Sophie pushed her feet against the end of her bed, overwhelmed by memories. She spoke the litanies of the Mater Dolorosa, of the holy angels and of the sacred heart, and ran in memory along Charvat Lane in the rain, put on her white linen dress with the blue-spotted cuffs, saw the tram stop and the straw hat, the Spanish Hall, the name on the door 'Olga Siebenschein', flew to Franzensbad, wrote the letter to Christine once more.

Hanna threw off her blanket and turned to Sophie. 'What are you thinking?'

'Of my vows.'

'Me too,' Hanna whispered, and with the knowledge that they had lied to each other, they lay awake until it got light.

Monsignor Atány celebrated the Mass for the Archbishop. He kissed the cross on the stole and looked through the peep-hole into the crowded church. He waited until nine o'clock had finished striking and stepped behind the acolytes on to the altar carpet.

'*Dominus Vobiscum*,' he sang.

'*Et cum spiritu tuo*,' came the answer.

After the Credo the postulants were given their dresses and the novices their veils. The novices took their vows of poverty, chastity and obedience. When they left in procession, the bells pealed and the congregation sang the Salve Regina. With the relatives of the other girls, the Sellmanns were invited to a small reception in the library where Monsignor Atány repeated some passages of his sermon. Betty was anxious to get back to their hotel in Bratislava. The Mass which had lasted more than three hours had exhausted her. Sophie kissed her parents goodbye. Then she sat down beside Hanna on her bed.

'Why are you so happy?'

'Since this morning I believe that one can touch God,' Sophie said and showed the little gap between her teeth.

2

Sixta's Letters

30th October 1939

Dear Fräulein Sophie. I have asked the local establishment of your Order whether I might write to you, and have been told that the decision must rest with the Mother Superior of your convent and with you. So if nobody forbids me, I'll write to you occasionally without expecting an answer. The conversation will be a bit one-sided, but I'm glad to know that somebody is listening to me. Budweis is the most boring town in the world, and this hasn't altered since I've been hired to explain chromatic scales and the sonata form.

Since the beginning of the school year, Georg, the sixteen-year-old son of a cousin, is living with my mother and me. I think that if it were up to him he'd stay for the rest of his life!

At night I'm working on an opera using as a libretto the drama *The Last Judgment* by Ödön von Horvath. I saw the first performance and got the text through an agency. The piece is very suitable for an opera since it has a simple story.

Hudetz, the stationmaster, forgets to set a signal because he is being embraced by Anna, the innkeeper's daughter, and causes an accident. Anna swears before a court of law that Hudetz had set the signal. Hudetz is acquitted, but Anna cannot endure the thought of her perjury. Hudetz kills her and confesses to the murder after meeting the dead engine driver killed in the accident to the express train. The rest of the cast is made up by Frau Hudetz, by Anna's father, Anna's fiancé and others.

It remains, of course, a project to be put aside for some future day. As far as I know the author has emigrated to France. But I'm not going to think ahead. In any case, I hate showing my compositions around. Perhaps the reason is that we all live outwards rather than inwards.

When I go to Prague in December, I shall try to telephone your parents. Do you know that the conductors on the Prague trams call out the stations in two languages now?

8th May, 1940

Spring has broken out like a silent war. The daisies advance to the attack, the apple-blossom explodes, the tulips draw their green swords, the corn is shooting up in the fields. Swallows and newly-weds are building houses. My mother thinks I ought to buy a piece of land – it's cheap at the moment – and marry, because I'm often ill. She's afraid I'll have no nurse if she dies. [The next sentence deleted by the Mother Superior.] But my ailments are really what keeps me alive! There's nothing better than to sit by the window with a cold and a pot of tea, and to look out at all the healthy people running after happiness on their strong legs.

You'll have to think of my opera *The Last Judgment* without spoken dialogue. I've remained faithful to the division into seven scenes, but I have drawn some parts together so that it sounds very 'recitative', or, to put it another way, it sounds as if the singers pulled one single big melody to pieces and threw the bits at each other. In the middle of it all trumpets bray, and when the imaginary express train goes past, two men – they needn't be professional musicians – scrape two sharp razors on the rim of a zinc bathtub. I'd like to use humming voices, but then it would sound like the thunderstorm in the third act of *Rigoletto*. It is frightening, but you mustn't worry, *The Last Judgment* will never be performed, and even if [the following lines deleted by the Mother Superior].

My nephew would like to start an amateur dramatic company with me and some others. He thinks, probably rightly, that his talent for cheating is a natural basis for acting. An older pupil, who failed the entrance exam to drama school, has explained to him the various exercises that each candidate has to perform at his audition. Since then he tries to imitate a man who bites into a lemon, scrubs some stairs, and – Exercise III – suddenly meets a lion in the street. My mother is sometimes taken in by him, especially when he practises at mealtimes. [The rest deleted by the Mother Superior.]

4th October, 1940

Dear Fräulein Sophie. Your sister Katharina has let me know that I deprive you of your monthly letter from your parents if I write to you outside the high holidays. But today is St. Francis', and I expect this is a special day of celebration for you.

I went to Prague for two weeks in the summer holidays and stayed with Professor Vavra. The hotels were crowded with Germans in uniform and civilian clothes. They were celebrating the victory over France with ham and chocolates. My former friends were out of town, and the first night I had to sleep in the station waiting-room. Next morning I went to see Fräulein Kalman, and she sent me to Vavra. Since his dismissal he works as an archivist and photographer (!) for his brother who is doing research for the Italian Academy of sciences. It concerns the reappraisal of the Roman fragments from Kouřim which have been lying in the National Museum for years. Good that, don't you think?

We went to visit a colleague of Vavra's who, until last year, was a professor of the psychology of language. He makes his wife lock him up every evening so as not to drink. He doesn't want to drink because he doesn't want to run into the street, and he doesn't want to run into the street because he doesn't want to scream, and he doesn't want to scream because he doesn't want to be locked up.

When one travels from Prague to Budweis, life gets slower and the key changes. The people from the provinces talk about how hard they find it to get used to driving on the right, and then they screw up their eyes and look out of the window because it suddenly reminds them of something they don't want to think about. When they get out, they leave these thoughts in the train *Praha locuta, causa finita* – that's all over. Prague held its peace, it did not speak.

I'm not sorry that I went. I think I wrote you that in the spring my nephew urged me to go in for amateur theatricals. Professor Vavra suggested *Lucerna* by Jirásek. The premiere is to be at the beginning of December. Georg wanted to play the miller's daughter! I don't know what's come over the boy. When, with a great deal of difficulty, he'd been dislodged from the part, he began to lacquer his nails and paint his lips, and my mother even caught him heating up her old curling tongs over the spirit stove. I gave him another part in the play, and he was hardly angry at all. It's enough for him just to be on the stage.

The Last Judgment is finished and put aside. Now I'm working on the *Song of the Sun* of St. Francis. (Do you notice now that I have a special reason for writing you today?) I don't want to translate it, but am leaving it in the original Umbrian. *Lo sole* is neuter in Czech, *la luna* masculine. Imagine what it would be like in German: 'Brother Moon' and 'Sister Sun'!

I find it hard to say goodbye to you, but I have to go to the rehearsal, and want today's datestamp on this letter.

11th February, 1941

I didn't send off my Christmas letter to you because I couldn't understand my stammerings myself. A week ago the lawsuit against my nephew came on, so I waited until today.

Our amateur dramatic premiere was a great success. The town council even asked some of the officers of the German garrison with their ladies, and though they presumably didn't understand a word, they applauded after every scene as enthusiastically as our Czech public. Afterwards Georg introduced me to Captain Groschup and his wife, and I found out that he has been frequenting their house. 'Frequent' is perhaps not the right word. Georg has been maid of all work there. For a few krone he has been helping with the washing and ironing. We'd arranged for a second performance for the following weekend, but I had to cancel it because Georg was on remand in prison. We didn't see him again until last week. He was accused of the theft of a passport, and unlawfully crossing the frontier.

On the Monday after the premiere, Georg had stolen Frau Groschup's passport, had put on women's clothes and shoes and a wig, and bought a ticket for Linz. He had no difficulty crossing the Austrian frontier, slept in a hotel in Linz, and took the train back to Budweis the following afternoon. By chance the same officials who had checked his passport the day before were on duty again and asked him, thinking he was Frau Groschup, whether he'd not liked Linz, coming back so soon. Georg had to answer in German, became confused and lost his nerve.

He admitted having taken the passport. 'I was practising,' he

236

said. 'I wanted to know whether I could play a woman so well that even the police didn't notice.'

Georg received a sentence of four years' juvenile detention, and the judge said that the 'magnanimous' sentence was due to the age of the accused. On the advice of his counsel, Georg accepted the judgment and apologised to us all for the bother he had caused.

You know that I've no time for heroes, but sometimes it seems to me that if nothing is changed, we're going to be a people of waiters, hairdressers, door keepers, interpreters, masseurs, shoe-cleaners, photographers, jazz trumpeters, castle guides, beer brewers, gardeners and chauffeurs. Nobody wants to make a mistake. Everyone wants security. Absolute security. It is as if one were waiting at a station which has only one line but kept asking the station master whether one were on the right platform. Why is it?

I've just been telling my pupils for the third time how Goethe took off his hat to their ducal highnesses on the Teplitz Promenade, but Beethoven didn't. I explain this year in, year out, for one can explain everything, but fundamentally I don't understand it. Why didn't he acknowledge the people who admired him? Because of the Eroica, or because of the F-minor string quartet? Do you know? [The rest deleted by the Mother Superior.]

Christmas, 1941

Thank you for your Christmas message. It was the best present you could have given me. My mother has learned the three lines of your letter by heart, and has put the sheet of paper in the drawer in which she keeps my father's wedding ring, her wedding ornaments, and my first shoes. I had to talk to her about you the whole evening, and it made me realise how little I know about you. I showed her the place where you were born on the map, and when she saw that it was on the Elbe she was pleased. 'The Fräulein isn't a stranger after all.' I played her the songs that you sang at our concert, but she was more interested in the dress you wore. She cannot understand that Bucovice is in another country which is called Slovakia and doesn't belong to us any more.

The geography teacher's subject changes from day to day. He reads the news from the front to find out where the Reich stops. 'Where exactly is Poland these days?' he asked during the last staff meeting before the holidays. 'In London,' the chemistry master said. Is Kiev German? And Norway, Holland, Belgium, France, Crete? Three and a half million Russians have been taken prisoner. Should one deduct that number from their total population? I stick my head in the sand and into books. (I've had to teach German during the last three months.)

In September I started a chamber orchestra. All old music is played too fast. People take the differences in tempi much too seriously, and the virtuosi's madness to reach the finale twenty seconds before other people make music into an obstacle race. I ask myself why these note-gobblers don't conduct at the railway station or the aerodrome. Do you know how I started the first rehearsal of my little orchestra? 'Long live amateurism! I'm sick and tired of frosty faces above instruments with sweat pouring on the double-fingering.'

Not a Christmassy letter, you'll be saying. But you'll understand and forgive. When the bells ring in the New Year, I shall be with you in thought.

28th July, 1942

Dear Sister Agnes. I am so happy that you have taken a 'Bohemian' convent name and congratulate you, also on my mother's behalf on your admission into the Order. When I heard from Fräulein Katharina that you would be taking your first vows in July, I asked for a passport to travel to Bucovice, but since the death of the Reichsprotector such requests are not granted any more. Perhaps you have heard that in revenge for the plot against Heydrich, the village of Lidice was [deleted by the Mother Superior].

A little while ago I received a summons to appear at the employment bureau with my identification papers, having 'washed my body all over'. The medical examination revealed that I am completely fit, and my employment book was stamped 'liable to service for the duration of the war'. So I'll be going to the Reich in the autumn to make grenades, cast iron, or build air-raid shelters. Many places need workers, including Dessau! But who will there be then to explain to my pupils why Dvorak preferred to breed pigeons instead of writing the symphony about Niagara Falls?

8th October, 1942

I am celebrating my thirtieth birthday in a barracks just outside Dessau. I am working at the Junkers factory, issuing tools. Why did you write to your father that I was liable for work in the Reich? Do you worry about me? In any case, many thanks.

We sleep eight to a room. In other factories there are hundreds in a dormitory. To distinguish us from the Germans with their

round insignia, ours are square, in several colours. Some benches
and public lavatories are marked FOR GERMANS ONLY, so
that one knows the people sitting there aren't foreigners.

We work from seven in the morning until six at night, with an
hour's break. I've already learned a lot of new words: beam-
compasses, punch, circular file, slide-gauge, worm-drill, flat chisel.
I live with two office workers from Budweis, an ex-student from
Prague, a waiter from Melnik, a joiner from Pardubice, and two
men who never speak, not even with each other. One's bound
to search for a while for one's pitch; none of us knows just what
tone to take. Only the waiter has had no difficulty. He's bellowed
from the first day. The office workers whisper, the joiner growls,
the two men who never speak have no problem, and the student
says everything in a deep bass, every word weighing two kilos. I
speak 'con sordino'. We are treated correctly, and misunderstand-
ings are usually our own fault. When a German engineer asked
about a certain delivery yesterday, I answered in too much detail.
He looked at me for a while and then said, 'I don't really want to
have a conversation with you when I ask a simple question.' He
could have said, 'Shut your trap', but he didn't.

Though I am free after work, I don't like the look of the barrier
between us and the outside world. Perhaps that's the reason why
I haven't been into the town yet. I can see a small pine forest out
of my window, and I already know how to reach the part of town
where you used to live. Your father was kind enough to give me
a letter of introduction to Herr Grützke, who is not only his
successor at the bank, but also lives in the same house. I shall
visit him next week.

20th December, 1942

Yesterday I went to see *Lohengrin*. Herr Grützke, your father's
successor lent me his box. The orchestra played splendidly. I love
the overture. It is as if a stone fell into water and drew great
circles, until the subject covers the whole surface and then sinks
down into itself. A huge stage! Even a real meadow on the banks
of the River Scheldt couldn't be any larger.

I was astonished by the ease with which people moved about
during the interval. I had expected them to march about in rows
of three in step through the foyer. Instead the place was crowded
with people in evening dress and dinner jackets like in the old
days. Very few uniforms, no Hitler salutes, no clicking heels. I
told myself: these are the people amongst whom Sophie Sellmann
grew up, her playfellows, schoolfriends and teachers. I'd have

liked to have gone up to somebody and asked them if they remembered a dark-haired girl with big dark eyes and a tiny gap between her front teeth and [deleted by the Mother Superior]. But I can't even approach those who are closest to me in my present situation. I long for friendship, but I can only manage the bare courtesies. In these three months my comrades have told each other everything that they know about themselves. I listen, but I can't give anybody anything. I feel that my soul is wounded, and I believe that I can protect my innermost being best by tucking my head under my shell like a tortoise the moment anyone comes close. My father used to say that there are two ways of chopping wood: you either hit the tree with the axe, or you hit the axe with the tree. [The rest deleted by the Mother Superior.]

11th July, 1943

I am writing this letter by the river at one of the beaches where foreign workers can bathe. Please excuse possible spots of oil.

In February, during the three-day mourning for Stalingrad, Herr Grützke took me for a walk through the town and led me to a place in the public gardens near the station where there was nothing but snow and rhododendrons. 'This is where the statue of Mendelssohn used to stand,' he said and quickly pulled me away. Now I've made a mess of the paper after all! Forgive me!

There are a lot of girls and women with children here. They look at us askance. They think of us as shirkers, lying in the sun while their men defend Sicily and Kursk. But the dear ladies ought to see from our Slav bullet-heads, our Mongolian cheekbones, and Kirghiz bandy legs how unfit for military service we are. Even I find that the waiter from Melnik makes me think, especially in swimming trunks, of Ghengis Khan *redivivus*. [The rest of the letter deleted by the Mother Superior.]

24th December, 1943

Everybody is writing. When I close my eyes, seven pens scratch over paper. It is as if seven mice were in the wall. The Budweisers have baked a Christmas bun, but the waiter, who is the senior in our room, doesn't want to cut it until tomorrow. The Italians have been given an extra allowance of red wine and are singing.

You can't imagine what your Christmas letter means to me. But why do you write that I must not despair? I don't feel like despairing. I've gained six kilos since I got here, and haven't been ill once. You'd hardly recognise me. In my blue overalls I look like a mechanic. I play football, drink beer, wash my hands in turpentine and pumice stone, and wear my hair three centimetres long, swear like a trooper and have muscles like a prize fighter. Once a fortnight I put on my disguise and eat dinner at the Grützke villa. I go for the Bechstein grand rather than the food. Frau Grützke has given me a suit which belonged to her son who has been killed, also two shirts. I can stay until coffee which means I have two hours alone at the piano. Last week I played and sang a few pieces from the 'Echo from Italian Folk Songs' and, at the request of Frau Grützke, the *Winterreise*.

No, no despair, Sister Agnes, only a certain aversion to life. But if you mean that I'm sad, then you're right.

At the beginning of October I bicycled to Zerbst. I went to the castle and looked at the cedar cabinet and the famous stairs in the east wing. Unfortunately I didn't go to the Wildfowler, but if the defensive battles go on as successfully as they do now, there should be plenty of time. What was the name of the village with the big chestnut trees? And your uncle? I have forgotten his name.

On the return journey I took the ferry. The meadows were very still, and the river smooth, almost without movement, although it pushed our boat across. I had bought myself half a pound of stewed plums in a crock. I sat down on the embankment, stuck my finger in the plums and finished the whole pot. I've always hoped for such an autumn. The horizon is wider than ours at home: one cannot grasp it. This is the landscape of the novel, not of music. I think composers always come from mountainous country. The first movement of the Dvorak G-minor concerto would be unthinkable here. One would imagine somebody was getting het-up, wouldn't know why, looking in vain for a reason.

Just before I got back to Dessau I was stopped by a military patrol. When they sounded their hooter, and I turned round, I made a face like the drama students in Exercise III: I see a lion behind me. But nothing happened. I always carry all my papers around with me, as well as a few extra passport photographs in case I have to fill in another questionnaire. The gentlemen were astonished by so much thoroughness from a Czceh.

26th February, 1944

This is a letter for Agnes day, so don't think I'm writing out of turn. Warmest congratulations! I have not much news to tell you. Our working day has been increased by an hour, and for three weeks I was the owner of a Bechstein grand which I was allowed to keep in the barrack canteen. It was taken away yesterday, and now if I want to hear music I'll have to play on the comb or listen to the Italians.

At the end of January, Herr Grützke asked me whether I would accept a present from him. I said yes without knowing what he had in mind. Two days later the grand piano arrived at the camp in a furniture van. We had to take the pedals and legs off to get it through the door. Then everybody stood around me and I played – don't ask me what I played! I made a musette of the Marseillaise for the French, so that the overseers didn't know what they were hearing, our national anthem, too, I paraphrased beyond recognition, and so it went on right across Europe, from Lili Marlene to the Well-tempered Klavier, from Chopin to Debussy, from Grieg to Donizetti, until, towards midnight I finally fell off my chair and was carried to my bed. My fellow workers collected money for a bunch of flowers for our benefactor, and the following Sunday I rode to his house with my newspaper-wrapped bouquet of hot-house roses. But nobody opened the door, and all the blinds were down. I was about to leave and go back to the camp when someone called my name from the house next door. The jeweller, a neighbour, knew me. He told me that Herr Grützke and his wife had been buried the day before. He said it with such emphasis that there was no need to ask about the circumstances of their death. I bicycled to the cemetery, un-wrapped the flowers, and laid them on the grave. (There was a wreath from your father.) I remembered that it was almost a year to the day since Herr Grützke had shown me the place of the Mendelssohn statue.

Night after night I sat down at the piano, until a lawyer appeared at the camp yesterday with a document in his hand. Herr Grützke's sister, as sole heir, had fought the gift successfully, and the same furniture van which had brought the piano was waiting outside the barracks.

These weeks have been the best of my life except for the years in Prague between '35 and '37. After twelve hours of hellish noise on the inspection stands, after a day of hammering, racket, and the din of motors, my friends sat around me and listened with such devotion that I was doubly ashamed of every mistake.

6th July, 1944

Many happy returns of your birthday. Stay in good health. Above everything, stay in good health. We must survive this war! [Several lines deleted by the Mother Superior.] When I went for a walk by the river the other day, I happened to step close to a man who was sitting on the grass. I suddenly found myself standing behind his back and was about to turn away when he said, 'Do sit down,' without turning his head. I asked him if I had startled him. He said no. 'But you couldn't have heard me.' – 'I heard your breath.' – 'And you weren't afraid?' – 'I'm not frightened of anything now,' he said. We talked for a while. His right arm was in a sling. A grey blanket covered his legs. He said he had been wounded in Russia, but didn't say anything else about it. I thought he was a man in his forties, but he was in fact younger than I. Some time later a Red Cross nurse came along, picked him up and put him in a wheelchair. He had no legs. He waved his left hand when she set off with him. He hadn't even told me his name, though I had introduced myself. An unknown soldier of twenty-eight whom nobody could frighten any more. If no bombs fall on the hospital he'll survive this war, and we too will survive and live differently than before. The world will change although it will not end. Do you remember amongst the paintings in the chapel of the Holy Cross of Karlstejn the one of the angel on St. Matthew's shoulder, giving the evangelist the joyful tidings? I too have joyful tidings for you, Sister Agnes! There is a new time coming. It will be quite unique, meridional, naïve and actual. I long for work! I am bursting with ideas. To create life, to change life, to lose life – those are the great themes! History is standing on its head – let's put music on its feet again.

In September I'll have been here two years. They may not have been the worst. But as in some places the interval comes just when great expectations are about to be fulfilled, so it is with my life. Perhaps I'll write my next letter – for the Assumption of the Blessed Virgin – in Prague. I have asked for travel documents, since to travel around Germany like last year in my holidays will be too difficult with the constant air raids. [The rest deleted by the Mother Superior.]

3

Catnip

WHETHER SHE WORE it straight or curled, smoothed down or
pinned up, her red lustreless hair always looked like a wig. It
started up on her forehead and ended in a straight line in the
nape of her neck. Katharina had tried every kind of hairstyle
from chignon to Eton crop, but for Sophie's twenty eighth birthday she looked the same fuzzy-headed, unkempt hoyden who
had, the previous year, climbed the convent's pear tree and had
picked the yellow pears though Sister Bursar had especially forbidden it. But, in spite of such misdemeanours, Mother Kasimira,
the new Mother Superior, had again asked her to come for the
holidays.

Unlike other convent guests, Katharina did not just turn up for
meals. She had scrubbed the corridors, ironed the altar cloths,
read to bedridden half-blind Sister Ignatia night after night from
the Legends of the Saints, and done all errands in town. Nobody
had blamed her for staying out until it was almost time for vespers,
though she had gone off on her bicycle early in the morning. A
worldly girl, a student into the bargain! Why should she not go
and enjoy the attractions of Bratislava, the beautiful rococo houses,
the Ganymede fountain, or the paintings of the church fathers?
What mattered was that when she was in the convent she went to
prayers, without being asked, at all times of the day and night.
The convent had another reason for gratitude of which neither
Sophie nor Katharina knew. Sellmann's regular financial contributions during the last seven years had improved the Sisters' budget
so much that they had been able to renovate the façade of the
convent, had installed an electric mangle, and were about to
commission a portrait in oils of Mother Kasimira.

On their family visits, which they called pilgrimages to Bucovice, Sellmann had said once and for all, 'Not a word about
Amery'. But the previous year, Katharina had asked Sophie out of
simple forgetfulness whether she wanted to add her name on a

244

postcard to Christine. 'Sister Agnes' had blushed and left the room.

Such touchiness, when so much water had flowed under the bridge, seemed silly to Katharina. One had to know how to forget. 'Forgetting is the great secret of strong and creative natures,' Balzac had said. Or Goethe. Or Lao-tse. Katharina had forgotten who. She had a strong nature. Other people's romances, even her sisters', left her cold. Except when it was a man like Mieke, Christine's favourite the previous year. He had categorised the Czechs into 'racially pure right-minded' (to be returned to the Reich), 'racially impure right-minded' (to be settled in the Eastern regions), 'racially pure wrong-headed' (to be shot), and had travelled the country with an X-ray van to supplement his findings by the examination of schoolchildren.

For Mieke's sake, Katharina had not missed a single one of Christine's 'days', and had made even Christine think that she was jealous of the stylish staff-surgeon. Together with Karol she had then written a broadsheet which had brought them personal congratulations from a courier of the illegal central committee.

As for Amery, Katharina had seen him sitting on a public bench in May. She had explained that she was hurrying to an appointment, which had been no lie. She had to deliver a pair of shears with wooden handles and sharp notches in the blades, for cutting privet hedges – or brake-cables on Wehrmacht trucks. In Katharina's eyes Jan was a spineless creature. Instead of getting a divorce, he served his wife's lovers sandwiches and champagne. She was certainly not going to tell Sophie that! She didn't begrudge her her memories of her former lover.

To be on the safe side, Katharina had said, the moment she arrived at Bucovice, that she had to escort a children's transport in August. Where to? Into the Tatra Mountains. She even showed Sophie the pink railway ticket. Recently she'd made several mistakes like that. She tried to show her innocence with such determination that she made herself suspect. On the journey to Bucovice she had worn her father's civilian war medal so that her cases should not be searched. But because he noticed the decoration, the customs officer had come and sat in her compartment and had helped her down with her two suitcases before getting off the train. In the tin trunk, beneath her underclothes, she was carrying a wireless transmitter. If he had noticed the weight, she might have had to jump from the train.

Birthdays were not celebrated at the convent. But in front of Sophie's plate at lunch lay an orange on top of Sixta's letter, and Mother Kasimira was delighted to see Sophie's surprise. After the meal she gave permission for Sophie to go for a walk in the convent grounds with Katharina. They didn't go far in the July sun, but sat in the cemetery and watched the bumble bees around the larkspur, and the wasps committing suicide in a glass of Slivovitz and sugar water. The hospital windows mirrored the sky, and when one of the window panes moved, it was as if a piece of a completely blue jigsaw puzzle had been turned over to reveal its dark back.

'Why can't I help in the hospital?' Katharina asked.

'Sister Blanka doesn't want you to,' replied Sophie. 'Because of the danger of contagion.'

'And if I want to visit a patient?'

'Herr Lasko?' asked Sophie. 'He asks about you every morning.'

'I've brought him something for his stomach ulcers,' Katharina said and turned so pale that her freckles looked as if they had been stuck on. 'He's a relation of Karol's.'

'No,' Sophie said. 'And he hasn't got ulcers. Before the X-ray he swallowed some silver-paper balls. I've explained to him that the spots will be somewhere else by the next X-ray, and he maintains that his ulcers move about.'

'That's possible.'

'Not from Monday to Friday,' Sophie said.

'So why do you keep him, if he's not ill?'

Sophie stood up and shook the dry juniper needles from her white habit. 'He's waiting for you. I let him rub the thermometer until he has a temperature.'

'But that's cheating!'

'We always have a few empty beds in the summer.'

Katharina walked behind her between the graves of former Sisters to a gate which looked out on the treeless Bratislava road. A dozen grey chickens were taking dust baths in the holes in the street where puddles formed in November, making the highway look like a chain of small islands.

'I won't let you visit him,' Sophie whispered. 'It would be too dangerous. I'll take the suitcase to Lasko. I'm on night duty.'

They parted in front of the convent. 'I'll go and sleep for a bit,' Sophie said.

When she went into Katharina's room that night, she told her that they still had an hour before she had to go on duty.

'Are you afraid?' Katharina asked and crossed her trembling legs.

'No.'

'Shall I turn on the light?'

246

'What for?'

'At least sit down for a bit.'

'I sit half the night.'

Katharina took the tin trunk from under the bed and put it beside the door, expecting Sophie to question her. She had prepared herself for this all afternoon, like a prisoner for his examinaton. Why was everything so still? Sister Melitta's sandals slipslopped through the corridor, the lavatory bolt shot home. Now Sophie had said something, or asked a question. Why did she speak in such a low voice? Oh, what had become of Jan?

'You really want to know?'

'Yes.'

An hour later Sophie went across to the hospital, put down the tin trunk in the washroom and told Lasko that it was there after the day Sisters had left. Lasko nodded, took his false teeth out of the tumbler of water and put them in his mouth. Sophie heard his braces slap his shoulders and the closing of the drawer of his bedside table. Then his boots came across the linoleum, and before she could do anything he had taken her hand and kissed it.

'Go through the cemetery,' Sophie whispered and gave him the key to the gate where she and Katharina had stood, and told him where to hang the key afterwards. Lasko showed his big porcelain teeth for the last time, then she was alone with four sleeping men.

During the following night Sophie was glad when she had to renew a bandage or turn a pillow, change a sheet, but she lost all her courage when she had to sit alone behind the screen again.

What was she really waiting for? Was everything not fine as it was? Should she despair because life held just what she had expected? Or was it easier to guess at the inevitable rather than look it in the face? Like twenty years ago when she had suspected that babies weren't found under a gooseberry bush but grew inside their mother, yet had almost died of fright when the midwife had taken the chromium-plated forceps out of the boiling water on the night of Heinrich's birth. The thought that Jan might have died of a broken heart had always struck her as ridiculous. Why did it depress her suddenly to hear that he was back in the old apartment, a little reserved and cold, but ready to make a speech for Sellmann's fifty-sixth birthday? He left Christine to deal with the business since its name had been changed because the original partner had been a Jew, and he spent the summers in the country, not now in Dubislav, but in a Moravian village where he lived on bread and wine and goat cheese.

247

All was well. It was well that she had loved him, it was well that she did not love him any more. But why all this feeling of unease when she compared her own memories with Katharina's report? Why should she be thinking of the day when she wrote to Christine and, too cowardly to send the letter, had written another one without a signature, her writing disguised? And a week later she had driven to Franzensbad with Jan and had told Jan everything just beyond Pilsen and the car had turned over.

No, nothing was well. Everything was wrong and disagreeable and beastly, and she had to remember sister Arsenia to recall why she was sitting in the hospital in Bucovice. If at least Hanna had stayed. But she had left the convent and married a widower, a cattle dealer with two grown-up children The only person with whom Sophie had been able to talk constantly in the last few years had been Sixta. She had learned his letters by heart, and puzzled out what Mother Regina's ink had deleted. She had sat next to him on the banks of the Elbe and put her fingers in the plums and wondered why musicians were born in the mountains and writers in the plains. But where were Wagner's mountains, she'd objected. In Leipzig? Lortzing came from Berlin. And what about Handel? Well, let's leave it at that. She'd listened to him play the *Winterreisse* at the Grützke's, and had tried out the effects of *The Last Judgment*, sharpening the breadknife on an iron washing-up basin until she had gooseflesh and was convinced of the success of the opera. She had tasted the bun the Budweis men had baked, and scratched out Grützke's sister's eyes when she had the grand piano removed from the camp, and she was startled, with Sixta, by the sight of the legless soldier. She saw Sixta with short hair, in blue overalls, and understood that the boy who had wanted to take his life because of a bad review in the newspaper, who had followed 'his' singer in the tram, and had come to the Mangl estate in his Sunday best to make her an offer of marriage, had became a man who impressed her as much by his convictions as he had amused her by his awkwardness. A new time is coming, he had written, and Sophie believed him.

But how would it start, this new time? With smuggled trunks? And where? In Bratislava, in Prague, in America? And when? Next week or not until next winter? Newspapers were only used as lavatory paper in the convent. In March Sophie had read on a piece that German troops had entered Hungary. In Bucovice everything had remained the same, despite the rattle of tank tracks, and the roaring of army officers, and she felt again, as on the day Monsignor Atány had handed her the veil, the security of this house where the world of time stopped on the doorstep.

When Sophie had not seen her sister for some days except at morning Mass, she went to Katharina's cell and found her winding up a long antenna attached to a radio under her bed. While Katharina told her how she had smuggled it into the convent, she sat on her heels in front of the yellow dials and moved the red pointer to Hilversum and Hörby, Lahti and Strassburg, Beromünster and Trieste. She would have loved to hear something, a voice or music, but Katharina disconnected the antenna and told her she could come and listen in the evening.

'I'll leave you the thing anyway when I disappear.'

After this, Sophie stole into Katharina's room as often as possible during her free time. They closed the door, hung a cloth over the handle, put the radio on the bed and turned it on as softly as possible, putting their ears against the loudspeaker.

'For God's sake don't confess that to Herr Dubravec,' Katharina warned. 'There'll be time enough after the war.' Sophie nodded, and Katharina allowed her a request concert after the news.

Since they did not only listen to transmissions from Vienna but, more and more often since the beginning of August, also from Bratislava, Sophie translated what Katharina did not understand. In mid-August, after the announcer had called the American landing on the Riviera 'a clever German manoeuvre to entice as many enemies into France as possible so as to destroy them', the news came through that the children's transport to the Tatra had been successfully concluded. Sophie translated the announcement and waited.

'What else?' Katharina urged.

'The weather forecast,' said Sophie and turned the radio off.

'Why are you looking at me like that?' Katharina whispered. 'I've lied to you, and if I were to ask your forgiveness I'd lie again. Apart from a few people whom you don't know, I lie to everybody, and I find it more moral than to lie to oneself.' She pushed herself away from Sophie but did not get up. 'Have you thought just once in the years since you have been in the convent that you all cheat? How would your Saviour like to see Sister Borromäa make the sign of the cross above her plate? What has the sign of His suffering to do with roast potatoes and sausage? Most of you are 'the brides of God' because you either can't find an admirer, or he has run away from you. And when you took your vows you didn't lie, you were completely convinced of what you were doing. But you've learned for years to lie to yourselves.'

Katharina took her handkerchief from under her pillow and blew her nose, as if to give herself and Sophie a moment's pause. Sophie took her feet off the bed and began looking for her shoes.

'You're lying too when you don't confess to listening to the radio with me,' Katharina said. 'Why do you reproach me?'

'Me?' Sophie asked. 'But I haven't said anything.'

She had found her shoes and put them on. Then she opened the window, untied the antenna from the trellis, and wound it up like a clothes-line, from her thumb to her elbow. When she was back with Katharina she put the wire into her lap and said, 'I'll come back tomorrow.'

But next evening Katharina waited in vain. Sophie and another nurse had to look after two patients who were small-pox suspects, and she was not allowed to leave the hospital until they were declared clear. During this time, Katharina bicycled to Bratislava almost every day. It was not until Thursday that they saw each other at a meal and looked long into each other's eyes as the heavy motor vehicles and military lorries roared past the convent.

That evening Vienna announced that Paris had been cleared of German troops, and the following week Bratislava station announced an important speech by the Minister of Defence. Sophie translated for Katharina.

'Officers! Soldiers! Citizens! Partisans have been parachuted into the country. They are invading our villages, robbing our properties, murdering peaceful people. For this reason we have asked the German army for their help. We will succeed in rebuffing the treacherous attack. Do not be misled by the partisans. They are our greatest enemies. Anyone who joins them betrays his homeland. We will fight them heroically and to the death. We will be joined by the German Wehrmacht. May God help us in our fight.'

Katharina began to pack without a word, and Sophie felt she could ask her no questions. She watched as the suit and the sweaters, the underclothes and the shoes went to lie on top of each other. Only when Katharina took her rain cape down and put it on, Sophie said quietly, 'You can't go until the morning. The door is locked.'

'Then I'll jump out of the window,' Katharina said. Despite her violent movements between the suitcase and the cupboard she had remained pale, and it seemed to Sophie as if she had shrunk under the dark cape. Suddenly Katharina bent her knees several times. Her hands were trembling, and she only just kept her equilibrium.

'It's good against fear, Karol says,' she panted.

'Do you have a gun?' Sophie asked and was astonished at her own courage.

'No,' Katharina replied, then changed her mind. 'A Browning.'

She sat down on the bed, and Sophie explained why it would be better to leave Bucovice in the morning. 'Give the Mother Superior the radio as a farewell present. Tell her it is for the school, so that the children can listen to the President's speeches. Have you understood?'

Katharina nodded.

'Now you're going to take a Veronal,' Sophie said firmly, 'We'll meet after early Mass.' She got up and went through the darkening room.

'Is that all?' Katharina asked.

'Yes.'

'Why don't you say something nice to me?'

'Because then I'd howl.'

'I'd howl with you.'

Sophie took her hand from the door knob and walked back. The distance to the bed seemed immense, and she seemed very tall, falling at last into her sister's arms. The same old scent met her from Katharina's hair, a scent of catnip and thyme, but their leavetaking was not a success. They kissed and stroked each other, but their tenderness had an aunt-like quality which they both disliked. They wanted to feel close to each other but couldn't really like each other. They were like children who had desperately looked forward to a visit to a chocolate factory, but when they stood in front of the machine that stirs a rancid brown paste, nothing in the world would persuade them to stick their fingers in it.

Two weeks after the defeat of the Slovak uprising, Sophie renewed her vows before Monsignor Atány.

4

A Full Day

WITH THE YEARS, Sellmann had got used to going on unsuccessful errands of mercy. Despite his efforts, Victor Lustig and Frau Eva Kulik had been deported to Theresienstadt. Herr Lilienthal, the former head of the Böhmische Landesbank had taken an overdose of sleeping tablets. All attempts to get Vavra a job on a paper had been frustrated. The Professor had begun to live one week as a Frenchman and the next as an Englishman. He read only numbers of *Figaro* and *The Times*, drank Bordeaux or whisky bought on the black market, cooked '*pommes frites*' for '*déjeuner*', or 'baked potatoes' for 'lunch', and refused to speak in any language but the relevant one.

Apart from one or two favours which Sellmann had been able to obtain for employees of the bank and business friends of his son-in-law's, he remembered only two cases where his intercession had met with some success: Eugen Lustig and Pavel Sixta.

But why not try to do something to help Fräulein Kalman too? For though they had never met, there was surely a tie that bound him to the lame singer. Had he and Fräulein Kalman not been the first to know of Sophie and Amery's relationship?

It was no more than a step from the bank to the Petschek Palace, headquarters of the Gestapo. Sellmann turned into the bright street and was glad that the March sun only came as far as the second-floor windows. It was a relief these days to step from light into shade, and for a while he imagined he was walking through the pre-war city. Then the placards with the Bolshevist hand grasping the silhouette of the castle reminded him of the present, and the reason for his visit to the secret police.

The previous week he had had a letter from Sophie's former teacher in which she had asked his forgiveness for the 'lessons that were not given', and had promised to return the unearned fees 'at the earliest opportunity'. He would have thought such a late repentance eccentric, if Fräulein Kalman had not given the central prison as her return address, and asked him if it might be possible to use his influence to gain a pardon for her, that her counsel would be glad to give him the details. A few days later the lawyer had told him that his client had been sentenced to death for the distribution of seditious leaflets. He thought a pardon unlikely, for the number of executions at the central prison now stood at one hundred and thirty-six, including twenty women, which constituted an increase of thirty-nine compared with the same quarter the previous year. In other circumstances there might have been a chance of quashing such a conviction, for Fräulein Kalman had been denounced by the caretaker of her building for storing leaflets, not for distributing them. But to try to go against a judgment of the special court bordered on suicide.

There remained Schwerdtfeger. At one of Christine's 'days', he had struck Sellmann by his fiendish cleverness. When the talk had turned to the early death of various geniuses, Schwerdtfeger had spoken of the mathematician Galois who had been killed in a duel. He had then proceeded to demonstrate how the doubling of the cube, which the Delphic oracle had demanded, was arithmetically impossible, though it could be done in figurative terms. The silence of the rest of the company had been impressive. The gentleman from the Gestapo had continued to develop his thought imperturbably, returning after a quarter of an hour, and to everyone's relief, to his starting point. An educated man, without a doubt, even if one should not use such an occasion to show off one's erudition.

Sellmann touched the Iron Cross under his coat before entering Gestapo headquarters. One did not go naked to the police. Originally he had meant to wear a rather more modest medal, but it had disappeared. He decided to treat Herr Schwerdtfeger, of whom he knew neither Christian names nor rank, like an old schoolfriend, as if his last chat with the top boy in Greek had been interrupted years ago by the school bell.

While he had, at Christine's, presented himself as a man who had read 'everything', in his office, Schwerdtfeger tried to make up for his physical insignificance by the power of his position. During the time it took his secretary to look for the 'Kalman, Josephine' file, he behaved like a clerk who exaggerates his efficiency immoderately. That did not displease Sellmann. Anyone who had to blow his own trumpet to that extent could hardly beat a retreat when things got tough.

Schwerdtfeger sat down at his desk, opened a folder, and proceeded to sign his mail.

'You'll excuse me,' he said and wrote his name with exaggerated movements, 'I needn't read through it, thank God. I can depend on my secretary. But these have to go in a hurry, and my letters of sympathy are famous because I really mean what I say. Many people have told me: all letters of condolence just go into the waste paper-basket, but I keep yours! I tell people the truth. That's what one has to do if one wants to give consolation. It's the same with a man who is about to be shot. He has a right to know why and for what reason. Otherwise he feels like a guinea pig. Don't you think so?'

'I quite agree with you,' Sellmann said, and noticed that he was careful how he moved his hands and held his head, as if he were a candidate at an examination. He couldn't bring himself to take his handkerchief out of his pocket.

'How many daughters do you have then?' Schwerdtfeger enquired.

Sellmann replied as if he had been asked about the foreign currency reserves of the Böhmische Landesbank.

'I've been told that the second is in a convent.'

'Yes.'

'And the youngest?'

'She is studying philosophy.'

'My own domain. Do you think she'll graduate?'

'I don't know.'

'One's own children are often strangers,' Schwerdtfeger agreed. 'Kish sent Saul into the mountains, but instead of bringing back the lost she-asses he brings home a kingdom. My son is a flak officer and wants to become an entomologist, studying insects, catching moths.'

'Why not?' asked Sellmann.

Schwerdtfeger pressed the telephone button. The secretary brought two files and took the mail folder. Schwerdtfeger opened the first file.

'Fräulein Kalman's counsel suggested . . .' Sellmann began, but Schwerdtfeger interrupted him.

'Let's go on talking about the children,' he said and tapped a pink carbon-copy. 'This form's been sent us by our Slovak people: Proceedings, Sellmann, Katharina. When was the last time you saw your daughter?'

'In July.'

Schwerdtfeger lolled in his chair and smiled, not maliciously or as if he had just thought of a joke, but as if he had made a pleasant discovery.

'Why did you write to the German envoy in Bratislava?' he asked. 'We're just round the corner after all.'

'I thought you were only responsible as far as the Protectorate was concerned.'

'That's quite true. But we are like the Saxonia. Where we can't act ourselves, we put in one of our people.'

Sellmann cleared his throat and sat silent.

Schwerdtfeger bent over the file and leafed through some papers. 'You know that the original enquiry as to her whereabouts has been changed to a warrant for her arrest?'

'No,' Sellmann replied.

'Yes,' said Schwerdtfeger, and extended the 'yes' until his breath gave out. 'Philosophy has gone into the mountains or joined the Russians. Now supposing we catch her – which is very unlikely – but supposing we do. What should we do with her?'

Sellmann shrugged his shoulders and remained silent.

'It depends on what she's accused of,' he said finally.

'High treason, illegal possession of arms, active participation in the insurrection, murder. That's enough. So, supposing I had your daughter in the cellar and a signed confession, would you ask for a pardon?'

'It would be difficult,' Sellmann said, and at last mopped his forehead. 'But I don't frankly see any connection with Fräulein Kalman.'

'Why are you afraid?' Schwerdtfeger said. 'We haven't proved anything, we're just inferring that we have proof. We are developing a joint hypothesis: *should* we shoot your daughter *if* we manage to establish the offences I've mentioned.'

'If it is a question of a hypothesis, why are you speaking of my daughter?'

'Would you rather have another girl?' Schwerdtfeger asked. 'Do you know the story of the young man who was asked whether he would wish an unknown Chinese dead if it would bring him happiness? No? You remind me of it.' Schwerdtfeger shut the Sellmann, Katharina file. 'Would you care to answer me?'

'Yes,' said Sellmann, 'I agree with you,' and knew that he was repeating a sentence he had already used some time ago.

'Thank you,' Schwerdtfeger growled and opened the Kalman, Josephine file and turned to the last page.

'I could ask for a meeting with the Reichsprotector,' Sellmann offered, and went on speaking until he realised that he was already too late. 'When did it happen?' he asked, getting up.

'The sentence was carried out yesterday afternoon,' said Schwerdtfeger and dismissed his visitor, after helping him into his coat, with a Hitler salute.

Sellmann walked to the main post office and sent a telegram to the convent of the Sisters of Mercy asking for Sophie's return.

At Gestapo headquarters his head had felt hot and his feet like ice. Now the blood went back into his legs, and his nose became cold, a sign that he was turning inwards. What embittered him beyond his humiliation was that there was no longer room for larger decisions. He could ask Sophie to come back as had been agreed at her admission to the Bucovice convent and confirmed by the new Mother Superior. What else? Escape? Packing one's suitcases and stealing away? Ridiculous. The words victory and defeat seemed to him irrelevant, they were so alike they were interchangeable. 'The failure of an idea is worse than the defeat of an army,' he had read in a biography of St. Francis. It hurt him to see both go down at once. Until today he had always said: I'm made of concrete. Nothing touches me. The earth trembles and I shake with it, but my soul is firm. Even the old gentleman on the bench at the White Mountain who had looked a bit like Eugen Lustig had not enlightened him. If there was this I-am-who-I-am it'd be all the same anyway, and if not, all right.

Sellmann walked for a while, until he finally knew where he wanted to go. When Amery senior's housekeeper told him that he was expected home any moment, he took off his hat and coat. In the drawing-room he unhooked the order from his jacket and moved an armchair near the faience stove.

At first the only thing he and Amery had had in common was that they were fathers-in-law of the same marriage. Only with the accident and its explanation had their relationship changed. Instead of blaming each other, they apologised for their children, and the memory of the cold compartment in the Pilsen express had helped them later over many a misunderstanding. They weren't close friends. They did not know what to call their intimate yet distant, familiar yet correct relationship, but it gave them a secret pleasure. Women and politics were tabu. What was left? Sometimes, by the time he was on his way home, Sellmann had already forgotten what they had talked about. He was nevertheless already looking forward to their next meeting. He did not need to announce his arrival. Amery had let it be understood that Sellmann's unexpected visits were the only thing left that did him good. He liked to speak of a fortune-teller whom he consulted every month. But her predictions could be made to lead on to many other things, and the subjects reached from hyacinths to sea-voyages, from Berlin and Prague first nights to comic papers which had gone bankrupt years ago, from the polishing of crystal to the ontological proof of the existence of God. And when the conversation lagged, Amery poured out some of his wine. The courtesies of the old man moved the younger one. He tried to repay him by his undivided attention.

'I beg your pardon for having kept you waiting,' Amery senior said when he returned. Darkness had fallen. 'I had an idea that you would be coming today, and I hurried back, instinctively, so to speak.' He held out his hand to Sellmann. 'What has my vacuum cleaner given you to drink? Tea, for God's sake! At least have a drop of rum with it! Excuse me for a moment, I'll just take off my coat.'

'I'm afraid I shall have to go,' Sellmann said. 'I want to be home for dinner.'

'Then I'll take you as far as the tram,' Amery said.

Outside, the air smelled of snow, and this was enough to keep the conversation going as far as the tram stop. There Amery suggested keeping Sellmann company as far as Wenceslas Square. 'Perhaps I'll look in on Jan,' he said. 'Tell me what is on your mind.'

Sellmann told him as they walked through the town. When he was silent, Amery stopped as if to say goodbye. Sellmann put his hand to his hat, but Amery made him continue down the street.

'I used to know a painter from Trieste,' he said. 'His name was Sigfrido Pfau and he did some designs for us. He was at the Vienna Academy of Art before the First World War and took his entrance examination the same day as Adolf Hitler. Sometimes I wonder what would have happened to us all if Adolf had passed the examination and Sigfrido had failed, and not the other way round. Sigfrido would probably not have invaded us, he lacked the means, especially the gift of oratory. But would Hitler have drawn us a decent flower pattern for our coffee services? I often wonder. Perhaps he would have created a new fashion with lots of swastikas around the cups. But one could have put one's thumb on them while drinking coffee.

'Then I ask myself: could one really have depended on Sigfrido? Because he was ambitious, too, in his way. I once asked him for an art-nouveau decoration, something between Klimt and Tiffany, and Sigfrido painted a red horse above a purple nude because he was experimenting with Expressionism. So I was left with a lot of plates I couldn't sell, and he had the last laugh. Imagine if they'd both failed the exam and pooled their rage! It would have been the end of the world. Then I say to myself, be grateful, Bohuslav, that you've been spared that misfortune.'

'You hadn't thought of a happier solution?' Sellmann asked.

'Such as?'

'That they'd both passed.'

'That's true,' Amery sighed. 'That's true. But to imagine that borders on arrogance.'

Conscious that they might go on walking together all night if they spoke one more word, they parted almost without a farewell, Amery going to a café, Sellmann taking the tram to Bubenech.

Betty and Heinrich had already eaten their meal, but left the dessert untouched so that Sellmann would not have to sit at table alone. Heinrich, who was a civilian member of the ambulance service at the German army hospital, unfolded his thin length to push in Betty's chair. Only when he was rowing did he know what to do with his bones, how to put his hands on the oars, his feet against the toe-board, and not be in anyone's way. In the tram the leather straps dangled in his face, all mirrors were too low, the arms of ready-to-wear jackets came just below his elbows, and the nurses stood below his breastbone.

When Sellmann told them that he had sent a telegram to Sophie, asking her to return to Prague, Heinrich blushed with pleasure. While Sellmann ate his meatballs they made plans for Sophie. Would she remain in Prague? Would she change her Order, or .. ? Neither of them would finish that question. She'd live with them at first, until things were settled, perhaps Papa would be moved to Berlin or would retire. One would have to find out whether Sophie could work in a hospital with another Order until the end of the war. She must have ration-cards and clothing coupons, her old things wouldn't be wearable any more.

After a while Sellmann felt as if he were eating his meatballs in the presence of people who lived in the Himalayas or on Tierra del Fuego although they went to the same air-raid shelter as he did. The Americans had crossed the Rhine, and Betty moved the furniture. The Russians were an hour's drive from Berlin, and Heinrich told them that he had added a golden oriole to the birds he was helping through the winter. They behaved, surely, as if the Führer had passed the examination to the Vienna Academy of Art, and Sigfrido Pfau were Reichschancellor.

'Do you want to hear the news?' Betty asked.

'No. I'm going to bed.'

'Don't you, at least, want to see your letters?'

Yes, he'd look at his letters.

'Dear Doctor Sellmann,' Fräulein Kalman had written.

'My counsel tells me that you are being kind enough to ask personally for a pardon for me. I shall be grateful if you succeed. But I already have a foot on the threshold, and it isn't as bad as I thought. It is just sad that I can't say goodbye to anybody. If I had a child, something of me would survive. Well, at least I had pupils. The day before yesterday I was transferred to another part of the prison, and the priest asked if I wished to make my confession. I did. I confessed the business with Sofinka and everything else. I hadn't been to confession for a long time. I was a bit surprised that he gave me absolution straight away. I don't hate a single human being except the caretaker, that Herr Volavka, and he isn't human. He informed on me because he had to climb the stairs so often to get me a taxi, and I didn't give him a tip on his birthday because he talked to me as if I were a bit of dirt.

'At one time, executions of people belonging to the Protectorate were carried out in Dresden, and I'd rather have died in Dresden, though it is bombed flat, one hears. I hope the Opera still stands. I heard the great Destinn in *Seraglio* there, she still had a wonderful voice but had difficulty getting down the ladder because she had become so fat.

'Please tell Sofinka that I admire her. For everything! I liked her very much. She was my favourite pupil. Please give my regards to Professor Vavra. He should be glad that he didn't marry me. My neighbour here has written a poem of which I send you the last two lines:

> When my life slipped out of my hands
> I burnt my fingers on freedom.

'With many thanks for your efforts on my behalf, I am yours sincerely Josephine Kalman, teacher of voice and piano. P.S. I've thought it over, and I forgive even Herr Volavka.'

'Something unpleasant?' Betty asked.

'No, no,' Sellmann said, and put the letter in his pocket. 'Just business rubbish.'

5

Christine's 'Day'

IT WAS TUESDAY. Chistine went into the drawing-room to look at
the arrangements for her 'day', the ice-bucket, bowls of pastries,
glasses, napkins and ashtrays. Then she turned on the overhead
light and looked at the wall above the sofa where, instead of the
'crooked village', the 'Avenue de l'Opera' hung. Three years before
she had lived in the Boulevard des Capucines in Paris with a
German staff officer. On an excursion to Reims she had seen the
original Pissaro and had had a copy made.

Christine owed the success of her 'days' to a trick. After the
occupation she had suggested to the Mayor of Prague that she
might offer the officials and officers stationed there social access
to her family, and had put the letter into an envelope addressed
to the press department of the Reichsprotector. A few days later
she had telephoned to apologise for her mistake. The recipient of
the letter had been delighted with her error, especially when he
learned that she had originally written to complain about the
irregular delivery of German newspapers. The following week
Christine had a full house for the first time, and it remained so for
six winters. Today was a sort of anniversary.

The room smelled aromatic, not just clean and cool. Blue
lavender bags scented the air, and when the candles were lit it
would soon feel warm. On the piano the Telemann fantasies stood
open at No. VI, *'flatteusement,'* which fitted in well with the
evening. She expected a guest whom she had not seen since her
skiing holiday. But the chairs stood too formally, as if she expected
the ladies' circle. Servants had no feeling for a little elegant confusion.

Half past eight already? The president of the senate was already overdue. Christine stood in front of the hall mirror. Did the
little black dress with the narrow straps look a little extreme? But
the major whom she had met on her skiing holiday had been

260

entranced by her shoulders. 'Like Pauline Borghese, my love!'

A little more powder on her nose, then she knocked at Amery's door.

'Coming.'

A pity Aunt Marketa had said that she was coming. But she had promised not to be there before ten o'clock.

What would they talk about? Christine did not like to depend on chance. She liked to throw subjects out like throwing crumbs into a goldfish bowl. The previous year it had been easy because of the many famous people who had died: Giraudoux, Munch, Maillol, Kandinsky. This year too people were dying in droves, the newspapers could hardly accommodate all the notices, but they were all people with lesser names. She hoped the stylish ensign who told such good stories about the Caucasus would come, or the solicitor from Leipzig who knew the best Yiddish jokes, or the editor of a historical-critical biography of Charles IV. No, nothing could go wrong.

When she came out of the bathroom, Jan met her in the hall. 'The president?'

'No, not yet,' he said and sat down in the drawing-room where Marianne was lighting the candles.

'Could you wait and not smoke yet,' Christine asked, and he put his case away.

The waiter, a heavy elderly man, draped napkins around the bottles and went to stand by the window. The back of his tailcoat shone like cat fur.

'Herr Geier's car,' he said after a while, not turning. A few minutes later he said, 'It's driving on.'

'Then it must have been somebody else,' Christine said. Then she wondered whether the downstairs door was locked and sent the maid down.

'No, it's open,' Marianne said when she came breathlessly back.

'Please give me a glass,' Jan asked.

The waiter poured the champagne into a flat goblet. Amery sipped and said to Christine, 'It's only a "day". Those who want to will come. Those who don't, will stay away.'

'The major would have sent apologies.'

'Yes, perhaps.'

'And the President too.'

'But it's only nine o'clock.'

'A quarter past, if you'll allow me,' the waiter said.

Christine sat on the edge of the sofa and tried to draw Jan's glance to herself by putting her thumbs under her shoulder straps and crossing her legs in such a way that her stockings hissed. He couldn't stand that noise. Like an alcoholic who had given up drink and in whose presence no cork must be pulled. He folded his hands and looked at the carpet.

Christine looked at him as at a stranger. He was forty-three, too old for an idol, too young for an uncle. He was turning grey, but imperceptibly because he was blond. In the winter he gained weight, but when he came back from the country in the autumn he was slim and tanned. A man for dinner jackets and without secrets, except the one: that he was bored.

Sometimes he frightened her with his love of the vulgar. One afternoon she had met him in the company of two drunk tramps whom he had introduced to her as 'Reichs Administrators'. She had smiled because she was afraid of being molested. Was he mad? If it had been women, she'd have understood. A man who shirks his marriage has to look elsewhere while there's still sap in him. Amery sublimated. In October he dug Aunt Marketa's garden, pruned the roses and mowed the grass, and had blisters on his hands by evening. In the spring he planted tulips.

Now he smoked and kept his cigarette between his lips until the ash fell on the ground. They're my carpets too!

'How late is it?' Christine asked.

'Five minutes after half past nine,' the waiter replied and re-filled Amery's glass.

'I would like a glass too,' Christine said, not because she wanted the drink, but because it annoyed her to see someone whom she employed with nothing to do. 'The President never comes after half past eight. Do you think you should phone him?'

'It's raining,' Jan said. 'Perhaps he's been called to the Front.' Even people who went off to a lost war should have good manners. One said goodbye or sent a card. 'On the thirtieth of May the world will end,' the convalescents at the ski-resorts had sung, 'We won't live very long, we won't live very long.' For the immediate future it was probably a good thing to be married to a foreigner. When the Americans occupied Prague, Jan would be all right. She'd become naturalised.

At last! She heard Marianne run along the corridor. The major? Jan rose and the door opened.

The maid asked, 'Did you want the *bombe glacée* in the kitchen, madam?'

'Yes, please,' Christine said.

When the bell rang again they heard Marketa's penetrating voice, and she came in immediately.

'Children, 'she said, 'how grand you are,' and kissed first Christine, then Amery. 'Isn't that a bit too much?'

'What?' asked Jan.

'To have to show one's papers to come in. Am I the only guest? Quite *en famille*?' She put her thin fingers up to her hair and looked for a place to sit.

'Who asked to see your papers?' Christine asked.

'The two gentlemen on the stairs,' said Aunt Marketa and decided on a chair with a straight back. 'So that I don't go to sleep,' she explained. 'Black suits you, Tina.'

Christine looked at Amery. He shrugged his shoulders. She went out, opened the apartment door and pressed the light button. On the stairs up to the third floor two men in long raincoats squatted. She felt the same assurance that she had felt when she had dealt with the Dessau door-to-door salesmen.

'What do you want here?'

'Just go back in again,' the elder of the two said calmly and put his wet hat on his head, its wide brim shading his face. The younger one stretched out his legs.

'What right have you to ask Frau Farel for her papers?'

'Go on back inside.'

'You don't seem to know whom you're speaking to.'

'It says on the door!' the young one said.

'I'll have to ask you to show me some identification,' said Christine and recognised, before the stair light went out, the silver letters on the collar which the younger man had revealed.

'Do you want to see again?' she heard him ask in the dark.

She pressed the light button, and the men came down the steps to her.

'I'm expecting the president of the senate,' Christine said, and smelled cigars, beer and bread on the black uniforms.

'He's already back home again,' the elder one said. 'The others too. No more visitors today.'

'I'm going to complain.'

'To whom?' the younger one asked and left his mouth open as if to swallow her reply.

'To Herr Schwerdtfeger?' asked the elder, and smiled out of the shadow. 'He sent us.' He pressed his thumb against Christine's stomach and pushed her into the corridor. 'Mind the step,' he warned before he closed the door on her.

She still felt the thumb on her stomach when she staggered into the hall. She remained outside the door to the drawing-room and leaned her forehead against the door frame. She heard the voices of Marketa, Amery and the waiter, and it seemed to her as if they spoke Czech simply to make it impossible for her to go in. As if they wanted to say: you don't belong to us, stay out. Marianne, behind her, asked something.

'Tell them that I'm not feeling well,' Christine whispered.

She went into the bathroom and took off her make-up, changed into her pyjamas in her bedroom. When she slipped into the bed she felt the sheets cool and stiff. She turned out the light and took the corner of the pillow between her teeth.

Cowards, she thought, slimy, cringing cowards! Time servers! All of them had turned around and gone away, all of them. Of whom were they afraid? Of Schwerdtfeger, that mouse? Why had they stopped her 'day'? Because of Katharina?

When she had come back ill from Venice, the doctor had recommended Coué's auto-suggestion. 'Every day, in every way I feel better and better.' I know another sentence to add to that. Every day, in every way I hate my sisters more and more and more. I have hated them from the day they were born, from their first breath. They lay in my pink crib. They tore out my dolls' hair. They messed up my schoolbooks with their sticky paws. They stole my silk stockings. When I was asleep they put my hand into a bucket of water so that I wet my bed. They put valerian on my shoes so that the cats followed me in the street. They put itching powder in my collars. They made a hole in my swimsuit and said it was the moths. During my first ball they looked down at me from the gallery and laughed when I slipped. They read my diary and wrote rude remarks into the margin. They followed me when I had a date.

'Good night, child, get better soon,' Aunt Marketa called from behind the door. 'She's gone to sleep already,' she added. 'Don't worry, Jan.'

Every meal, every visit, every journey they've spoiled for me. It's enough to see their beastly faces to lose all pleasure in life. They've jumped around on me like a trampoline, the more I yielded, the higher they flew. My weakness makes them strong. One takes my husband, the other my friends. Now they've got what they wanted. I hate them more every day and every night, more and more and more.

She heard Jan go to the bathroom. He would take a shower and dry himself. He would put on his blue and white striped pyjamas. He would wipe the splashes the toothbrush had made from the mirror. He would go back to his room with wet feet. Then he would lock his door. Why do I blame him for every-

264

thing, she wondered, and the thought that Amery might be helpless and lonely suddenly moved her to tears. While she searched
for a handkerchief she suddenly remembered his embarrassment
in his bachelor apartment about her swollen lips, remembered the
Venetian lace dress, and *La Bohème* in the Teatro Fenice. She
blew her nose and listened. The waiter said goodbye to Marianne.
Marianne vanished into her room. Amery turned out the light in
the corridor. The key turned in the lock.

The previous year she had seen his room for the first time. Now
she wished she were there, in the moss-green armchair beside his
bed. I don't want anything from you, she would say. Don't take
any notice of me. Just go on reading. I'm only looking at you. I'm
a bit lonely, you know? Wouldn't you like to hang the 'crooked
village' back in the drawing-room? Did I hurt you? Did you hurt
me? My heart is a pin-cushion. Funny that nobody came today,
isn't it. Actually these people mean nothing to me. Not even the
major, nor any of the others with whom I've slept. Sometimes I
think I only love you. But you needn't be afraid. No, please, just
go on reading, Jan. I really don't want to disturb you. I just have
cold feet. May I put them under your covers? Have you forgotten
what I look like? Good God, I've got lacquer on my nails. Forgive
me. And my nose is red. I caught cold at the office yesterday. The
heating doesn't work. But I'll fix it. And now I'll go away. I just
wanted to see you. One lies alone, and next door someone one
loves lies in his bed, and one doesn't have the courage to tell
him because one is ashamed, or afraid, or because one can't find
the right words. Good night, Jan, sleep well, and many thanks for
warming my feet, and if you want me, just call me, or simply come
to my room.

Christine sat up and listened. It was very dark and very quiet.
She pushed her hair from her face and put her bare feet on the
carpet. On her way to the door she wiped her sweating hands on
her pyjama trousers. If he's asleep I'll leave him alone, she decided.
She went on tiptoe along the corridor to his room, and saw the light
shining through the key-hole. She knocked. For a moment she
thought she heard a step. Then she knocked again, and after an
interval she beat her fist against the door. Then bedsprings
groaned, a switch snapped, the light in the key-hole went out, and
immediately the light came on in the corridor. Marianne came
around the corner in her nightdress, with her long plaits over her
breast and asked, 'Are you looking for something, Madam?'

'Get out,' Christine shouted. 'Clear off to bed.'

The maid turned and stumbled back to her room in her thick

slippers. Christine pushed herself from the opposite wall and flung her right shoulder against Amery's door. She felt no pain but sank to the ground, turned on her back and stamped her heels against the door until the wood boomed and trembled. She had closed her eyes and put her fists under her chin. She gasped for breath, and her feet hammered empty air when Jan opened the door.

'What do you want?' he asked, and his eyes were small with anger.

She slid back against the opposite wall and pressed herself upright. She stood on tiptoe and spat in his face. She could see his jaw muscles contract.

'You're a coward,' she panted, 'A shit-bag, a louse!'

Amery wiped his pyjama sleeve across his mouth, and she thought he was about to slap her face.

'A coward,' she repeated when he lowered his hand.

'I'm sorry. I should have killed you earlier. Now there's no sense in it any more. Go to bed!'

When he closed the door behind him, Christine sank to her knees and called for Marianne. The maid put her arms around her and carried her to the bedroom. In the dark she put her on the bed, found the bedside light switch. Then she ran to the bathroom, fetched a towel, and put it under her mistress' bloody heels. When she had put plasters on the cuts she sat down on the bed and held Christine's feet on her lap until she grew tired and toppled over. When Marianne had fallen fast asleep, Christine crawled down to her, rolled against her warm body, and pulled the covers over herself and the maid.

6

I'm Coming

FOR DAYS LINES of refugees had blocked the road from Bratislava to the Hungarian border. Constable Illin climbed the church tower with his telescope and reported that it was the same on the other side of the Danube. Deacon Filo, trying to take a service in an outlying village, had to turn back as the refugees wouldn't get out of the way of his carriage. At night you could see fires burning, and the flashes of gunfire on the southern horizon, and on the Monday morning a Russian biplane flew over Bucovice and fired both machine guns into the grain silos.

On the Tuesday of Holy Week, the Mother Superior offered to take the unmarried daughters of the villagers into the convent. When she came back from the parish office, the Portress gave her Sellmann's telegram. Mother Kasimira immediately let Monsignor Atány know, and he arrived with the necessary forms in the late afternoon. The formalities were without precedent since the novice didn't want to leave the Order, but no one had ever needed a leave of absence before.

'An apostasy is child's play compared with this,' Monsignor Atány sighed, and finally arranged for Sophie's transfer to the Mother House, though it had been burned down some time ago. By the unusual title of the document, *'traductio ad monasterium sororum misericordium Hohenzollerarum'*, he hoped to prevent any question as to the future validity of her vows. 'The archbishop will have to decide that,' he suggested, and the Mother Superior seemed content while Atány pressed the diocesan stamp across his name.

When he wanted to take his leave he was told that Sophie did not yet know about her 'transfer'. He had to make an effort to keep his temper, for the Mother Superior now asked him to speak to 'Sister Agnes'. 'We can't just put the child in the street,' she said and had Sophie called from the hospital.

Atány raised her from her knees and explained what had been decided, stressing that she should first go to her parents in Prague, so as to go on from there, as soon as circumstances permitted. Tickets and money had been obtained, he continued. Sophie looked irresolute and shook her head.

'We have so many wounded at the moment,' she said. 'I'd rather stay.'

Monsignor Atány sent Mother Kasimira on an errand and asked Sophie to sit down.

'What did you vow?' he asked.

'Poverty, chastity and obedience.'

'And what did you promise your father?' he asked. 'Do you think it is easy for the Sisters to let you go? They love you.' He flattened his soutane and allowed his hands to rest on his thighs. 'You wear your habit and stay with your parents until . . .'

267

'Yes?' Sophie asked.

'What I'm telling you is between ourselves. By Easter the Russians will be here. You know what you may expect as a German.' He was sorry to have said it, and wanted to add something comforting. 'But everything is in God's hands, and blessed are those who are persecuted for the sake of righteousness. But the Lord also says, "Be ye cunning as serpents but beware of men, for they will deliver you to the councils." You understand?'

'Yes, Monsignor.'

'It is a time of transition,' Atány said mildly and pointed to the place where her signature was needed.

'May I stay until Maundy Thursday?' Sophie asked before signing.

'In the name of God,' Atány said and gave her the blessing.

On Maundy Thursday Deacon Filo preached. Sophie had said farewell to the Sisters the day before, quickly and without tears, only Sister Blanka cried, the others were too busy settling the village girls into the dormitories. Sophie saw a young Slovak girl taking off her boots and putting them under her own bed. She took her suitcase and went to the entrance, and not long after Mother Kasimira came with the money and ticket.

'I shall pray for you,' she said and kissed Sophie on the forehead. 'Go with God. The deacon is waiting.'

In front of the iron fence stood Filo's carriage. The deacon sat down next to Sophie. As the carriage passed into the road, she turned and recognised the Portress waving to her with both arms. I should have gone to Modesta's grave, she thought as they passed the cemetery.

Apart from lorries and the families who were returning to their villages from Bucovice, there was no one about. Nevertheless the noise of a motor made the deacon jump, and he looked carefully at the sky. 'If you hear a low plane,' he said, 'we'll lie between the wheels.'

In Bratislava Sophie had to get out because Filo could go no further. He showed her the direction in which the station lay and was immediately surrounded by men who wanted to buy his carriage. When Sophie looked back a little later, the deacon had taken off his round hat to hit at the money held out to him.

The station was cordoned off by military police who would only allow travellers with tickets inside. When Sophie asked from which platform the trains for Prague left, she was sent to an express train whose compartments, corridors, steps and roofs were already full of people, while those left behind were fighting for the best positions to get on to the next train, though nobody knew for sure when it would arrive. Shortly before the train was due to leave, some soldiers got on and threw the luggage of those who wouldn't come down from the room onto the platform. Most of them followed their bundles, and when the train left at last there was much quarrelling and fighting over the various possessions.

Sophie stood as if bewitched. Every sound, every word did her good and yet hurt her. She did not notice the passage of time. She was jostled and pushed aside, but was always in the middle of the crowd, and no nearer the edge of the platform. When she saw that it was midday she felt hungry. She forced her way out of the crowd, put her suitcase against a closed ticket office, and ate her goosefat sandwich which the kitchen Sister had made her. While she was licking her fingers, her face to the wall, she remembered that she had forgotten to say Grace. 'I'll make up for it tonight,' she promised herself.

On the town map she found the road to Brno and started along it. Though it began to drizzle, Sophie went on to the next village and billeted herself on the local priest. The clerical gentleman was impressed by the Latin inscription on her papers, her habit, and the signature of Monsignor Atány. When she took her leave on Good Friday morning he gave her a smoked sausage, and his brother, a pottery merchant, took her to Malacky in his delivery wagon. After going to Mass in Malacky she went to the station but found that the barrier had been closed since the platform was already crowded, and the trains from Bratislava, the railways inspector told her, only stopped in open fields to give people a chance to relieve themselves without losing their seats.

Unable to get away, she spent the night in a Franciscan convent and joined a group going to Brno on the Saturday. But their carriage was taken off the train, and she had to get out at a small station. At the post office, where she tried in vain to get in touch with her parents, she met a shunter who promised her a place on a train to Brno for five hundred krone. She gave him half in advance and spent the day in his kitchen, between nappies and cabbage soup. She went to sleep at nine o'clock as usual and had to be woken up at midnight. The shunter took her suitcase across the railway lines and helped her into the brake-van of a goods-train. He shone his carbide lamp on to his purse and put the money in it, then whispered in the darkness, 'If anybody asks you, say Hiesel sent you.'

'God bless you,' Sophie thanked him.

She could feel the soot on the plank walls, and stood straight up until it occurred to her to sit on her suitcase. When she woke up it was dawn and the train was creeping across a river. Though Sophie sat with her back to the engine, the sun rose through the right window. She shook the dirt from her sleeves and wondered, but it took her a while to realise that she was travelling south once more. The bells of Malacky were ringing in Easter Sunday as she ran across the railway lines, her habit dirty, her veil fluttering behind her.

It annoyed her to think that she had only accomplished forty kilometres in four days, but she did not lose her courage. She stood beside the main road and waved with her sausage until a milk delivery van stopped and took her on a bit. From now on she trusted her legs rather than any promises, and walked to Brno in three days. She asked a clergyman for directions to a convent, and was at last able to telephone Prague.

Sellmann urged her to hurry. 'The Russians are in Bratislava,' he said. 'I'll talk with our Brno representative immediately and he'll help you get on. Take the train via Jihlava or hire a car.' He paused, and she asked whether he was still there.

'Yes, darling, I'm here. I'm looking forward very much to having you back. We all are.'

It sounded as if he were blowing his nose. Then the line was disconnected.

Sophie took a grey dress out of her suitcase. The fine fabric ran over her arms like a shiver. She went to the bathroom to wash her habit. She only knew her face from the window panes and the chrome steriliser in the hospital. She stood in front of the mirror and touched the pale scar at the hairline. Her lips were tight. Her forehead white and ruthless. She could not hide the scar, her hair was too short. Sophie sat on the edge of the bath and looked at the floor. Where can I hide until the summer when my hair will have grown? She crumpled the habit into the boiler and scattered soda between the folds, filled it up with cold water. He who loves father and mother better than he loves me is not worthy of me. Eight years they've lived without me. And he who loves son or daughter better than he loves me is not worthy of me. Why call me back now? I can't help anybody. She pushed the boiler under the wash basin and looked once more into the mirror. This is the dress I wore last time I saw him, on the Mangl estate. I want to marry you, he'd said, and turned pale. Why did your composer run away, Jarmila's father had asked.

Next morning Sophie collected money from the branch of the Böhmische Landesbank and received travel tokens for bread and meat. The news that there were no trains to Jihlava did not disturb her. She bought a map of the district and followed the road with her finger. Budweis was the most boring town in the world, she knew, the daisies advanced to the attack, the apple-blossom exploded, and the sky hung like a bell over the fields. The milestones and the cherry trees in blossom went westward along the highroad. Quite empty from sheer happiness, Sophie sat down at midday under a blossoming tree full of bees. Every crossroad was a proof of her freedom. Wherever she went, it was in her own direction. People who came towards her did not stop her. The men took off their hats when they saw her habit, the women smiled under their headscarves, and the soldiers waved from the tanks. At night she asked for shelter at the presbyteries, washed her clothes, mended her stockings, and started off again early next morning.

In mid-April she arrived at Budweis. She asked for the street which Sixta had mentioned in his letters. The whitewashed house was divided from its neighbours by a stretch of grass. She put her suitcase down outside the low fence, but did not dare stretch her hand over the gate to draw the bolt. She took up her suitcase when a curtain moved in the ground-floor window. A white-haired woman opened the window and called, 'Wait, Fräulein Sophie! I'm coming!'

7

The Barricade

SELLMAN WAS ABLE to follow the progress of the war in the behaviour of the door keeper at the bank who, since the fall of Brno, had stopped giving the Hitler salute, but called out, 'My respects, Herr Direktor!' Four days later he said, 'My compliments!' When Pilsen capitulated he silently laid his hand on the peak of his cap, and it was easy to foresee that one day he would greet him with, 'Morning, old boy!'

On the first Friday in May, when Sellmann arrived at the bank at his usual time, the door keeper did not turn round from watching the metal plate with 'Böhmische Landesbank' being unscrewed from the front of the building. Sellmann opened the door himself, went into his office and found it cold. He was told that the stoker had not come to work. Sellmann kept his coat on and asked for some tea with rum. He put it on the window sill and looked into the street. No military, but many civilians in slouched hats, the brims blown by the wind.

Halfway between Brno and Jihlava, partisans had blown up the railway bridge. Sixty-five dead and over a hundred hurt. Had Sophie been among them? For weeks he had telephoned the Brno branch of the bank daily until the line was shut down.

When his secretary announced Herr Amery junior, he gave her the empty cup and his coat. Jan was pale and looked as if he had not slept. He opened the parcel he had under his arm, took out an electric fire and plugged it in.

'How do you know our heating isn't on?' Sellmann asked and looked at the glowing filament.

Amery rubbed his hands in the mounting warmth.

'It's my fault,' he said smiling, and pulled two chairs to the fire. 'We need the man.'

'The stoker?'

Amery nodded and looked Sellmann in the eye before he lit a cigarette.

'For the business?'

Amery shook his head and blew the smoke through his nose.

'I'll explain everything in a few years' time,' he said and took his scarf off. His blue shirt was without a tie. 'Drive to Karlsbad today with Betty and Heinrich. Take my car because of the number. I parked it three houses down the road. The tank is full. Or do you want to stay until the Americans arrive in Prague? The Americans won't come. They'd have to make it by tonight, but they won't come. Don't ask me how I know, simply believe me.'

Amery had spoken in a low voice and with pauses, when his adam's apple had slipped out of his collar and under his chin. He looked at his thumb-nail as if he were considering cutting it.

'There's going to be a new Government. The President will speak on the radio tomorrow.'

Sellmann leaned forward.

'But he won't be making his speech,' Amery said.

'How's that?' Sellmann asked.

'Because I don't want him to,' Jan smiled and stubbed out his cigarette.

Sellmann wondered about such extravagance.

'What does Christine think?' It occurred to him to ask.

'She thinks that I've spent six summers in the country in Moravia just to eat goat-cheese,' Jan said and looked Sellmann in the face. 'You believe that too, don't you?'

Sellmann got up and stumbled over the heating flex as he went to the window.

'At first I wasn't quite sure,' he heard Amery say behind him. 'I was afraid of myself. Sometimes I thought that one had to be a German to love one's country. Then a man came to see me in black socks . . . No, excuse me, you won't understand that. But at a crossroads in the Böhmerwald I saw a Czech officer cry because he had to keep the road open for the retreat, without a shot having been fired. The tears ran into his mouth. He licked them, then he folded up, collapsed like a pocket-knife, and I picked up his cap out of the mud. He's pursued me, if you know what I mean. He has eaten from my plate and drunk from my glass. He has woken me up every night. He spent the whole war with me, and he's with me still.

'But he's not angry with you. Do you understand that? Nor does he mind Christine. After all, he's married to her – how does it go? – "until death do you part". Now and again he asks me whether German officers cry too when they have to give the signal to retreat. A few tears mightn't be a bad thing. But he is not vengeful. Mind you, he has friends who are already looking for torches, and he knows a man who had to conduct the triumphal march from *Aida* while his wife was taken to the gas-chamber. When he comes back to Prague it'll not be with a conductor's baton. Wouldn't it be better if you took my car? If that conductor is still alive he'll be just about at Dresden now. He's always a step behind the first tanks. Tomorrow it may be too late.'

'I'm staying,' Sellmann said against the window.

'Are you waiting for a miracle?'

Sellman put his hands in his jacket pockets and turned around. He saw Amery sitting in the armchair with pale lips and closed eyes, his legs stretched out, his coat open and his scarf over the back of the chair.

'You know what I'm waiting for,' Sellmann said.

'I can imagine,' Amery said and opened his eyes. 'You want to experience it.'

'No,' said Sellmann, 'I am waiting for Katja and Sophie.'

'It's the same thing,' Amery replied and got up. 'But you're too correct to admit it. Or too vain. You don't want to be a trouble to

273

anybody, especially for the sake of your own convenience, do you? May I at least give you the electric fire?'

'Thank you,' Sellmann said. No forgiveness, but at least something conciliatory. They smiled in a slightly embarrassed way as if they had met in a dogs' cemetery, and bowed as after a cancelled duel. Amery wound his scarf around his neck and buttoned up his coat, and Sellmann helped by looking for his hat. Oh yes, hats weren't being worn today. He accompanied his son-in-law as far as the stairs. They walked along with a good deal of determination, now that they knew the battle was over, and when they shook hands it was as if two clamps were saying goodbye. Then came the stairs of imitation sandstone and reinforced concrete, a fireproof construction, the bare balustrade and a head vanishing into the stairwell.

Sellmann went back to his desk. The telephone reminded him that he was not under arms. His wife asked whether he would be back to lunch, she had herring salad made of bottled rollmops. No, Betty, I'd rather eat that tonight. His very first boss used to tell him, when you have nothing to do, learn the rate of exchange by heart, or tidy up your desk. Work as if everything stopped at your death, and talk with the clients as if there was a Last Judgment.

Sellmann made a tour of the bank. On the first floor the employees sat in their coats. They opened letters from somewhere and sent off replies somewhere. The lady at the invoicing machine wore her gloves very reproachfully. The head of one of the departments followed Sellmann into the corridor and asked whether the Herr Direktor was interested in silver candelabra. The estate of the Countess of Ledur would be auctioned on Monday, the auctioneer was a schoolfriend.

Sellmann sneezed when he returned to his office. The sky had cleared, but it remained cool in the large room. On his way home in the tram he was sweating. He ate jacket-potatoes with the herring salad, took two Aspirins, drank hot camomile tea, and listened to the news. A new Government had been formed, its members had been confirmed by the Reichsprotector. A division of the Russian army of liberation, led by General Vlassov was advancing. Otherwise: better weather prospects.

Though he had a temperature, Sellmann went to the bank on Saturday morning and sat by Amery's fire until the bank closed. The new head of Government was due to speak over the radio at one o'clock. Instead, the announcer shouted, 'Death to the Germans!' Sellmann switched off the radio, opened the window, and saw a soldier run across the road. The soldier appeared to stumble in the tram line and fell on his face. His right leg extended slowly, shifting the trouserleg and exposing a white calf. The street remained empty for a while, then men came out of the houses and passed the dead soldier. They looked very much like the ones he had seen the day before, but they did not talk to each other but looked as if they had already agreed on what to do. A tram braked before the dead man, the driver and the conductor dragged him to the gutter, and the conductor pulled the signal bell after he had made sure nobody had got on.

Sellmann shut the window, pulled out the flex of the electric fire and telephoned Christine. The maid sobbed into the receiver until Sellmann shouted at her.

'Wouldn't you like to come to us?' he asked Christine.

'Not on your life,' she said. 'The bath-tub is full of water and there are enough candles, and Marianne is starting to cook to-morrow's dinner. It's beef olives, why not join us?'

'The situation is serious.'

'Yes,' Christine said. 'An hour ago they broke our shop windows. You must have heard it. Or are you speaking from Bubenech?'

'I'm just starting for home.'

'Ring again when you get there. Have you got another cold?'

'Yes,' Sellmann said, 'I'm afraid I have.'

As he went along the street, he looked at the faces above the coat collars: fitters after an early shift, their hair still wet and combed flat so that one could see the teeth of the comb in the parting, subtenants from the suburbs, customers from the neighbourhood bars, embittered employees, braggarts in civilian clothes. The young women too seemed changed, desirable and beautiful in their light-coloured rain-skins with strong legs and open throats. It sounded silly when there were shots, as if somebody were touching a burning cigarette to a row of balloons. Sellmann felt that any one of the people, amongst whom he moved, might suddenly kick him, without anybody being surprised. He saw a man eat a sandwich, throw a stone into the window of a bookshop, and then look at the clock down the street as if he wanted to make sure he wasn't late for an appointment. Machine gun barrels rose out of the windows of the barracks. At the corner of the street, two women were leading a skinny salesman between them. They had pulled their shopping-nets over his head. They pushed him in the knees, and showed him off like a hare they had caught.

Workers in blue overalls stood in the middle of the Stephanik

Bridge. Sellmann wondered whether he should go another way, but the danger drew him forwards. He was asked for his papers, first in Czech, then in German, shrugged his shoulders and said in English, 'I don't understand. What do you wish?' The man called to the others that he'd met the first American, and gave Sellmann a friendly blow in the neck. His glasses slid down his nose, but he smiled and was allowed to pass.

Further along they were tearing up the pavement. A white-painted door fell from a second-floor window, and an open dust-bin rolled down the steep street, scattering potato peel and ash. Sellmann turned right and reached his house through side streets. He was exhausted, but the excitement and hurry had driven the fever out.

When Frau Sellmann asked him to telephone a Wehrmacht colonel whom they had met at Christine's, he shook his head, which, from experience, he had found was sufficient answer. But this time he was wrong.

'Perhaps he can find us a lorry,' Betty said, 'so that we can take the things we need most. I'm not waiting any longer. I never wanted to come to Prague. Only because of Heinrich.' She looked at her son who lowered his eyes. 'I don't understand the people here, and when they understand me, they understand me wrong. I don't know how Christine puts up with it, but that's her business. The girls are grown up now. They left us when they thought they should. I don't blame them, but I'm sorry. If you'd given up your job after Heinrich's operation, we'd have been spared a lot. Or after the accident. But you went through fire for that nice old Jew, and we didn't do so badly, I must confess. But do you think your Herr Lustig will come back from London next week with his millions and thank you for having saved his bank through the war? I'm not twenty any more. I don't want to start again. Can't you imagine what they'll do to us? The caretaker has already offered to hide the silver. Do I have to look on when Heinrich . . .' She had reached the end. She cried and knew that she could do nothing against Sellmann's silence. She laid her spoon on the side of her plate and went out. Sellmann nodded, and Heinrich followed her.

He went into his study and looked out into the green park. When he had been wounded in the previous war, Betty had written him cheering letters. She looked after him, put up with him, and spoilt him. After Heinrich was born his marriage lived on the memory of those early, happy years. Heinrich was a part of Betty. He belonged to her. When he went blind after measles, she had howled like a wolf, and bitten her knuckles until they bled. She had made God into her own secret doctor and consulted him every night, and he had calmed her into sleep. If Sellmann had not married Betty, he would never have known what it was like to be loved by a warm, gay woman for ten years. Later she had longed for solitude and disliked company, especially if anything was discussed that she did not understand. After Heinrich's operation she had spent months with him so that he got to know every line of her face, and she had forgotten Sellmann and the girls in the process. Why should he not ask the colonel to take Betty and Heinrich? But when he contacted the orderly, he was told that the colonel might possibly be reached the following day.

When a cease-fire was arranged between the Prague National Council and the German chief of staff towards midnight, Sellmann went to bed. Next morning he tried to reach the colonel again, but was put off until Monday. On Monday the shooting began again, but with heavier guns. The caretaker brought the news that American tanks had been seen in the town. He did not remain in the hall as had been his habit, but preceded Betty into the drawing-room. Sellmann gave him a bottle of brandy and asked him to help buy some groceries. The caretaker promised to do his best and came back towards evening with a packet of noodles. Betty thanked him, but did not let him come into the hall. A bottle of brandy for a packet of noodles, that would never do.

Sellmann played chess with Heinrich, but lost both games. Then they heard firing outside the house.

'Lie down under the windows,' Sellmann called, turned out the lamp and remained in his armchair. There were more shots, and a grenade exploded. The windows trembled. 'Fifty metres,' Sellmann said in the dark. Then they heard metal-studded boots clattering down the street.

'Shall we go into the cellar?' Betty asked, but there was no need for a reply. A booming bass voice suddenly began to sing in the street. Sellmann did not know the tune but felt its strength, and noticed how the hair in the nape of his neck stood on end. The song pursued him into his dreams.

It was Tuesday morning before Betty noticed that a bullet had gone through the bedroom window, curtain, cupboard wall, and through Sellmann's top hat.

Heinrich put the hat on and stuck his finger into the bullet-hole. Sellmann laughed and put his arms round Betty. They breakfasted in pyjamas, and Frau Sellmann left her hair hanging loose over her housecoat. She poured tinned milk from the silver cow Amery senior had given Heinrich. Sellmann reminded them how Heinrich had looked at cake crumbs through his microscope one Christmas. When Heinrich denied it, Sellmann demanded that the microscope be found, so that he could demonstrate.

'We haven't had such a good time for ages,' Betty said an hour later.

'And now we've got to get dressed,' Heinrich grumbled, and in protest pushed the coffee spoon through the bullet-hole into the top hat.

'It isn't really necessary,' Betty said to Sellmann. 'If you aren't going to talk to the colonel anyway!'

'Well he isn't going to see you on the telephone,' Heinrich said and took off his slippers. 'I'll stand beside you and go "bang",' he slapped the soles together. 'And the colonel will think you're clicking your heels.'

'Please,' Betty said, and Sellmann got up.

When he came back and reported that the German troops would be leaving during the day but could not take any civilians, Betty was the first to regain her composure.

'Then it'll be noodles for lunch again,' she said.

'And then the Russians will come,' Heinrich said.

'My God, the Russians are human too,' Betty said, and began to stack plates and saucers. 'Every nation has its peculiarities. I'll tie up my head in a scarf and go to market in wooden clogs.' She lied for Heinrich's sake. Sellmann took the tray and carried it into the kitchen.

In the afternoon Heinrich asked what he should do with his bust of the Führer. 'I got it for my final exams, but it'll have to go. I'll bury it tonight.'

'Break it with a hammer and put it in the dustbin!'

'Anything else that ought to vanish?' Heinrich asked and blinked behind his thick lenses.

'No, thank you,' Sellmann said. 'And mind you don't hit your thumb.'

Why don't I invite him to stay? he asked himself when Heinrich left the room. Why don't I explain to him what lies before us? Why don't I stroke his lean neck, even if he thinks such a caress humbug? Don't I love him? Perhaps I don't love him. Whom do I love? In the days when he had travelled by plane, he had wondered what would happen if they crashed, and had looked over the rim of his paper for a single person on whom he might depend. If he found a young man who reminded him of Heinrich, he felt that all was well. So he loved him after all? He did not know the answer, and knew no one he could ask. He felt like an old, choleric cripple who had been shut up alone in a room. In the course of the evening he felt his anger rise without reason, and when Betty snored he broke out in a sweat with fury.

On Wednesday morning he shaved, showered, sprayed his face, neck and arms with eau de cologne, and dressed with care. After breakfast he opened a city map and asked Heinrich to translate the radio news. He traced the occupied suburbs until the noise and shouting came so close that it was enough to open the windows to know the state of affairs. The neighbours ran out of the houses, waved tricolours and red flags, kissed each other, and ran down into the park. When Heinrich wanted to take the dust-bin with the broken bust into the courtyard, the caretaker sent him back into the apartment.

After lunch – Betty had cooked white beans, but they remained untouched – an open cattle-truck stopped outside the house. Sell-mann saw white hands clasping the high open sides. Then the ramp was let down, and two men with guns and red armbands jumped over the manure-covered planks into the street.

'I really don't need a coat,' Sellmann said to Betty when the bell rang. 'It's warm today.' He kissed her, embraced Heinrich, and went to the door on his own. The caretaker stood between the armed men. He hung a cardboard notice saying 'Collaborator' around Sellmann's neck and asked for Heinrich.

'He is ill,' Sellmann said.

The men with the guns pushed him silently aside. Betty went and stood in front of Heinrich's door, but he opened it himself, and the caretaker found it difficult to pull the string over the tall young man's head.

'Give them something to eat to take along,' he said, and Betty went and filled a saucepan with white beans.

One of the men pushed the cardboard against Heinrich's nose, and the other hit him in the back with a gun butt. Sellmann took Sellmann and Heinrich had climbed into the truck, she called, the saucepan, and Betty accompanied them downstairs. When 'I shall wait! I shall wait!' Over the closed back of the lorry Heinrich saw his mother collapse, but he was not sure that he had really seen it, for his eyes were full of tears.

Sellmann put the saucepan handle over his arm and put both his hands on to the sides of the truck to keep his equilibrium. He counted eleven men including Heinrich and himself. At the first stop he asked the man next to him where they were going. He shook his head and spat some blood on to the floor of the truck.

There were three newcomers, and the armed men, finding it too crowded, stood on the running-boards of the cab.

Then Sellmann saw the first Russian tanks. The soldiers wore flowers in their caps. Girls in light-coloured blouses sat on the tanks, waved and laughed, or tried to pull the soldiers out of the turrets. When some more prisoners were put in the truck, Sellmann did not need to hold on any more, they were pressed so closely together. When they were stationary he felt the heat, and the sweat ran into his eyebrows, but the breeze, when they were travelling, blew his skin dry again.

When the truck stopped at the Troja Bridge and the ramp was let down, he slid and staggered down with the others. It was impossible to hear the orders the armed men shouted above the booming martial music from the loudspeakers, but it was easy to guess that they were expected to form a line. A photographer took a picture, and after they had all been issued with shovels, a second one, but when an elderly collaborator fainted and fell down, the guards demanded a third photograph in case the earlier one was spoilt. Then they led the column away from the loudspeakers and explained the work. The bridge had to be cleared before evening, and the roadway made smooth. The barricade which, apart from the breach made by the tanks, obstructed the whole width of the bridge, was made out of paving stones, tar barrels, doors, balcony railings, car-wrecks, soap-boxes, fire-grates, and other rubbish. When one of the prisoners asked for wheelbarrows and rams, the guard hit him on the forehead with a shovel. The guards chose the strongest of the men and sent them up to the barricade to disentangle the crushed and bent iron pieces. The weaker group formed a chain to pass the smaller pieces back, and, after the arrival of another transport, this chain went all the way to the river bank.

Sellmann put his saucepan of beans in a safe place and tied up his cardboard notice under his chin so that it would not dangle between his arms. He was glad that Heinrich was working near him, and looked at him now and again through his dusty spectacles. When he had pulled an interior-sprung mattress out of the barricade, he waved to him, and they carried it to the river bank. Now that the fog created by the heat, fear, and blaring music had lifted, he noticed the spectators in the grey tenements and behind the police cordon. They had put cushions in the windows or had brought chairs with them, and expressed their opinions on the proceedings as if they were watching a football game. On the way back, Sellmann showed Heinrich where he had hidden the beans and threw his jacket over the saucepan. At that moment, not ten metres from him, one of the prisoners swung himself on to the parapet of the bridge and hung there for a moment before jumping with outstretched arms and legs into the river. The nearest guard laid his gun against his cheek, waited until the fugitive's head came out of the water, and emptied his magazine into it. But he did not appear to have hit him, for other guards fired at the man, and the people on both banks ran alongside the swimmer.

Sellmann looked over the balustrade but felt himself held tight by the collar so that he could not move his head. I should go after him, he thought, but the guard turned him in the direction of the barricade and kicked him in the seat of his pants with his boot, so that Sellmann stumbled over his shovel and grazed his face in the fall. He got up quickly and joined some others who were trying to pull a car out of the wreckage. Because the metal of the wings was too hot, he grasped a piece of the windscreen, felt the pain for a second, but continued to pull until all four wheels were back on the street. Then he wiped the blood on his trousers and began to make a pyramid of the paving stones that were lying around, so as to make room to move the car. He did not look at the water again, even when the shout of joy from the spectators announced the end of the chase. It was enough that Heinrich was beside him.

When, later that afternoon, Sellmann climbed into the sandy bottom of the barricade to throw out any remaining pieces, the handle of the shovel felt wet. He licked his right hand and spat into the left as if to make it better for gripping. He was surprised that his left hand was bloody too. He wiped the sweat from his forehead and saw that his shirt-sleeve was full of blood. I'm not a butcher, he thought. The sand and the stones turned red too, and when Sellmann looked up, the sky was a deep red, rather like a stormy sunset. He pressed his chin on the handle of the shovel, straddled his legs, and closed his eyes. Behind his lids it was red too, not as red as before, but rather as if brickdust lay on his eyeballs. He breathed slowly and carefully, like a pair of bellows, and made his way back to the heap of stones, supported on his shovel like Amery senior with his silver-headed cane. He felt Heinrich's hand. Let's sit down. For a tired behind, paving stones are as comfortable as a club armchair. Put the shovel between the knees.

The guard who had been watching Sellmann stagger to the

heap of stones, knotted a bucket to a rope, let it down from the bridge, and brought it up half full.

'Go away,' he said to Heinrich who stood beside Sellmann. Then he poured the water over the head of the director of the Böhmische Landesbank. Sellmann opened his eyes, took his shovel, swung it high and brought it down on the guard's shoulder. He wanted to do it again, but the shovel slid out of his hand.

Only the people on the bridge heard the shot that threw him to the ground. Heinrich kneeled beside Sellmann and tried to turn him on his back. The guard who had got the water, and the guard who had fired the shot helped him. Heinrich took a corner of his shirt and cleaned his glasses between thumb and forefinger so as to look into Sellmann's face. He put his arms under the neck and knees.

'Wait,' said the guard and ran to the end of the bridge.

One of the stains on Sellmann's shirt got darker and larger, and blood seeped through the cardboard shield. Heinrich put his hand on Sellmann's chin and felt the short bristles. He wanted to close his father's eyes, but did not dare take off the gilt-rimmed spectacles. The guard came rattling along with a two-wheeled vegetable-cart, and the prisoners laid the dead man into the green-painted box.

When Heinrich saw his father's jacket near the parapet, he remembered the white beans. He stopped the cart and fetched the saucepan and the jacket. Then the guards cut the cardboard notice from his neck and put their feet on the rope dividing the bridge from the road, so that he could push his father across.

8

Bite Into An Invisible Lemon!

THE WEATHER REMAINED fine. Sixta, still pale from his winter hiding-place, went into the city.

The previous September, at the end of his home leave, he had stopped off in Prague on the way from Budweis, and instead of taking the train for Leipzig had gone back to live with his landlord in the 'vale of tears'. When he left there, the Mannlicher gun lay under the score of *The Last Judgment* in his suitcase. Through the good offices of a trombonist from the Philharmonic Orchestra he had found lodgings with a painter who, because he had a studio beside the Bottich river, was known as Botticelli. Living with the painter had been both tiring and tiresome. Botticelli spent hours standing naked in front of a mirror, his sexual organ in his left hand, his pencil in his right, drawing, while Sixta had to read to him from *The Life Story of a Viennese Whore*, or other 'suitable' books.

When he moved in with Vavra, Sixta noted that he had exchanged a monomaniac for a lunatic. He wasn't bothered by the fact that the professor wore not only his belt and braces, crossed over his chest, but also an army gun belt, but he was much confused by the professor's insistence on speaking English and French on alternate weeks. He had understood nothing of what the professor said except that he must not go out on the streets, and when Vavra went shopping, he heard him secure the safety lock behind him.

It had probably been a mistake on Sixta's part to show him, in an attempt to calm him, his gun. 'Throw it away!' he had exclaimed in English (despite his difficulties with the aspirated 't'), and with a suitable gesture. No, the weapon was Sixta's pillow, his life insurance, the last resort. Whenever he couldn't go to sleep because he had smoked too much and had forgotten where he had put his hands which had lost all feeling, when he heard steps outside the house, dogs barking in a nearby park, or the elevator coming to rest with a sigh, the memory of the gun was enough to make him feel not utterly lost.

But on gloomy mornings when he rose with the dim sun, he felt that he had searched for America and found the Indies. The experience of the camp failed him in his sanctuary. He did not know whether he was a free man or a deserter. In the camp there had been clear distinctions between friend and enemy. In Prague everyone seemed suspect. The trombonist advised him to be careful of the painter, Botticelli warned him of Vavra, Vavra distrusted the painter, and all of them doubted Sixta's reliability. Yet the trombonist played without pay for the wounded, Botticelli sold his oil paintings of the castle to German officers, and Vavra had, through his brother, worked for the Italian Academy. How would Sixta justify himself if asked to whom he owed the comfortable position at the aeroplane factory? How could he explain why, during the rising, he had written the last movement of his string quartet, *vivace ma non troppo,* instead of shooting out of his window?

The professor had put a piano at his disposal which Sixta had modified so that the felt hammers did not touch the strings. He had sat at his silent instrument for six months, deaf *'comme le vieux Smetana'* according to Vavra. The result could be seen if not heard: the quartet in D-minor whose parts he played for the first time while machine guns marked the beginning of the revolution.

An actress at the stage door of the local theatre reminded him of Sophie. His letters to the convent had seldom received a reply. Sophie had mostly sent Christmas greetings or birthday wishes, picture postcards of fat saints in whose hands the incunabula looked like cookbooks. He couldn't explain to himself, especially in this brain-softening weather, why he had continued to write to Bucovice. He had poured out his heart without ever being explicit, and had posted the letters himself so that no one in the camp should read the address. When the water was up to his neck, he had tried to prove how good a swimmer he was. He would have liked to have demonstrated to her what life was like without her. He would have liked to have been more specific, to torment both Sophie and himself, but his affair with a married student had to be kept secret from the Bucovice censor as did the Budweis stenographer and the Dessau bookseller, let alone the anaemic model in Botticelli's studio at the beginning of November when he had, in any case, ceased to write, so as not to give away his whereabouts.

A loudspeaker outside the National Museum was broadcasting the proclamation of the new Government. There seemed to be general agreement that one should use the victory while it was hot. In the Conservatoire Sixta discovered some old acquaintances with whom he sat down in the library. No dreaded questions were asked. A saxophonist told them how he had played for the Americans in Pilsen, a hundred cigarettes and a tin of corned beef per man per night. The prostitutes had arrived walking along the railway lines, since there were no trains. The Russians only paid in embraces, and anyway they made their own music, so one would have to play for one's own people. His uncle, who ran the Café Manes, wanted to make up three orchestras. He wanted musicians who played jazz, proper 'blues', boogie-woogie, Dixiland, bebop, swing, no rumtata, or 'I kiss your little hand, Madame'. Shouldn't one jump at it before the professionals snapped it up? Just temporarily, until one could see ahead a bit? He'd brought some music along.

'Why not?' Sixta said to his own surprise, and left the Conservatoire as pianist of the Original Swing Serenaders. They were engaged next morning, and the same evening they gave their first concert, and the manager counted out their payment in cash on the grand piano.

'We live again,' he explained the change of circumstances when Vavra came to his room.

'*Ce n'est pas de musique,*' said the professor. '*C'est beaucoup de bruit pour rien.*' And added, suddenly comprehensible in Czech, 'You shouldn't be doing that.'

'I owe you money.'

'Give me a ticket for the first performance of your quartet and we're quits.'

Sixta took a ticket from his breast pocket and gave it to the professor. 'Unfortunately not for anything of mine,' he said. 'The reopening of the National Theatre with Beneš speaking, this evening. I'm going too, but can only stay until the interval since I will have to play at the Café Manes afterwards.'

'I'd really meant to . . .' said Vavra.

'Yes?'

'Have you any idea what's happened to the Sellmanns?'

'No,' said Sixta and turned around on the piano stool.

'I've telephoned again and again. Nobody answers. Oughtn't we to go and have a look for them?'

Sixta frowned and nodded. He was angry not to have thought of this himself. They arranged to visit the Sellmanns that afternoon, and then to go to the opera together.

Wenceslas Square and the adjacent streets were closed to traffic because of the victory march. They could not get a tram to Bubenech until they reached the station. Vavra wore a dinner jacket, the trousers attached to the shirt with safety pins, Sixta a black suit the professor had lent him for his performances at the Café Manes.

'We look rather old-fashioned, don't we,' Vavra said in English as they rolled across the bridge, translating it himself when they had got off. Sixta smiled and looked at himself in the shop windows. He was pleased. But he'd have to grow his hair a bit longer. To celebrate the revolution, Vavra had shorn him like a village barber. A nice nose, though a little sensual, but did his mouth not deny what the nose promised? Sixta licked his lower lip until it shone, pushed it forward as if he were about to be photographed.

The prospect of meeting Sophie's parents daunted him. He hoped they'd be off and away by now, otherwise one would have to drink tea, stand up when the lady of the house stood up, bow, say thank you, and Vavra, polyglot like a sleeping-car attendant and gaudy as a peacock, would prophesy the future and hold his cup so crookedly that the lukewarm orange-pekoe dripped on to his knees. But perhaps they were in jail and one might be able to do something for them with food or character references. It was difficult to think of that family needing assistance, but the broken window and the flags – the professor pointed his chin at them – led to some such expectation. The brass plate had been taken away, the bell was silent. When they knocked, a stranger opened the door. He wore Sellmann's white dinner jacket with a five-pointed red star on the collar, and smelled like a field of lavender.

'Who are you?' Vavra asked without introducing himself and rather too brusquely for Sixta's taste.

'The caretaker,' he said. They stepped closer, and now he smelled of rotten eggs.

'Sir, you've shat in your pants,' Vavra said point-blank.

'Yes, indeed. I saw you come. Everything is still here.'

'We're neither from the police nor the funeral parlour,' Vavra explained, taking a pace back. 'Nevertheless we have the means of forcing a statement from you, if only by my reciting the original text of the *Edda* to you. Do you understand?'

The caretaker nodded, shattered.

'Where are the people who used to live here?'

The caretaker told them.

'The wife and son were taken away after the funeral. They were allowed to take their rucksacks and a few blankets. They're probably at the Strahov Stadium like the others.'

'And the girls?' Sixta asked.

'None of them were here.'

Sixta suggested to Vavra that they telephone Christine.

'Not from here,' Vavra said and shook himself.

They tried to telephone from Bubenech market, but there was no reply from the Amery apartment. By the time they left the phone box Vavra's forehead was wet. Because of the victory parade they were unable to get a tram, and they walked for a long time in the heat. Before they reached the stadium, Vavra had to take a breather, and Sixta smoked a cigarette. He suddenly thought that they should have enquired where Sellmann had been buried, and Vavra nodded his head as if he could read his thoughts.

In front of the ticket office of the stadium, soldiers with red armbands sat playing cards. The flags made it impossible to look through the railings. While Vavra asked where the Germans were housed, Sixta watched a flag balloon out and then slap back against the bars. Behind the gap stood a two-wheeled bicycle-trailer in which a dog lay, perhaps a chow, a dog with a red-brown coat, his blue tongue hanging out. Sixta whistled, but the dog did not open his eyes.

'He's snuffed it,' the soldier called.

'Can we go in?' Sixta asked.

Vavra shrugged his shoulders and stood waiting for an officer who was hurriedly approaching them. Sixta could hear from Vavra's voice that he was angry because he had to repeat his request.

'What sort of Germans,' the officer asked, still out of breath. 'We only have Fascists here.'

'No women?' asked Vavra.

The officer grinned. 'Any objections?'

'There are even dogs,' Sixta said to make a joke, but nobody laughed.

'If you could give us a list,' Vavra said, 'We'd soon be able to find the lady we are looking for.'

'Go to the Ministry of the Interior,' the officer said and leaned against the flag.

'Couldn't we just simply look around the stadium?' Vavra asked.

'Come along,' Sixta said to him. 'Come along!' and took the professor by the arm.

'I was a legionnaire,' Vavra roared over Sixta's shoulder. 'I'm going to complain about you. My brother knows the President personally.' He went on swearing and shaking his fists, and stamped his feet so much that Sixta was afraid he would lose his trousers. They stopped at an open-air café, and he quieted down but would not listen to any excuses Sixta made for the officer. He dipped a salt stick in the beerfoam and sucked it, stupefied by the cheering and shouting of the crowds and the braying of the brass band. When Sixta asked whether they should go straight to the opera he nodded, but after he had eaten a second salt stick he corrected himself.

'Give my ticket to that fellow,' he said, pointing to a drunk who had just lifted his head from his plate and wiped the onions

287

from his forehead. 'He's in the right mood. Or ask the caretaker in Bubenech.'

'You're unjust.'

Though the music snatched every word from his mouth, Vavra answered at length. He did not need anyone to listen since he did not want to prove anything, he might even have been speaking in English. They paid for their beer and wandered through the dusky park. At the crossroads lanterns burned. Sixta wondered how the people in the stadium lit their sleeping quarters. Did they sleep on the seats, on the grass, on the cinder track? In Dessau, searchlights had lit up the barracks of the foreign workers until there were so many air raids that it was better to risk an escape than a direct hit.

Sixta told this to Vavra and the professor remained silent, then said suddenly, 'I'm afraid, you know. I wasn't afraid during the war. After all, I wasn't a German. But now I'm afraid. You'll be earning a lot of money soon?'

'I hope so.'

'Do you think your salary will run to renting your own apartment?'

'Certainly,' Sixta said, surprised that he wasn't furious. 'I could move out tomorrow.'

'Give my compliments to your mother.'

'I've been thinking of writing to her,' Sixta said. 'I'll just nip into the Café Manes and do it.'

'Do that!' said Vavra and held out his hand. 'Goodbye.'

On his way, Sixta realised that he had forgotten to ask Vavra for the ticket, but did not feel like turning round. The seat beside him might as well remain empty.

In the Café Manes the evening clients were taking the place of the *thé dansant* crowd. Sixta fetched paper and stamp from the office and sat down on the terrace. He soon gave up trying to explain the circumstances of his flight and the events of the past weeks, but emphasised that he was in good shape, mentally and physically, and closed expressing his regrets that he could not give her an address because he was looking for an apartment. A mixture of vague news and propitiatory emotion, he decided when he read through it, but mothers needed such letters. Then he remembered that he had forgotten Vavra's message and added, 'P.S. Professor Vavra, with whom I went to Bubenech today (Sellmann lost his life last week, his wife and son are being repatriated), sends you his obeisance and kisses your hand.'

While Sixta was putting the sheet of paper into the envelope, he heard his name called, and saw a young man mount the terrace steps. As far as he could see by the light of the lamp, he was fair and wore a dark brown double-breasted jacket. It took Sixta a while to realise that it was Georg, the little actor, his cousin's son. He stood up and took hold of his sleeve, and they fell round each other's neck. Georg sat down at the table and looked closely at Sixta as if he wanted to make sure he hadn't got the wrong man. When Sixta had been in Budweis nine months before, he had heard that Georg, having completed his sentence, was helping to build an army training ground.

Georg's smile was so affectionate, their family connection could not have been the only cause.

'Exercise I,' said Sixta, 'Bite into an invisible lemon! Exercise II, clean invisible stairs. Exercise III – do you still remember?'

'The lion,' Georg said and wiped his eyes. His left thumb had been cut down to the middle knuckle like the docked tail of a dog. 'A tip-up truck,' he explained as if he had felt the glance. 'On stage I'll have to wear gloves or an artificial limb. Horrible for Romeo, what?'

Georg explained how he had come to Prague and been told at the Conservatoire that Sixta played with the Original Swing Serenaders. He had even found an apartment on Wenceslas Square, two rooms, kitchens, bath, completely furnished, telephone, the windows at the back, but chestnuts in the courtyard. Sixta remembered that the Minister woud be making a speech before the performance and that he did not want to miss it.

'I'll come and see you,' he said. 'I'm afraid I've got to go to the opera now.'

'Can I come with you?'

'I have only one ticket. But if you . . .' he didn't know why he was hesitating.

'Well?' Georg asked as if ready for anything.

'If you'd like to stay here . . . I'll be back in two hours.'

'Good,' said Georg and laid his hand on the letter. 'I'll see to that in the meantime.'

Irresolutely, Sixta scratched his chin and suddenly wanted to snatch the envelope as in a game, but missed and felt his hand crushed against the table.

'Sorry,' said Georg and freed it. 'Sorry,' he repeated. 'A habit from clink. A trick, you understand. I could show you how to break someone's neck in passing.'

'No need,' Sixta said, and rubbed his fingers.

Georg held the envelope towards the light and read the address.

'To your mother?'

Sixta recaptured the letter, and Georg called after him, 'I'll be waiting.'

The windows of the National Theatre gleamed like holes in a huge cardboard box which is lit from inside. The chauffeurs of the parked cars leaned against the bodywork, squatted on the running-boards, or stood on the quay smoking, throwing the fag-ends into the river. Sixta smelled the biting smoke of the cigarettes and the scent of violets. He entered the foyer from the quay, but was told that he could not go to his seat until the Minister had finished speaking. He went to drink a lemonade and was surprised to see Professor Vavra running towards him, waving the forgotten ticket.

'There you are at last, forgive me for my carelessness.'

'That's all right,' Sixta said and took the ticket.

'Thank God I arrived before the performance had begun,' Vavra said and walked beside Sixta. 'If the Minister is talking about Smetana he won't stop in a hurry. Do you know why? No? Well, fifty years ago he wanted to marry Dvorak's daughter, but was refused. Since then Smetana is his favourite. Why didn't you know that?'

Sixta shrugged.

'It's very interesting,' Vavra went on, not realising that Sixta felt him to be a nuisance. 'I'll tell more about it tomorrow.'

'I'm moving,' Sixta said, more sharply than he had meant to.

'That's why I'm here,' Vavra said. 'I've thought about it, and really, it's very nice to have you in the house. You won't find a better room in a hurry. We could arrange for you to practise in the mornings, and in the evenings you'll be at the café. Give it time. I would miss you, *mon cher.*'

'I've already got a room with my nephew,' Sixta said and regretted that after this lie he didn't have the heart to go down the two steps that divided him from the professor.

'Ah well,' Vavra said. 'Ah well. I didn't know. Forgive me for keeping you.' He smiled sadly as the applause on the other side of the door announced the end of the Ministerial speech, and bowed while Sixta, overcome by his own pose, tore up Vavra's ticket with sharp fingers.

Sixta squeezed past evening dresses, dinner jackets and uniforms to his seat, and hoped he might be able to forget the unpleasant incident in the same way that he had tried to forget his toothache as a child by sitting in the dark cellar. But when the curtain rose he felt sick. The dead chow stuck out its tongue, Sellmann's caretaker rubbed a spot from his white dinner jacket, Vavra wiped his tear-stained face on a plush curtain in the theatre foyer, Georg picked his nose with his docked thumb. Sixta put his head between his knees, clenching his teeth against his retching. When there was applause before the scene change, he stumbled out and was sick, before the attendant could show him the way to the toilets, into a tub of laurel. He gave the girl all the money he had on him, and left the theatre.

Next morning a young man appeared at Vavra's and handed him a black suit and a piece of paper. When the professor gave his permission, he packed Sixta's clothes and scores, shut the lock of the suitcase with a cripped left thumb, took the gun from under the mattress and put it in his coat pocket.

'That's it, do you think?'

'*Absolument*,' said Vavra.

9

A Visit

KATHARINA'S ARRIVAL IN Prague continued to be delayed. In the winter she had become pregnant and a partisan doctor had arranged an abortion while Karol was away at a session of the National Council. When he returned in April in his new olive-green field-service jacket, he entrusted her to a Russian Red Cross column. She asked to be taken to the Bucovice hospital but had a relapse when she heard that 'Sister Agnes' had left the convent before Easter. Karol visited her every day and remained in Bratislava though his father urged him to join the delegation which was negotiating the eventual representation of Slovak interests in the Prague Government. Karol promised to come the moment Katharina was able to accompany him. Dr. Djudko, who had spent the war in Moscow, went on ahead and succeeded in getting his son appointed a member of the committee preparing for the National Assembly, and as an officer of police. Karol showed Katharina the announcement in the newspaper during their first walk together.

'Now I've got to get well, Captain sir!' she said, holding her face to the sun.

On the evening before their departure for Prague, Karol had a long telephone conversation with his father and heard of Sellmann's death and the expulsion of Betty and Heinrich.

'No, no,' Dr. Djudko assured him. 'That has no bearing on Katja. I've already arranged for her residence permit. You can go and live in the Sellmann apartment. It looks a bit wild because the caretaker has been keeping house in it, but I've had him thrown out. I hope you're not expecting me to wash the curtains? Have you prepared yourself for the constitutional debate? There are a few people here who question the President's continuing in office because he resigned, and his successor had a three-fifths majority. They don't talk about it openly but ask awkward questions, and we can't just put them up against a wall – they're our allies after all – you understand?'

'We could simply refer them to Hitler's protocol,' Karol said. 'A President who puts the destiny of his state into the hands of a foreign nation, denies his own position.'

'Exactly. I've thought of that too,' said Djudko. 'If you go on like this, you'll be Minister of Justice before long.' When Karol said nothing he added, 'May I, though you're thirty now, give you some advice? Not as a father but as a comrade! Wait a little before you marry.'

'We never discuss it,' Karol said.

'That's as may be, but you threatened it eight years ago. Unfortunately we can't be at the station since we have to attend a banquet for Marshal Konyev, the emigrants in ready-made lounge suits, the resistance in full evening dress, the ladies in organza, and the Alexandor Choir in parade uniform! May I, as your father, give you one more piece of advice? Buy a litre of vodka, get drunk, and leave enough in the bottle for tomorrow morning. But for heaven's sake don't tell your mother. The keys are with the neighbours. If the door is locked and nobody hears at first, don't shoot at the windows.'

The more Dr. Djudko joked, the more certain Karol was that his father was either afraid or, and it came to the same thing, had had an experience which refuted the optimism with which he had gone to Prague.

When he had finished telephoning, Karol tried to read himself to sleep with Marx's *Critique of Hegelian Dialectic and Philosophy*, but its well-proven soporific effect failed for once.

Karol followed his father's advice and drank three-quarters of a litre of vodka and kept the rest for the morrow.

Next morning he drove to Bucovice in a jeep. As a present for the Sisters he brought a gilt processional cross which he had bartered for a dozen pairs of pink corsets with a Russian parachutist. Katharina climbed into the car and fixed the window so that the wind blew her hair back from her forehead. At the station they got into a first-class compartment which was to be attached to a military transport towards noon. Karol distributed their luggage all over the compartment and attached his gunbelt with gun and cartridge pouch to the window handle, to stop anyone asking for a seat. While Katharina drank the last convent tea from a thermos flask, Karol leafed through a book. When Katharina suggested that instead of reading them, they should tear out the pages and make aeroplanes, he gave her the book and, to facilitate the despatch of the squadron, opened the window.

'A pity it's raining,' he said. 'They won't get far.'

Katharina threw out a few aeroplanes, but they were beaten down by the heavy rain or were blown back into the compartment. Karol shut the window and said, 'Your father is dead, Katja.'

'Yes,' she replied. 'I spoke to Christine on the telephone a few days ago, but I didn't want to tell you until we were on our way.' She stretched her face and lifted her eyebrows in a way that was familiar to Karol from his mother, who always stared in this way when she didn't want to spoil her make-up with tears. But it made Frau Djudko look offended and quarrelsome, while Katharina looked astonished and disconcerted. She flicked the last of the paper aeroplanes from the grey upholstery. One couldn't tell whether she mourned more for her father or the crashed planes, and Karol resisted a feeling of half pity, half mistrust as he had done six weeks previously when he had found out about Katharina's pregnancy by being told of her abortion.

'Don't look at my nose, Captain sir,' she said. 'You know I don't like it.'

'I'm sorry.' He leaned his temples against the window and listened to what Katharina had to tell him.

'Christine is very proud of Amery. He belongs to a commando that stormed the radio station.'

'With coffee pots and flower vases, I suppose,' Karol said without turning.

'Christine thinks he'll go into politics,' Katharina said. 'All sorts of people have already approached him, but he hasn't made up his mind yet.'

'China is safer.'

'Then I'd better go and live with them perhaps,' Katharina said. 'My sister has offered to have me.'

Karol did not reply. He felt Katharina sit down beside him, move his arm out of the way, and put her head on his lap. For a while he enjoyed feeling melancholic, hung over, and morose, looking out of the window into the rainy landscape. But then he asked, clearing his throat, 'Shall I close the curtains?'

'You can't make love to me yet,' Katharina said. 'Anyway, the door won't lock, didn't you notice?'

'Yes,' he said and looked out again, first a bit desperate and ready to grind his teeth, but eventually smiling and quite happy again. At Brno he bought some Slivovitz and sipped it as an accompaniment to the salami which the Bucovice Sisters had given Katharina.

Most of the people in the train got out at a station of which only a shed could be seen. When the train stopped at Prague goods station, Karol took both the trunks and ran along the empty platform, hoping to find a taxi, Katharina took the hand luggage and waited while Karol tried to telephone. When his efforts took too much time, she went into the street and stopped the first car that came along with outstretched arms. 'You driving to Bubenech,' she said in a Russian accent when the man at the wheel had opened the door. When Karol came out of the station with the trunks and looked about him, perplexed, she was sitting in the car and laughing.

In Bubenech they had neither to ring the bell nor shoot at the windows. The neighbour had remained awake and threw down the keys, closing the window before Karol could thank him. They did not look closely at the apartment and slept in Katharina's room.

Next morning Karol went to the Ministry of the Interior. Dr. Djudko had told him which department to go to, but the head and other members were at a meeting and could not be called out. The secretary suggested Karol bring four passport photographs. He telephoned his father at the Czernin Palace and arranged to meet him for lunch at the Hotel Ambassador. He decided against asking Katharina to join them; she would lunch at Christine's. On the way he had himself photographed. The photographer tried to make him smile, but Karol insisted on his usual expression. He felt as if he had reached his goal and didn't know where to go on to now. He hoped his father would enlighten him, but had difficulty in understanding what Dr. Djudko tried to explain over bouillon, a lung-roast and cranberries.

'Victory has made us too many friends,' he lectured, and praised the sauce. 'It makes the individual into a type. We were wrong to expect political extravagance, adversaries, factions. Instead we have to encourage people to remain true to their parties. They don't want discussion, they want decrees. Resolutions are passed unanimously. Well, then, your good health!' Dr. Djudko wiped his mouth and looked at the rim of his glass before drinking. 'And what does that teach us?' he asked, smiling, and put his glass down on the damask tablecloth. 'We have all the power, but cannot admit it. Or, to put it differently, we govern on our own, but have to pretend to depend on a coalition. I think our position is pretty unique. I fear we shall have to institute one day a week when it is illegal to shout "long live the Soviet Union"! Sounds a bit cynical, no? Don't worry, you'll have your difficulties.'

'Because of Katja?' Karol asked.

'I hope she realises that she has to stay at home for the time being?' Djudko handed a paper across the table.

'She is with her sister,' Karol said, and thanked his father for the residence permit.

'Very thoughtless,' Djudko warned. 'What if she is asked for her papers on the way?'

'But what can happen to her?'

'If I were you I'd go straight to the Amerys' apartment. Or shall I drive you? Well, it isn't far, you'll do as well on foot.' Karol put his knife and fork on his plate and looked at his father in astonishment.

'But . . .'

'Do as I tell you.'

Karol got up and shook his head.

'If you need me, you have my number. But I'm with the Minister today. If I'm lucky he'll send me to the United Nations. Keep your fingers crossed that I'm not made Ambassador to Ulan-Bator. We'll be visiting you within a day or two. And now, run!'

Karol went through the revolving door into Wenceslas Square. He would have liked to have hurried, but everyone looked so much as usual that he went along quite slowly. He felt like turning round and asking Djudko not to make such jokes at his expense again, but the memory of certain events in Bratislava, and the sight of two women with close-cropped hair drove him on, so that after a while he did not care if he ran into people walking in the opposite direction.

Amery opened the door and asked him in. Yes, Katja had said she would come to lunch. 'We're still waiting.' Christine appeared in light-coloured calico with blue batik flowers. She stretched out both hands to greet Karol. He only took her right hand and asked if he might use the telephone.

'We've been trying for the last hour,' Amery said. 'I'll drive you home,' he said when Karol put the receiver down.

'She probably doesn't answer,' Christine said. 'I won't answer the telephone either. I ignore the whole business. People want to have their fling; it's understandable in a way.'

'Yes,' said Karol and looked from the cornflowers of her dress to the pattern of the carpet. But he refused the offer of a lift.

'How would you like us to come by for a moment this evening?' Christine asked.

'I think Katja would be pleased,' Karol said against his own belief.

Amery accompanied him downstairs.

'Is it true that you are going to be a candidate for the next Parliament?' asked Karol.

Amery shook his head. 'My chances of election are too small.' He smiled. 'Since I've met our new masters I've decided on a one-man party. No, one moment,' he said when Karol wanted to say goodbye. 'I'll come with you for a bit of the way, I want to tell you something for which I won't have the opportunity if we visit you tonight. You're in the best possible frame of mind for it now.' He put his hand on Karol's sleeve as they crossed the street. 'You'll have your own reasons for thinking little of my wife or myself. This is not the time to discuss it, and probably it is unnecessary anyway. But I sometimes remember a winter morning in Dubislav when I walked with your father and Doktor Sellmann . . . well, let's leave that. You're in a hurry. Would you rather talk about it tonight? No, wait. It's quickly said. Has anybody suggested you should hide Katja? Yes? Your father? That's understandable. But one day you will be accused of having lived with a German. It would be nice if you showed the same keenness then as now. Otherwise you'll have to reckon with me, captain.'

'Is that a threat?' Karol asked.

'No,' said Amery and turned to him. 'I just want you to know that I am at Katja's disposal if she needs anybody. Forget it, or remember it some time, it's your choice. There's a taxi.'

Karol went to Bubenech, but there was not even a message in the apartment. Katharina's case stood beside the bed. On top of her clothes lay the embroidered shepherd's belt he had brought her from the mountains. He looked in the cupboard, but did not know Katharina's clothes well enough to see what was missing.

He lay down on the drawing-room sofa and looked at the mutilated picture of the Wildfowler. After a while he jumped up and went into Sellmann's study where in prehistoric times, in the days before the Flood, two serious children had sworn eternal faithfulness, the girl in a high-necked green dress, the boy in a grey linen suit.

In the wood of the bookcases the letters USA and USSR had been carved beside the initials of the caretaker. The topaz paper-weight lay in the splinters of the glass-fronted cabinet. The wallpaper was lighter where the Mortlake Tapestry had hung.

Where should he look for Katja? Had she taken the train to the frontier? Had she gone for a walk, gone shopping, gone for a stroll? Had she been stopped and arrested? Would she defend herself? Bite, scratch, kick? Suddenly he thought of asking his mother what a girl in Katja's position would do.

'She's at the cemetery,' Frau Djudko said without hesitation.

'Thank you,' Karol said and put the receiver down.

Beyond the chestnut walk he saw the red bush of hair above her black dress. Katharina saw him and waved. She walked slowly towards him as if she wanted to finish her thoughts before putting her hand through his arm.

'We've got to put up a cross,' she said. 'The gardener has given me an address. The grave looks so empty, you know.'

'I'll see to that,' Karol promised and told her that he had lunched with his father and had been at Amery's.

'My God,' Katharina exclaimed. 'They telephoned from the Ministry.'

'When?'

'Soon after you'd been there. The head of the department apologised for not being there to receive you. He wants you to come tomorrow morning without fail, even without the passport photos. A nice man.'

'How did you manage to talk?' asked Karol and put his forefinger inside his collar.

'He speaks perfect German,' Katharina said 'He was in Dachau for three years.'

'Wasn't he surprised?'

'Why?'

'That I didn't wait for him this morning,' Karol lied.

'No,' she said, and hopped to get into step with him. 'He respects you. I told him that I respect you too. Then he said, "my respects, Comrade Sellmann". So we all respect each other. Or don't you respect me?'

'I do,' he said and put his arm around her hips. 'But don't jump around so.'

'If I were a housewife,' Katharina said when they returned to the apartment, 'I'd have cleaned up. But I thought it'd be quicker for two.'

'Hm,' grumbled Karol.

When Jan and Christine arrived that evening, he was still busily mending the picture of the Wildfowler with sticking plaster. Katharina welcomed her sister and brother-in-law in an apron, to save herself, Karol supposed, from Christine's embrace. Amery brought cold meat, wine and glasses. The conversation between the sisters began with questions, the answers to which did not seem to interest either of them. Karol was grateful when Amery asked how the Slovak rising had been organised. He told him how his group had operated, and the more wine he drank, the more detailed his descriptions became. When he spoke about the crossing of the Vàh, Christine interrupted him.

'Excuse me, this doesn't have anything to do with it, but as you were speaking of that river – what will become of Papa's country house on the Sázava?'

'Oh, I think . . .' Amery said, trying to stop her, but she would not be interrupted.

'It was registered before the occupation,' she said, beaming. 'Could one simply seize it? What do the police think?'

'I have nothing to do with houses,' Karol said and turned back to Amery.

'I don't care a hoot either,' Katharina said.

'Yes, but I care,' Christine insisted. 'We could sell it, or have you more money than you know what to do with? Have you considered how much rent you'll have to pay here?'

Amery leaned forward and asked Karol, 'Don't you think the help given by regular troops during the uprising is being under-estimated these days?'

'Possibly,' Karol said.

'Would you like to see Heinrich's collection of badges?' Katharina asked.

'Yes, please,' Christine said, and the sisters went out.

When they returned half an hour later, Karol and Amery sat smoking over the empty bottle. At that moment the telephone rang.

'That'll be your father,' Katharina said.

'Djudko,' Karol announced himself and pushed the drawing-room door shut. There was no reply. 'Djudko,' he repeated and thought he could hear breathing at the other end. 'Hullo,' he called, 'Who is it, please?' He did not know what made him keep listening to the breathing for almost a minute. When he realised that it was fear, he said, 'Please have your line checked. Goodbye.' With his hand on the door handle it occurred to him that now he could get rid of his visitors.

Amery was obviously telepathic. 'Official business?' he asked, getting up.

'Yes, I'm afraid so,' Karol said and they both smiled.

When they said goodbye, no further meeting was arranged, and nobody pretended that they were sorry.

'A beautiful night,' Christine said at the street door.

'Yes,' said Karol and wished them a good trip home. He watched them drive away, then went out into the street and a little way towards the next corner. Yes, it was a beautiful night, he thought, so peaceful and quiet. It was different from the silence of the nights before the attack, when silence was a hiding place, the magazines resting in the machine guns, metal parts of the gun carriages clinking against each other, and the heart beating like a drum. To think of somebody breathing into a telephone receiver to frighten another person seemed so absurd to Karol that he was ashamed of his fear. He saw Katharina against the light of the room and waved to her. She had her elbows on the window sill and did not move. 'Katja,' he called, but she remained silent. He ran into the house and up the stairs. When he entered the room she said, 'Beautiful, isn't it?'

'Didn't you hear me?' he asked.

'No.'

He took her into his arms and kissed her.

'What is it? You are trembling.'

'It's been a bit much today,' Karol said and undid his tie.

'Who rang?' she wanted to know before he left the room.

'My father,' he said. 'He'll either be going to New York or Outer Mongolia. Kindest regards.'

He had a cold shower, dried himself, and put on Heinrich's pyjamas, turned up the long trouser legs and ran through the dark hall. He fastened the safety chain, felt for his gun belt and unbuttoned the holster.

When they had cleaned the apartment they had left the master bedroom untouched, but had carried Heinrich's bed into Katharina's room. Now he thought of the other room as Katharina told him of her sister's curiosity.

'She wanted to go into all the rooms.'

'The bedroom too?'

'I just couldn't get her out of it. I think she was looking for something.'

'Did she look into the cupboards?'

'No, but under the bed. She thinks we've hidden the tapestry, the bitch. I'd cut it into pieces and send them to her piece by piece if we had it!'

'She didn't drop any hints?'

'She didn't want me to notice that she was spying. "That was our childhood," she exclaimed, and went on her knees in front of the picture on Papa's bedside table. And then she looked under the beds. If I wasn't sorry for Jan, I'd say: immediate expropriation for those brutes.'

' "The democratic revolution is bourgeois",' Karol quoted. 'Lenin, *Two tactics of Social Democracy*.'

'It's nonsense nevertheless.'

'And if I'd written it?'

Katharina turned her head to one side and smiled. 'That would be different, of course.'

As he climbed into bed the doorbell rang.

'Who can that be?'

'I hope it isn't anybody to borrow money,' Katharina said crossly. 'Ask who it is before you open.'

'Don't worry,' he assured her and went out. In the hall he wiped his sweating hands on his trousers and took the gun out of the holster. When he opened the spy-hole in the door, the stair light went out. 'Who is it?' he asked and heard a step. The light went on again. He saw a coat, white like a burnous and above it the shadowy face of a woman. He took off the safety chain and opened the door.

'Good evening.'

'Who are you?'

'I am Sister Agnes,' said Sophie.

Karol stuck the gun into the waistband of his pyjamas, but it slipped down, and he knew he did not cut a very impressive figure as he bent over and held the weapon with both hands below his stomach.

'Are you ill?' Sophie asked.

'No, no, on the contrary. Come in,' Karol said and took the gun out of his trousers and put it down. 'Blessed be Jesus Christ,' he groaned in Slovak.

'For ever and ever, amen,' Sophie replied in the same language, stepped into the hall and stood still until Karol had turned on the

300

light. Then she put her suitcase down.

'I don't want to be a nuisance,' she said and shook her habit as if it had been raining out of doors.

'Did you phone earlier this evening?' asked Karol.

'Yes.'

'Why didn't you at least give your name?'

'I wanted it to be a surprise.'

Karol took the suitcase and sighed. 'You've certainly succeeded. An hour ago the surprise would have been even bigger, but it's quite enough as it is. Sister Katja's cell is the third door on the right.'

He watched Katja run towards her sister. Then he squatted on the floor, laughed, and put his arms around the suitcase.

IO

Seven Pens, Seven Mice

IN MAY, SOPHIE had fled from Frau Sixta's house to the Sisters of the Budweis Old People's Home. It was there that she had read the letter Pavel had written on the terrace of the Café Manes. When she had heard a Requiem Mass for her father it came to her what she must do: go back to Germany with Katja.

But breakfasting in Bubenech, she found that Katharina wanted to stay in Prague, and Karol explained that one could not cross the frontier without first going into a camp and joining a transport.

'I'll arrange for a temporary permit of residence,' he said. 'You won't have to wear a yellow arm band. You helped us. Now it's our turn.'

'Lasko,' Katharina reminded her. 'The suitcase with the wireless transmitter.

'Fill out the forms and get yourself photographed,' Karol suggested. 'But not in those clothes. It would be better if you didn't wear the habit while you are here.'

Sophie remembered the pearl-grey dress in which she had walked about Brno all one day. She wanted to protest, but the kitchen wasn't the right place. It was difficult to keep up an argument with marmalade in your mouth. In Prague, coffee strainers, frying pans and oven-clothes were nothing but useful objects. In Bucovice even the urine bottles and feeding cups were holy. Now she stood by the stove, waited for the water to heat, looked at the dirty dishes in the sink and couldn't think for whom she should wash up.

She went to the photographer, but when, a week later, she collected the photos, she hid them from Katharina. Only Karol had to see the passport photographs, because of his official position.

'You ought to have those enlarged,' he flattered her.

Sophie blushed to her shoulders, and her arms itched under her pullover. When Karol brought her the permit of residence, Sophie asked whether she might look for work now she had this document.

'Try it,' he said.

She telephoned several hospitals and asked whether they needed nurses. Yes. But when she went to the personnel department and showed her papers, she was turned away. She did not try the University Clinic because it was in a part of town which she avoided, even if she had to go a long way round.

She was used to fixed hours from the convent, so she was up by five every morning, went to early Mass, and bought rolls and newspapers on her way home. When Karol and Katharina came into the kitchen, she had already laid the table and made coffee. If Karol went off on his own, she spent the morning with her sister. If Katharina went with Karol, she dawdled through the rooms, opened drawers to look for lost memories among the bits and pieces. Did Aunt Marketa still crack violet lozenges? Did Fräulein Kalman still sing scales with her bunch of keys hanging over her turquoise pullover? Did Professor Vavra still wear a belt and braces? Did the world still turn as if nothing had happened?

Katharina had changed, smoked in the lavatory, cut her hair and fingernails short, wore men's trousers, and read the editorials in the morning papers. She even demanded that Sophie read the chapter about dialectical and historical materialism in the history of the Communist Party of the Soviet Union, so she'd learn a bit of sense. Sometimes she spread out a map of Slovakia, stuck pins in the Tatra Mountains, and cried without discernible reason. At night she shut herself in the bathroom, waited until Karol rang the bell, then ran to the door and embraced him as if she had not seen him for weeks. If he was late, she reproached him. If he went to meetings or social gatherings to which she had not been invited, she sat in the drawing-room which she now called sitting-room, and drank lemonade and vodka. 'Don't go to bed,' she said to Sophie whose eyes wouldn't stay open after nine o'clock, and spoke of the uprising and the hiding place in the mountains, and of her fear when the anaesthetic mask was put over her face, and she had felt the cold forceps between her legs.

In July, to celebrate her birthday, which neither Karol nor Katharina had remembered, Sophie went to see Professor Vavra. On the way she read her mother's birthday greetings.

'Since I heard that you are well and with Katja,' Betty wrote, 'I can sleep again. We're living with Uncle Wilhelm at the Wild-fowler for the time being. Heinrich works on a farm. I help at the inn because Aunt Rosa has sciatica. There is a lot of coming and going here, many Russians, refugees and bombed-out people. We only go to town on Sundays. Everything has been destroyed except the barracks. The market, the old bridge, the castle, everything is gone. It seems a miracle that our church has been spared, and now the Protestants come to us. However much I'd like you here, I advise you not to be hasty. As you know, the Freiburg convent where you want to go has been burnt down.'

Sophie pushed the letter into her handbag and looked out of the window when the tram turned into Wenceslas Square. The display figures in the shop windows, and the girls in the street, were showing off the latest summer fashions. Men in straw hats went in and out of shops, banks and cafés.

After she had said goodbye to Vavra and was travelling down in the elevator, she wished the ride would never end, that she would go right through the earth and come out in the antipodes among rabbits and kangaroos, where nobody knew of Fräulein Kalman and Victor Lustig, the Prankraz prison, Theresienstadt and the Gestapo. In the street she went up to a stranger and said in Czech, 'I am a German'.

'Kiss my arse,' he snarled and went on.

When she repeated the performance with a postman, he said, 'Then go hang yourself.'

I've got the wrong people, she thought. At least I ought to get my face slapped.

She saw an elderly man who wore a carnation in his buttonhole. She went up to him and said it again.

'Sorry, dear lady,' he answered in German. 'I'm afraid I haven't got a penny on me,' took his hat from his head, exposing dyed hair, and walked towards a woman who came to meet him.

On the bridges the lights had been turned on. The darker it became the brighter the lamps shone on the riversides, and the water reflected the lights.

'Please forgive me,' Katharina said when she opened the door. 'I'd totally forgotten your birthday – with my memory for dates! But someone else hasn't forgotten. He's been waiting an hour.'

'Who?' asked Sophie and kept her handbag in her hand.

'You'll see him in a minute,' Katharina whispered and pulled Sophie along behind her. 'I'm no sadist.'

Beside the table in the drawing-room stood Sixta, tall and slim in his black suit. He smiled shyly like an examinee who has given up all hope. He gave Sophie his flowers and wanted to say something, but only his lips moved. Sophie heard Katharina leave the room. She took a step forward and leaned against him with the bunch of flowers and handbag. Sixta said her name. She hadn't heard it said that way since Hanna had left Bucovice, the 's' soft and silky.

'Say it again,' she said, and would have remained standing like that, but Karol shouted in the corridor, 'Because today is Tuesday!'

'And when will you be home?' asked Katharina.

'As soon as it's over.'

When Karol slammed the apartment door, Sophie put the flowers on the table and Sixta pulled a chair out for her. Both were waiting for the door to open, but Katharina went into the kitchen and put the coffee things into the sink. Sophie threw her handbag beside the flowers.

Next evening she sat at a reserved table in the Café Manes. The Serenaders played a blues, and the dancers rocked, belly to belly. In the interval Sixta took her down to the island. Sophie looked at the lock by the small weir as if she could keep the Vltava back with her eyes. When Sixta put his arm around her, her knees became soft, and when he took her back to her table she was afraid she might stumble. She did not dare look in the mirror, for she was ashamed of her straight hair, her old-fashioned velvet dress. To stay awake she drank several cups of coffee and went back and forth between her table and the lavatory. She felt old because nobody asked her to dance.

When Sixta climbed down from the platform at midnight, she did not hear what he said to her. She was deaf from the music. But no doubt all that he'd said was that he would take her home.

They strolled along behind the last customers. In the street, the boys gave their jackets to the girls, rolled up their sleeves as if they wanted to fight or chop wood, took the jackets back, hooked them over their index finger and made them revolve. Sixta took off his tie and unbuttoned his collar. When he turned away from the National Theatre, Sophie thought they were making a detour. Unlike the boys who had been silent the moment they were alone with the girls, Sixta talked without taking breath, told her how he had got the job at the Manes, asked how she had got on with his mother, and saved her the trouble of replying, 'She's marvellous, isn't she!'

'She wrote straight away that you were in Prague. No, not immediately, otherwise I'd have come to see you sooner.'

A little further on he kissed her, but immediately went on talking. Every time they reached the darkest spot between two street lamps he kissed her, and eventually she noticed that they were walking neither towards Bubenech nor to a tram stop, and that he was talking so much to distract her from the direction they were taking. For a while she thought of saying goodbye. But why? Didn't she love the man who had written her, 'When I close my eyes, seven pens scratch over the paper. It is as if there were seven mice in the wall. We will survive this war and live differently...' Perhaps tonight was the night when peace began.

She licked her dry lips and put her arm into his open jacket, feeling his perspiring back. He stopped and stared into a shop window, then took off his jacket, hung it over Sophie's shoulders and rolled up his shirt sleeves as the young men had done. He stuck his index finger through the loop and swung the jacket until it turned in front of Sophie's face like a propeller.. Then he let it swing to rest and asked, smiling, 'Good?'

She nodded. She blamed the way her heart beat on the coffee.

Diagonally across from the museum she followed him through the door of an apartment house. He opened a door on the first floor, and Sophie entered a cool corridor. When he turned on the bedside lamp in his room, she saw the score of an opera, written in pencil. She would have liked to have asked what it was, but was afraid of saying the wrong thing, yet felt that the fear of making a mistake was a mistake in itself.

On the couch lay a flowered cover, and green and white pyjama trousers showed underneath. She suddenly felt as if she had shrunk to nothing, so light that her handbag was huge and heavy. She saw Sixta close the window, but it seemed to take a long time before he turned. Why did he give her so much time? She wondered where she would be now if she had taken the train to Prague from Brno. Would she be standing on this carpet, under a ceiling that appeared as far away as on a stage, a theatre-sky under which she was to play the part of her life without make-up or costume or prompter? She heard Sixta draw the curtain, and he glided towards her as silently as on a revolving stage. He kissed her and pressed her head back as if the play had started with the happy ending. Then he said something which she did not understand, but which must have been the cue for the beginning.

In the morning she put on his pyjamas, pulled the curtain, and looked into the back yard. A grey-striped cat ran into a spot of sunlight, fell on its back and pushed a chestnut leaf into the air with all four feet as if lifting a heavy weight. She thought of the convent, smelled the bitter malt coffee, felt the hot rolls in her hand, and heard the creak of the bread knife when it cut through a crust. She remembered that Katharina and Karol would be waiting in vain for breakfast and newspapers. The tram passed the back of the house and made the panes tremble. Other people were on their way to work while she, Sophie Sellmann, stood by a window as she had done at her parents' and asked herself why she wasn't allowed to work. The night before she had noticed a dairy at the corner of Wenceslas Square, but she didn't have enough money to go shopping. She bent down and rubbed her finger over the floor boards. The room needed cleaning. In Bucovice she had learned to put the handle of a bucket down so softly, to wring out a floorcloth so soundlessly, that even the half-blind Sister Ignatia did not hear it. Sixta slept on, his face to the wall. She pulled the cover over his naked shoulder and went out.

In the kitchen a man sat at the table and dipped croissants in his coffee. He was blond, younger than Sophie, and wore a chequered shirt over his trousers. He did not seem surprised to see her. He greeted her as if they knew each other and urged her to come in, though she was already apologising and turning to leave. He introduced himself, and Sophie mentioned her name, but still remained by the door. He walked across the blue and white tiles in his grey army socks, fetched a second cup, and pushed the basket of croissants across the table. When she made no move to join him at breakfast, he said, 'You don't need to worry about having stayed the night with us. I know you are a German, but I'm a policeman and therefore nothing can happen to you. Until three months ago, Germans used to live here. Look!' He pointed to a spice shelf above the gas stove where the spice jars bore German names. His voice was high and boyish, but he smiled with pointed lips, like a woman who is afraid of wrinkles or wants to hide a gold tooth. When he poured her coffee, she saw that his left thumb was missing.

'I'd rather wait for Pavel.'

'He sleeps like a log,' he said. 'I won't look at you if it bothers you.' He turned his head and looked at a calendar on the wall, offered her a chair with his mutilated hand. 'You can pray if you like,' he said when Sophie had sat down. 'Or have you given it up?'

'No,' Sophie said and blushed.

'Well then, pray,' he said, his mouth full. 'I'm not religious, but you can pray for me too. It can't do any harm. Sugar?'

'No, thank you.'

'I just want you to feel at home,' Georg said and dipped a second croissant in his coffee, 'even if you think me a bully.'

'Yes,' she said, because she knew he expected it. Her openness pleased him, and he became more friendly and told her that he had to leave at the weekend for two or three months' duty in the frontier region. But that didn't mean she'd have to leave the moment he came back. On the contrary. He'd like it if she stayed. She was not to worry about reporting to the police. He'd do that. As long as her permit of residence was in order, there were no difficulties. He would find himself another place later. At the worst he could live in the barracks. When Sophie wanted to contradict, he interrupted her, 'I can understand your position very well. Much better than you think. I tell you quite honestly that I'm not thinking of you. You may want to go back to Germany. Who knows? Not today, certainly not today, but in a month, or in a year. I'm thinking of Pavel, you understand. He has something that we don't have. May I look at you again now?'

'Yes,' said Sophie and saw that he had pale blue, almost colourless eyes.

'When he was a teacher in Budweis, he said in a music lesson: the greatness of an artist is that he gives people something which they might otherwise never have seen or heard. A good definition, don't you think? I've remembered, and Pavel has forgotten. He strums on the piano so that those ladies and gentlemen can rub their navels together. Do you think that is right? No, I don't think that is right, either. But when I tell him he nods, but doesn't believe me. He'll listen to you. Don't ask me how I know. But I've talked much too much already. Now go into my room and ring your sister, so that comrade Djudko doesn't have the militia out looking for you. Wait, one more thing. Concerning art – I suppose you think I'm talking like a virgin about babies? But my horoscope

307

didn't say I was going to be a policeman. That's other people's fault. Well, go and telephone. But don't be alarmed – I haven't tidied up my room.'

After her talk with Katharina, who had not noticed Sophie's absence, she went back to Sixta. He was awake but still in bed, and had spread her black velvet dress over the flowered bedcover.

'You live with your nephew?' she asked.

He sat up. 'That idiot swore he'd be sleeping in the barracks. I am a victim of the housing problem,' he said and laughed. 'I can't make love to you without half the Republic knowing about it.'

She put out her hand for the dress, but he held on to it.

'Let go,' she begged.

'No,' he said. 'I'll tear it to pieces so that you can't run away. That copper isn't my nephew but my cousin's son, and my cousin's mother is only my father's sister-in-law. So in actual fact we aren't even related, although we have the same name.' Pavel whispered, 'I bet he's just behind the door and listening to every word.' He got out of bed, draped the dress around his hips and tiptoed to the door, opened it quickly and shouted, *'Canaille!'* along the empty corridor. 'He's so artful, he doesn't wear boots in the house.'

Sophie sat down on the bed and laughed.

After lunch they got dressed, and Sixta rapped against Georg's door as they left the apartment.

In front of the National Museum hung a canvas with the profiles of Stalin and the little president who had led Sophie through the Spanish Hall. He didn't look quite as helpless as before the war, his blond beard quite self-confident beside the black moustache. But when the tram turned, and the canvas moved, he looked once again like a frail old gentleman who wasn't helped much by being kissed by a real live generalissimo.

Sophie bought a tomato-coloured bathing dress in a shop in the lower part of Wenceslas Square but wanted to change it because it made her skin look so white. But Sixta was in too much of a hurry. She begged him to go to one of the river beaches further up, where there were fewer people on a weekday. By the way he agreed she realised that he thought she wanted to be alone with him, while she just wanted not to expose her white legs to other people.

Sixta was demented with happiness. When they got to the beach, she had to remind him to take off his suit and shoes before jumping into the water. His fever was contagious. Even diving did not make her feel cold. When he crossed his hands in the nape of her neck, she let herself sink so that he could not look into her eyes. When they were drying themselves he told her that years ago someone had advised him to take her swimming if he didn't have the money to buy her orchids.

'Was it Vavra?'

Sixta shook his head.

'Katja?'

'No, you don't know him.'

She guessed that he was lying, but she did not really want to know.

'It was Fräulein Kalman,' he said after some time, and did not at first realise that it had been unnecessary to say anything. 'I can hold my tongue as little as I can stop writing.'

'I did want to know,' she reassured him, rolled on to his out-stretched arms and asked him what had become of the opera of which he had written to her in Bucovice. When he did not remember the letter, she repeated it by heart. He was moved. But when she admitted that she knew all his letters by heart he turned away and looked for a cigarette. He had to admit, he said, that the music he had written pleased no one but himself. And if the quartet he had composed at Vavra's was also refused . . .

'What then?'

'Everybody is on holiday until September,' he said dismissively and would not tell her to whom he had shown the work.

Towards evening Sixta took Sophie back to Bubenech in the tram. 'I'll come,' she promised, but did not say when. In the hall Katharina ran to meet her but was disappointed because she had expected Karol. They exchanged a few words, then Sophie went into her room. An hour later, while Sophie was mending stockings, Katharina appeared with a jug of suspiciously pale orangeade and two wine glasses. She pushed the red fringe from her forehead and poured.

'I need money,' she said and sipped at her glass.

Sophie tasted the orangeade and smelled the potato spirits under the orange scent.

'Couldn't we sell the house on the Sázava? Do you know anyone whom we could ask?'

Katharina drank down the mixture at a gulp. 'I can't bother Karol, with it.'

'No,' Sophie said.

'You don't have to bother either. It's been seized. I need a lot of money.' She was silent and rubbed her nose as if she was wondering whether to continue. 'I have to have an operation. I want to have a child. If I have a child, everything will be all right, you understand that, don't you. Then Karol would be allowed to marry me and would come home at night. I wouldn't drink any more, but knit baby-clothes. Why are you looking at me like that? Karol doesn't want me to have the operation. He's afraid I'll die. That isn't an excuse. I believe him. But if I don't have a baby,' she said like a threat, 'I'll go away with you. It's possible to register for voluntary emigration. Have you registered?'

'No.'

'Karol has difficulties. They've fired him from the personnel commission because he didn't finish his studies. Those are reactionary reasons. The uprising was our University!' Katharina exclaimed and thundered her little fist so hard on the table that the darning egg fell off. 'He can't defend himself because he's got me round his neck. He's hiding me. We're being watched. Many people would give their right arm to find out something discreditable about Karol or his father. Perhaps they'll arrive one day with a search-warrant.' She took Sophie's glass and drank it. 'Have you come to some arrangement with Sixta? I don't know how else to say it. Has he got an apartment? Why don't you move in with him? You mustn't think you're in our way. I'm only saying it in your best interest. Wait. I'll show you what I've found.' She slid from her chair and moved on her knees to Sophie's bed. 'Will you promise to keep it between the two of us?' She pulled out a box, opened the lid, and let Sophie look inside.

'When father bought his monstrance you were already in Bucovice. He had the money from Eugen Lustig. Do you remember how we drove to Wörlitz with Herr Croissant?'

'Yes,' said Sophie. 'And since when has it been down there?'

'You'll sell it. Half is for me. It's solid gold.'

'Why did you put it under *my* bed?' Sophie asked.

'You're a nun,' Katharina said and shut the lid. 'Why shouldn't you sleep above a monstrance? In memory of the victory of John of Austria over the Turks. Lepanto, 1571! I've got all the dates in my head except your birthday.' She got up, gave the box a kick which sent it back under the bed, and gave an embarrassed smile because she had to hold on to the back of a chair. 'Why don't you hit me. Go on then, you holy cow!' She shouted so loudly that her voice cracked. Though she tottered, she leaned forward as if she expected to have her face slapped. When Sophie did not move, she said disdainfully, 'If someone spoke to me like that, I'd murder them.'

'But then you're not a nun,' Sophie said and looked at her watch.

'I suppose you want to go now,' Katharina wiped her mouth with her sleeve and pushed the chair aside. 'Don't leave me alone,' she begged, and staggered towards Sophie as if about to put her arms around her. 'Karol will be home late. The Ministry is forming a council for the settlement of the frontier regions. Isn't that wild?'

'Yes,' Sophie said.

'Perhaps he'll get a post there, and we'll return to Bratislava. I speak much better Slovak now.'

Karol came home about ten, and Sophie took the tram to Sixta's apartment hoping that Georg was at home. On the way she worked out that she had just enough money for a week of tram rides. When nobody answered the bell, she looked under the mat and found an envelope which contained a note and the key.

'Dear Fräulein,' Georg had written. 'My so-called uncle has probably forgotten to give you a key. Please be kind enough to tell him that I shall be sleeping in the barracks, and that I've watered my African violet.' A child's writing, thought Sophie, put down her bag, tied on her apron, and got to work.

When she had cleaned Sixta's room, the kitchen and the corridor, she showered, put on the green and white striped pyjamas, and lay down on the bed with the score which still stood on the piano. It was headed *The Last Judgment*, Overture. The notation was strongly written and easy to read. It started with a piccolo flute and a trombone chasing along in dotted crochets, until bassoon, violin and double-bass join in on the next page. Since it was well past midnight, she got up and struck a very quiet 'a' on the piano and tried to follow the instrumental parts, but the changing key, and the need to switch from bass to treble clef tired her. She turned the pages quickly and came to the voices and hummed the soprano part through the first scene, but when the express train thundered past behind the backdrop with cymbals, rattles and kettle-drums, and stationmaster Hudetz sang his regret that he had not set the signals, her eyes closed. She did not even feel it when Sixta took the music away from her.

After Georg's departure, Sophie moved into Mezibranska Street. So as not to pass Amery & Herschel, which was now once more the name of the china store, she continued to make a detour whenever necessary. She was annoyed that she lacked the courage to speak with Sixta about Amery. It was so easy to talk to him about anything, but she comforted herself with the thought that there was really nothing left to talk about, since Sixta knew it all.

In August, when Sixta went to Budweis with the Swing

311

Serenaders to give a concert and visit his mother, Sophie went to Bubenech and took some of the clothes her mother had left behind, and out of the honest dresses and worthy suits she made herself a fantasy-dress with a brocade sash. When she wore it to welcome Sixta back, he took her in his arms and carried her into his room like a bride.

'I just can't believe that you are here,' he said. 'In Budweis I sometimes thought I'd come back and the apartment would be empty.'

'What would you have done then?'

'I'd have searched for you.'

That evening Sixta at last played her *The Last Judgment*.

'Who has turned it down?' she asked when he shut the piano lid after two hours. He pushed his hands into the small of his back and laughed.

'I haven't submitted it to anybody. Nor the quartet. Forgive me. It is so senseless. I know that the theatre managers would put my score with hundreds of others and send it back after six months. It's the same for everybody, I'm not complaining.' He got up and stretched out on the bed. 'I haven't got a society for private performances like Schönberg, nor a rich wife like Stravinsky, and I haven't got patience like Janacek. Sometimes, when I hear my own music, I tell myself, you've overrated your work, my dear sir! You give what you have, but it's not enough. Perhaps one has to be sixty or seventy before one can write something decent. From sheer superabundance without coffee and cigarettes.'

'Why pay such a price? Why should I tremble and sweat and drink valerian tea so that some drunken dramatic critic – they're all drunken, believe me – can stick his red nose into my music and then write, "with the greatest regret . . ." I have no aptitude for posterity.'

'I think your opera is marvellous.'

'What's that got to do with it?' he said and sat up. 'You're marvellous.' He lay back again and smiled. 'You are marvellous. It would be much easier to sell you than my music. But I won't part with you. We shall never part again. When I saw you the first time you wore a blue dress with white – what do you call the things?'

'Cuffs,' said Sophie.

'When you had a sore throat I wrote a funeral march,' he hummed the tune and banged an invisible drum with his right hand. 'Did you know that?'

Sophie lay down beside him and kissed him.

'I won't let you sell me,' she said.

'Where do you think the interval should be?' Sixta asked.

'After the waltz. When Anna makes her appointment with Hudetz by the viaduct.'

'That's what I thought myself,' he exclaimed and ran to the piano. He asked her to sing a few passages of Anna's part, and did not criticise when she breathed in the wrong place or missed a transition.

'Cool, remain cool!' he said. '*Secco, secco,* not with the soul but with the stomach!'

The next evening Sophie went to see Aunt Marketa. She was afraid of the meeting, and her fear proved justified.

Since April when her friend Dr. Kavalár had been killed, Frau Farel saw nobody, not even her brother-in-law Amery. She asked Sophie to come in, but did not ask her to sit down, and stood with folded hands beside the stove. She wore black, had pinned back her hair at the temples, and she seemed much like before. Confused because she was being treated so formally, Sophie stated her request. She knew that Frau Farel was acquainted with the chief conductor of the National Theatre, and she explained simply what she wanted.

'I'm sorry not to be able to help your friend. I do not run a concert agency.'

Sophie waited for a while for a word that revoked the refusal, or at least made the leave-taking easier, but Aunt Marketa said nothing. The honey-coloured parquet gleamed at the edge of the carpet, mother-of-pearl fringes hung from the table-lamp, and the smell of cold coke drifted about the stove. The visit was over. Years ago the 'little niece' had had to write her name in the guest book even if she had only come for a cup of coffee. Now they could not even shake hands, they had moved so far away from each other.

One evening Sophie went into Georg's room and telephoned the presbytery of the church of St. Salvador and asked for Svoboda. A woman, presumably the cook, insisted that there had never been a priest of that name at St. Salvador. Sophie asked to speak to the priest. Was he wanted to administer the Last Rites, the cook asked in a tone of voice as if she would refuse in that case. No, but it was important. The reverent gentleman told her that Svoboda had been moved to St. Apollinaris, and gave her his number.

313

11

Christmas Presents

A GERMAN HAD lived in the apartment in Mezibranska Street, and all Sophie and Sixta knew of him was that he had worked in the administration of the Protectorate. During the general confiscation in May, Georg had seized the rooms on his own initiative. The furniture had remained, also the curtains and carpets, bedlinen, china and the African violet. Only the pictures had been taken by the previous tenant, or Georg had thrown them in the dustbin. On the wallpaper, above Sixta's divan, there was a lighter rectangle, tall and narrow like a window pane.

After she had seen Svoboda, Sophie went out less often. She did her shopping in Wenceslas Square where the crowd in the shops was so great that the salesgirls did not recognise her if she returned. It seemed to her as if the passers-by were forming up to march along the boulevards, they appeared united and threatening as if they were about to stamp down anything in their way. She often went through the small back streets to avoid the attack.

The manageress who distributed the food ration cards in the house asked, in September, why the foreign Fräulein received meat coupons, though the Germans were put on the same rations as the Jews during the war. Sixta shut the door in her face and did not mention the incident. But Sophie had heard every word. She smoked too much and spent hours looking down into the courtyard where the autumn wind shook the first chestnuts from the trees.

One day Sixta received a letter asking him to visit the Cellar Theatre in the town centre, and returned towards evening smelling of rum, with an armful of roses. Since she didn't have enough vases, Sophie stuck the long stems into milk bottles and beer mugs, and while Pavel told her all about it, she made coffee.

The superintendent of the theatre had asked about *The Last Judgment*. He had already read the play by Horvath. He wanted to put on an experimental performance in his theatre, and he'd be ready to arrange for some further performances if the opera was a success. There were conditions. Sixta would have to provide the singers, orchestra, and scenery. He could offer nothing but the stage, costumes and technical personnel, neither salaries nor royalties. Rehearsals would have to finish by three o'clock in the afternoon because of the scene changes for the cabaret in the evenings. And yes, did Sixta trust himself to produce the piece by 14th February? That was a Thursday, the critiques would appear in the Saturday papers, and there'd be plenty of time to be angry over the weekend – *d'accord?*

'You're going to do it?'

'I wouldn't have had a drink otherwise,' Pavel said and smiled as if to say, 'I wouldn't have bought you flowers.'

Before leaving for the Café Manes he told her that he'd be home later than usual since he would be meeting friends to discuss preparations. From the doorstep he asked, 'Does anything strike you about this affair?'

Sophie frowned as if considering.

'Who told the fellow that I'd written an opera?'

'Didn't you ask?'

'No.'

'Perhaps one of your friends told him . . .'

'Yes,' Sixta said and wanted to add something but a neighbour came to her door, and he only waved goodbye. Sophie waited a little while, then tied a black scarf over her head and went quickly to Apollinaris Street.

Father Svoboda, who had been promoted to hospital priest during the war, had just returned from supper in the kitchen of the psychiatric hospital, and, because of his slipped disc, had stretched out on the woden chest in his study. At their first meeting in August, Sophie had hardly recognised him. The plump chaplain with the pearl-onion nose and matronly hips had become a haggard cleric. Sophie had confessed to him on that occasion, at greater length than to the priest at the Budweis Old People's Home. It was a *confessione ambulante* as Svoboda had said – that is, between the beds of the botanical gardens – before he took her to St. Apollinaris and granted her absolution.

Now he wanted to get up from the chest, but Sophie begged him to remain, pulled a chair close, and thanked Svoboda for arranging for the performance of Sixta's opera so promptly.

'A premiere is the only thing we can still manage,' he said and put his high lace-up boots back on the arm of a chair. 'Even that

315

may not be for long, but one mustn't give up. We've survived the Austrian Empire, the First and Second Republic, why should we founder with the Third?' He closed his eyes. 'Was Herr Sixta pleased?' The great virtue of the fathers confessor was their forgetfulness, but he had remembered that name. 'That's the important thing. Sometimes it is easy to give pleasure. At St. Salvador we had a tramp who used to sleep in my confessional. The sacristan wanted to call the police, but I told him the gentleman was an impoverished aristocrat, and from then on he was always called the "Herr Baron". But we had to be careful during High Mass because he sometimes pushed the door open to stretch. He was an incredibly long fellow, and always drunk, but in a manner in which even a teetotaller would like to be drunk.' Svoboda took his feet from the chair arm, and put them on the ground. 'Would you like me to give you the blessing? Then I must go back to the hospital.'

'There's something else,' Sophie said. 'Herr Sixta wonders how the superintendent heard about his opera. Couldn't you tell me who .. ?'

Svoboda smiled. 'You don't need to worry. He won't be thinking about it for long. A man who has success doesn't enquire into its cause.'

Sophie kneeled down and looked, while Svoboda gave her the blessing, at his dusty toecaps.

At breakfast Sixta told her that he had already engaged half the orchestra. In the afternoon he'd go and listen to a few singers in the Conservatoire, and tomorrow he'd be meeting a scene painter. 'You'll help me copy the parts, won't you? The theatre is lending me a copying machine. I only need to buy the paper, ink and such,' he counted off on his fingers. 'Anyway, I know who must have recommended my opera.'

Sophie pressed her knees together.

'It can only have been Vavra. He sits on the scientific committee of the Ministry of Education. That's where they decide which theatres should be subsidised. Well, he's a good fellow, it's just that I don't trust myself to go and see him.'

'At least send him a ticket for the premiere,' Sophie said.

'Of course. And I behave with the superintendent as if I had simply no idea.' He quickly finished his coffee and went to fetch the copying materials.

By evening, Sophie had already copied and duplicated several pages of the baritone part. After a week, the pencil edge had made a dent in her middle finger. She stuck a bandage over it and went on writing. Even in her sleep she scribbled sharps and flats, drew bars and ledger-lines, numbered measures, and sketched the curl of the crotchet-rest. When Sixta saw her reddened eyes, he gave half the score to a copyist. He continued to play at the Café Manes as it was his only means of livelihood. He was still looking for a baritone and an alto, and even auditions cost money since he had to ask the candidates to a meal. When the theatre director asked whether Sixta had acquired the performing rights for the Horvath piece, he was thunderstruck. The agency which had sent him the text of the play had gone out of business. He telephoned the theatre where the piece had been performed, and they remembered *The Last Judgment*, but had not heard that the author had died seven years before. Sixta found a solution by making it a club performance and putting any profit, which was scarcely expected in any case, into an account for the author's heirs.

Sophie worked. If she was anxious, it was only about Sixta. Therefore she gave him courage. She kept him from changing the finished parts, not because she would have had to have written them out again, but so as not to let him lose his enthusiasm. She could not hear the music as she wrote it, and when she followed the pale minims and streamered quavers along the lines, or if she went to the piano to play a few measures, she wished herself back to the evening when Sixta had played *The Last Judgment* for her, and when she succeeded in bringing the occasion back, she was happy.

In the last week of October she yielded to Katharina's wishes and went with her and the Lepanto Monstrance to see Botticelli. The painter named a price which Katharina wanted to accept immediately because it was more than her doctor demanded. When Sophie hesitated, Bottichelli fetched a parcel for which, he said, he had already been offered a Doctorate of Philosophy, a suckling pig, and a twelve-year-old virgin. The parcel was full of nylon stockings. They agreed that the painter should deliver the whole sum the following morning in Bubenech. They left the monstrance with him, and took the nylon stockings. Sophie did not ask him not to tell Sixta of the deal. To have secrets with this man seemed to her in bad taste. And why bother Sixta with such a tale? She would not in any case accept her half of the money, only taking a few pairs of stockings out of the parcel. She had agreed on a sentence with Katharina which the redhead should say casually on the telephone the moment the painter had delivered the money.

Next morning Katharina rang, said breathlessly, 'The Turks

have been routed,' and hung up. A bit clumsy for a partisan, Sophie thought. And why the hurry? Today, Saturday, Katharina could not have her operation.

The next day, Sunday, while Sophie and Sixta were looking at the models of the stage sets, a celebration was held in Wenceslas Square to mark the nationalisation of heavy industries, banks and insurance companies. The voices of the speakers rang in the backyard and through the closed windows right into the Wild Man, the miniature inn where Pavel moved thumb-high tables and chairs. When the Internationale was being sung at the end, he sat down at the piano and played the waltz with which station-master Hudetz says goodbye to Anna, the innkeeper's daughter.

A little later Georg came in and sat down as if he'd left three hours, not three months ago. He liked the last scene best, where a police-doll stood under a silver-paper moon.

'What does he sing?'

Sixta told him.

'Very good,' Georg approved, and had the plot explained to him. 'So the stationmaster murders Anna?'

'One can tell you're with the police,' Sixta said.

'Not right on the stage? Do you think the audience will under-stand about the murder?'

'It becomes apparent in the next scene,' Sophie said quickly.

'It's obvious from the very beginning,' Sixta objected, and shook his head as if Sophie still hadn't understood the piece.

Georg noticed Pavel's irritation, put his hand in the pocket of his uniform and took out two crackling bank-notes, purply-brown and blue-red.

'Have you seen the new money? A five hundred note and a thousand note! Printed in England! With watermark!'

'When were they issued?' Sophie asked.

'Yesterday,' Georg said. 'But you can't change as much money as you want to. We're letting the big money-makers cool their heels a bit. Just be glad you're broke!'

'Excuse me please,' Sophie said and went into Georg's room and dialled the Bubenech number, but there was no reply. When Sixta called her from the corridor, she put the receiver down.

'I didn't mean to hurt you,' he said. Sophie rubbed her forehead on his jacket as if she had forgiven him.

Since Georg wanted to come and live with them again, she cleaned his room, changed his bedclothes, dusted the violet, and combed the carpet fringe.

'Without you, Pavel would never have made it,' Georg said

when he came home. 'And if you don't go on helping him, he'll
fall flat on his face. So battle on!'

Katharina arrived at Mezibranska Street towards midnight. She
had been to the Café Manes to make sure Sixta was playing with
the Swing Serenaders. Though Sophie told her that Georg was
not at home, she whispered, and sometimes her words had to be
guessed at. She opened her fur coat and showed Sophie the money
hidden in the lining.

'Karol would be suspect if he went to the bank with such a
sum,' she said. 'Anyhow, I don't want him to know anything about
it. You know why. Will you give it to Sixta to change for the new
money?'

'And how am I to explain where it comes from?'

'Just tell him the truth.'

Sophie shook her head. She wasn't afraid of telling Pavel that
she had gone to Botticelli with Katharina, but why should he be a
party to something that had to be kept from Karol? And
what would happen if Pavel were asked where he got such a sum?
Why should he be questioned or arrested for Katharina's sake?
Why endanger his opera to save Captain Djudko's career?'

'No,' Sophie said. 'I'm sorry.'

'I'm so stupid,' said Katharina after a time.

'Why?' asked Sophie, unsuspecting.

'My own sister cheats me, and I don't notice. How much is
Botticelli giving you for this fraud?'

'Me?'

'Yes, you,' Katharina spat. 'The two of you have done me down
properly. You knew exactly when the new money was coming
out, and that I couldn't change this!'

Now Sophie understood. She took the nylon stockings out of
the cupboard and threw them at Katharina's feet. Then she held
the door open for her. But Katharina was not yet ready to
capitulate. 'I've found the tapestry,' she said, ready for reconcilia-
tion. 'Under a mattress. Christine suspected it. She's practical, like
mother. The tapestry will bring us as much as the monstrance, perhaps even more.'

'You know the painter's address,' Sophie said with finality.

Katharina had an answer on the tip of her tongue. It was the
kind of answer that had to be bellowed, and she swallowed it
with difficulty. Then she buttoned up her fur quite slowly as if
she wanted to give Sophie time to change her mind. No? Another

glance like a bayonet thrust. Still no? She stepped over the stockings and went into the corridor without turning back.

The rehearsals for *The Last Judgment* took place in the Conservatoire, because the theatre would not be available until January. Sixta asked Sophie to come with him, but did not repeat the invitation when she refused. How could he have explained her presence to the orchestra? She bore her loneliness like a duty, but was angry that she was not allowed to work. Sixta ate with the musicians in a bar, Georg in the canteen. Once when she cooked herself a chop she ate it out of the frying-pan because she couldn't think why she should lay the table. In the afternoons she used to go to the Conservatoire to wait in the street for the end of the rehearsal. When it rained she stood in the entrance of a house, but when the first frosts came she had to walk up and down to keep warm. In December she fell ill. Good Lord, a bit of 'flu, nothing more. She looked after herself and was sorry for Pavel who had to sleep on the camp bed beside the divan. When she had recovered, he gave her some money for warm boots. She kept some of the money for Christmas presents, and bought a pair of black buckle shoes with high heels.

'I'll wear them for your premiere,' she said and turned round and round until she was giddy.

'And how are you going to get through the winter?'

'Don't you like them?'

'That's not the point.'

'That's the only point,' Sophie said and asked what he wanted for Christmas.

'I don't need anything,' he said. 'Really nothing at all.'

She nevertheless began to search for presents, bought a shot-silk tie for Georg, and wondered what Pavel would like. In the store opposite the Cellar Theatre she had seen a red leather box for paper, stamps and pencils. She went down the street and allowed herself to be pushed into the doors of the shop, between gingerbread, wafers, and honey-cake, until she was pressed against a table full of pink marzipan pigs above which green balloons waved. There could be no question of retreat. Those who had pressed in behind her would not give way. When she reached the stairs to the first floor, she had to hold on to the banisters. In the leather department she asked a salesgirl about the red box. Sold? No more until January? She went on to the cosmetic department. No, no shaving soap, she thought. We're not married, after all. If I had enough money for a gramophone, that would be good. But not shaving soap.

She went to stand by a display case, looked at her pale face between damp fingermarks on the glass, and read the price tags. She was about to turn away when she noticed the reflection of the head of a man behind her shoulder, and the turned-up collar of his herringbone tweed coat. She bent forward to read the name on a bottle, and came so close to the glass that she could see the pale scar on her forehead. The letters on the label blurred, she pressed her fingers against the glass as if she wanted to push herself away from his face, but he still stood behind her, with blond or grey hair, indeterminate in this light, with thin, almost sunken cheeks and wrinkles running to his mouth which made him look like his father. She felt that he was looking at her, that he was seeking her eyes in the spotted glass between the bends and curves of people's hands, and the yellow glass flagons. I'll move on, she decided. I'm no: going to turn round, just move on. It's twenty steps to the jewellery counter, and not as many from there to the stairs. I'll go on without turning, into the street, and if he follows, I'll run across to the theatre and into the office of the producer who knows me, and I'll tell him that I've come to enquire about the plan for rehearsals. But a woman with two shopping baskets was in the way. She asked Sophie a question, and when Sophie had replied and looked back into the display case it was empty: Amery had vanished.

Was it very late? She remembered that she had planned to make ham omelettes for supper, that she still had to iron Pavel's white shirt. He had to be at the Café Manes at seven.

She was home by six. Sixta stood in the kitchen, ironing the cuffs on the ironing board. Sophie took the iron out of his hand and told him to have a rest while she finished the shirt and made the omelettes. When they sat down to eat, he told her that he intended to get another singer for the Public Prosecutor in *The Last Judgment*.

'The fellow is incompetent,' Sixta said. 'But if I don't find a tenor by tomorrow, all the instruments will have to be draped with mourning-crêpe. Farewell lutes, farewell violins!' He stood up to change his shirt. 'But he'll have to learn the part over Christmas, and it isn't easy.' He pulled the shirt over his head and felt the sleeves. 'It's still warm,' he said and smiled.

Next morning Sophie thought up a job that would keep her busy all day. After Sixta had left for rehearsal, she took down the curtains. While the muslin soaked in the bath-tub, she ham-

321

mered hooks into the walls and put a line criss-cross along the corridor. Then she washed and rinsed the curtains and hung them in front of the open doors, so that they would be dry by evening. But by early afternoon she was bored. Why should she watch the water dripping from the curtains on to the cloths she had spread on the floor? She went for a walk in the town, then waited for Sixta. He came out of the doors of the Conservatoire with some of his orchestral players, and hesitated a moment before coming over to her.

'I've got an appointment,' he said a little hurriedly as if he did not want to introduce her to his companions. 'We're off to see a tenor. Perhaps he'll help out.'

'Good,' she said and turned away.

She took a tram to the store and went to the leather department to ask again about the red box. 'No,' said the salesgirl and smiled because she recognised Sophie. 'But I'll keep you one in January.'

Then I'll have to find something else, she told herself. On the second floor she went through rows of jackets and lounge-suits, felt the sleeve of a brown tweed jacket. She did not know Sixta's size, did not want to buy a jacket in any case, and was embarrassed when a salesman took it from its hanger for her. She went up to the third floor behind a group of Slovak women in wide purple skirts and black headscarves printed with roses. She went through suites of walnut furniture and Chippendale imitations, through varnished kitchens and bedrooms until she reached the windows and looked out.

Had he really stood behind her, or had it been her imagination? Why had she not turned round? Why had she thought he would come again today? And if she still believed he would come, why did she not stand and wait for him in the same place? She might even have him paged over the public address system. Why did she want to see him, and yet had run away from him?

In the offices opposite, office workers sat at their desks. The dimmed headlights of the cars lit up the wet street and the coats of the passers-by.

'Are you looking for something?' Amery asked. His hair was streaked with grey and his eyes were dark under the bony fore-head, his mouth soft.

'Yes,' she said.

'Me?'

'Yes,' she repeated.

'I've been looking for you ...' he said, leaving the sentence trailing.

She went ahead of him through the bedrooms and kitchens, down the stairs, and put her reddened hands into her pockets. She felt neither the steps underfoot nor the elbows which jostled her.

They walked slowly along the street and spoke to each other like two pupils during a lesson: very quietly and without looking at each other. When she left him, she did not turn round though Amery followed her with his eyes until she vanished in the crowd.

When she opened the door to the apartment she heard Georg call, 'At last!' He had taken the curtains from the line and draped them over his shoulders. Sophie took her coat off quickly and went to help him. 'I look like Salome during the dance of the seven veils,' he said. 'If only I knew where those damned hooks go! Which is top and which bottom?'

'Didn't you learn that at Frau Groschup's?' Sophie laughed and showed him the hem.

'Where?'

'At the captain's lady in Budweis,' Sophie said and carefully took the curtains from his shoulders, making sure they did not snag on his epaulettes. 'We'll put them over a chair, and when I've finished attaching the hooks, you can push them on the curtain rail. I'll hold the ladder.'

'Good,' Georg said and sat down on the bed.

When she was ready with the curtains she said, 'Would you be so kind now?' But Georg remained where he was.

'Do you know about it from Pavel?' he asked. 'About Frau Groschup?'

'Yes, he wrote me about it.'

'When?' Georg asked and took the curtain.

'After the law suit,' Sophie said, holding up the hem as Georg went up the ladder. 'I thought it was marvellous that you disguised yourself so well. Did the police really think you were a woman?'

'Yes,' Georg said and felt for the rail. 'But that wasn't the reason why the Germans gave me four years' forced labour.'

'Forgive me,' Sophie said and hung the rest of the curtains by herself.

When she walked with Sixta to the Café Manes after supper, she told him of her clumsiness. 'I'm afraid I've hurt his feelings.'

Sixta laughed. 'Nobody can hurt Georg's feelings. He's only afraid that his superiors will find out that he wasn't in the camp because of political but criminal proceedings. No, forget it! Tomorrow is Christmas. Put your tie around his neck and give him a kiss, but not too big a one, else I'll be jealous. Then it'll all be over. Just be happy that I've found a tenor.'

'Is he good?' Sophie asked.

'I listened to him for half an hour. He warbles a bit like a nightingale, but I'll soon cure him of that. He has to crow like a cock on a dunghill. That's how a public prosecutor should sound, don't you think?'

'I can well believe it.'

Instead of parting at the Café Manes, they went down to the river.

'You'll be late,' Sophie said as he put his arms around her, and she closed her eyes when his lips touched her forhead. She put her face against his damp coat and felt his lips in her hair. She did not hear what he said, but felt the pressure on her hair slides and the warmth of his breath.

Next morning, Christmas Eve morning, Sophie went to the market. The salesmen in their rubber aprons stood beside the barrels, pulled the golden-bellied carp out of the water, threw them on to the metal bowls of the scales, and moved the weights until the bar was horizontal. Then they called out the price and stunned the fish with a greasy club. Sophie bought a four-pounder, had it wrapped in newspaper, pushed into her shopping net and carried it home, still jerking against her calves. Georg had promised to clean and scale the carp. Sixta had gone off to buy a Christmas tree, so there was still time to look for a present. She put a few Botticelli nylon stockings into her handbag and ran to a small antique shop. The owner soon realised that Sophie was waiting for him to finish with the rest of his customers. He looked into her handbag, enquired about the size of the stockings, and brought a drinking-glass from his back room. It was enamelled with a four-leafed clover and violet flowers, tied with a gold ribbon.

'Early nineteenth century,' he said, and packed it in a box with woodshavings.

'And how many of those have you got?' asked Sophie.

'I beg you to believe me, a single piece, a rarity!'

Sophie couldn't bring herself to tell him that one could exchange nylon stockings for a suckling pig, a doctor's degree, let alone virgins! She took the glass.

Georg had already cut up the carp. He wanted his third steamed, Sixta's third should be baked, 'And how do you want yours? Like Pavel?'

They did not bother with a midday meal. Sophie helped Sixta decorate the Christmas tree and put cardboard plates with nuts

324

and honey-cake on the small table. Towards evening she went into the kitchen, made potato salad, and prepared the fish. Then she hid Pavel's glass and Georg's tie under the tree and put on her fantasy dress. While she was laying the kitchen table, the men put her presents under the tree, and when the bells chimed seven, they sat down at table. Georg poured out some of his special-issue 'Ludmilla', proposed a toast, took a fishbone from between his teeth, and kissed Sophie and Sixta, which rather pointed to the fact that he had already sampled the wine during the afternoon. He rolled his eyes, complimented Sophie on her dress, and, later in Sixta's room, sang 'Silent Night' with such fervour that neither Sophie's soprano, nor Sixta's piano could be heard. When presents were exchanged, Georg received two ties, one from Sophie, the other from his 'uncle'. 'Very original,' he said when he thanked them, and hung both ties around his neck. Sophie opened a parcel, and when she had unknotted the string she found the handwritten score of *The Last Judgment*, and read Sixta's dedication, 'For Sophie, my only love', on the title page.

'No,' she said and turned pale. 'You mustn't do that.'

'But I've got the copies you made,' Sixta said.

She closed the lid and went blindly along the corridor and locked herself in the bathroom. She pulled a towel from the hook, crumpled it up and pressed it against her mouth to stop herself from screaming. She went down on her knees and laid her chin on the side of the bath-tub.

'The best is still to come,' Georg shrieked in the corridor. That was an expression to make one weep, yet she had to laugh, and with the laughter came tears. She cried into the bath-tub and thought: I am crying into the bath-tub. She wiped her nose with her brocade sash, and could not believe she had done such a thing. When she went back to Sixta and Georg, she felt as if she were calling for help after drowning.

In the meantime Georg had unwrapped his present, a large gilt-framed, vertical oil-painting, a three-quarter profile, naked shoulders and body laced into black taffeta, of a young woman.

'For you both,' Georg said when Sophie entered. 'It exactly fits the stain on the wallpaper. I've tried it. It might be a duchess, or a countess. Anyway, it comes from Dux. There's a coat of arms on the other side. Do you like it?'

'Very much,' said Sophie.

'Did you steal it?' Sixta asked, smiling.

'What are you thinking of?'

'Requisitioned?'

'I've paid for it,' Georg shouted and only calmed down when Sophie kissed him. 'And what does Pavel get?' he asked.

'I didn't want anything!' Sixta exclaimed. Sophie pointed to the small parcel under the tree. When Sixta had unwrapped the glass, Georg ran into the kitchen to fetch wine.

At eleven o'clock Sophie sent the men out of the room to change her clothes to go to Midnight Mass with Sixta. Going down the stairs, Georg ran after them with a handful of carp scales. 'I'd laid them on the radiator,' he apologised, 'Put them in your purses. The scales will bring you wealth and happiness.' He bowed in the draughty downstairs hall, 'And wealth and happiness is what your nephew and friend Georg, son of damnation, ghastly fiend and black sheep, wishes you.'

When they were walking back from St. Stephen's, Sixta asked, 'Did you see your sister just now?'

'No,' Sophie said, holding her scarf over her mouth.

'Funny that I should have thought of her earlier today, and that she should go to Midnight Mass alone .. ? But perhaps it was someone else.'

'But Karol is a Communist,' Sophie said through the scarf.

'I'm talking about Christine,' and he told Sophie how, years ago, she had asked him about the origin of the gilt frame. 'It was very much like the frame around the painting Georg gave us. Not exactly, but like. She even offered me money to tell her. How should I know where the frame without a picture came from? That woman is sick somehow. Have you ever visited her since you got back?'

'No,' said Sophie and put her arm in Sixta's.

12

The Upper Castle

THERE WERE TWO roads that led to the Upper Castle, the Vyšehrad, and a lane with steps for pedestrians. From spring to autumn, lovers and married couples, mothers and nannies with children, came up here, and even Eugen Lustig, like others who preferred to think while walking rather than sitting down, had once made a habit of walking here, dictating brief directions to a secretary and looking over the yacht harbour or the tennis courts. Even in the winter there were plenty of people there, schoolchildren and tourists from the provinces who came to look at the view of Prague and the National Cemetery.

Sophie usually came up the tunnel from the tram stop, while Amery went up the ice-covered steps, and they met at the rotunda of St. Martin. If it was sunny he spread a newspaper on a bench facing south. If it turned cold they stood out of the wind near the old priory.

They had arranged the first meeting, but after that they came every day at the same time, except at the weekend. In the tram every day, Sophie felt as if she were a Bucovice cucumber seedling, taken from the greenhouse and put into the open air. She promised herself not to tell Jan of her silly comparison, but told him immediately they met. He smiled and stroked her sleeve as if to encourage her.

Amery did not talk to re-live the past but to make up for earlier omissions, and Sophie was not silent out of thoughtlessness, but because every word weighed eight years. Sometimes she confused her experiences so much with his, that she could not have said whether he was speaking of her or of himself. When he mentioned that he had noticed that even clever books had stupid answers for stupid questions, she thought she'd known that from childhood. Had her father not been such a clever book? When she had asked him if the Good Lord could look through walls, he had said, 'Certainly,' and she had waited night after night for his finger to pierce the bricks, and had been afraid of his huge fingernail.

Walking along, Amery leaned forward and spoke without turning his head. When he stood still, he lifted his shoulders and tried to find a point on which to fix his eyes so as not to look Sophie in the face. Once, when she took off her headscarf and pushed her hair to one side, revealing the white scar on her forehead, he turned away to show her the view towards the mountains. She felt his tenderness, though he did not touch her.

She wore the same open pumps every day, and rubbed her insteps and ankles the moment she sat down. One afternoon he brought her a pair of lined boots, and stepped aside while she put them on. When she changed out of them before saying goodbye, he nodded and took them away with him.

Sometimes he spoke about his time in the sanatorium, and how he had invented a crossword puzzle where there were two answers to every question, either of which fitted in with all the other alternatives. As if one could find a place in life where one could have taken another road and lived another life.

Sophie understood what he said but could not have repeated it. She liked his careful and thoughtful way, and felt safe and realised that he took her seriously. But in the middle of January, when she explained that she could not come the following day, he dropped all restraint.

'That's impossible,' he said.

'It can't be put off.'

'No, no, you've got to come,' he insisted.

She was so upset that she forgot to change the boots for the pumps when they parted, and only noticed when she got to the tram stop. She took the tram around the castle and met up with Amery.

'Where are my shoes?' she asked, since he was not carrying the box.

'Where I leave them every day,' he said and collected them from a pawnshop and held her arm as she put them on. She asked Amery to drive her to Wenceslas Square to be home before Sixta, but he told her he didn't have a car any more, and found her a taxi.

The following day at three o'clock Sophie had an appointment at the Cellar Theatre. Sixta knew nothing about it. For the first time in years she put on rouge and lipstick. The theatre director kissed her hand and offered her an armchair. On his desk stood the photograph of a young woman with a baby in her arms. 'What can I do for you?'

'I'd like to ask you something,' she replied. 'And I'd be glad if you didn't tell Herr Sixta.'

The director pushed a button, and they were able to hear Sixta's rehearsal on the stage of the theatre. 'Absolutely one-way,' he said. 'We have him, but he can't get us.'

'Could you give me a few complimentary tickets for the premiere?'

'How many?'

'A hundred?'

'Don't you believe in his success?'

'Oh yes,' Sophie said and forced a smile. 'But I want to make sure.'

The director listened for a while to the duet between the injured engine driver and the linesman, and grinned when Sixta stopped the rehearsal and called, 'You're already dead, Pokorný! Don't shout as if you were dying all over again! And you're quite calm, Ferda! It says, "I have no face". Hold the D on "have", that's a minim, not a crotchet or whatever it is you're singing. Eight, nine measures back! No, eleven. Sorry! And it's the trombones who make the wind, not you!'

The director pushed the 'off' button, folded his white hands and asked, 'Have you ever heard of Robert-Houdin?'

'No,' said Sophie, surprised.

'A French magician and theatre director. Long dead. I only mention him to point out that the wisdom I'm about to pass on to you isn't just out of my own head.

'An audience with complimentary tickets won't allow itself to be impressed. Anyone who is given a ticket by the director or the author goes to the theatre with the firm conviction that without him it would remain empty. If he finds the theatre full, he believes that everybody else has complimentary tickets too, and expects the performance to be a miserable failure. If it isn't he won't applaud because he's afraid of being taken for a man with a complimentary ticket. That's the reason why I don't give anyone complimentary tickets.

'Apart from that, I'm not worried. Do you think I would have accepted the opera otherwise? Never!' He paused and looked at the picture of his wife, then went on, 'The libretto is good. Unfortunately Horvath was a Hungarian, but he was an anti-Fascist,' he sighed. 'What a fate! To be killed by a falling tree in the Champs Elysées! Frightful!' He shook his head.

'The music is very modern. I could tell you today which newspapers will tear it to pieces. The rest will say all sorts of things, from *très bien*, to *très* godawful. If Herr Sixta doesn't steal any silver spoons before the premiere, or at least isn't caught at it, I see no reason *pourquoi avoir du chagrin*. We'll do it! The theatre is a lottery where we draw the blanks and the audience the winning tickets. You needn't laugh, dear lady, unless you want me to hire you. It's an old number, but well rehearsed and the plain truth.' He stood up, took her cold hand, and bowed his pursed lips over it. 'I give you my word of honour that our talk will go no further.'

Sophie took the tram to the Old Castle, ran through the tunnel and up the road. At the door of the rotunda Amery was waiting. She ran towards him, saw that he was coming to meet her, and heard the shoe-box fall to the ground as he took her in his arms. She felt her feet slide away in the snow.

'I can only stay a quarter of an hour,' she said when Amery wanted to give her the boots. 'It's not worth it.'

They walked under the black acacia trees. The streets down below were already quite dark, and every street lamp that came on made the evening come nearer.

'Do you know where I live?' Sophie asked.

'Yes.'

'And with whom?'

'Katja told me.'

'I must go home,' Sophie said.

Since the rehearsals had moved to the Cellar Theatre, Sixta had given up playing at the Café Manes. His mother had sent him enough money at Christmas to last until Easter, if necessary, and the Conservatoire had announced that it would invite two representatives of the Ministry of Education to the premiere, to 'procure the most favourable conditions for bestowing a State commission or stipend'. In the evenings, Sixta prepared himself for the following day's rehearsal, or took Sophie to the late show of an American film. He spoke of his work superficially, as if it were a matter that had long been settled. But Sophie noticed that it was only for herself and Georg, and perhaps for his own sake, that he behaved as if everything were going as he would wish. The nearer the day of the first dress rehearsal came, the more often he got up in the night, added to his notes, or sat, as once at Vavra's, before the silent keyboard.

He moved on to the camp bed so as not to disturb Sophie, put an armchair at its head so that his reading lamp should not shine in her face. He did not suspect that she woke up when he wrote, and that she could hear him tossing and turning on the canvas bed after he had turned out the light. They often both lay with open eyes until morning.

When she asked at breakfast whether he had slept well, he said, 'Marvellously! And you?'

'Yes.'

Once, when she asked him if there were any difficulties with the production, he glared at her and asked, 'Whatever makes you think a thing like that?'

After that she was afraid to offer him encouragement. The only way in which she could help him was by putting up with his moods and not letting him out of her sight until the premiere. He lived in a kind of delirium, from which he only woke when he was alone. When he happened to pick up some of his earlier compositions, he threw them away and was furious when Sophie took them out of the wastepaper basket and locked them into her suitcase. He quarrelled with everyone, even his 'nephew'. When Sophie discovered the Mannlicher gun under the webbing of the couch, she gave it to Georg, thinking it had been left by the German, the previous tenant of the room. Sixta demanded the gun back, and would not be put off when threatened with the law on arms. To pacify Sophie, he did not put it back under the couch but behind his big encyclopaedias on the top row of the bookshelves.

At the end of January, when they were having a meal out, he asked Georg how he might manage to get into the pathology department of the police.

'Simple,' Georg said. 'Just die.'

'No, seriously,' Sixta said. 'I want to see proper corpses. I've written an opera called *The Last Judgment*, and apart from my father, I've never seen a dead person.'

'Do you think Rossini became a hairdresser to write *The Barber of Seville*?' asked Sophie, and Sixta laughed so much that the other diners turned to look at him.

He came home late from the first dress rehearsal. 'The director has shown me some letters,' he called out before taking off his coat. 'The theatres in Brno and Pilsen will put on performances of the opera if it is a success. But I haven't told you the best yet. Fräulein Vesela, who sings Anna, today introduced her boyfriend to me. His great-grandfather was a commander in Magdeburg under Napoleon. He has eyes that look as if they'd fall in the soup any moment! I think she's only having an affair with him because he drives a sports car. He is Prague correspondent of *Le Monde*, and his brother-in-law is in the Opera Comique. He is a producer there, and we could invite him to come to the premiere. The only question is, who will pay his travelling and other expenses.'

'I'll put my mind to it,' Sophie said.

'And next winter we'll go to the premiere in Paris. *Le Jour Du Jugement Dernier* – is that right?'

'I think so,' she said and hung up Sixta's coat.

'It's madness,' he said and took her in his arms. 'But hope is better than cash in advance!'

That same evening Sophie managed to be alone with Georg. 'I want to sell something,' she said straight out. 'And you've got to help me. My sister and I have a wall hanging, a genuine Mortlake tapestry. Perhaps that doesn't mean anything to you, but it is a very valuable piece.'

'Am I a carpet dealer?'

'We've already sold one thing,' Sophie said and blushed. 'But the man was a swindler. I thought, if you . . .'

'A policeman?' Georg laughed.

'For that very reason.'

'I'll lend you a thousand krone,' Georg said and made to get his wallet.

'That isn't enough,' Sophie said and told him why she needed the money.

'But that's all nonsense,' Georg exclaimed. 'He only shot off his mouth because Vesela was there. But even if he has a brother-in-law, and the brother-in-law is really a producer and comes to Prague at your expense, do you know what he'll do? He'll live in the best hotel, stuff himself full of food, and lay a few girls. That's the French for you. And if he really goes to see the opera, he'll say, "I'll see what can be done, Monseeeur." And that's the last you'll hear from him, or I'll eat my hat. If he's interested in the opera, he'll pay the fare himself. The End!'

During the last week of January, Sophie only had an hour each afternoon for Amery. When she told him that she couldn't meet him again before Sixta's premiere, he nodded, but when she went shopping or went to meet Sixta at the theatre she often thought she saw him standing near the National Museum. She looked neither to left nor right and went faster. A man like Amery had other things to do than to wait for hours in the rain. But one evening she recognised the herringbone tweed coat in front of a restaurant, and pulled Sixta on to the other side of the road. From then on she knew that he was following her, and it didn't help if she took the tram. She had only to turn, and there he was in the second carriage. He gave no sign, did not stare at her. But he was always there.

On the second Monday in February, around noon, the telephone rang. Sixta had been asked to lunch with a conductor from Bratislava, and planned to take him to the rehearsal. Sophie went into Georg's room and picked up the receiver.

'Who is speaking, please?' asked Amery.

'Me,' Sophie replied.

'Just ten minutes. I have wonderful news.'

'Tell me,' she begged.

'I've got to look at you when I tell you.'

'And if I can't come?' Sophie asked and changed the sweaty receiver to the other hand.

'Today is the 11th, my birthday.'

Sophie crossed Wenceslas Square as through a fog which weakened her head, her ribs and her knees. While she was waiting for the tram she felt for her pulse. I've either got a heart made of cotton wool, she thought, or I've died and nobody has told me. The conductor took her under the arms to help her up, and she clung to the brass rod of the back window. Then the streets flew by. In the tunnel she almost turned back, but when she saw Amery she ran to him and fell into his arms.

They walked along under his umbrella. 'You'll soon understand everything,' he said. 'Do you remember the golden window you gave me . . .'

'Nine years ago,' Sophie said.

'Christine burned it,' Amery said. 'Are you sorry?'

'Why?' Sophie asked. 'There isn't a Fräulein Siebenschein any more.'

'We'll have to wait two or three months,' Amery said.

In her confusion she did not ask 'What for?' but 'Why?'

'Christine signed the papers only yesterday. She wants to be naturalised before being divorced. Otherwise she'll be expelled. Or perhaps it's because of the business. I've promised that I'll wait. The shop is the only thing that is left of the business. You knew that all our enterprises were confiscated? No? I thought I'd told you.' He tipped the umbrella forward so that the rain ran down as from the edge of a bucket.

'I was in custody for a few weeks last year. It was more a matter of conversation than investigation. It wasn't really about me personally. After all, I was a sort of revolutionary. But I wasn't able to make a profession of it. No, somebody had denounced Christine because of her "day". But I took most of the blame and put the rest on to Dr. Sellmann. I hope he'll have forgiven me if we meet again! My father wanted me to go to court, but there was no sense in it. Why do you think old Lustig didn't come back to Prague but took his money to Argentina? Because he knows that we're finished. It's so stupid. People are looking forward to the elections in the spring as if politics were like the weather. They don't notice that the climate has changed. The world ends, and they think it's a cloudburst.

'Originally I wanted to take you to England. I have a few friends in Worcester and Chelsea. But I don't want to see anyone who knows me. I need a new country. Perhaps Sweden.'

333

Sophie let go of his arm and stepped from underneath the umbrella.

'Or America. Do you get sea-sick?'

She held her face up to the rain and smiled. Amery stretched out his arm with the umbrella and pointed to its ribs with his free hand.

'You've got to imagine a huge roof made out of glass plates and carried by a steel construction. If you put metallic oxide into the glass you can heat it, and the snow runs off. That's the kind of thing I'd like to build. In Canada.'

Sophie wiped her wet hair and blinked the rain out of her eyes. She remembered the country she and her sisters had imagined when they were at the Wildfowler, the meadows made of honey-cake, and the river made of raspberry juice had been what Katharina wanted. And Christine had asked for a sky made of plum-pudding, with clouds of meringue.

'I know what you were wearing yesterday,' Amery said. 'But I won't follow you any more. You're going to come to me. I've taken a room for Friday. The premiere is on Thursday, isn't it? I hope it is a success. I really wish him that. Do you know the Hotel Paris?'

'My father stayed there once,' Sophie said and went ahead.

Amery held the umbrella over her. 'In the evening, between seven and eight,' he said. 'Room 402. Shall I write it down for you?'

Sophie shook her head. 'One doesn't forget that sort of thing.

13

The Last Judgment

SIXTA'S MOTHER HAD planned to come the day before the premiere, but she arrived in Prague on the Tuesday because she was afraid that the dark suit she had had made for Pavel in Budweis might have to be altered. Thus she suddenly appeared at the door, the rim of her lead-coloured knitted hat down on her forehead, in her left hand a suitcase and two bags, in her right the parcel containing the suit. She expected pity because she had got lost in the city, and thanks for the prompt delivery of the suit, but was told that her hotel room had not been reserved until Wednesday. That wasn't the kind of welcome she had anticipated, and the thought that she would have to sleep in a hotel instead of 'with the children' confused her. If Sophie hadn't made coffee straight away, she would have turned round and gone home. But after some sweet black coffee, the successful trying on of the suit, and a tour of the apartment, she decided she really could not expect Georg to sleep on the camp bed in the kitchen for three nights.

Sixta's close relationship with his mother had withered during their separation in the war to a respectful exchange of letters and postcards. Her way of asking him when he'd at last get married, start to save, go to bed earlier, smoke less, or have his hair cut, and then asking the same thing again the following day as if she had forgotten his replies, had made his visit the previous year a misery. When he spoke of her in her absence she was always 'a wonderful woman', but if he had to be with her for more than a day, her obsessive sense of order and her superficial solicitude for him provoked him into bursts of fury which he regretted once it came to saying goodbye.

The morning after her arrival – Frau Sixta had spent a sleepless night in Georg's bed, she said – Pavel carried her suitcase to the hotel before taking Sophie to the dress rehearsal. But his mother told him that they had decided that Sophie would come with her to do her shopping.

'After all, she knows your opera by heart, and we'll be seeing it tomorrow evening. I need rubber rings for preserving jars, flower seeds, darning yarn, a cigarette lighter for Herr Volny, fishing hooks for Herr Dycha, a cable-release for Dr. Havlitschek's camera, razor blades for Herr Nechansky, that's my butcher ...' the list had no end. Pavel looked at Sophie who stood behind his mother. She shrugged her shoulders and smiled helplessly. 'And then some things that one doesn't talk about,' Frau Sixta finished.

'And what do you think?' Pavel asked.

'Oh we've agreed,' Frau Sixta answered for Sophie.

'Renunciation is the price of family life,' Sixta thought on his way to the theatre and convinced himself that it had been up to Sophie to make the decision. But presently he felt he had made a mistake and telephoned Sophie from the theatre office to tell her that she should send his mother to do her shopping alone.

'Wouldn't you like to tell her yourself?' she asked.

'But of course,' exclaimed Frau Sixta when he explained that he needed Sophie because one of his assistants had not come. 'Nobody could foresee that, dear boy!' Sixta threw the receiver down. He was furious that he had been too cowardly to tell her the truth.

Sixta had broken the usual custom of asking some critics to the dress rehearsal, and there was no audience. He introduced Sophie to the director and watched as they sat down together before he left the auditorium.

On stage he greeted the singers, waved to the lighting engineers, and after a last word with the stage-manager, went into the orchestra pit. When the 'ready' light came on, he looked at the piccolo flutes and trombones and lifted his baton.

The change from the first to the second scene went well, but the interval before the third scene was too long.

'Four months go by between these scenes,' Sixta called when the curtain rose again, 'but we want to do it in four minutes.' He was told that a defect in the hydraulic lifting system was the cause, and he grumbled, 'Well, take your time.' He turned for a moment to look at Sophie, and to show that she had seen him, she put her right hand on her left shoulder. Her gesture seemed to him to show more tenderness than any other hand could convey.

During the interval, Sixta thanked 'Anna' and the stationmaster for the way they had sung the waltz, then climbed under the stage to make sure the hydraulics were functioning properly. When he went back to the musicians, they looked at him expectantly. Most of them were of his own age group, and some had been through much the same as he. He knew that they supported him, and that to see him acknowledged meant a sort of acknowledgement to them all.

'I feel,' he said and unwrapped his sandwich, 'that the last three months haven't been in vain.' That was just what was wanted.

In the last scene Sixta felt his excitement transferring itself to the singers. Anna's solo, taken out of the twelve-tone scheme, sounded like a folk-song, 'Heaven was a strong angel, we heard the words and were afraid to understand them,' and, after the stationmaster's question, 'Did I hear trumpets?' the chemist replied, 'It was the wind,' then the quiet finale, the violins and the basses repeating the waltz theme of the third scene. Everything remained silent for a while. Sixta squatted down on the step to the podium, took a handkerchief out of his jacket and wiped his wet hands.

'Could you see the green signal on the railway embankment today?' he heard the stage-manager call.

Sixta got up, clung to the podium and shouted back, 'If it shines as brightly tomorrow, Herr Polatschek, I'll kiss your arse.' He bowed to the musicians and was about to leave the podium when someone touched his shoulder.

'What do you think of our announcing the second performance for Sunday?' the director asked.

'Yes, that's fine.'

The director told him that he had ordered a table at a restaurant for after the premiere, but Sixta was not listening. He watched as Sophie came slowly down the gangway and looked into the orchestra pit. 'I've given the Fräulein the tickets for tomorrow,' the director said and brought his scented shirt within smelling-distance of Sixta. 'I didn't know she sings. She told me in the interval. Maybe she'd have been better than Fräulein Vesela. Pity she's a German. As it says in *Cyrano*, "*Que diable va-t-elle faire dans cette galère!*" Don't you feel that too?'

'I don't know French,' Sixta replied.

'What the devil is she doing in this place,' the director translated.

'That'll soon be different.'

'You think so?' the director asked sceptically, thus turning Sixta's assurance from the particular to the general.

'Don't say anything,' Sixta said to Sophie.

She pushed her hair into the turned up collar of her coat and smiled. 'I'm buying fishing hooks for Dr. Havlitschek's camera this afternoon, and a cable release for Herr Dycha, or the other way round. We won't be home before seven. If you like, I'll take your mother to the cinema . . ?'

'On no account,' Sixta said and heard someone call for him.

'I've just learned French from the director. *Je t'aime*, is that right?'

Sophie nodded and, as he said goodbye, he felt her hand on his neck.

When the four of them were having their meal at home that night, it occurred to Sixta that he might suggest that Sophie invite Christine and Katharina to the premiere. But at the last momen he remembered that he had felt at Christmas that she had given up her sisters for his sake, and he decided not to ask any questions. It seemed ridiculous to him not to have spoken of Amery once during the last months. But wasn't there a whole lifetime left for that?

'Don't you like your food, my boy?' Frau Sixta asked.

'On the contrary,' he said and looked at the portrait Georg had given them for Christmas.

'Sophie won't say a word,' Frau Sixta said. 'But you could at least tell me whether you were pleased with the rehearsal.'

'Very much,' he said and put half a dumpling into his mouth to get a bit of peace. If the gilt frame round the painting had not brought back a memory, he would not have asked after Christine at Christmas, and he did not want to talk of Amery in case it hurt Sophie. Words, when spoken at the wrong moment, could do damage.

'Delicious cranberries,' Frau Sixta said.

'Would you care for some more?' Sophie asked. 'And you?'

'No thank you.'

Sixta wondered whether he ought to tell Sophie again that he wanted to marry her. His proposal was nine years old and was as valid as ever. Perhaps it would be a good idea to repeat it when the occasion arose. He would ask at the registry office whether he could marry a German wife.

Later he took his mother to her hotel room. While she unpacked her shopping bags and ticked off her list, he was suddenly sorry that she had to sleep in the hotel like a stranger, and when she put her open-work taffeta-lined evening dress on a hanger, he embraced her and she cried. She became very gentle. That's how she could be when they were alone together. Before he had had to go to work in Germany, she had shown him his first shoes, and he had confessed that he had cheated her out of four krone when he was a child, but she had piled memory on memory. Even in the train his head had been heavy with all her stories and reminiscences. Now he had to look under the bed before he left her. No robber, no black dog behind the fringes?

At breakfast Sixta read the detailed announcement of the premiere and gave Sophie the newspaper.

'Marvellous,' she said.

'How much do you think the theatre paid for it?'

'Nothing,' she smiled. 'You know that very well.'

They ate out at noon, and after Sixta had accompanied his mother and Sophie to the hairdresser's, he went to the theatre. When he saw the 'Sold out' notice at the theatre ticket office, he asked the girl whether that was for tonight's performance.

'Yes,' she said without looking up from her magazine. 'But you can have a ticket for Sunday. But the only ones left are in the sixteenth row.'

He went along the street, then turned and came back and

looked at the 'Sold out' notice as if he had only just seen it for the first time. He went on again, turned and ambled back and saw an elderly lady outside the ticket office.

'The next performance is on Sunday,' he said to her when she came out.

'I don't want opera,' she said. 'I want cabaret.' That sobered him. He would have liked to have thanked her. He went home, bathed and lay down on his bed.

When the lights went out in the auditorium that night, he mounted the podium, bowed before the black abyss with the white shirt fronts, heard welcoming applause, and waited for the signal from the stage manager before giving the sign to begin. He suddenly felt that the sleeves of his new suit were too tight, but the express train bringing disaster to stationmaster Hudetz could not now be stopped.

The applause after the first scene was polite, after the second it lasted long enough for the scene shifting, and during the third scene the waltz was applauded for so long that Hudetz and Anna had to repeat it. During the interval Sixta gave his jacket to the wardrobe mistress to undo the lining and went into the washroom. People made room for him at the wash basin, but when he went back to the sewing-room he noticed that he had not washed his hands at all, but had wiped the liquid soap on his trousers. He wanted to ask Fräulein Vesela whether she had some chemical cleaner, and saw her admirer at the door of her dressing-room.

'Get back to your seat,' Sixta hissed. The eyes of the great-grandson of the commandant of Magdeburg almost dropped out, but he went away.

'The best thing is water,' Fräulein Vesela said. She rubbed a damp sponge against Sixta's hips. 'And be a bit nice to my Frenchman, else you won't be photographed later. Our picture will be in *Le Monde.*'

'On the front page?'

In the sewing-room he stood by the radiator to dry his trousers. At the first bell he put on his jacket and ran to the orchestra pit.

When the curtain rose, the audience liked the scenery so much, two grey pillars under a brass moon, that they applauded until the policeman came on. But when the stationmaster sang the mawkish words about Anna's death in the sixth scene somebody laughed, and Sixta felt the sudden coldness at his back. The applause was friendly, but the change to the last scene took painful minutes, when paper rustled, shoe soles scraped and hand-bags snapped shut. Sixta waved for the drummer to go to the tub for the ghost-train. 'Scrape nicely,' he whispered and took up his baton. Everything depends on Fräulein Vesela now, he thought and looked at the light-button on his podium.

When the curtain kept showing the legs of the singers and then hiding them again, and when he couldn't hear what the first violin was whispering into his ear, Sixta realised that he had won. He saw Fräulein Vesela's admirer with a flashlight, then Sophie, his mother and Georg. The theatre director and his young wife smiled as if it were their birthday. A gentleman in the second row shook his hands above his head and then suddenly clutched his waist. That would be Vavra. He had given the rest of the audience the signal for a standing ovation and now sat down again.

The cast was already at the restaurant before Sixta left the theatre with Sophie, his mother and Georg. He would have liked to have walked a little, but the director had ordered a car, and Frau Sixta warned him of colds. She enjoyed sitting beside the chauffeur and asked him to go slowly over the Charles Bridge because of the panorama. In the restaurant, the embraces began all over again, and it took Sixta some time to fight his way to his table. Nobody had waited to start drinking, and the director was evidently afraid of being too late, for the moment Sixta sat down, he tapped on his glass. After him came the representative of the actors' union and Ministry of Education, and after the head of the conducting class of the Conservatoire had finished his toast, Sixta rose. He wondered whether to get up on his chair and looked at Sophie. She smiled at him. Her face was very pale around the red-painted lips.

'Friends,' Sixta called and stopped. He noticed how excited he was, and held his glass with both hands. It sounds too solemn he thought when he thanked the cast and the previous speakers. I must make a joke like the others. He told them how he had wiped soap into his trousers during the interval, and Fräulein Vesela shrieked with pleasure.

'Don't forget the kiss you've promised me,' the stage-manager called.

'In its own good time, Herr Polatschek,' Sixta replied and took care not to spill his wine while he calmed down the laughter. 'Now I want to say something else,' he continued. 'I want to make up for something that has for a long time . . .'

'. . . lain on my soul,' the director prompted.

'Yes, exactly. And it concerns someone at this table. I could tell her at home. Perhaps she would prefer that. But I want my friends to hear it.' Frau Sixta bowed her head and produced a crochet handkerchief out of her sleeve. ' "What I give you, I give to no one else," Nezval said. 'I give it to you, Sophie, and I drink to the two of us.'

'Bravo, and no tears!' the director called and held out his glass to Sophie after Sixta and clinked glasses with her. Then it was the turn of Frau Sixta, Georg and the others, and Sixta made sure no one shirked.

'Thank you,' Sophie said, and, 'Your good health', and then again 'Thank you.'

The critic of a former Legionnaire paper took Sixta aside and asked, 'May I bring a tiny mistake to your notice, maestro?'

'Please do,' Sixta said and smiled across at Sophie.

'What Nezval actually says is, "what I *wanted* to give you, I shall never give to another". There is a slight difference.'

'What?'

'I wanted to point out to you that Nezval did not write "give" but "wanted to give".'

'Go chase yourself.'

'I expect you heard someone laugh in the sixth scene,' the critic said and looked at his watch. 'I think one could build a nice little theory about modern opera on this laughter. An annihilating one, of course. Just because there are more composers nowadays doesn't mean the music is getting better. Perhaps I'll develop this a little more in my review. Even at the risk of being the only bad fairy amongst so many good ones.'

'It'll be a pleasure,' Sixta said and bowed.

'Oh, quite mutual,' the critic said and went to collect his coat from the cloakroom.

When Sixta woke up at midday on Friday, he thought he remembered going on to other places after the restaurant. But where? He wanted to ask Sophie, but she was not beside him, and he noticed that she had slept on the camp bed. She was sitting in the kitchen with his mother. Frau Sixta had, by herself, brought the suitcase and the shopping bags from the hotel, and was already 'booted and spurred' as if her train were due to leave in half an hour. Sixta sat down with them and ate a sour gherkin. He nodded in reply to everything his mother said, and only objected when she wanted to heat some soup for him. Sophie gave him a bottle of beer, and Frau Sixta told them how Herr Hrbek, in Budweis, had had a duodenal operation because for years he had drunk cold beer on an empty stomach.

'I'm only doing it today, Mama,' Sixta said.

He went and soaked in the bath, and when he pulled the plug, and the water gurgled down the drain, the previous evening unwound in his mind, all the places they had been to, until he was back in the restaurant and remembered the critic. What was his name? Schramek, Schima, or Jamal? Jackal would have been the right name for him. Carrion eater and howler in the night! His review would be in the Saturday edition, but by going to the printer's one might be able to get a pull of the proof before midnight. Sixta turned on the hand-shower and splashed cold water over himself.

The train to Budweis left towards six o'clock and the station was fifteen minutes' walk, but at four o'clock Frau Sixta put on her knitted hat, and Pavel had to promise that they would leave the house at five at the latest. When she picked up her bags to put near the door, it came to her that she had forgotten something. She asked Sophie to take off her shoes and stand on a piece of newspaper. Then she licked an indelible pencil and began to draw the outline of Sophie's feet on the paper.

'I've had a look at all your shoes,' she said. 'I'm going to get Herr Pravda to make you a pair of boots, fur-lined.'

'You shouldn't be buying me things,' Sophie said.

'Don't contradict,' Frau Sixta panted from the floor. 'A lot of the winter is still ahead.' She asked for a tape-measure and wrote down the measurements of the instep, the ankles and the calves. 'Don't be so ticklish, my child. Do you want them black or brown?'

'I don't want them at all,' Sophie said, stepping into the high-heeled buckle shoes she had worn for the first time the day before.

'Black is more elegant,' Frau Sixta decided.

When Sixta kissed his mother goodbye at the station, and saw her blueish tongue, he remembered the chow at the Strahov Stadium. For the next kiss he only gave her his cheek and took the case and bags into the compartment while Frau Sixta said goodbye to Sophie. He wiped the window with his coat-sleeve and watched how they hugged each other, and how Sophie put her forehead on Frau Sixta's shoulder. Then Sophie shook her head and his mother seemed to wish to persuade her. Then they suddenly seemed to agree, for they kissed, and Frau Sixta climbed into the compartment.

'I'll be thinking of you on Sunday,' she said to Pavel and sent him out on to the platform. He went to Sophie, and when the train began to move, his mother came to the window and waved.

On the way home, Sixta suggested they eat out. Yesterday, the director had given him an envelope with some money so that he could treat a few people, and there was still some left. But Sophie wanted to go home. 'I'm cold,' she said. Sixta put his arm around her and felt her trembling. On the stairs to the apartment Sixta had to let go of her to get his keys out of his pocket. Sophie stumbled and fell on the stone steps. She laughed as if to show that she had not hurt herself. In the corridor Sixta tried to take her coat, but she went ahead of him and sat down on the piano stool.

'I am so happy for you,' she said, when he came in after her. He told her about the critic.

'You mustn't let it annoy you,' Sophie said. 'One can only believe in the good reviews if there is at least one bad one.'

'I'll go and get it from the printers presently,' Sixta said and fell silent when he heard steps in the corridor. Georg came into the room.

'How does one recognise alcohol poisoning?' he asked. 'I wish I hadn't told the stage-manager that I am with the police. I'm sure the swine put cigar ash in my wine.' He asked after Frau Sixta, but when he noticed that nobody wanted to talk to him, he pressed both fists against his temples and left.

'If the theatre in Brno puts on *The Last Judgment*, we'll look for another place to live,' Sixta said. When Sophie did not reply, he asked, 'Why don't you take your coat off?'

'I'm going out again.'

'The shops are shut.'

'I don't want to buy anything. There's enough of everything in the house. But you'll have to buy bread in the morning. I've paid for it, so that you don't have to wait.'

'Where are you going?' Sixta asked and saw her turn with the stool to the piano.

'I can't stay here any more,' she said.

'What did my mother want you to do, at the station?'

'That in the summer . . .' she couldn't go on.

'What.'

'That we should stay with her in the holidays, but I told her that I wouldn't be here any more in the summer.'

'Where are you going?'

Sixta looked at her, saw Sophie at the piano, the black hair on the black coat. He shut his eyes and saw a girl walk slowly towards him through a maple avenue, first in a military blouse with a green tie, then in a hospital gown with a white bandage round her head, and at last in a grey silk dress with a white collar. She stopped in front of him and, showing the little gap between her teeth, said, 'You know that I'm going away?'

I want to marry you, he'd said on that occasion. Now he said, 'You have met him.'

'Yes,' Sophie said and turned around.

'When?'

'Every day since Christmas until the end of January. Then once more this week.'

'Did you sleep with him?'

'No.'

'Why did you meet him?'

'Because he wanted me to.'

'And now?'

'I'm going to him.'

'Home?'

'He lives in a hotel.'

'Where?'

Sophie tried to smile.

'I must at least know where to send your post,' Sixta said calmly.

'Hotel Paris.'

Sixta wanted to take a cigarette, but it suddenly seemed to him as if his arm were too short to reach them. He got up and pushed the packet so hard against his left fist that several cigarettes fell on to the table.

'So you were only waiting for the premiere to be over?' he asked and put a cigarette in his mouth.

'No' she sobbed.

He put the cigarette back on the table, picked up Sophie and carried her to the divan. He sat down beside her and took her face between his hands.

'I love you,' he said. 'Did you know?'

She nodded, wanted to wipe her tears, but Sixta would not let her.

'You're staying here,' he said.

'But he is waiting,' she whispered between his hands. 'If I don't come, he'll fetch me.'

'Let him wait,' Sixta said and kissed her wet lips.

'Are you going out?' she asked when he got up and put the cigarette packet in his jacket pocket.

'I'm only getting the proof from the printers. I must know what that fellow has written, otherwise I can't sleep tonight. I'll be back in half an hour. Then we'll talk about it all again.'

'Why don't you ask Georg to go?'

'He's giving himself cold compresses,' Sixta said. 'But they wouldn't give him the proof anyway.' He helped Sophie to take

344

off her coat and hung it on a hook in the hall. 'In half an hour,' he called, 'At the latest!' Then he shut the door and went to see Georg.

'I'm running over to the printers,' he said to him and took the wet towel from his face. 'Go and sit with Sophie and don't let her out of the house. Understood?'

'What's the matter with the child?' Georg asked.

'Tell her how you acted in the play at Budweis, that'll make her think of other things.'

When he ran down to Wenceslas Square, the pedestrians turned in front of his eyes like the silhouette targets on a rifle range. On he ran and only slowed down when his breath burned in his throat. Then he stopped under the overhang of the Municipal House, took the envelope out of his coat pocket and counted the money left in it. He walked the last few yards to the Hotel Paris like everybody else who was out that night in that weather, quickly and with his head down.

He went through the leather-bound draught-curtains into the hall. A waiter with white whiskers stood by the entrance to the restaurant so immobile that he looked stuffed. Beyond him on the tables stood the sugarloaves of the napkins, and batteries of sherry, wine and champagne glasses. Sixta did not know that Sellmann had once stayed here. He smelled the scent of leather, eau de cologne, Creme Caramel, and Turkish cigarettes.

'I want to see Herr Amery,' he said. The reception clerk looked at the key board.

'Room 402,' he said. 'Is he expecting you?'

Sixta nodded and got into the elevator. He pressed the button, and suddenly felt so light that he might have been floating to the fourth floor under his own volition. He went down the corridor, found 402 and knocked.

Amery hesitated before he asked Sixta to come in. He was wearing a navy-blue pinstriped suit and a grey tie. The curtains were drawn, and between the deep armchairs stood a low table with an ice bucket, an open bottle of champagne and two glasses, one of which was half full.

'What can I do for you?' Amery asked.

'I still owe you some money,' Sixta said and put the envelope on the table. 'Perhaps you have forgotten all about it?'

'No,' Amery said.

'I'm afraid it isn't the full amount. I'll bring you the rest next week.'

'Your premiere was a success, I hear?' Amery asked.

'And something else,' said Sixta and pointed his chin at the table. 'You can save yourself that expense.'

'Aha,' Amery said and sat down in one of the chairs. 'You mean Sophie isn't coming today? Have you locked her up?' He sipped at his glass and refilled it. 'Well, then she'll come tomorrow,' he said and crossed his legs. 'Not then either?' He smiled. 'I think I must explain something to you. Won't you sit down? Do.'

While Sixta stood and listened to Amery it seemed to him as if he were being crushed by an invisible vice which attacked all his muscles and joints. Its pressure crushed his fingers into his palm, pushed his ribs into his lungs, turned his eyeballs round, sank his ears into his skull, so that he felt as if he were falling into himself, into a sweaty, bloody depth where he came as near the truth as never before.

'It is all the same if Sophie comes today or tomorrow,' Amery was saying. 'Perhaps she'll come next month, or perhaps you'll marry her first. That is quite unimportant. She'd come to me even if she had your child. Why do you try to convince yourself that she'll stay with you? Do you really believe you are capable of keeping a woman like Sophie? Then you don't know her. Do you want to run after her all your life? Do you want to have her watched? Do you want to go through her pockets in fear of finding an address or a telephone number that will reach me? Spare yourself all that.

'I remember very well how you came to me and demanded money. Yes, I thought at the time you wanted to blackmail me. I beg your pardon. I'm also sorry about what happened in your room. But I wasn't able to apologise for that because I . . . And then you didn't live in Prague any more. I'm sorry for you, you understand? I'm quite serious. You're the kind of person who rings up a newspaper and says: I'm so unhappy, what should I do? Or was that at the Conservatoire? And didn't you tell me about a lady with whom you spent the holidays? A girl from Wittigau, wasn't it? When you were with her you felt like a newly-discovered Indian, wasn't that it? No, you wanted to marry into a bakery. You see I have a good memory. Wouldn't that be a solution?

' "Let the floods clap their hands . . ." something like that? You should be glad that you have compensations, and even if the theatre doesn't work out, weren't you a music teacher during the war?

'Wait! Don't bother. I'll pour you . . .'

Amery managed to lift his hands as far as his chin, then his

346

body jerked over the back of the chair and his feet pushed against the table before he slipped to the floor. Sixta saw a large green splinter between the upset glasses. He opened his hand, and the neck of the bottle fell on the carpet. He bent down and felt Amery's curly hair under his hand. When he stood upright, Amery's face turned once more against the folds of the armchair valance.

In the elevator mirror Sixta noticed that champagne had squirted on to his coat. He mopped the collar with his handkerchief.

'Good day,' the reception clerk said when Sixta went past him.

Whiskers was speaking to a waitress and fell silent when the draught-excluder was pulled aside. A liveried page pulled a brown trunk into the hall.

From the Hotel Paris, Sixta went to the print works and asked the night porter whether he could have a pull of Herr Schima's review.

'Doctor Schimal,' the foreman corrected him in the booming office. 'With an "l" at the end. But the edition isn't ready, and I can only give you the pull if I have the Doktor's personal permission.'

Sixta was about to leave, but the foreman was bellowing into the telephone, sticking his index finger in the other ear. Then he went and got the proof.

'Thank you,' Sixta said and folded the paper and put it into his coat pocket.

Outside the house in Mezibranska Street he took the keys out of his trouser pocket and heard them fall on the ground. He did not pick them up.

'You said half an hour!' Georg complained.

All voices were suddenly very loud.

Sixta went ahead through the corridor. Sophie was sitting in his room. On the table stood a chess board. White was winning.

'Where is the review?' Georg asked.

Sixta put his hand in his pocket, gave him the paper and leaned against the door. He looked at Sophie. She sat under the gilt frame.

'. . . and what distinguishes him from all others of his generation . . .' he heard Georg read.

As in the days in the hospital when she could not speak, Sophie lifted her right hand. What had it meant? Yes or no? She smiled. So it had been yes? He wanted to go to her and sit down beside her, but at the first step the room spun around him, and he bent down as if he wanted to hold on to his shoes so as not to fall on to the ceiling.

'It's nothing,' he heard Georg say. 'That's only happiness.'

He stretched out. The turning and booming became less. The sky under his lids became gentle, and he breathed as quietly as when he was a child.

14

When the Chickens Fly South

AFTER GEORG HAD put the Mannlicher gun into his own room, and impressed upon Sophie not to mention the weapon to anyone, he accompanied Pavel to the police. Half an hour later an ambulance took the unconscious Amery to the University Hospital where he died the following morning of a brain haemorrhage. The theatre director who rang up at noon to congratulate Sixta on the reviews, heard from Sophie that Sixta had been arrested. On the Sunday, stickers saying 'Postponed owing to illness' were stuck across the theatre placards that had advertised the second performance of *The Last Judgment*.

The preliminary investigation included everybody who had had any connection with Sixta. At first Sophie was a suspect as an accessory, but she was soon cleared, though she and her sisters were forbidden to leave the country before the trial. This was especially unfortunate for Katharina who had asked for voluntary repatriation as early as January. Karol had resisted the idea for a long time, though Dr. Djudko, who was still waiting for his call to New York or Ulan-Bator, had tried to persuade him to part from her 'in a sensible manner, as was usual amongst comrades'. Karol had wavered when some newspapers began to disclose the background of the 'Murder in the Hotel Paris'. But only after the elections which were an unequivocal victory for his party, and with the certainty of promotion for himself, did he cease to stand in the way of Katharina's return to Germany.

Frau Sixta and the foreman of the printing works were summoned but did not add anything to the known facts, nor did the questioning of Bohuslav Amery. The old man, who had gone out of his mind when he heard of his son's death, refused to sign his statement with his name, but wrote 'Kaschka, Clown' instead.

The reception clerk, on the other hand, testified that Sixta had nodded when he had asked him if Amery was expecting him. The prosecutor used this statement later, since it strengthened the case for premeditation and appeared to justify the indictment for murder.

The trial opened in July, the choice of a jury having been delayed by the elections. Wearing the same suit that he had worn to the premiere, Sixta was led into the dock. When the judge addressed him, he answered quickly and in a low voice. Then the witnesses were taken to a separate room and told that they must not speak to each other.

The sergeant in charge leaned against the cool radiator. Georg blew his cigarette smoke through a gap in the window. The hotel reception clerk read an illustrated paper and apologised when he kicked the table by accident. Sophie and Christine, who were seeing each other for the first time in nine years, had entered the witness-room without a word to each other, and waited in opposite corners.

Christine wore a black hat with a kind of veil at the back. When Georg was called into the court-room she took off her gloves and laid her white hand with the two wedding rings on her leather handbag. The sergeant took a dusty glass from a shelf, rinsed it at the wash basin and looked questioningly around him. The reception clerk refused and brought out a propelling pencil to work on the crossword puzzle. The sergeant drank the water with such noisy gulps that Sophie felt she could hear the heat in the small room. The reception clerk was called to the court-room, but Georg did not return. The sergeant went and stood by the window and breathed as if he were having his lungs tested. 'It's calming,' he said, between drafts of air, but the sisters did not reply. Their eyes went slowly from each other's hem to collar, until they met and locked, as if they were playing a game they had played as children when the one who blinked first lost. But there was no winner now.

A long time after Christine, Sophie was led into the court-room and sworn in. The judge asked her to describe the events of the evening of the killing. The prosecutor, a young, tall, and almost bald man, treated her kindly. From his questions it was clear that he wanted to show that the accused was the victim of confused circumstances. He underlined Sophie's statement that before he left the apartment, the accused mentioned neither his visit to the Hotel Paris nor the payment of his debt.

The short, energetic, and equally bald defending counsel tackled the matter quite differently. Asking whether the witness had been a Sister of Mercy until the end of the war, he made the public laugh, and one or two of the jury coughed behind their hands. His tactics worked. Could they imagine the accused running, after the triumphant success of his first opera, to the Hotel Paris to do murder for this woman, as the prosecutor maintained? Wasn't he in fact showing mistrust of the witness by not telling her of his debt? Did she not admit that she was merely his assistant, that she had even been excluded from the rehearsals?

Sophie looked across at Sixta who had lowered his head. At the end of her examination, the judge adjourned the proceedings for two hours.

Sophie lunched with Jarmila who had got in touch with her in February, announcing herself with their old watchword 'Frinz'. The former Fräulein Mangl was now called Podzemma, but was divorced, and was not much changed from earlier years. When the case resumed at two o'clock, Sophie sat once more in the witness-room, now alone with the sergeant.

The case continued through the afternoon. The psychiatrist gave his opinion that the accused was mentally normal and responsible for his action, and that his responsibility had not been diminished by a heightened sense of self-assertion or a hysterical anticipation of the reviews of his opera. With regard to Sixta's forced labour in Germany and his life in hiding, the psychiatrist suggested that people with such a background often acted compulsively against people who had come out of the war unscathed. In his opinion the fact that he had gone to the police himself showed not so much a feeling of guilt as that the accused possessed an elementary consciousness of right and wrong, clearly shown by his courageous appearance at the Budweis anti-Fascist trial.

Towards evening Sophie was told that she would not be needed any more, and the judge adjourned the case. The following morning, Botticelli, the theatre director, the critic Schimal and 'nordic' Vavra were questioned, but without any useful result. The professor, who had ceased to work for the Ministry of Education since the elections, made his statement in such a mixture of French and English that neither the prosecuting nor the defending counsel wished to question him.

In the afternoon, Sophie was taken into the court-room. The defending counsel rested his outspread fingers on his papers and asked the witness whether she believed Amery to have been capable of using force to make the accused part from her.

Sophie remembered how Amery had shown her his bruised hand in the room in Charvat Lane. 'I know who wrote that letter,' she heard him say. 'There's no more danger from that quarter. I've already dealt with that.' And also the conversation at the Mangl estate, before her departure for Bocuvice. 'I shan't bear him a grudge,' she heard Pavel say. 'That would be silly. But why did he beat me?'

The judge objected to the defending counsel's question, and the defending counsel reformulated it, 'Do you know of any facts which would lead you to believe that the dead man would have been ready to use force to assure himself of your person?'

She knew from Georg that Sixta had maintained that he had been attacked by Amery. She suspected that this statement did not refer to the evening at the Hotel Paris.

'Yes,' she said in a low voice. Had Christine gone so far as to tell them that she had thought that Pavel had written the anonymous letter? Or had she held back because she had been afraid he would then mention the business with the gilt frame?'

'Which facts?' asked the defending counsel.

'It's a long time ago,' Sophie replied softly and had to unbutton her coat because she suddenly felt hot.

'I'm sure you have a good memory,' the judge urged her.

'On Maundy Thursday nine years ago I drove to Franzensbad with Herr Amery. On the way I told him that I had written to tell his wife of our relationship.'

'And then?'

'I saw him turn the steering wheel to the right.'

'Are you trying to say that he caused the accident on purpose?'

'Yes.'

'I must remind you that you are under oath.'

She nodded.

'Why did you not mention this when questioned for the preliminary investigation?'

'I didn't think it was very important,' Sophie whispered.

'And why did you not report it nine years ago?' the prosecuting counsel asked in the silent court.

I could say because I'd bitten off my tongue, she thought. She looked at Sixta. He was pale. She turned to the prosecutor and said, 'Because I wouldn't have minded dying with him then.'

'Any more questions for the witness?' the judge asked both counsels, and jury, and lastly the accused. Sixta shook his head and was pressed back on to his seat by his guards because he had leaned over so far that he threatened to fall.

Two days later the jury announced their verdict. They agreed unanimously that the accused had not murdered the merchant

Jan Amery from low and dishonourable motives. The court sentenced Pavel Sixta to ten years penal servitude for manslaughter.

Katharina came to Mezibranska Street for Sophie's birthday. She had already made contact with German comrades and wanted to go to Berlin as soon as possible.

'And Christine?'

'Tina is already in Bavaria. She wants her business manager to join her there.'

Towards evening they went for a walk. The castle swam above the city like a stone ship. '*Niyatam kuru karma tvam*', Katharina said and laughed because Sophie did not understand the Russian sentence. 'The revolution knows no homeland,' she translated freely, and made a fist in front of her thick nose.

A few weeks later Sophie received her expulsion order. She told Georg that she would put the score of *The Last Judgment* behind the encyclopaedias on the top shelf of the bookcase.

'Why don't you take it with you,' he asked. 'Pavel gave it to you after all.'

'It will be better if you keep it for him until he returns,' Sophie said. Then she went to St. Apollinaris to say goodbye to Svoboda, but he was not at home.

Georg and Jarmila took her to the station. When the train started, Georg made a thumbs up sign with his stump, and Jarmila called something which must have been 'Frinz'.

Sophie put her feet in the black buckle shoes on her suitcase and tried to imagine who would be the first to welcome her to the Wildfowler. The windows were dirty. 'The glass is brown from your eyes,' Jan had said. White clouds drifted across the August sky. Some looked like mountains, and some appeared as large as continents, but measured against what had been, they lasted no longer than a smoke signal. Some day everything would stop except one thing, Sophie still believed. 'Once, once only did love touch me,' Vavra had said. We live but once. One day we will turn around and around and spread out our arms. One day everything will become easy. One day even our feet will become light and will lift off the ground. One day the blood will rush into our fingers, we will turn, lay back our heads and lift our feet. That day will come. One day everything will be easy, the blood will rush into our hearts, we will turn and spread our arms. Then the time has come of which Uncle Wilhelm says, 'The chickens will fly south.' Then comes the time that's now passing.